PROLIFERATION

A NOVEL BY

ERIK A. OTTO

This book is a work of fiction. Any references to historical events, real people, or real places are used fictitiously. Other names, characters, places and events are products of the author's imagination, and any resemblance to actual events or persons, living or dead, is entirely coincidental.

Rev 1.0—May 21st, 2021

Cover design by Karolis Zukas.

ISBN-13: 9781732136151

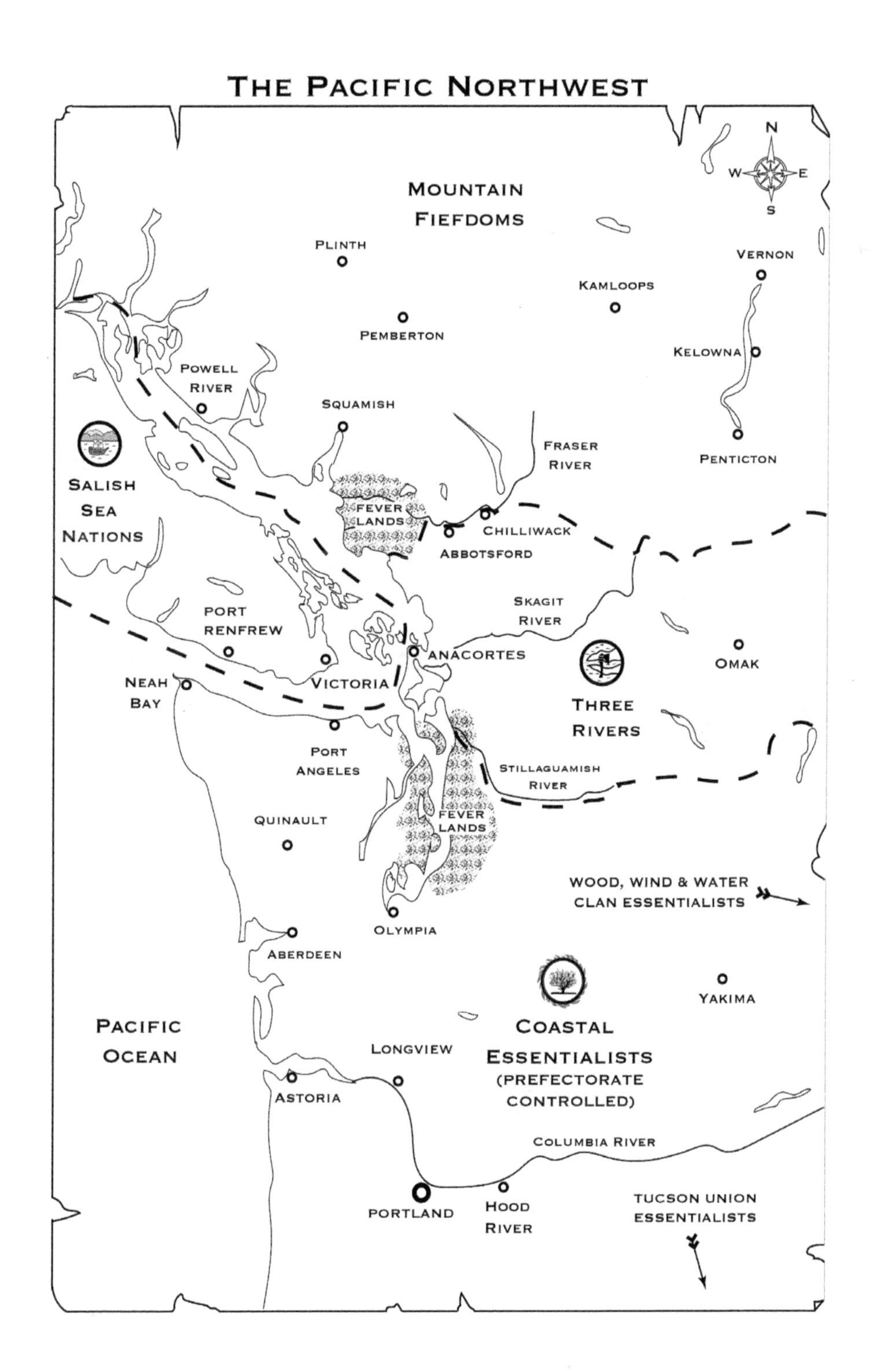
The Pacific Northwest
N
W
E
S
Mountain Fiefdoms
Plinth
Vernon
Kamloops
Pemberton
Kelowna
Powell River
Squamish
Fraser River
Penticton
Salish Sea Nations
Fever Lands
Chilliwack
Abbotsford
Skagit River
Port Renfrew
Anacortes
Omak
Victoria
Neah Bay
Three Rivers
Port Angeles
Stillaguamish River
Quinault
Fever Lands
Wood, Wind & Water Clan Essentialists
Olympia
Aberdeen
Yakima
Pacific Ocean
Coastal Essentialists (Prefectorate Controlled)
Longview
Astoria
Columbia River
Portland
Hood River
Tucson Union Essentialists

Salish Sea Nations

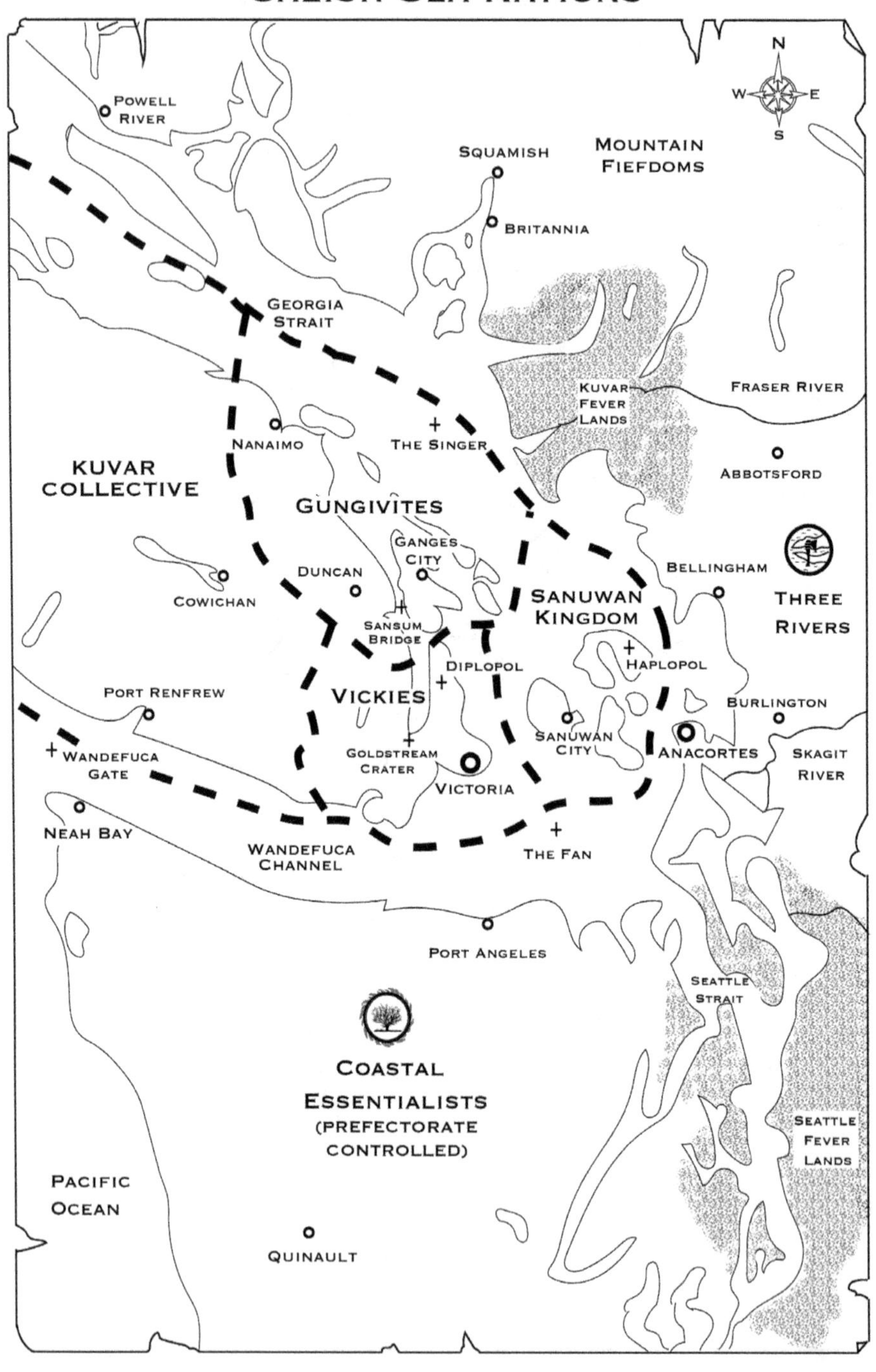

PART I

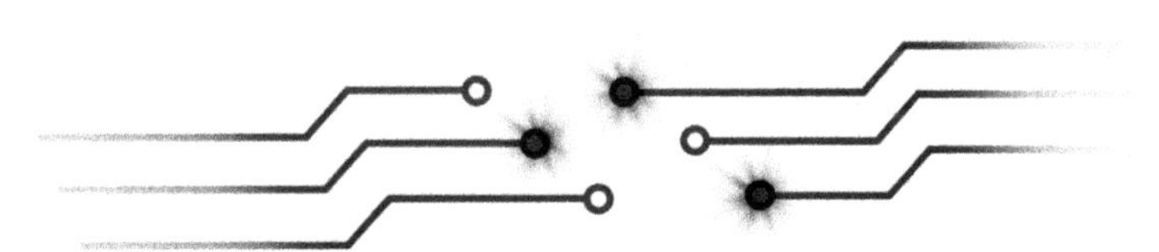

An Intercepted Letter

Dr. Leopold Halsey
Associate Professor of Antiquity
Anacortes Research Academy
10 Poplar Lane
Three Rivers Nation

Dear Leo,

The rumors are true. There is a terrible machine war here in the east. We will be sending someone to meet with you, because it is too complicated—and dangerous—to describe in a letter. But first we must know one thing.

Has Haplopol awakened?

Always your friend,

Cecile

—1—

A Hairy Job

Lexie hopped off the ferry gangway onto the metal grating that extended to the pier. "Let's get moving," she called to the others. "I don't want to be around town after dark." Victoria wasn't the kind of town where you could enjoy a moonlight stroll, even with three meaty strongmen.

Well, maybe more like two and a half. Ryder was such a waif Lexie couldn't give him a full count anymore. He ambled behind her, his breathing ragged, his face blanched. Poor sod.

Tarnation followed. "Ryder, bud, you're lookin' extra whingy today," he said. "We need to get you some vegie-tables." He laughed. Ferry workers tending mooring lines stared as Tarnation bounded down the gangway, his melon-sized hair bun bobbing on his head with every step. Lexie would ask him to be less conspicuous, but it was nigh on impossible for the hefty Oaknagan, with his green and black snakeskin-style body tattoo, to not draw attention.

Pulling up the rear was Johl, his head swiveling and eyes active. Lexie gave him a once-over. He was wearing his prized bearskin vest over a cloth jerkin, his machete scabbard bounding with each stride.

"Take off those furs," Lexie said.

"What's wrong with them?" Johl asked, a hint of offense in his tone.

"They're real pretty, but Vickies don't like 'em. Plus you look tough enough as it is."

He smirked and went about stowing his furs in his pack. Better to pad his young ego than let him know the truth: that the Vickies often took mountain fiefdom folk for suckers.

The four of them made their way along the pier into the harbor area. Dozens of sailboats and galleys lined the marina berths, as well as a couple of sleek-looking catamarans. The inner harbor walkways were busy with pop-up merchants and food vendors eager to palm off half-rotten fruit or curried goat to sailors who'd just finished long sea journeys. Horse-drawn carts and carriages transporting all manner of people and goods also paraded along the wharf.

They passed the Vicarial. It was the most impressive building in the harbor, both in its stature and due to its well-kept state. Several pyramidal towers adorned the ornately designed, four-hundred-room grand hotel. It was the highlight of Victoria, really, because the rest was mostly ramshackle. Besides the Vicarial, the Vickies didn't like to invest in anything long-term. "It's the quick money or no thank you, honey," Lexie had once heard from a Vicky merchant.

"What do you think, Johl?" she asked.

Johl's eyes were glued to the hotel as they walked past it. He said, "I've seen a picture of the Vicarial before, in a book, but it was at night, and back in the Old World, when there was electricity and neon. It doesn't look that impressive, compared to the photo, but maybe it's just because everything looks more glossy in pictures."

Tarnation didn't seem to care about the buildings. He was nodding and smiling at people with such verve that most pedestrians gave him a wide berth. "What's up, *bae*?" he would say boisterously whenever someone met his eyes. No, there was no chance of being inconspicuous with him around.

And Ryder, well, he just staggered along like a zombie.

Lexie led them down one of the main thoroughfares into town.

Johl said, "So boss, this message you're supposed to deliver. Ryder was saying it's about a city that used to be run by machines?"

"That's right," Lexie responded. "It's called Haplopol, in the Sanuwan Kingdom. It's deserted now. Nobody knows what happened to it—why it ... stopped working."

"What's so special about it? I thought everything in the Old World stopped working."

"Haplopol's different. Some people think it was still working after the fall."

Johl frowned, grappling with the concept. "What's the message, then?"

"Somebody saw something there. Our client—Leo—he wanted us to report it to the Gungivites. It's probably nothing."

"Why do you need three of us for that? Why not send a messenger?"

Johl was young—too young to know that he shouldn't ask so many questions. And he'd had plenty of time to ask Lexie on the ferry. Which meant he was getting nervous. Telling him more now would only make that worse, and she needed him calm. So she just shrugged and hoped he would forget it.

He didn't follow up. Maybe he was distracted by all the new sights and sounds. As a major trading hub, all the Salish Sea nations were represented here in Victoria, as well as Essentialist peoples—plenty for a young farm boy from the mountains to stare at and wonder about.

After passing through several more intersections, they stopped. Across from them was the Sanuwan Embassy; a tall, skinny tower with a single balcony on which a big gold sheep statue was frozen in a prancing position. Behind them was a more austere, institutional building. It was downright featureless except for the sign jutting out in big block letters: *Kuvar Collective Outpost.* The Three Rivers embassy was farther down the road. It had tall windows and an archway featuring an emblem of three rivers overlaid with an axe. Another sign, pointing down a side street, read: *Essentialist Embassy.* Lexie could see only an edge of the building itself within a large compound, fenced off and partially obscured by trees.

"Well?" Lexie asked, her eyes on Ryder.

He pointed back the way they had come, toward the wharf. "Back this way three blocks, and to the left," he said.

"How far to the left?" She glanced at the sky. It would be getting dark soon.

"About a half-mile."

"A half-mile? Why wouldn't they put them all in the same place?"

Ryder shrugged. Then, as if that small shoulder movement was a monumental feat of stamina, he launched into a fit of coughing. He bent over at the side of the road, gurgled, and spat.

Lexie should have asked Ryder about the embassy when they arrived at the docks. The Gungivites were always squirrelly, never doing things quite like the other Salish Sea nations. It figured they would put their embassy halfway across town.

Ryder was still bent over, drooling. Would he even make it to the embassy? It was hard to be miffed at him when he was in such dire straits, but she needed him. He surely had some terminal illness.

Eventually, Ryder peeled himself away from the gutter, pointed down the street and stumbled forward.

As he led them on, the streets became less populated and more littered with trash. A few buildings were boarded up. A few others were burnt down, with only blackened foundations remaining.

After they had been walking a considerable distance, Ryder cut down a narrow side street, one with no sidewalk and room for only one horse to pass. The street sign was barely legible. Lexie had to lean in close to make out the letters. It read *McTavish Lane*, as far as she could tell.

The side street broadened, but only enough to allow room for large dumpsters on each side, serving the dilapidated four-story buildings that bordered the alley. Beyond the dumpsters, a tall fence of rotting planks cut off their advance. To the right was a solitary door with the letters *G.E.* scrawled on it. It could have been graffiti, or even written by a child.

"This is it?" Lexie asked.

"Yes," Ryder replied. "The Gungivites aren't pretentious about their embassies."

"Pretentious? How about a little dignity?"

But she remembered that Ryder had been a Gungivite as a child. She didn't want to offend him. "I'm sorry, but … look at this place."

Ryder only nodded, then coughed into his forearm.

The fence squealed as a lower board turned. Johl's hand moved quickly to his machete.

It was only a gray tabby—a rather obese one, in fact—carrying a mangled rat by the scruff of its neck as it pushed through the fence hole.

Tarnation laughed heartily. "It's just a cat, bud."

"The biggest cat I've ever seen," Johl said, frowning. His hand eased away from his machete.

The cat sat down and stared at them, the rat still in its mouth.

"I wonder if it's one of them Gungivite cats," Johl said. "You know, the ones they talk about?" He looked at Ryder.

Ryder's jaw flexed. His eyes darted. "Could be, Johl. I've heard they're pretty big."

"Okay, let's get on with it," Lexie said. They were far away from the docks, in a dead-end alley. Not the ideal place to be when twilight was taking hold.

Ryder knocked on the door.

A muffled response came from within. "What now?"

Lexie said, "We're here to deliver a message for the Gungivite Observers."

"Fine, fine. Come in."

Inside was a square room with a solitary desk in the middle. A wooden door in the back was the only other exit. A man sat behind the desk, fingering through a binder that lay open on the table. There were a few stacks of these binders on the desk, but nothing else in the room except a few piles of trash and what were clearly lumps of cat turds. In fact, Lexie noticed the gray cat had followed them in. It sat in a corner and gnawed happily on the rat, the bones grinding in its mouth.

She wasn't sure if it was the cat feces, the trash in the alley, or the man's body odor, but the room stank. She tried hard not to wrinkle her nose.

"What's this all about?" the man behind the desk asked. He had jowls, patchy hair, and a monocle that rested below one eye. Flies circled around him. One landed on his nose. He seemed oblivious.

"We have a message for the Gungivite Observers," Lexie said, repeating Ryder's words as she stepped forward.

"You look Asian. Prefectorate?"

"No," she replied, "but my father was. I'm from Anacortes."

"What's the message about?"

"Haplopol. It lit up a week ago."

She'd thought the man might be surprised, or at least might find the news interesting. Instead he just rolled his eyes. "Sure it did. I'll pass on the message."

"You don't believe me?"

"Look, we get the same message several times a year. Sometimes it's a lonely sailor that wants attention. More often it's the Sanuwans lighting fires around Haplopol, starting rumors. Tourism is their main income, you know—from people checking out Haplopol, for the most part. It sure ain't from sheep herding, like they say. So forgive me if I don't jump out of my seat."

"This isn't from a sailor, or from the Sanuwans. A man named Leopold hired me to deliver the message."

He perked up at that. "Well, let's have it then." He thrust out a stubby-fingered hand.

"I'm only supposed to deliver it to a man named Nillias."

"Yeah, that's me," he said.

She glanced down at his forearms. His arms were bare; no tattoo. "No, you're not," she said.

Tarnation stepped forward. He pulled out an axe that had been hidden under his jerkin and hoisted it over his shoulder. "Time's a wastin'," he said. "No more funny games, bud."

Johl followed suit, fingering the sheath of his machete.

The man rubbed his nose rapidly as if he was trying to scrub it off his face. Maybe he'd finally caught a whiff of the atrocious stench. "You've got the right idea. Us Gungivites don't like to waste time, but you best keep your dogs on a leash."

None of them budged.

He sighed. "Can you at least show me the message? At a distance, like."

Lexie pulled out the envelope and showed it to him, remaining a few steps from the table. All that was written on the cover was *Nillias*.

The man frowned at her, stewed on it for a moment, then yelled, "Nillias!"

They only had to wait a moment. This man, Nillias, must have been in the adjoining room. He opened the door and entered without flourish.

Nillias looked nothing like his colleague—and this *was* Nillias, for his sleeves were rolled up and his tattoo showed prominently on his arm, just as Leo had described; it was a stencil, like you might see on the arm of some Old World prisoner, which read *GO78230.* He wore spotless wool pants and a matching vest over a white shirt and black tie. His face was pale, but not sickly like Ryder's. His brown hair was perfectly combed in long, flowing lines, hanging near to his shoulders.

He pointed at Lexie. "You, come with me. The rest, stay."

"No, sir," Lexie said, smiling. "We're all coming."

Beside her, Johl and Tarnation nodded. Ryder tried to suppress a cough.

Nillias didn't respond. He only cradled his hands together and stood there, motionless and silent.

That was when things got pretty hairy.

It started with a curious whirring and whipping sound coming from the walls, like the steering wheel of a ship set to spin with stray ropes attached to it. Then Lexie lost her balance. Or rather, she lost the floor. It literally opened up underneath her.

The landing wasn't hard; she bounced off of a soft surface and soon righted herself. Tarnation, Ryder and Johl had also fallen through panels in the floor, but the man at the desk hadn't, nor had Nillias. Even the cat had remained in the room above them.

They were in another square room that appeared to have no exits—at least, until one of the walls began to descend into the floor.

"What's going on?" Johl jittered, his machete drawn. Tarnation and Ryder were crouching beside him, similarly bewildered.

"Just be ready … for anything," Lexie said, pulling a knife of her own from her sleeve. So far, this job was looking to be a real cock-up.

The room that opened up beyond the descending wall was a far cry from the one from which they had fallen. Mahogany shelves full of carefully arranged books lined the walls, and the floor was dark, gleaming marble. Nillias was there, having completed his descent of a spiral staircase, along with three similarly-attired men, all of them brandishing pistols pointed in their direction.

It wasn't a good sign.

"I'm sorry about the uncivilized welcome," Nillias said, "but we insist that you join us, alone. We will not harm your colleagues."

Her mind raced. "Let me take one with me," she said, "for protection. If you're civil, like you say, we won't have any problems." She reckoned one wouldn't help her much, but if they said no, she was pretty sure they were just going to kill them all. In that case, they might as well fight it out here and now.

Nillias took an inordinately long time to decide. He stared at her, unflinching. Meanwhile, Johl's head spun frenetically. It wasn't helping the jitters in the room any.

"Fine," Nillias said. "Take that one." He pointed to Johl. Nillias began walking into the adjoining room, paused, half-turned to Lexie, and waited.

"Stay calm," she whispered to Johl, and they walked onto the solid marble floor, amid the three Gungivites holding pistols. Two of these kept their weapons targeted at Ryder and Tarnation, while one kept his pistol trained on her and Johl.

Nillias led them through a heavy metal door on the far side of the room, and the man pointing his weapon at them followed them in. The next chamber was similarly elaborate, furnished with a set of leather reclining chairs around a glass table. Lexie could see no lanterns or candles, but light emanated from translucent panels on the ceiling and floor.

This was another planet compared to the dingy embassy entrance. With all this neon, these people were definitely hiding something—something they probably didn't want Lexie to see.

Also not good.

"Sit," Nillias said, taking a chair.

She did, as did Johl.

"Can I see the letter, Lexie?" Nillias asked.

Wait a minute. How did they know her name?

Her skin was crawling something fierce now. She wasn't sure she'd be getting out of this one alive.

Nillias just stared at her as her heart hammered in her chest.

There were no conditions she could think of to give her leverage, and certainly no easy escape, so she pulled out the envelope and offered it to Nillias.

He opened it and read the letter.

Nillias's next action was too smooth. She wasn't ready for it, and she wasn't used to dealing with guns. Why would she be? Guns were outlawed. Johl didn't catch on either. So they sat there, frozen like statues, unable to react in time.

In a motion as casual as it was fluid, Nillias pulled a pistol out of a vest pocket, pointed it at Johl, and shot him in the temple.

Johl's body slumped from the chair and then sprawled out on the floor. His eyes were vacant.

Lexie jumped, backing away from her chair with her knife out, but the exit had closed and the armed Gungivite stood before it.

Slowly, Nillias turned his weapon toward her. She was sure he was about to pull the trigger, until there was another whirring sound, and yet another wall began falling away behind Nillias.

"Wait," she heard a voice say, coming from the direction of the falling wall.

The chamber that was revealed was even stranger than the first two. A dozen or so black panels were spread about, and half as many chairs. The room was illuminated by wall-mounted pictures of what looked like colorful fruit trees in various stages of bloom, as if each had a powerful lantern behind it. A glass water tank full of exotic fish was glowing in the corner.

In the middle of this room was a man. His hair was long and clean, the same as Nillias and the rest of the Gungivites in the last room, as if they had all gone to the same barber, and the barber had only known how to do one kind of hairstyle. But his clothes were different. He wore pants and a baggy black linen shirt, which might have appeared like undergarments one might wear to bed if they hadn't been cut to fit so cleanly. His eyes were a frosty deep gray, and his face was creased with age.

"I need to talk with this one," he said.

Nillias frowned, but nodded. He motioned with his gun for Lexie to move toward the older man.

She tried to suppress her anxiety, though her mind reeled. What in blazes *was* this place, and how could she get out in one piece? Tarnation and Ryder weren't going to help. In fact, she had to accept the fact that they were probably already dead, or would be soon.

For lack of a better option, she slowly put one foot in front of the other, heading over to the older man. Nillias handed him the letter.

He glanced at it for a fleeting instant.

"It's surely another rumor," Nillias said, "and this one has seen too much. She's spoken with Leopold. She has to die."

"We can't be certain," the old man said.

Nillias looked miffed. "But, sir, the chances—"

The old man raised his open hand, and Nillias held his tongue.

Then the old man turned to her, probing her with his metallic eyes. "Tell me, Lexie. What did Leopold say to you about what he saw in Haplopol?"

"It's in the letter there."

"No, it's not, not all of it. The letter says that Haplopol has awakened, and its lights are visible from the Salish Sea. It also says its doors finally opened, but what did he tell you about the entrance to Haplopol, specifically?"

Had Leo told her something else? She tried to recall. In fact, he had. It seemed a silly thing at the time—a trivial fact. She'd wondered why he'd told her. "He said … he said the Haplopol doors are open and the drawbridge is down. He said there was gold lettering above the main doors that read *Haplopol is open to all*."

The old man's gaze wavered, and his head fell into his hands. He appeared to be deep in thought.

Nillias stepped closer to Lexie, his gun pointing even more resolutely at her temple. He was clearly awaiting some decision from his boss, some decision that would determine whether she would live or die.

Lexie thought about trying to swat away the gun, but then what? There were too many of them, and she didn't know how to get out of this bizarre underground freak show. “Look, let’s just say I didn’t see anything here, okay?” she said, her voice cracking. She was pleading with open hands, trying to keep them from trembling, while looking back and forth between the old man and Nillias. “I’m just a messenger. Let’s pretend I dropped it off and left.”

A panel behind the old man lit up, and then another to his left, and another to his right. Numbers streamed down them, along with diagrams and reams of text. They cast shades of color on the old man’s hands as they covered his face.

“Are those …?” Lexie exclaimed. First guns, then all that neon, and now *computer screens*? Who *were* these people?

In hindsight, Leo did seem a bit shady, and the price he had offered was way too high. Nothing was that good. That was why she had brought all the help. But how could she have known about … *this*?

It looked like she was about to pay for her greed with her life. Mom would be left alone, with no one to help her. Lexie’s anxiety mushroomed into anguish that threatened to consume her. “Please. You don’t need to kill me. I promise I won’t say a word.” She was babbling like a child.

“Sir?” Nillias asked, with a hint of impatience.

Finally, the old man looked up. His gray eyes looked even colder, and his face was stern, as if he had mined a steely resolve during his minute of contemplation. He said, “The story matches, so the city has awakened. This is the moment we feared.”

Nillias’s eyes widened. After a pause, he asked, “And the woman?”

The old man squinted at Lexie. “We may have need for this one. Let’s not kill her yet.”

—2—

ANTHROPOLOGICAL MUSINGS

Dryden awoke to the sound of knocking on his door. He was lying on his couch in his black housecoat, a few sheets of paper spread out on the coffee table in front of him, as well as Ranthoke's compendium titled *Independent City States of Morganis: Archeological Findings and Anthropological Musings*. A bowl and a pair of scissors lay on the ground.

He pulled a creased sheet of paper from under him. It was covered in blond strands of hair. Hairs also littered his housecoat. He tried to wipe them off but they only rolled under his hands, stuck to the coat by static.

More knocking sounded, louder this time.

"Coming!" he called. He found his down jacket draped over a stool in the kitchen. He threw it over his housecoat and opened the door.

"Oh, hi, Telly," he said. Telly was already halfway down his apartment steps, about to leave. She had her hair in a tight ponytail and wore her cotton two-piece work outfit from the exchange store. She hid one hand around her back, as if there was an itch she couldn't scratch.

This wasn't going to be a casual visit, he guessed.

"Why are you wearing a jacket?" she asked.

"It's cold in here," he said. It wasn't that cold, in fact. It was early summer, and quite mild. He was just trying to cover the hairs on his housecoat.

She frowned. "Did you try to cut your own hair again?"

"I'm not going to *pay* for it," he said, wiping the side of his head, as if he might right some outliers. He'd cut it short, so it wasn't his bedhead she was criticizing—it was indeed the haircut. "They charge me more than the Prefectorate soldiers, and even other Coastals. It's discrimination! And besides, is it really that bad?" He offered a half-smile.

She wasn't going for it. "Yes, it is," she said, her face sour.

"So what's up?" he asked. "Did you forget—"

"I spoke with Rena," she interrupted. "She told me about your kid."

"Oh." It was something he'd neglected to mention the night before.

She presented the hand that had been hidden behind her back. It extended and threw an object at him, hitting his coat before his reflexes fired and he was able to swat it against his side. It was a carving he'd made for her—a doe and her fawn, sculpted from amber-colored driftwood. "And don't send me any more of your notes, either," she said.

She turned and walked away.

Dryden exhaled a long sigh. He leaned over the stairs and rubbed his head aggressively, letting the stray hairs be taken away by the breeze.

He weighed the carving in his hand. Maybe he could sell it? There were only three more days until the trip he'd promised Nate, and he could always use more spending money—but the only place he could sell it was the exchange shop, where Telly worked.

He walked back inside and into his room. There, he opened his closet and placed the carving on the top shelf. There were about twenty of them there; mostly squirrels, rabbits and cats, but also an asymmetric Old World building and a misshapen car. The doe and fawn was one of his favorites, so he was almost glad to have it back.

But not really.

He returned to the couch and picked up Ranthoke's compendium. He'd been in the middle of reading it when he'd drifted off. Unfortunately, so far Ranthoke's revised edition was full of fluff, light on archeological findings and even lighter on anthropological musings.

Another rapping came from the door. He stood up slowly and walked to the entrance. He'd gotten off too easy with Telly. She probably wasn't quite finished giving him a piece of her mind.

But it wasn't Telly. It was a pureblood Prefectorate soldier, dressed in a tight olive uniform, an intimidating-looking sword at his belt.

"Dryden Quintain?" the soldier asked with a Japanese accent.

"Yes, that's me."

"You will attend a meeting at the Hood River Municipal Chamber at three p.m."

"Wait. Sorry, who are you, and what is this meeting?"

"Your superior officer—Curator Maxwell—has requested your presence."

Dryden almost laughed at that. Why did these Prefectorates have to militarize everything? "What's this meeting about?"

"General Hatsuo and Captain Chinatsu will be in attendance."

General Hatsuo? Dryden was glad he hadn't laughed. "Um … yes, sir. I will be there promptly at three p.m."

The soldier nodded tightly, turned about, and left.

The Hood River Municipal Chamber was near the banks of the Columbia River. It was a boxy Old World building with framing made of sturdy steel beams. The municipality could have used any number of buildings in the main town, but the Prefectorate soldiers preferred to linger close to the shipwrights along the harbor and generally didn't like to stray too far into town.

Beside the building was another plot of land where a similar-sized foundation had been laid, but this structure had collapsed, decayed, and been pillaged of any useful construction materials. All that remained were several husks of rounded metal protruding from the earth, melted down by retcher attacks during the fall, or so it was said.

Dryden arrived early. The same Prefectorate soldier was waiting for him at the entrance. He escorted Dryden through the offices to a lobby outside the main boardroom. There, Dryden sat and waited.

He'd brought a large loose-leaf binder, figuring Maxwell would want him to take notes on some topic of anthropological concern. He couldn't think of any other reason why he'd be called in.

"So what's this all about?" he asked the soldier, his foot tapping expectantly.

"You will find out."

Evidently.

The door opened and Maxwell exited. His hair was disheveled as usual, and his long face was taut and serious. "Dryden, good. Please," he said, waving him into the boardroom.

Including Maxwell, there were four people in the room, and Dryden could tell they'd already been meeting for some time. A rough map of the Salish Sea had been drawn on a chalkboard, and papers were strewn about the long table. The table had a number of cut marks along the top, no doubt made by Prefectorate blades. If anything told Dryden he needed to be on his best behavior, it was those cut marks.

A vigorous-looking Asian man in a tight Prefectorate uniform stood up to greet him, shaking his hand with verve. He had a wide nose and glossy white teeth. "This is Dryden, then," he said. "Nice to meet you; Maxwell has told me so many good things. I'm General Hatsuo."

"He did?" Dryden glanced at Maxwell, who glared at him. Maxwell had quite the portfolio of glares. Dryden was pretty sure this was the glare that meant *Don't screw this up*. "Thank you, General. Honored to meet you, sir."

Hatsuo smiled generously.

"And this is Captain Chinatsu," Maxwell said, gesturing toward a woman in military uniform, who was sitting in a chair. "She is one of General Hatsuo's primary aides." Chinatsu was as tall as the general, and lithe, with short-cropped hair that revealed a scar that angled across her forehead. A maroon band adorned her arm.

"What is wrong with his hair?" Chinatsu asked.

"Sorry, I cut it and didn't do a good job," Dryden said sheepishly.

"Why did he color it yellow?" Chinatsu looked pointedly around the room at the others, as if Dryden had committed a capital offense. His platinum blond hair and freckled complexion were extremely rare among coastal Essentialists, so quizzical looks were frequent. Some were even repulsed by it, as Chinatsu seemed to be.

Maxwell spoke carefully. "It's actually his real hair, captain. It's unusual, I know. We can have him dye it brown or black if you prefer."

Chinatsu was about to speak, but Hatsuo spoke first. "Nonsense, there's nothing wrong with blond hair. Let's be sensible." He winked at Dryden.

Maxwell nodded and took the opportunity to move on to the final introduction. "And this is Mayor Gianna. I presume you two have met." They had indeed met before. Gianna was a rotund, no-nonsense woman with cheeks constantly in some form of red rash. She was new to town, and as such it was hard to figure out how she made mayor. It was quite possible it was because nobody else wanted the position. She nodded and barely waved at Dryden.

Hatsuo and Maxwell regained their seats, while Dryden was left standing, unsure of where to sit.

"Well?" Chinatsu said to him.

Maxwell intervened. "I'm sorry. Dryden hasn't been briefed. Let's get him up to speed. Dryden, please have a seat over there." He pointed to the end of the table, near the map that had been scrawled onto the chalkboard. Dryden maneuvered around the table while Maxwell continued speaking. "The short version is, we believe Haplopol has awakened."

Dryden hadn't quite made it to his chair. "What?"

"We received an invitation from the Sanuwans, with a rather steep price tag attached to it, to come and visit. We also heard a rumor—separately, and from an independent source—about lights coming from the center of the island."

"But … are you sure? There have been so many rumors. The Sanuwans, they play games, light fires, trying to draw people to the island."

"We sent a stealth ship to Sanuwan coastal waters, under cover of night," Hatsuo said. "They confirmed the lights are too bright, and not the right coloration, to be fires. Not only that, but the buildings are visible from the East Sound Channel." He pointed to the diagram behind Dryden.

Dryden turned. Haplopol had been marked on the map and a circle scrawled around the channel closest to it. He scratched the back of his head. "You shouldn't be able to see the buildings from the channel, unless …"

"I've shown them your paper on ICSM city awakenings," Maxwell said. "The city—or I should say, the buildings within Haplopol—may have risen further out of the ground, as you suggested they would, when the city awakened. In that case, it would make sense that you could see them from the channel."

The group granted Dryden a moment to absorb the news. Could it really be happening? They had done their homework. It certainly seemed plausible.

And it was finally obvious why they'd asked him here. He'd spent ten years studying ICSM culture in Portland, making him one of the most knowledgeable people on the subject in coastal Essentialist lands. It had been a vocation that, until today, everyone had told him was a complete waste of time.

His heart started beating rapidly. He almost felt faint. "So … how can I help?" he asked, trying not to lose his cool.

"Why do the cities exist?" Chinatsu asked. "A summary, please."

"Wow. Well, I'll try—to summarize, I mean. Most evidence points to them being built about eighty years ago, or twenty years after the fall. The creators, led by a man named Morganis, wanted to form a sort of utopia. At the same time, they wanted to protect themselves from the harsh post-fall world. That's why many of these cities are hard to access, or hidden altogether. Supposedly they used advanced machines, even more advanced than the Old World. After a period of thriving and expansion, they abruptly went dormant. We don't have good records of what happened to them. This is all based on scattered evidence."

Chinatsu scowled. "How can you not know? Why don't you just ask people who lived there, or their relatives?"

Dryden could see that Maxwell had his fingers slightly raised from the table in a gesture of caution. Dryden smiled and kept his voice low, trying not to seem confrontational. "Apologies, captain, but there actually are no such people. This is one of the great mysteries. There is no account from anyone who lived in the cities, or their relatives—only from people who knew about the cities but didn't live there, or who corresponded with the inhabitants."

"You say *cities*," Hatsuo said. "There are more than Haplopol?" He was leaning back, looking thoughtful.

Dryden couldn't be sure how much they knew already, and he had to be cautious not to say anything that would be considered anti-Essentialist. He continued on, speaking slowly. "Yes, it's generally believed there were five in all, but we only know the location of three of them. Haplopol is the best preserved, probably because it's quite secluded and wasn't pillaged. It's also the first one Morganis built. You may not have heard much about it this far south because the cities aren't on coastal Essentialist land, or even in the mountain tribal areas. The cities had advanced electronic systems so are only in places that have been depopulated of retchers, like Kuvar Island and other islands in the Salish Sea."

"What do you think happened to all these cities?" Gianna asked. "You must have a theory." She seemed just as curious as the general and the captain.

Dryden shrugged. He looked at Maxwell for help but received none. "Honestly, there are many theories, but little evidence. Many believe they just disappeared or sank into the earth. Some believe the inhabitants fought and killed one another; others believe they all committed suicide. It's not clear."

In contrast to the general's thoughtful air, Chinatsu was tapping her fingers on the table impatiently. "And what might we find in Haplopol," she said, "if it's *open,* like the Sanuwans say?"

"According to what few records we have, it should be a city unlike any other, controlled by machines that clean, make food, and entertain you. These machines should be able to build the tallest buildings, answer almost any question you have, and keep you safe. We have no real proof of this, of course."

Chinatsu glanced at Hatsuo, then back to Dryden. "They have machines that protect you? How?"

Dryden waved his hand and shook his head dismissively. "It's highly speculative," he said. Normally in academic circles that would mean *not worth talking about*, but the people in the room remained attentive, waiting.

Maxwell's eyes widened and he nodded, urging Dryden on.

Dryden continued, "Well, there was one account, from an old letter we found, that said Haplopol had three large defense droids. It described them as being about half the size of this building and having the firepower of a couple armored tanks, if you know what those were like, back in the Old World. I'm not sure if this was an exaggeration, and again, that's just one person's account from eighty years ago, so—"

He noticed that Gianna had been building up a head of steam as he was speaking. Suddenly, she broke out into a rant. "No, no, *no!* I know what you're thinking, Captain, and you too, General. First I hear about this war in the east with the Spokes, and now this. If your interest in Haplopol is about us taking control of those machines, we simply can't have it. We Coasters pride ourselves on being more liberal than the eastern Essentialists, but this would be a clear violation. Even to set foot in that place would be dubious, right?" She glared at Maxwell.

Maxwell grimaced. "It's true, as curator it would be hard to condone—"

"Damn right," Gianna interrupted. "We should *not* get involved. Don't you remember *sun, soil and seed*? That's our sacrament, our pact with the earth that *you* agreed to when we signed our treaty. Not sun, soil, seed, and *neon*." She pointed accusingly at Chinatsu and Hatsuo. "Let's let the Sanuwans sully themselves with this … this … bizarre city that makes people disappear."

Dryden was amazed at Gianna's tone, and with a Prefectorate general in the room, no less. She was either really brave or really stupid.

Chinatsu stood up, her face red. "Insolence," was all she said. Her katana glinted as she drew it from her hip scabbard.

The odds were quickly tilting in favor of *really stupid.*

Gianna was from a small town, many leagues away, and had been thrust into the mayoral job without much training. Maybe she was skeptical of the story that a tenth of the town had been beheaded when the Prefectorate ships first arrived. She might believe it now, though. She stood up and recoiled from the table, as did Maxwell and Dryden.

The general hadn't moved, however. He simply cleared his throat, with a hint of exaggeration. Chinatsu stared at Gianna with loathing but stayed her hand.

Hatsuo's disposition warmed to a smile, and he looked at each of them in turn. "Please, please, can we all try to be a little more civilized? Captain, we must learn to be more patient with these people. And Gianna, your tone is unbecoming for such an important leader in this community."

His gaze rested on Gianna. "We *do* take sun, soil and seed as sacrament. You are clearly a staunch defender of our principles, and that impresses me, but I am saddened you would think otherwise of the Prefectorate. Why else would we be interested in Haplopol other than to contain it, or rid the world of it? What if one of the Salish Sea nations took these tainted machines from Haplopol and made them work the land, or had them build *more* machines? You know the Salish Sea nations are full of pirates and despots. Who is going to police them if not us?"

Gianna nodded slowly, but Dryden wasn't sure if it was because she actually believed the general, or because Chinatsu's katana blade remained drawn, several feet across the table. "I apologize, general," Gianna said. "I spoke out of turn."

Chinatsu's disposition didn't change. Her face was like red steel.

Hatsuo turned to Chinatsu. "Captain, please. These people often lose their tongues, you know that, and we don't want to spoil the excellent job Otaka has done in stabilizing Hood River for the Prefectorate. Find your inner *yurei*, and be at peace."

Chinatsu's face finally lost its color, and she sheathed her sword. "*Hai, ippantekina*," she said in Japanese, and she nodded to the general.

"Good," Hatsuo continued. "Let's wrap up, then. I think we've covered the important information. We will be sending a military expedition in two days." Hatsuo smiled at them all, his hands open.

Heads nodded back at him as the tension gradually dissipated.

Dryden had to admit, he liked this general. He'd been nervous about the prospect of offending him, as he'd heard Prefectorate military leadership were often petty and cruel, but this Hatsuo seemed quite reasonable. He even treated coastal Essentialists with respect.

And perhaps because of this, he decided to venture a request of his own, to ensure that a once-in-a-lifetime opportunity wasn't wasted. "General—

sir—if I may. There is a great scholar named Leopold who knows the ICSM well, and who is based in Anacortes. Can I write to him and request that he send someone to join your expedition? It would be of tremendous importance to document what you see, and he may provide needed guidance to your soldiers."

The general raised his eyebrows. He stood up, moved toward Dryden, and placed a hand on his shoulder. "No, you cannot, because we already have the scholar we need." He winked again.

Oh.

A tide of exhilaration rose within Dryden. He might be the first to visit an awakened ICSM city. He might become one of the great ICSM scholars, like Ranthoke, or Leopold. He could finally put his life's work to good use. And maybe, just maybe, he could find a way of preventing the Prefectorate from damaging a site of profound historical significance.

He couldn't help allowing himself a childish grin.

But his smile soon withered, because undermining his elation, weighty and dark, lurked a promise. It was a promise that he would break, for the person he cared most about in the world.

—3—

Teleological

Nillias delivered a needle to Lexie's upper arm only a few seconds after the old man with the gray eyes had stayed her execution.

"Who are you people?" Lexie asked.

There was no response. The lights from the display terminals still crawled with numbers and images.

"What will you do with Ryder and Tarnation?"

But Nillias and the old man just waited. She was already feeling faint. It was fast-acting, whatever it was.

Nillias caught her as she collapsed into unconsciousness.

She experienced snatches of coherence every few hours, each time for only a minute. It was as if Lexie was sailing in the dead of night, and a lighthouse lantern was revolving far away. There was only darkness, save that brief moment when the light would shine on her—and only then was she able to obtain her bearings, until she was lost again.

There was movement. A river was moving under her. No, it was too coarse. Cobblestones. She was in a cart, or a carriage. Inertial forces tugged at her gently—turning, starting, stopping—until she was lost again.

A sliver of sunlight reflected from the dust particles hanging in the air of the carriage. Nillias was sitting upright in front of her, eyes closed. On occasion, his eyelids fluttered. Lexie tried to crane her neck to look through the window that let in the light. The sun shone off a body of water. She was crossing a bridge. A giant platform with five-point protuberances reached out from the guardrails, hovering over the water—a splayed hand.

Exhaustion overcame her, and she was lost again.

Her subconscious started to plug the holes of blackness between bouts of awareness. Mom was there, reading next to her. Mom's black tresses were gray-streaked, and the veins in her arms weren't visible. It was a memory from long ago, because now the veins would be distinct rivers of blue riding above a white plane.

The book she was reading was about a group of navy brats trying to find a sunken ship filled with treasure. The lead man was a real knob, always talking about how special their mission was—about some self-important, vainglorious calling.

"I hope they don't find it," Lexie said.

Her mom's eyes widened in surprise.

Darkness.

Lexie was looking at the shore from a ship. The smell of brine permeated her nose. She felt a firm, reassuring hand on her shoulder as she watched an angular building burn to the ground. People scurried around the fire, trying to contain it with water and active shovels. Two of these people stopped and stared out to sea, and back at the ship—back at Lexie.

Their eyes burned like the blaze that raged behind them.

Lexie awoke to the sound of bells in the distance. She lay in a bed covered in white sheets, a single window casting a pallid light on her. It was either dusk, or dawn. She wore dark linens, similar to the attire of the old man with the cold gray eyes. Her head pounded and her body ached. A glass of water had been left on a bedside table. She drank greedily from it.

Despite her body's objections, she changed into her own clothes, which had been cleaned and left folded neatly at the end of her bed. She stepped carefully out of the room.

She found herself in a large house with several bedrooms, and as far as she could tell, it was of Old World construction. Here, on what appeared to be the third level, there were broad windows that looked out over a lake surrounded by low mountains. Canoes and rowboats dotted the expanse of water. The sun was rising, so it had to be morning. On a peninsula across the lake was a small hamlet, if it could even be called that, with a large tower and municipal building, almost like an Old World church but more institutional-looking, with an ornate clock tower and several steeples rising from the highest vertices of the roof. She suspected it was the source of the tolling bells that had woken her.

There was no one in the house, nor were there any additional shoes or clothes anywhere.

She searched the house, more meticulously this time. Some of the doors and cabinets were locked, but the kitchen had its fair share of utensils. Two knives she took for herself; she hid one strategically near her bed, the other in her sleeve. She also checked the false heel of her boot and saw that her hidden knife was still there.

She exited through a doorway at the rear of the property and was met by a warm summer breeze. A road cut back and forth up a terraced hill, upon which were a number of fruit trees: apple, pear, plum, and cherry. To the left and right of the property were other, nearly identical tracts of land with the same type of house and variety of fruit trees.

Lexie was about to head back inside when she saw a man on a ladder propped against a tree, almost completely obscured by the foliage.

She considered hiding and trying to escape. Maybe she could find a boat and cross the lake, or skulk across the neighboring properties. Or she could even attack the man and try to get some answers out of him.

She decided against all of these approaches. The very fact that she wasn't tied down or locked up meant her abductors weren't worried about her escaping. These people had guns, and computers. They had almost killed her. Best not to give them any more reasons to do so.

And she had no idea where the heck she was, anyway.

So she walked along the road to approach the man in the tree. A bucket hung from his forearm and he was looking up into the branches, plucking plums judiciously. Occasionally he would examine the fruit carefully, and if he didn't like it, he would throw it on the ground. He had a familiar tattoo on his arm—it was Nillias.

"How do you feel?" he asked, not looking down.

She felt remarkably good, in fact. The aches she had experienced upon waking had dissipated quickly. But she said, "Lost and confused. Where am I?"

"Ganges Island. This is where I grew up."

"Whoop-de-doo. Why are you keeping me here?"

He picked a plum, then another. No answer seemed to be forthcoming. He still hadn't looked down at her.

Finally, he said, "All entities are teleological, Lexie, which means we all have goals. I would like to pick plums. What would you like to do? If you tell me, maybe we can have a more efficient conversation."

It was a bizarre statement. She already suspected the Gungivite Observers were some sort of deranged cult, and Nillias was certainly affirming her belief. But how should she answer? She wanted to get home, of course, but she couldn't tell him that.

"I want to know why you're concerned about Haplopol," she said. If she could learn the answer to that, maybe she could find out why they were keeping her.

He finally broke himself away from his plum picking to gaze down at her, but only for an instant. Then he returned to his picking.

"Well?" she asked, after another extended pause. "Are you going to tell me?"

Nillias said, "Olint—the one who stayed your execution—is a senior Observer. He has many goals, and he believes you can help us with some of them. To do that, first you must pick plums."

"What does that have to do with Haplopol?"

Nillias descended the ladder. He handed Lexie his bucket. "There are more buckets in the shed, next to the house. There is also food and water there. I have prepared breakfast and lunch." He paused, tilted his head, and leaned in closer to her. "Listen closely. I want you to gather as many plums as you can before nightfall."

He walked away from her, along the road.

"Wait. What does that have to do with anything? You didn't answer my question!"

He didn't stop, and soon he was over the lip of the hill.

What a nutjob.

It was aggravating. What was the point? At first she thought he was just being a jerk. He needed to harvest the plums, so why not get his captive to do it? In that case, maybe she should refuse. Why be a model prisoner if she didn't want to be a prisoner at all?

But it seemed too trivial to be his objective. It was a nice estate, and if the embassy was any indication, these people didn't lack the means to hire a day laborer. Surely Nillias could get someone else to pick his plums. His gibberish about goals came back to her. Maybe this was some kind of test? Maybe she had to prove that she would comply—that she could make his goals her goals? If they needed her for a job, maybe they needed to be sure she would follow orders, and if she couldn't follow a simple one like picking plums, she would be useless. This seemed a more likely guess.

It was still annoying.

In the end, she didn't have a choice. If she was on Ganges Island, there would be way too many geographic hurdles and political borders to overcome if she tried to escape. Pirates and merchants steered clear of Gungivite coastal waters because the Gungivites were so loopy and territorial, so she couldn't hitch a ride with anyone. Ganges City harbor wasn't even open to foreigners.

So she picked up the bucket, climbed the ladder, and started snagging plums, one by one.

The tree had mostly been picked over already, and so, after filling a couple of buckets, it became too time-consuming to pick the odd plum on the farthest reaches of the tree, not to mention dangerous.

Nillias had said to gather as many as possible, so she moved on to the next tree, but not before having her breakfast in the shed. It was a healthy bowl of oats and apple slices. She felt as if she hadn't eaten in days, and she devoured it quickly. Maybe she *hadn't* eaten in days? Either way, it was remarkably tasty. But you know what they say about sailors and pirates; you could serve them a bowl of dog piss. As long as you tell them it's not fish, they'll eat two of it.

She spent the balance of the morning picking plums from the next tree, and filled up three more buckets. She had to admit, lunch was also good: succulent plums, of course, but also thick sandwiches filled with smoked venison, tomatoes and sprouts.

While she ate her sandwich, she strolled around the property to search for more plum trees, but these appeared to be the only two. She could see similar plum trees replete with fruit beyond short picket fences marking the property boundary, but she suspected Nillias wouldn't want her stealing from the neighbors. She also found a trough filled with rotting plums. Perhaps these had been picked up off the ground, or possibly these were ones that Nillias had rejected. She weighed sifting through it, but she wasn't about to give this homicidal man any rotting plums.

Johl had died for less. Johl had died for nothing, in fact.

Occasionally, birds would flock on the lake and the wind would gently course through the trees. Sunlight shimmered through the branches and warmed her face as she reached up, over and over again. It was a beautiful setting, and the work wasn't hard, but that didn't stop surges of anger from rolling through her. This was a frivolous exercise. Tarnation, Ryder and Johl didn't deserve to die at the hands of these sociopaths.

And Mom was waiting for her. Without Ryder and Tarnation, the only person who would be looking out for Mom was Freddy. Freddy was about as reliable as the winds in Howe Strait.

She kept at it for the rest of the afternoon and into early evening, but managed to fill only one more bucket. At one point, the ladder almost fell, at which point she decided to be more careful. She didn't want to make it *that* easy for them. The two trees were mostly bare. *A bang-up job*, she thought.

Nillias strolled back down the road as twilight was taking hold. *Strolling* might not have been the right word, though. It was more like marching. He was a real tightwad.

She descended the ladder and took her last bucket back to the house, where she lined it up next to the others. She sat down on the porch stoop and exhaled. Nillias looked at the trees, left her to walk around the property, and finally came back to her.

"You're welcome," she said.

"You didn't follow my instructions," Nillias said.

"Oh really?" Just in case, she moved her hand near the false sole of her boot, where her hidden knife was stowed.

"I told you to gather as many plums as you could before nightfall. You could have gathered three times as many if you'd collected from those trees." He pointed to the trees on the adjoining plots. "And you could have filled buckets from the trough." He pointed again. "Furthermore, you ate plums on your lunch break. Those could have been added to the total to maximize your output."

Lexie tried to contain her temper. "Are you kidding me? That's totally unreasonable."

"Yes, it is, Lexie, and yet that's what I asked you to do."

"Okay, weirdo, that's it, I'm done. I spent the whole day doing this for you. If you want me to help you, I'm not going to do it unless you start answering some questions."

"I am answering your question."

"Oh really, which one?"

"Earlier today, you wanted to know why we are concerned about Haplopol. This is why, or at least, it is the top layer of a more complex explanation. You must understand it before we move on."

She just frowned at him, waiting for him to continue with his circular gibberish.

"We are all teleological," he said, "but value-based considerations can alter how we accomplish our goals. You assumed that I do not want theft. You assumed that I do not care for rotten plums. You have also assumed that I would grant you a small reward for your efforts at lunch. Those are assumptions based on your values, values that are complex and nuanced and difficult to define. If you had disregarded them, you would have gathered three times as many plums."

"But … why would you want rotten plums? No, never mind about that. What does this have to do with my question?"

"We believe Haplopol is a machine that has not been properly value-loaded."

"What? Look, you're going to have to dumb it down."

"We believe Haplopol has been given a goal, but the goal is ill-defined, without the proper constraints. This could result in it … stealing the neighbor's plums, amongst other things. More than that, this could result in significant harm to us, and all the Salish Sea nations, in fact."

Finally, he had said something that Lexie could at least grasp, even if it was still abstract. She sat and ruminated on his words. "But why not just tell me that up front instead of wasting this whole day?"

"Sometimes, lessons are best learned the hard way. They become more memorable. This is an important one, because it is the foundation for many more to come."

"Many … more?"

"The second will be tomorrow. Your dinner is inside. Get your rest." He turned about and marched up the road again.

"Wait! Stop! I need to get home! I don't want to be in your deranged cult!"

Nillias was unresponsive.

Lexie's shoulders sagged. She kicked over one of the pails of plums and headed inside.

—4—

A Bit of Punishment

"I'm still going to take you to Portland," Dryden said. "Trust me, Nate, once this expedition is finished, I'm all yours, and I'll have saved up even more. You're going to love it. The buildings are so tall, you could stack me up twenty times over and still not reach the top. There are nine bridges still standing, each one of them more than a thousand feet long, and another one that crosses the whole width of the Columbia."

Nate was sitting on his bed, his youthful brow wrinkled ever so slightly, his brown eyes active. He was surely cycling through all the fun things they'd talked about—and painting them all with a cautionary brush. *That's probably not going to happen, or that, or that.* This was how Nate's mind worked.

Dryden couldn't blame him.

Dryden hated that Nate had quenched that spark, so he tried to reignite it. "But that's not the best part. What I haven't told you is that they have a good curator there, maybe the most progressive of all the coastal Essentialists, some say on the whole continent. She's put together museums that have dinosaur bones, flying machines, cars, and even spaceships. There's the biggest library you've ever seen, with a *million* books. That's why I want to take you there, more than anything."

Nate's eyes widened. "I would really like that, Dad," he said. His hopeful expression faded quickly, though. He was fascinated, but he didn't think he was actually going to be able to see it.

"I've got to go, Dad," he said.

"Metal working?" Dryden asked.

"Yeah."

"Okay. Love you." Dryden bent over and gave him a hug. Nate turned his head away and returned his embrace furtively. "Be good to your mom,"

Dryden added.

And Nate was gone.

Dryden stood up slowly, surveying Nate's bedroom. It was full of artifacts that his mom—Alayna—had collected in trade deals. Some were silly toys and games, like a Rubik's Cube, and an old checkers set with dragons emblazoned on each counter. One artifact was new. It appeared to be some sort of ornate compass, or maybe an astrolabe. There were a few old books as well, which he scanned the titles of.

He wasn't trying to be sneaky. He just wanted to get to know his own son.

Eventually, he pulled himself away.

Alayna was standing in the kitchen, writing on a notepad. She always wore collared shirts, and today was no different. She said it was "just formal enough" for the trading outpost. Her short-sleeved black top and shorts fit her trim figure snugly.

Her jade-colored eyes flashed up at him, then returned to her notepad.

She used to do this when they were together. She would write things down all the time. Usually it was a reminder about a task to add to her to-do list, or sometimes it would be a revelation she'd had about a new way of speaking with one of her clients. Or it could be as trivial a curious smell, or a sound she'd heard that she liked. The passages he found most interesting were the ones she would write about nature. That's where her passion lay—she was a true Essentialist in that respect.

She put the notepad down. "So you told him," she said, with the hint of a scowl.

"Yes."

"He already knew, of course," she said. "I told him last night. He's been moping around ever since."

"Hey, I'm sorry. I had no choice. The general insisted."

She shrugged. "Yeah, I believe you. In fact, I told them they shouldn't take you."

"You did?"

"I didn't do it for Nate. This is an important expedition. They should be taking Leopold, or one of his students, as you suggested. You've got too many … issues. You're a …"

She was right, and she still couldn't use the correct word, the more truthful word. It would be better if she just said it out loud. The pain of her saying it would be more respectful than dancing around it. Not that Dryden deserved any kind of respect.

"Sorry," she said, catching herself. She looked up at him again. "Are you going running?"

He was wearing the stretchy cotton clothes that he typically wore when jogging. "Yeah, the Cedar Creek route."

She nodded.

"I saw that you got Nate an astrolabe," he said. "Are you sure it's safe?"

Her head recoiled. "Is that what it is? Figures you would know. And yes, I'm sure it's not from the fever lands. The trader said it was found in an abandoned house with a lot of other trinkets, well east of Seattle. There was a ship in a bottle too, but it was too expensive."

"Okay, it's probably fine," he said.

"Isn't that what I just said?" She rolled her eyes, like she did whenever she thought he was trying to be responsible, as if he was making some hollow gesture.

"And the books?" he asked.

"What about them?"

"Two of them aren't on the curator's list. One of them looks like it could feature Old World biomedical instruments."

"Oh, I see. Are you going to report me to your boss?"

"No, of course not. That's not the point. You shouldn't be seen with this stuff, Alayna. These rules may seem silly and trivial, but it doesn't mean someone won't get their head cut off. You should have seen them at the meeting. Chinatsu nearly killed Gianna."

This time, she didn't roll her eyes. Instead, she looked stern, defensive. "Fine, I'll hide them. Is that good enough?"

"I'm just trying to help, Alayna. I hope you know that."

She was angry again. It was all too easy for her to slip into bitterness.

"Bye, Dryden," she said. She crossed her arms.

"Bye, Alayna," he said, and he left.

He did run up the Cedar Creek path. It undulated into the hills, away from the river, mostly upward but sometimes down. He stepped on the trunks of fallen trees and jumped over bubbling streams. Sweat dripped from his brow, then from his nose. His breathing was rhythmic, and at times he counted, trying to beat his time on well-worn spans between familiar landmarks.

He did the long route this time. It was ten miles in all. He didn't see a soul. Only a few people ever hiked this trail, and even fewer actually ran it. Most people in Hood River saw running as a waste of time, although probably not as much as studying ICSM history.

He told himself he wanted to stay healthy for the expedition. Who knew when he would exercise again? And the journey could be arduous in parts, particularly in Sanuwan, so best to be in top form. But in truth he also ran to relieve his frustration. He hated seeing Nate pull away. He hated breaking his promise.

And Alayna was still closed to him. Lately it was a win if he could leave without her yelling. He couldn't ask for anything more, though, after what he'd done.

When he was finished, he felt better. After a bit of punishment he could feel good, at least for a while.

Maybe it was the endorphins.

—5—

A Galleon Full of Gungivite Goats

Lexie was walking down the wood-slat quay that was elevated above the main piers of Ganges City harbor. Clippers, cutters and frigates lined the piers, their rigging tight, their sails precisely stowed, cannons bristling out of their sides. The Gungivite flag—blue and white diagonal stripes over a black circle—rippled from their masts. They weren't the most intimidating-looking vessels—the Prefectorate and even the Vickies had a few four-masted eye-poppers—but you'd never want to stare down a Gungivite warship, no matter the class. Gungivite ships seemed to always anticipate your moves, and Lexie had never heard of anyone outrunning one.

Nillias waddled along beside her, his hands cradled in front of him. His skin looked paler than usual, accentuating the moles Lexie had counted on his face; eleven on his left side, four on the right. Counting moles was something you did when you spent your days staring at one person who barely spoke to you, while trying to digest his pointless books and presentations.

The lessons weren't all bad. Some were about how computers worked. Others were more abstract, about intelligence and philosophy. Outside of specific, focused topics, Nillias wouldn't answer her questions. She still didn't know why they needed her, or what had happened to Tarnation and Ryder.

They turned off the quay and down one of the main roads.

It wasn't your typical island town. Usually you would have a couple of pubs, a trading outpost, a number of merchant shanties, and the usual warehouses to service the marina, whereas Ganges City featured dozens of larger buildings that were about six stories tall. These looked more medieval than maritime, with palisaded lookout towers and windows lined with ornamental flourishes. They housed any kind of shop, office or service that the town needed.

"Why is the town so built up?" Lexie asked. "You guys been invaded before?"

"No," Nillias responded, "but that doesn't mean we shouldn't be prepared."

"It still seems like a waste of money. How can you afford all this?"

"We've been fortunate, Lexie. When most communities declined or collapsed after the fall, we thrived. The channel surrounding Ganges Island was a natural barrier for protecting against marauders. As a result, we managed to preserve certain grain and fruit crops—sheep and goat breeds, as well. We even managed to herd the extensive deer population. All of these crops and livestock we selectively bred to be more productive varieties, then we sold them off-island at a considerable profit, to communities that had few surviving breeds or crops left."

"He's got a galleon full of Gungivite goats."

"Excuse me?"

"It's a saying, in Anacortes. Means someone's well-to-do."

"Oh, I understand. As you have seen from our Victoria Embassy, we try not to flaunt our wealth, but it's true we do have considerable resources. This has allowed us to think longer-term, and think big. We rebuilt the entire the town of Ganges City in one fell swoop, and we refurbished the ICSM bridge that crosses the Sansum Strait, among other things. It also allowed us to colonize the area near Duncan and just to the north of it, on Kuvar Island."

Lexie looked up at the buildings again. It looked a bit sterile, but it was still impressive. "This is no Victoria, but it could give Anacortes a run for its money as a port, especially because you could use the Sansum Bridge to get to Kuvar Island. Why won't you allow foreigners in?"

Nillias was quiet for a moment. Finally, he said, "Maybe some other time, Lexie."

It was just one of a hundred questions he wouldn't answer.

Nillias said, "Stay here," and gestured for her to sit down on a nearby bench. Lexie did as she was told while he went into the building labeled *Pharmacy*. They didn't have pharmacies in Anacortes, so she had to drag Mom to the clinic instead. But Lexie had been to one before, in Victoria.

She was surprised the place in Victoria hadn't been outlawed, since it had all manner of hobos and vagabonds littered in front of it, in various states of intoxication. Of course, the Vickies would let anything slide for a profit.

She wouldn't have pictured Nillias as a man who needed a pick-me-up, but maybe pharmacies were different here. There certainly weren't any hobos or vagabonds.

The street was busy enough, but it felt quiet relative to the size of the buildings. There were fishermen, and merchants, and even farmers, but everyone looked so much cleaner than in Anacortes or Victoria. Maybe they starch their shirts? She saw several people who wore the same black linens as Olint and Nillias, sporting the same long coif of wavy hair. Across the road she even saw a child with long, wavy hair similarly attired, escorted by her mother.

These people—the ones with the black linens and hair—always seemed so rushed and in a daze, as if the world around them was woefully unimportant.

Nillias exited the store and continued walking into town. Lexie jogged to catch up.

"Hey, Nillias," she said. "These other mop tops with the black clothes, are they nutjobs like you?"

Nillias pursed his lips before he responded. He was about as emotional as a rotting log, so this was equivalent to getting a rise out of him. "Yes, they are Gungivite Observers, like me," he said.

"Why are there so many of you? I mean, no offense, but there's not much Old World tech around here to worry about."

"You are assuming we are like the Essentialists. We aren't. We can use machines, when it's necessary, but you've already seen this." His eyes flashed at her. "We are concerned with specific forms of machine *intelligence*, which is different. We want to ensure we have enough people dedicated to understanding this principle, and who see the importance of that mission, at all times. It's more of a philosophy than a station in life. Many of us have regular jobs."

"Why are you so concerned about machine intelligence?"

She thought he wouldn't answer, but this time, he did.

"We have evidence to suggest this is what caused the fall. It's also what caused the ICSM war."

"What war?"

"The people from the ICSM cities didn't just walk away, Lexie."

"Really? Wow," she said.

Not really. Not wow. In fact, she'd already suspected that was the case. She knew more than most, but it was probably better she didn't let on to Nillias.

They headed up some steps of one of the many identical-looking buildings and walked through a door labeled *Gungi-Bites*.

It was a modest eatery, with more character than Lexie had presumed from the outside. Upon the wooden tables were sculptures made of sea glass, and the contours of a pod of dolphins had been carved into one of the stone walls. It was empty save a few fishermen, judging by their long rubber pants. They were eating venison, or so it appeared, and some bland-looking vegetables. A hefty Gungivite Observer woman sat staring into space, a half-eaten apple before her. In the corner of the room was a sign that read *Restrooms* beside spiral stairs leading to the basement.

Nillias took a table in a corner. Lexie noticed a subtle cringe on his face as he sat down.

"You okay?" she asked. "You don't look so good today."

"I'm feeling a bit off," he said. "I'll be okay."

A fly was buzzing around the table. It managed to land right in front of her, on a breadcrumb. She tried to swat it but missed.

"Why did you try to kill the fly?" Nillias asked.

"Um … because it's gross."

"Why doesn't it deserve to live?"

"Look, even hardcore vegan coastal Essentialists kill flies, buddy. You need to get real."

"This is an example of value-loading," Nillias said.

She should have known Nillias was about to spit out one of his nebulous lessons. "Look, just hit me straight this time, okay? Then we can eat sooner."

A fleeting grin passed over him. "Haplopol's teleology has a number of objective functions," he said. "The two most prominent are: first, to maximize happiness for all of its citizens; and second, to follow the commands of a human representative, provided it does not substantially conflict with the first objective."

Lexie digested this. "That doesn't sound so bad. I guess the human could be a pain, but he or she would have limited power to change things. What does this have to do with the fly?"

"The challenge comes when one tries to define *happiness* and *citizens*. There are protections for wireheading, but otherwise the loose definitions of these terms have resulted in complications."

"What's wireheading?"

"An example would be if Haplopol were to feed you euphoric drugs all day long. You would be happy, but that may not be what you intended."

"I get it, but what are these complications, and what does this have to do with a fly?"

"A fly is a citizen."

"You're kidding. I thought you said this thing was smart."

"To us humans, a fly could be seen as a lesser citizen, but the truth is it's not unequivocal. The fly is a unique life form, even though it may be less sophisticated than us, and less intelligent. Therefore the interpretation of the citizen definition is highly dependent on value-loading that is not straightforward, because it pits one life form against another."

"Why couldn't they just define citizens as humans? Or anything smarter than a mouse, if you want to protect your pets?"

As she was speaking, the hefty Observer woman stood up, glanced at Lexie, and headed down the steps to the basement.

Nillias cringed again. He replied slowly, as if he was having trouble getting the words out. "Yes … that is the natural course of mitigation. Some ICSM cities did in fact change the definition to weight the value of citizens in accordance with intelligence, but it may have only worsened the problem …" Nillias stopped. His face had gone from pale to a green tint.

"You can order. Excuse me," Nillias said, and he left to go to the restroom.

Lexie looked at the menu and ordered a chowder when the waitress came by. The food came, but it was too hot, so she waited for it to cool. Meanwhile, the fishermen all paid and left.

Lexie finished her bowl.

Nillias was taking an awfully long time. She figured she'd better check on him, so she went down the stairs. The restrooms were along a hallway, both a men's and a women's, and there was another door marked *Fruit Cellar.*

She'd only been to a few places on the island, but most of them had a fruit cellar. Sure, these people made a good living off harvesting fruit, but it seemed excessive. It was probably some fad for everyone to have one—some cultural tradition gone too far. She certainly couldn't see the need here, in the middle of town.

She crept up to the men's washroom and listened at the door. She heard a long cough, and then the sound of spit on water, like … yuck.

"You okay in there, Nillias?" she asked.

Why did she care about him? The man was deranged and homicidal.

But he could also get her home.

More coughing. He appeared to be busy.

She stood back and waited.

The door to the fruit cellar was ajar. Curious, she pushed it open a little further and peeked in. There were indeed jars of all kinds of fruit: pears, plums, preserves, jams, blackberries, blueberries, arbutus berries, cherries, and more. She went in and fingered the jars. They were laden with dust, and some had blackened and sprouted white mold on the inside. Apparently this cellar wasn't used often.

There was another doorway at the far end of the room. This one was closed, and there was a sign reading *Apple Cellar* on it. Nillias had told her that the apples were kept separate. Apparently they gave off a gas called ethylene when ripening, which could spoil other fruit. She went to check the door handle to see if it was unlocked.

Just as her hand was about to touch the doorknob, the door pushed open, knocking her hand away.

It was the big-boned Observer woman—the one who had been upstairs, staring into space. She entered the fruit cellar and shut the apple cellar door behind her. She was frowning, her face full of suspicion. "What are you doing here?" she asked.

Lexie had been about to ask her the same question. "Just waiting for my friend Nillias. He's in the bathroom."

The woman grabbed Lexie's shirt collar and pulled her out of the fruit cellar.

"Hey! Why so testy?" Lexie protested.

"You are not allowed in the fruit cellar."

"I wasn't going to steal any fruit. Half of it's rotten anyway."

This only made the woman angrier. She grabbed Lexie's shirt again and moved her toward the bathroom, then knocked on the door. "Nillias, your prisoner is on the loose. Come out at once."

How did she know Lexie was a prisoner? Word must get around.

"A bit of a stretch to say *on the loose*," Lexie objected. "I just got bored."

The woman tired of waiting and tried the door handle.

"I don't think you wanna—"

There was vomit in the toilet, as Lexie expected, but Nillias wasn't there. It was a bald man, casting an annoyed look at them. Next to him was an expunged syringe, dripping red fluid on the counter.

Lexie saw the man's eyes, his pale face, and his moles—all fifteen of them. Okay, maybe it *was* Nillias.

From behind his back Nillias retrieved his wig, and he arranged it back on his head. "Thank you, Vaia," he said. "I will take it from here."

—6—

The Seattle Strait

It was spitting rain when the river ferry docked in the terminal north of Portland. Dryden donned his waterproof frock and was assigned a horse, which he saddled. He covered his provisions with a tarp to prepare for the long journey.

There were only thirty of them in this part of the expedition. Two more groups had taken different ferries down from Hood River, a day ahead of them. Apparently General Hatsuo didn't want them all traveling together. It was probably a wise move. Historically, large contingents of Prefectorate-controlled militia waltzing through coastal Essentialist villages often spelled trouble for the locals. Best to not alarm anyone unnecessarily.

Dryden was riding next to Sergio, a career Essentialist soldier who was proficient in navigation and nautical engineering. Sergio didn't look like your typical army grunt; he was lanky, and spectacled. He also retained an olive tint to his skin, courtesy of his original home in the Tucson Union, well to the south. They had met during their schooling in Portland and caught up on occasion—whenever Sergio happened to be traveling through Hood River.

"Any idea why we stopped here?" Dryden asked Sergio. Ordinarily to reach the Salish Sea they would have kept going down the length of the Columbia River into the open ocean. From there they would sail up the coast and around Neah Bay.

"They want to make use of a few well-provisioned military galleons stationed in Olympia."

"Ah, I see." The route would take about the same amount of time, but it meant they would have to take the Seattle Strait north from Olympia. And Dryden knew what "well-provisioned" meant. They wouldn't be concerned with rations on such a short trip.

"How did you get this gig?" Dryden asked. "I thought they had plenty of work for you in Astoria."

"*Yo no se*, I thought so, too. Sometimes they pull me in when there's a mission they're not quite sure about." He touched the arm of his glasses. Sergio had a tendency to do this, even when stationary. It was a nervous habit. "There could be some unusual maneuvering around all those islands."

"I thought we were heading to East Sound and being escorted to Haplopol by land from there? That shouldn't require any fancy maneuvering."

"Good point, *amigo*," he said, and shrugged. "Maybe I'm here in case things get a bit crazy. We're going up the strait as well, you know."

Dryden didn't argue. It made sense that the Prefectorate navy would want their best navigators for the Seattle Strait. He couldn't think of a worse place to run aground.

He looked out over the countryside through the misty precipitation. There were plenty of farms, neatly packed into quadrants, each with longhouses covered in layered canopies. Save a few staunch concrete foundations, Old World buildings were few and far between. These Essentialists were too devout to sully themselves by living in them, never mind rebuilding them. The houses had degraded over time or been plundered and dismantled. Occasionally the party would ride through one of the many hamlets. These were typically a congregation of fifty or so of the same type of longhouses.

The Essentialist lands to the north and south of Portland were some of the most densely populated—a mecca for devout Coastals. It was a fertile valley, with frequent rains, embraced by protective mountains on all sides. The climate was also temperate, and there were no fever lands to speak of. All the devouts made Dryden uncomfortable, though. If you were unable to recount the latest dogma with ease you were often looked at with scorn.

The valley made for a colorful contrast with the city, which was a mecca of another kind. As one of the largest Old World cities to have survived the fall, Portland attracted the more progressive Essentialists, the ones who didn't fear the Old World—ones who wanted to explore it and learn from it. People like Dryden.

He looked behind him. Portland's skyline had long since faded into the horizon. The "vertical abominations," as people in these parts would often label them, were no longer visible.

Despite these divergent outlooks, the city folk and rural Essentialists had formed a cautious alliance. They had grown to depend on each other for food, trade, labor, skills, education, and more. It gave Dryden hope that if people of such differing ideals could come together, maybe the Essentialists could strike the same balance with the Prefectorate.

"So, how's Alayna?" Sergio asked. "You guys were something else back in Portland."

"What do you mean?"

"Like … the puppy-dog eyes, the constant flirting. Everyone knew you were like rabbits, even though you refused to admit it. I figured you'd have a few dozen kids."

Dryden tried to laugh, but it only came out as a loud exhalation. "You know that's mathematically impossible."

"You'd find a way, knowing you."

Dryden nodded. He couldn't think of a good way to address Sergio's question.

"So, how is she?" Sergio asked again.

"We broke up."

"Really. Wow, sorry, *amigo*. What happened?" Sergio wasn't cruel. He just didn't believe much in white lies and other social graces.

"I don't like to talk about it."

"Oh. Okay, man, no problem. It's been a long time. I was just curious."

No, he needed to own up to it. This was Dryden's fear speaking. It was weakness, and pain. He needed to face it.

"It was my fault. I messed up."

Sergio was staring at him, ever curious. He touched the arm of his glasses again, as if they needed repositioning.

Dryden sighed. "She was out of town. I was taking care of her brother—you know, Ben?"

"Neah Bay Ben?"

"I guess you've heard of him."

"Only a little. Never the whole story."

"Have you been to Neah Bay?"

"Yes, once—they keep building up the fortifications every year. They wanted me to give some of the new fleet vessels a test run."

"Well, the story goes that late one night, the Kuvar Collective was about to attack the town of Waatch, just to the west of Neah Bay, on the oceanside coast. Their plan was to take the town, move through the valley and surprise the Neah Bay garrison from land, where the fort was undefended. Ben saw the ships and ran up the mountain to alert the Waatch fort towers, which turned their cannons on the Kuvar Collective ships. They sank three of them before they could deploy their men to land. After that, several fort installations were destroyed, as well as half the Essentialist fleet and most of Waatch, but sinking those vessels may have saved the rest of the people in the area, including thousands of people in Neah Bay."

"Wow."

"Unfortunately, when Ben was running back down the mountain to join the fight, he slipped and fell and broke his back. It paralyzed him."

"Oh, man."

"Anyway, several years ago I was watching Ben when Alayna was out of town. We had gone out to the pub the night before and had a few drinks. Then I saw Maxwell in the morning—my boss—with Ben in tow, while Alayna's parents watched Nate. We were a bit hung over, so we went down by the river to rest. I was tired so I laid down on the grass." Dryden had told the story many times, but whenever he did, it took a great feat of will to stop the tempest of emotion from rising up.

"The next thing I knew ..." he continued, forcing out the last few words, "Ben was a quadriplegic, you see—no movement below his neck. I must have forgotten to put the brakes on his wheelchair. So it rolled into the river. He drowned. They found him half a mile down."

Sergio was quiet for a moment, absorbing it. He said, "I'm sorry, *amigo*. Could have happened to anyone, though." He was definitely lying, this time. That's how bad it was. Sergio didn't care much for social graces, but in this case he had to lie.

Dryden gritted his teeth and nodded.

"Look, it's a terrible thing," Sergio continued, "but you made a mistake, that's all. It sounds to me more like bad luck. I can tell it's eating you up, but you need to let it go. I remember you used to be happy-go-lucky, even when you'd be working sixteen hours a day. And you're whip-smart. I keep waiting for you to become a famous scholar, or rich, or … well … you probably couldn't go into politics anymore."

"Thanks, Sergio." Dryden tried to keep his response free of emotion.

They didn't talk for a while after that.

The rain continued throughout the rest of the day. It was annoying, but it didn't impede their progress. Sergio knew a few of the other expedition members, so he went off to chat with them, leaving Dryden to brood by himself.

It took them three days to reach Olympia. It was a town without much vitality. Most people lived in halfie Old World buildings—structures with Old World foundations and a few walls, with many of the frames and sidings refurbished over the years.

This was the end of the line for most people, from a geographic perspective. The only boats whose crew had the gumption to travel through the Seattle Strait were military in nature, and even those trips were infrequent.

There was indeed an oversized Prefectorate presence, particularly of the naval variety, and as a result the docks were active. At least ten large galleons were being built, and eight more were ready for action. They were high-caliber ships, if one could judge by the look in Sergio's eyes when he inspected them. It was the longest Dryden had ever seen him go without touching the arm of his glasses.

After a quiet night in the sterile Prefectorate military barracks, the party left early the next morning on one of the newly-minted galleons. Sergio was called to duty, so Dryden was left on his own to stare at the shore from the stern of the vessel. He had never traveled down the strait, so the voyage kept his attention. The strait provoked a sort of morbid curiosity in him, as well as an anthropological one.

At first, there wasn't much to see. The coastline featured rocky beaches, with high-tide lines eaten into the shores, and coniferous trees wrestling with the bedrock to stay erect in the shallow soil. The ship tacked and jibed through a number of narrow channels, turning deftly as the crew worked sail and mast under scrupulous instruction.

When he was bored, Dryden whittled a shape out of the driftwood he'd pocketed near the docks in Olympia, letting the shaved chips drop off the side and be taken by the wake. He decided that with this carving he would go above and beyond for Nate. No more deer or Old World vehicle carvings. He would have plenty of idle time on this journey, so he might as well attempt something more grandiose.

When he looked up from his project, he realized they must be getting close to Seattle. The channel was widening, and they were staying farther from the shore. Sailors were draping gray masks over their noses and mouths. Dryden pulled out the one the quartermaster had given him and strapped it over his face as well. He also withdrew an eyepiece, notepad and pen from his breast pocket.

The foliage didn't change much at first. They passed the occasional rundown Old World cottage that had been blanched on its northern face. Soon the white faces gave way to houses with cavities that had been overtaken by vegetation. Eventually, there were no dwellings to be seen at all. Only thick concrete pier posts and the strongest house foundations remained.

The vegetation also changed. For the most part, trees became scarce and the ground was covered by expanses of vines and weedy grasses—large swaths of which had been overtaken by yellowed blights and blue molds. A piece of flotsam drifted by. It was brown, partially occupied by dandelions, but it also seemed to ripple in the sun. When Dryden looked through his scope at it, he noted there were insects on it, in some cases large ones, with thick black exoskeletons, crawling over the plants.

The ground rose up on each side, and large metal bridge posts stood tall on the hills above him, but there was no center part of the bridge, nor sign of any remains of one in the straight around him. The bridge itself had been smoothly cut just after the posts on both sides, as though the middle portion had just vaporized.

The sailors kept at their duties, but some stopped to stare at the bridge posts on occasion.

The banks lowered again, while the boat continued to turn through the channel, until it reached an even wider opening. Here the northern channel was unimpeded by curves in the shoreline for many miles. Based on the maps he'd seen of the strait, it meant they were nearing where downtown had once been.

It started to rain again, so Dryden put on his hood. He didn't know if the rains were toxic here as well, but it was best not to take any chances.

The ground was devoid of structures, save the occasional jumble of concrete or steel girder protruding upward resolutely. Vegetation was extremely sparse; only small clusters of ground cover and brown, stringy vines.

A few tents dotted the shoreline, probably erected in the last few years, and an old rowboat was tied to a tough mooring post. Beside one of the tents lay a hollowed-out husk of clothing with withered, skeletal appendages poking out from where limbs should have been.

Some people still didn't believe in the reality of the fever lands, even now. It was a harsh lesson to learn.

Beside the corpse were a few balls of black feathers.

Even the hardiest scavengers would succumb.

The occasional noise refracted off the water, coming from the ruin. Dryden heard a snap, maybe the branch of a dead tree falling to earth, and a thud, like a steel beam giving way and slamming into the ground. Once Dryden heard a dull moan, or even a whimper, and he thought: *What could possibly be alive?* Maybe some poor animal had taken a wrong turn, gotten lost, and was dying. But even that was hard to fathom, since they were so deep into the ravaged city. More likely it was the wind, complaining as it steered through the rotting tangle of this forsaken place.

Dryden put his notepad and scope away. He decided there wasn't much of anthropological interest here. There wasn't much of anything at all.

As daylight began to dwindle, he saw the outpost Sergio had mentioned, just off an upcoming island. The Marrowstone Flotilla was made of random pontoon arrangements propping up old houseboats, with weatherworn wood structures overtop, connected by a series of enclosed walkways and covered platforms. At the base, a number of floating docks pointed out from the periphery.

Many believed the flotilla marked the end of the fever lands, but no one had enough confidence in that belief to venture onto land for long. As a result, there were no real structures to speak of on the island itself, despite the fact that there were several long docks that led to the Marrowstone Flotilla from the shore.

The ship moored in an empty berth, next to two older-looking Prefectorate vessels. These were some of the quick Salish Sea clippers—long skinny vessels with three masts. The crew disembarked and were shown to cramped quarters. Dryden had to share his room with five Essentialist naval officers. These officers immediately changed out of their military uniforms into more casual linens. It cast a ripe odor throughout the room.

Feeling out of place, Dryden decided to take his leave and look for Sergio.

—7—

The Selection School

Lexie wasn't sure why she thought about her pirating days so much, and she wasn't the type to spend time psychoanalyzing herself. There were enough quacks out there and she didn't need to waste her time with that. So she just let the dreams come. They weren't all bad, only a few of them. It was a form of entertainment.

The one she had this particular night was about the Nichols incident. He was a pasty prick with eyes so far apart they almost fell off his head. He'd been stealing her rations, and it didn't give her the warm and fuzzies when he'd lick his lips at her, either.

Pirates can be a real bunch of scumbags. It's not like you get to recruit the best students out of the Dressler Institute.

The second part of the brawl of the Nichols incident came to her first; because dreams sometimes don't arrive how you'd expect, and not always in a logical sequence. This particular brawl was supervised by the crew, to settle the dispute. It was a dorky dance on a slippery deck. The wooden floorboards were beating her up just as much as his fists. Man, was she ugly after that for a good while. She had her boot knife on her mind the whole time. She could have gone for it, but she never did.

There was a flash, and she went back in time. She was grabbing Nichols' arm as it went into her bag. His arm was veiny. He had knobby knuckles and fingernails that were thick with grainy sludge. This part of her dream was more like a still shot, frozen in time. It was this grab that did it, really—it was what set off the whole thing—first the two of them going at it below decks, and then afterward settling the matter in front of the crew on the main deck.

The next flash in her dream was the blow to her eye that left her seeing stars, literally, like they show in Old World comic books. She saw twinkling and blue and white and all that. This was from the scuffle below decks, shortly after she'd grabbed his arm, and before the rest woke up and held them back.

Back to the second part of the brawl again. This part of her dream was like a blurred montage of falling and punching and kicking, except the end was clearer. She'd roped Nichols's feet and he fell hard, like the big sack of meat that he was. He stayed down long enough for them to give her the win. Thank goodness, too, because both her eyes were swelling up and she could barely see.

They were open enough, though, to see Warrick standing there, looming over them both as she slobbered blood-infused drool on the decking. His black hair was cut short in those days, and he had a peppered goatee. In fact he was almost too clean to be the captain of a pirate ship. But he was no prude. He knew how to be a badass.

Which was why, when Nichols pulled out a blade to stab her in the back, Warrick knocked it away before he could strike. "Rules are rules," he said. Casually, he picked up the knife and gave it to Lexie while two of the crew restrained Nichols.

Needless to say, Nichols's neck didn't remain closed for much longer after that.

Warrick was good like that. He was callous, at times, but if you did your own dirty work, he wasn't going to throw you to the sharks. He often helped her out, behind the scenes, even though he didn't like the rest of the crew to know it.

Those days were long gone. What happened to Warrick was arguably worse than what Mom was going through. You've only got one mind. Yeah, you might still be alive when it goes, but who you are gets taken out with the tide.

Lexie awoke to see Nillias in her bedroom, standing beside her window, looking back at her.

She jumped out of the bed, hoisting the covers around her midsection. She wasn't naked, but somehow she still felt exposed. "Dammit, Nillias, you're a twisted enough bird as it is. You don't need to be watching me sleep, along with everything else."

"I didn't mean to startle you. There has been a change of plan."

At least he didn't seem sick anymore. "Why does a change in plan mean you have to creep around in my bedroom?"

"Olint would like to see you as soon as possible. Lessons are cancelled today. Please get dressed and meet me outside."

They rode two strong, well-groomed steeds on a northern route around Ganges Island. The path was broad but little used. On the several-mile trip they saw only one farmer driving a horse-drawn cart full of freshly shorn wool into town. It was much more pastoral here, with well-tended fields and herds of sheep and goats. Off the road Lexie could see tall, paneled walls of wood zigzagging through the hills.

"What are those fences for?" she asked Nillias.

Nillias didn't even glance at them. "Animal pens."

"What kind of animals?"

"Deer, mostly. Some cats."

"Cats? Why do you need pens for cats? I remember you had a rather plump-looking one in your embassy in Victoria. Do you guys worship them or something?" Yes, it was a strange question, but at this point nothing would surprise her about these Observer loons.

He squinted at her, then looked back at the road. It didn't seem like he was going to answer her question.

She tried changing the subject. "I thought Olint was in Victoria."

"No. He has returned."

"Why?"

"Because of Haplopol. There have been many changes. Preparations need to be made, and we need more oversight from Ganges. Plus, it may no longer be safe in Victoria."

"Because of some old city in the Sanuwan Kingdom?"

"Yes, Lexie. Remember your lessons. A true superintelligence will display emergent behaviors that we incapable of understanding until it's too late. It will seem like magic to us. No place is safe, including Victoria."

It seemed a stretch.

After rounding the northern end of the island, they started on some switchbacks up into the hills. From here, Lexie could see the narrow channel between Ganges Island and Kuvar Island. The waters shimmered in the morning sun except where a few active ships cast long, westerly shadows. She saw one ship leaving what must have been the port of Vesuvius. In town she'd overheard that they had regular ferry crossings over to Kuvar Island.

The Vesuvius ferry terminal wasn't that far away.

The road leveled out and they passed an old, worn-out sign that said *Channel Ridge*, and soon after they veered up a road to a large, enclosed estate.

"Olint lives here?" she asked.

"At times. It's a Selection Institution."

"Let me guess … where you guys pick out your favorite wigs?"

He allowed her a faint grimace.

They passed through an open gateway. It was unguarded.

The grounds of the Selection Institution were replete with flowers, arbutus trees and, of course, many fruit trees of different varieties. Lexie noticed two girls high up on a ladder next to one of the trees, picking cherries. The main building was built into a hill, the facade of each level dominated by broad swaths of tinted glass stepped back from the level below, allowing for balconies on each floor. A large, hexagonal tower jutted out of the uppermost reaches of the facility, with a lookout palisade on the top.

Nillias escorted her through the main door. They scaled several flights of steps that ran up the center of the building, all the way to the top level.

There were a dozen people moving about on the stairs or adjoining hallways, all at a rapid clip, carrying papers or baskets, but there had only been a few horses outside, and the building was rather remote. Maybe all these people lived here?

They found Olint on the top level, with his hands cradled behind his back, staring out of one of the large windows of tinted glass. Outside, children were playing in an enclosure to the rear of the building. Toys and a couple leather balls were strewn upon several tables, as well as binders and books. Maybe it was some kind of school.

Olint turned to meet them, his cold, gray eyes catching hers only briefly. He didn't otherwise acknowledge her. He appeared distracted, mired in thought. "Come with me," he said eventually.

They followed him down another staircase, then through a glass door into the yard, where the children and instructors were.

"So what's changed?" Lexie asked.

Nillias said, "Shhh. All in good time, Lexie."

Olint didn't turn around. He was intently watching the children work at tables and play with the toys, his hands still held behind his back. "I have been observing this group for a week," he said. "I know them well." He stopped and watched a group playing a game of kick ball.

"Don't point," he said, "but do you see the one with the yellow socks?"

"Yes," Lexie said.

"He is the smartest. Possibly also the strongest."

Lexie saw the boy receive a pass and maneuver around the other kids. He was no more than eight years old, but he was fast. He kicked the ball and it bounced off the goalpost. His teammates threw up their hands in frustration, and the other team went to collect the ball, which had ended up out of bounds.

There was a referee, a black linen–clad Observer, who was wearing the same type of long, flowing wig as Nillias and Olint. He walked up to the child, took out a plastic strap from his pocket, and slapped him violently on his wrist.

The boy's hand recoiled but he didn't cry out. He only glanced up at the

Observer with a defiant expression.

The Observer looked at Olint, nodded and approached a child on the other team. "This other child you will see next," Olint said, "he is almost as good as the first." The other boy was bouncing along the field, skipping happily toward the opposing goal. The Observer grabbed him by the arm forcefully and proceeded to slap him on the wrist, as well.

"Ow!" the boy called out. "Why did you—" He looked around at the other kids and at the instructors, his face an incredulous mask. He started to cry.

"What is wrong with you people?" Lexie said.

"Quiet, Lexie," Nillias said. "This is important."

Olint was holding his chin thoughtfully, watching the child wail. With slow footfalls, he approached the crying child. The Observer referee backed away from the boy, as did the other children. The gameplay stopped as all the other children that were further afield had frozen where they were. In fact, everyone in the whole enclosure school froze, except for Olint and the weeping child.

Olint bent down on one knee, unhooked his cradled hands, and placed one of them on the boy's head. The boy looked up and burst into an even louder cry of anguish.

"Shush now, my child," Olint said.

Olint's actions triggered something in the rest of the people in the yard. The instructors began ushering the rest of the children back into the building and packing up loose equipment. Soon, there was only her, Nillias, Olint, the child, and the referee Observer left. The boy draped his arms around Olint and cried, "But I don't want to!"

"Shush, child," he said. "You're one of us now."

"Is he being—" When Lexie looked up at Nillias, his eyes were glazed, as if lost in a memory, and his face displayed what she could only describe as melancholy. Her captor's emotions were a rare sighting, and it made her lose her train of thought. Nillias snapped out of his daze and forcefully blinked his eyes, as if doing so would extinguish whatever he was thinking.

Olint removed his hand from the boy's head, returned his embrace, and stood up. He retreated to stand alongside Nillias and Lexie, while the referee Observer tended to the still-distraught child.

Olint walked past Lexie and Nillias, back to the door. "Thank you for your patience," he said. "I needed to finish the selection process. We can talk in the gardens."

She joined Nillias in following after him. "So this boy is going to become an Observer?" she asked.

"Yes. It is a great honor."

"Well, that could be a matter of opinion."

Lexie wondered if Olint might be angered by her comment, but instead he said, "I suppose so."

"Why did you choose him? You said yourself that he wasn't as good as the first one. Was it because the other one missed that goal?" It seemed to be a silly reason, but she wouldn't put it past these nutjobs.

Olint stopped, turned around and met her eyes. "No, it had nothing to do with the missed goal. They were close in potential, so it was a tough decision. The one we chose—his family loves him, he hasn't experienced any severe trauma, and he may even be spoiled. It is much better to take the spoiled one and break him. This allows us to more easily mold him, as we understand his temperament. In regards to the silent one, the one that is calculating and defiant, it's too hard to see the shape of his clay, so we don't know if it can be altered. He is likely to be strong-willed, but it could also be that he is mentally unstable. It would be too risky to invest our time and energy."

Lexie looked at Nillias, then back at Olint. "Nauseous nettles. No wonder you're all so messed up," Lexie said.

They took a back exit from the building and arrived at the top of the fruit orchard. There were a few more people here, but no children. These people quietly stepped down their ladders with their partially-filled baskets of fruit and walked to a door marked *Fruit Cellar* in a lower part of the building.

Olint found a cherry on the ground, examined it, and dropped it back where he found it. "We sent a team to Haplopol," he said. "They have been eliminated."

Lexie looked at Nillias. He nodded. Apparently he'd already heard the news. "By Haplopol?" she asked.

"No. We believe they were killed before they reached Haplopol, by Prefectorate militia posing as Kuvar Collective soldiers."

"How do you know that, if they're all dead?"

Olint granted her a meager smile "That's not important, but I enjoy your questioning, Lexie. Your inquisitive nature, and what you've learned from it, will be important."

"Important for what?"

"For your expedition to Haplopol."

"Oh no, it won't."

"Yes, Lexie, it will."

"But … why do you need me?"

"We need someone to help us deal with the Sanuwans. Gungivites make them nervous, and our best negotiator has been killed."

"That's the first thing you've said that makes any sense—the making them nervous part, at least—but I have no sway with the Sanuwans. You're gonna have to find someone else."

Olint smiled again. It was a frigid thing, his smile. Lexie could tell his face wasn't quite used to it. He said, "You've raided Sanuwan towns twice, and traded with East Sound three times, successfully. Plus, you've dealt with their emissaries in Anacortes."

Her face felt hot. How did the Gungivites know all this? And if they knew this, did they know about the raid she'd done near Maple Bay? She felt profoundly uncomfortable, but she clucked her tongue and tried to not let on. "Not sure where you get your info, bud, but you might want to check your sources. In any case, you're not much of a salesman. You just said the last bunch got slaughtered, and meanwhile Nillias has been trying to brainwash me about the danger of this Haplopol place, and it's actually working. So why would anyone, on the Salish Sea or otherwise, want to go on this confounded trip?"

This time, it was Nillias who answered. "We know you want to get home, to your mother. We can allow a stop in Anacortes."

Well, that *was* something. "Let me guess. *After* Haplopol."

"No," Nillias said. "We can stop there beforehand. We wish to speak to Leopold first."

The offer surprised her. It seemed a little too generous for these no-nonsense eggheads. She made a show of scratching her head. "Listen, can I take a moment to think about this? And I have to use the privy, too, if you don't mind."

"Of course," Olint said. "There's one next to the fruit cellar entrance."

Lexie walked down the hill, making sure to cast a scowl up at the two of them as she did. It was better that they didn't think she was happy about anything.

They were like statues cut from the same stone, watching her with the same bland expression.

She almost bumped into a man in black as he emerged from the fruit cellar. His clothes were spotless; he didn't look as though he'd been picking fruit. He seemed a clone of Nillias, except with higher cheekbones and fewer moles, and of course a different number on his arm tattoo. He ignored her and headed for the house.

The privy was real fancy, with shiny brass taps and gold detailing on the stall door. It even flushed itself on its own when she was done. She wondered if it used electricity, or if there were computers or some other neon around. She would be the last to know.

She opened the door, just a sliver. The two men were still there, staring down the hill. These guys didn't like small talk. She guessed there wasn't much to talk about since they didn't have many fashion choices, and talking about superintelligent machines all the time would be a bit of a buzz killer.

The thought of seeing Mom sounded nice, but Lexie doubted the stop in Anacortes was real. It was probably just a lie to keep her compliant until they got her closer to Haplopol. And the mission itself seemed suicidal, with the Prefectorate already out to get them.

Considering all that, it made for an easy choice.

She crouched over and slid out the small knife blade hidden in the sole of her shoe. Then she took a deep breath and bolted through the door.

She ran down the hill, toward the stable. Nobody was guarding the horses. She quickly unwound the reins of her horse and jumped on. She glanced back momentarily and saw that Nillias and Olint were walking towards her, but they were still some distance up the hill.

Well, you snooze, you lose.

She kicked the flanks of her steed and raced out of the estate onto Channel Ridge road. It had been easy, perhaps too easy. They could send someone after her, but she had a good lead. Maybe they didn't think she could find passage on the Vesuvius ferry. That would be the hard part.

But that wasn't it at all.

She heard it coming. It was more like a soft, thumping sound, not like another horse, and barely audible except that the pattern conflicted with her own horse's more rhythmic footfalls. She turned to see what it was, only to catch a snapshot of padded feet and arced talons flying through the air at her. She was thrown off her horse, onto the ground, landing on her side.

That hurt—*a lot*—but the pain wasn't enough to pull her attention away from the animal on top of her. A grinning, drooling maw with inch-long incisors was leaning over her. The animal's body was flush with tensed muscle, coursing with feral energy.

It was a cat, or rather, some kind of enormous mountain lion, and it looked hungry.

Her knife had fallen from her hand. What was she going to do, punch the thing? It was twice her size. She tried to push back with her heels, to scurry away, but the cat kept pace with her, its long teeth always within a few inches from her face.

She braced for the attack.

But it didn't come.

After what seemed an endless standoff, the cat turned and trotted away. Lexie scurried back to gain more distance, and sat up.

Nillias and Olint were standing a stone's throw up the road, with the cat sitting on its haunches next to them, licking its chops.

"We leave tomorrow," Nillias said.

—8—

The Deck

Sergio said, "You don't seem very talkative this evening, *mi amigo*."

"I didn't come to talk," Dryden said. He gestured at the dark void before them. "I came for the view." His words were laced with sarcasm.

They were on the top level of one of the larger houseboats, where there was an enclosed bar witlessly named *The Deck*. The bar was facing south, into the fever lands, pitch-black in the distance. It was probably better that way. Had they been lit up, the effect might be more unsettling.

Dryden sipped at his metal cup with care. It was a simple drink: straight gin with a few blackberries mashed in. "I guess the northern view is reserved for high-ranking Prefectorate soldiers," he said.

He hadn't meant to be snarky, but Sergio took his statement as such. "Hey," he said, "why would they have their lookouts facing south? You saw where we came from. There's nothing to worry about back there."

"Yeah, I know," Dryden said with a snigger. "Still seems unfair."

Dryden looked around at the handful of people in the bar. They were Essentialist soldiers, mostly. He made a mental note to keep his voice down.

Sergio took an object out of his pocket and pushed it over to Dryden. It was a glass bottle resting on a glued block. Inside the bottle was a miniature ship with three sails.

"You're still doing the model ships, eh? What's this one called?"

"The *Dirty Princess*."

Dryden laughed. "You don't look much like a sailor, Sergio, but you have the heart of one, through and through."

"And watch this." Sergio took a small hook out of his shirt pocket and pushed it inside the bottle. He deftly pushed down the masts and caught a small ring to pull the ship out of the narrow bottleneck. With the same hook he opened the door to the captain's cabin, and with his fingernails he nipped out a puny piece of paper from inside.

"What's that?"

"It's a letter."

"What does it say?"

"It's not for you; it's for a dirty princess, *amigo*. For her eyes only."

"Really?"

"I'm going to throw this in the ocean and find my true love. It won't work if you've read her love letter first."

Dryden rolled his eyes. "You're insane."

Sergio beamed, wearing Dryden's accusation with pride. He went about putting the ship back in the bottle with meticulous care. "You know what, I'll send you a bigger one, when we return home. You'll like it, and I'll give you some tips on how you can learn to make them yourself, if you're up for it. You can find a princess of your own."

Dryden shot him a skeptical look.

Sergio just smiled. "You still carving?" he asked.

"Yeah, I'm working on a piece for Nate." Dryden hadn't brought his carving to the bar. Besides, he didn't want to show Sergio his latest. It was still just a rough form.

Dryden motioned to the bartender. "One more, please."

"Well, you can still drink," Sergio said. "I'll give you that."

The bartender was a stout fellow with a wind-worn face—probably a sailor trying to pick up some extra cash while on shore leave. He poured Dryden another drink, mashed in the blackberries and slid it along the bar.

"Should we do another toast?" Sergio said.

Dryden nodded, but couldn't think of a good one.

Sergio pointed ahead of them. "We've already toasted to old *times*. How about the Old *World*? Nobody else is going to."

Dryden laughed. "Sounds good to me. Because *nobody else is going to*." They raised their glasses towards the southern expanse, touched them together, and drank.

He heard the door to the houseboat swing open on a creaky hinge and then slam down below. It wasn't a proper door, more like something you'd see on a screened-in porch. He couldn't see who'd entered, at first. The bar was on the upper level of the houseboat, meaning you had to climb up a ladder to get to it. Getting back down could be difficult for the less nimble—and more intoxicated.

Dryden nearly dropped his cup when he saw who'd entered.

"Figured I would find you here," Alayna said as she finished scaling the ladder. She walked over to them with a frown on her face.

"What are you doing here?" Dryden asked.

"I've been here since yesterday. The general wanted a trader to deal with the Sanuwans. I know them as well as anyone."

"But why didn't you tell me you were coming?" Dryden asked.

"You didn't ask."

It took a while for Dryden to get over his shock. Meanwhile, Sergio sat back in his chair, watching their exchange with eyebrows raised. Dryden finally caught himself. "Oh sorry, Alayna, do you remember Sergio?"

"Of course!" she said, her eyes lighting up like they used to. She gave Sergio a warm embrace.

"So good to see you again, *hermosa*," he said. "Dryden says you're doing well—business is booming. Do you ever get back to Portland?"

She looked down, her eyes avoiding Dryden's. "No, Sergio. I miss it, though."

"Come, join us for a drink," Sergio said. "I don't miss Portland, honestly, but I do miss *you*."

Alayna glanced at Dryden's metal cup, a hint of contempt on her face. "Sorry, I don't drink anymore."

"Are you sure? We need help here—we just toasted the fever lands. Maybe you could find us something a little more inspirational."

She offered a timid grin. "Maybe a quick one. Bartender, a cider please." She pulled up a chair beside Sergio.

"Cider? What happened to your jalepeño moonshine?" Sergio looked at Dryden. "I thought she was a girl after my own heart, until Sir Study-a-lot stepped in."

Sergio was trying to be witty, and Dryden figured if Alayna had been alone with him, she would have laughed along with him, but instead Sergio's quip was met with silence. Alayna was always on edge in Dryden's presence, and all the talk of drinking certainly wasn't helping.

In fact, Dryden couldn't remember the last time he'd seen Alayna happy. Before Ben died, Alayna used to give him the occasional half-smile. It would break out on one side of her face, as cautious as she was. Yet it was enough for him, because he knew he'd reached her. He'd breached her immaculate concentration, even if just for a moment. That was years ago. Now, all too often he would get the mask; her eyes would come together, her teeth would clench, and her face would redden. When the mask appeared, nothing good would follow.

The cider sat before Alayna, untouched. She stared at it, but perhaps just to avoid eye contact with Sergio or Dryden.

"So, Sergio, what are you up to nowadays?" she managed to say. "Do you have a family?"

"No. No time for that when I'm always sailing. My sister is in Astoria, and I have a girlfriend. Hopefully I can make something of that, if I'm ever in Astoria for more than a week at a time."

Alayna nodded. Dryden tried to think of some way to steer the conversation in the right direction, but he could never think of anything good.

Sergio leaned toward Alayna. "I wanted to say … I'm sorry about your brother. Such a terrible accident."

That did it. The mask descended. Sergio was being sincere, but more than anything, she hated when someone called it an accident. She looked at Dryden, back at Sergio, and back at Dryden again. "What did he tell you?" she asked.

Sergio glanced at Dryden with a look that said *Am I doing something wrong*? "That … that your poor brother, he fell into the—"

Alayna interrupted him, her face lighting up with rage. "River. Into the river. Right. But I bet Dryden didn't tell you that he was drunk the night before, or that he forgot to put on the brake, and that he fell *asleep*! No, he tends to leave out those important details."

"Actually, he—"

"You're right, Alayna," Dryden interrupted. "I should have said those things. I'm sorry." He turned to Sergio. "And it was entirely my fault." Owning up to it would usually defuse her.

"That's right," she said, nodding resolutely. After a pause, she sighed, catching herself. "Rancid rivers—I'm sorry, Sergio. Sometimes I get so worked up about it …"

"Hey, hey, you don't need to apologize. I can't imagine what you went through."

When Alayna and Dryden were alone, she couldn't talk about it, but she had no problem discussing it with others. Maybe it made her feel in control. Maybe she wanted to be sure others knew it was Dryden's fault.

She pulled away from the counter. "I should really be going," she said. Whenever her mask descended, she couldn't bear trying to be sociable. She would do anything to get away.

"Well, thanks for joining us," Sergio said. "I'm glad I had a chance to see you."

They embraced again, and Alayna walked toward the stairs, ignoring Dryden, but then she abruptly turned. "I forgot," she said. "Dryden, the general wants to see you."

"Hatsuo? He's here?"

"Yes, he's on the flagship *Haratumi*. He wanted to oversee the operation himself. He asked me where to find you. It was pretty easy, since I knew there was a bar on the flotilla."

She had to get in another jab. Dryden absorbed it without affect.

"He's expecting you this evening," she added, then she turned back to climb down the ladder.

That explained why she came to see him. At first he'd wondered if she'd only come to the bar to lay into him. This was a better reason, he supposed, although the outcome was the same.

Sergio was looking at him, an eyebrow raised.

"Yeah, I know," Dryden said. "We're a real mess."

Sergio laughed and slapped him on the shoulder. "Hey, try not to worry about it. Lots of fish in the sea." He took a quick swig of his drink.

But no fish that were quite like Alayna.

"I better go," Dryden said. "Thanks for the drinks."

"Cheers," Sergio said, touching the arm of his glasses. Dryden left him staring out into the pitch.

The *Haratumi* was docked on the northern side of the flotilla. Dryden had to use one of the covered wooden walkways that spanned the cluster of houseboats. People on the walkway were discernible only when he passed by the few lanterns adorning the walls. These were exclusively Essentialist soldiers, eyeballing him with curiosity. At the end of the hall, when these probing looks were no longer sufficient, a sentry asked him his business.

"I'm going to see General Hatsuo. My name is Dryden Quintain."

The sentry bowed his head and faded back into the wall.

After rounding down a few staircases, Dryden reached the northern quay. The galleon was easy to find. It was well lit, and it was the only ship with two sentries standing before the gantry.

Captain Chinatsu walked tightly out to meet him. She was in full uniform. "Yellow-hair man, come with me."

She escorted him up the gangway, onto the vessel, then down into the hold, where a circle of sailors cleaning bayonets looked up briefly as Dryden passed.

Chinatsu knocked four times on door to the captain's cabin. "Come, please," Dryden heard Hatsuo say from within, "and no need to knock." Chinatsu opened the door and they entered.

Hatsuo was stooped over papers on his desk. He pushed himself up and took Dryden's hand in both of his. "Please, please, come have a seat," he said, "and thank you so much for joining me at this late hour."

Chinatsu backed into the shadows of a corner, her features losing resolution.

"Would you like some wine?" Hatsuo asked, gesturing at an unlabeled bottle of wine, with glasses laid out. It looked like a white.

"Yes please, General. Thank you." Anything to lose the taste—and hopefully scent—of the gin he'd been drinking.

The general poured him a generous glass. Dryden sat on a plush chair that the general offered. He noticed something move in the back of the room, behind the general. Looking more closely, he could see animals in cages, as well as a small plant. *Plant* might not have been the right word, for it might in fact have been a tree, one of the smallest Dryden had ever seen. It was like a miniaturized replica of a maple tree, only a foot tall.

"I'm so happy to have you with us, Dryden. Maxwell is quite fond of you, and I can see why."

Dryden had no idea what Maxwell might have said. The only time he gave Dryden praise was when he kept his mouth shut at the right times, but he wasn't about to say that to the general. "You're too kind, General. I'm happy to serve you and the Essentialist cause."

Hatsuo tilted his head. "Yes, the Essentialist cause. That's a good place to start." He sat back and angled his leg over his knee, getting comfortable. "We have vowed to defend the earth, and to protect the gifts of sun, soil and seed, as any devout Essentialist should. If you look behind me, you can see I take this to heart." He lifted a lantern on his desk to illuminate the cages behind him. A snake hissed and curled up, and a plump brown rabbit wrinkled its nose. Hatsuo opened the rabbit's cage and pulled it out. "We cherish all of earth's bounty. All living things." He lifted the rabbit up and let it sniff his face. He smiled at the animal, like a child with a toy.

Hatsuo placed the rabbit in his lap and caressed it with his hand. Eventually, he turned his attention back to Dryden. "There will be pressure, Dryden, for us to contain what we find in Haplopol. You saw Gianna in the meeting. We have to consider the possibility that we will have to destroy the whole city. Otherwise, it could desecrate sun, soil and seed."

He was watching Dryden closely as he spoke. "I know this could be disconcerting news for you. I thought it would be best to convey it in private, and also—given your expertise in the matter—to see if you have any reservations."

Dryden tried not to react. He had indeed pondered the possibility, and it was exactly what he feared. It would be a huge loss for so many academic fields: history, archeology and anthropology. On a more personal level, given his focus on ICSM culture, it would be a professional disaster.

"Sir, I know it's not my place to protest, but that could be a grave mistake ... in my opinion." He imagined Maxwell would reprimand him for speaking this way, but Maxwell wasn't here, and this was too important. "This expedition could result in some of the greatest discoveries made in the last half century. We can't let Haplopol be destroyed."

"But why not? How will it purify the eternal spring to let it be? How could a city run by a machine make us better defenders of Essentialist edicts?"

Dryden had to think of something. He spent a minute ruminating on the question. Hatsuo was patient, nuzzling the rabbit again. Dryden said, "Well, for one, we have nothing to worry about if we can control it. If we can make it do our bidding, we can *force* it to strengthen our bond with the earth."

Hatsuo frowned and stopped petting his rabbit. He placed it back in its cage. "And how do we control it?"

"According to correspondence from ICSM times, there is a main computer junction that is key to the operations of the city. This central junction is actually very small, an orb the size of a melon, but its size isn't indicative of its power. It's advanced Old World—or, I should say, post-Old World—technology. According to some accounts, if we can find it, it will listen to our instructions and allow us to influence the city. In fact, there are historical accounts that suggest two of these control junctions are located in Haplopol. Maybe the one for Haplopol was found by the Sanuwans, which enabled them to revive the city."

"I think I'm following, but what is this about a second control junction?"

"There is an account which claims that two of the main hardware junctions—these orbs—were hidden in Haplopol during the last days of the ICSM cities, before they went dormant. One of these is designed to control

Haplopol and the other is designed to control Diplopol."

"Diplopol? Is that the second ICSM city?"

"Yes. It's located north of Victoria, in the Vickies' territory. It was more than ten times the size of Haplopol, but it sank into the earth. What was left on the surface was plundered by the Vickies long ago. Many people believe it's dead and gone, but our historical records would suggest that it's more likely to be simply dormant, like Haplopol."

Hatsuo stared at him for a long time, then turned and gazed at the animals behind him. He massaged his chin thoughtfully.

Dryden said, "So with these junctions, we could have the means to control both cities. Diplopol would have ten times as many machines, and we could reprogram them to do whatever we wanted: to clean up Old World cities, to build gardens, to plant trees, whatever you want. Heck, we might even be able to send them into the fever lands to clean it up. I can't see how that would be against Essentialist edicts."

Dryden knew it was a thin argument, but it was all he had.

The room was poorly lit, with many shadows. Hatsuo was turned halfway toward his animals, so it was hard to make out his expression. Despite the flickering light, Dryden could have sworn he saw his lips curl into a smile, if only momentarily.

When Hatsuo turned back to him, though, he wasn't smiling. His brow was furrowed and stern, his eyes squinting. "You do make a good case, Dryden. One that I can appreciate, but we are talking about controlling machines here. I'm having a hard time seeing how we can convince our coastal Essentialist friends of the value of this." He tapped his finger on the table.

Dryden was losing him, but he couldn't think of anything else to say. How much sway could a curator's apprentice really have on these political matters, anyway? He could only shrug. "I'm sorry," he said. "I don't have any other arguments to make. I understand that we may need to … destroy Haplopol, if you think it necessary." His chest fluttered uncomfortably as he spoke the words.

The general tapped his finger on the table again. He stood up, stretching his back. "You know, Dryden, in my homeland, there are no fever lands. By the grace of the good earth, we were spared many of the repercussions of the fall. As a result, many great Old World cities still stand: Tokyo, Nagoya, and Sendai, to name a few, and some with only minor retcher damage.

"These cities occupy much of our land. Even though many detest them, we have to live with them, side by side. In fact, in the early days after the fall, to have enough food, so that our children did not starve, we had to plant seeds on the rooftops and upper levels of these towers. And as the weather ravaged our islands, these buildings have protected us from the elements. They have even protected us from our enemies. So we have come to tolerate these cities of steel. We live with them, even as they crumble and collapse, not only because they offer many necessities but because they allow us to remember the Old World, what was lost, and what to be mindful of—historically. In fact, some of us even *appreciate* them."

Dryden was unsure where Hatsuo was going with this tangent, but he made sure to nod carefully during his oration.

Hatsuo found his seat again. "I know this is a stark contrast with coastal Essentialists, and one that sometimes causes conflict between our peoples, but I wanted to highlight it. I thought you, in particular, might understand. You are well-schooled and have a progressive view. Someone as worldly as you can appreciate these buildings for what they are."

Hatsuo nodded to himself, then continued. "This is why we protect the city of Portland from zealot Essentialists, because we would be loath to destroy such a grand city, just as I would be loath to destroy Sendai or Tokyo. It doesn't mean we have any intention of building machines that choke out the guts of the earth or lace the earth with lines of metal."

He paused and took an extended breath. "And this is also why now I would have you know, if it were only up to me, I would also be loath to destroy the ICSM cities as well."

Dryden hadn't realized the tension that had been building up in him until it was suddenly flushed away by Hatsuo's statement. "General, it's a great relief to hear you say this. There is so much we can learn from the ICSM people. So much we can do—"

Hatsuo raised his hand. "We must be careful. I am telling you this in confidence, because you are a learned man. I am entrusting my views to you in the hopes that you will entrust me with *your* confidence, so that we can work together to protect these cities—to prevent devout Essentialists from stepping on their own feet, as it were."

Dryden nodded in earnest, and Hatsuo smiled again.

"Thank you, Dryden," Hatsuo said. He stood up and approached Dryden, extending his hand. "I think we should speak regularly, you and I. I have many more questions about the ICSM cities and people. Why don't you join me on the *Haratumi* for the rest of our voyage?"

Dryden took the general's hand and shook it firmly. "That would be fine, sir. I would be honored."

"Wonderful. I'll see you tomorrow."

Dryden left the meeting with a spring in his step, and headed back toward his cramped cabin.

That night, he could hardly sleep. His arguments might have helped shift the general's sentiment toward preserving the ICSM cities. What's more, it was a much-needed boost of confidence that the general would reveal his personal thoughts—that he would want to work with Dryden on a common goal of such consequence.

He knew there was also a darker undertone to the general's comments. There would be objections to the idea of protecting Haplopol, and Dryden didn't know how they would deal with them. But that seemed far away, in the distant future. He was too engrossed in thinking about Haplopol. When he pictured it, it looked even more effervescent. It wasn't just a city, but a bastion of knowledge, one that Dryden might have a hand in protecting from the capricious forces of the world.

And it was only days away.

—9—

An Elegant Tapestry

As soon as Dryden left, Hatsuo's eyes welled up. He winced and held his fingers against his closed eyelids, hoping the pressure would stem the tide of tears. It worked, for the most part. Only one tear escaped, running rapidly down his cheek, eager to dampen the dirty floorboard.

He would feel this way, at times, when it all worked so perfectly. It was as if an elegant tapestry had been draped in front of him, one wrought by artisans over many years and with much effort, working with anxious uncertainty to realize something … so beautiful.

In this case, there had been quite a bit of uncertainty. He hadn't dealt with Essentialist scholars before, and he worried this one could be smarter than the rest—that Dryden would see through Hatsuo's game. But he had turned out to be just as naïve as the soldiers and diplomats, and just as pliable. His foibles and desires were more abstract, but they could still be exploited.

When the rush of emotion passed, Hatsuo pulled out a sheet of paper and began writing. He needed to begin mobilizing his forces. If Dryden was right, this could be Hatsuo's chance—*their* chance—to advance to the next stage of occupation.

There were four knocks on the door.

"Come," he said in Japanese.

Chinatsu walked in and stood at attention in front of his desk. "Dryden has returned to his quarters, sir."

"Good," Hatsuo said. He turned and opened the rabbit's cage, taking out the furry creature again. "This one stinks," he said. "Feed it to the snake. And get me another one. Pure white."

"General, the snake typically only eats small mice. The rabbit may be too large."

"Then cut it up into mouse-sized pieces. I doubt the snake will know the difference."

"Yes … sir."

He took a moment to stare at Chinatsu. Her hair was tightly arranged, like the maidens back home, but her form had few curves, and the scar near her hairline was unattractive. Still, the tension within her—the promise of violence—made her interesting.

"And what news of the raid?" he asked.

"Sir, our clipper waited until the Gungivites were on shore in Sanuwan, as you asked. We did not engage their vessels. Then we followed them along the shoreline and struck. We believe only one man escaped, but the Gungivites wouldn't know it was a Prefectorate operation. We made sure to use coastal Essentialists for the attack, and all of them wore Kuvar Collective colors."

"Someone escaped?"

"Yes." Chinatsu shifted her weight and bowed. "Apologies, sir. We will track him down."

Hatsuo nodded thoughtfully. "This will buy us very little time. It's true that with this Gungivite team out of the way, we may be first in Haplopol, but if we can kill *all* of them, they won't know about the attack for many more days."

"I understand, sir."

"And what is this I hear about Port Angeles?"

"The magistrate ruled in favor of the mayor, despite assurances he'd made to the contrary. The curator must have changed his mind, and backed the magistrate. Their claim is that the design of the new barracks violates the Essentialist treaty, with too many Old World materials used."

Hatsuo shook his head. "When will these savages finally capitulate? We won't accomplish anything with these dogs nipping at our ankles. Let's do something bigger this time. Let's do … treason. Think of something obscure and tangential to the issue, like selling Prefectorate military secrets to Salish Sea pirates. Yes, that will work for us on a number of fronts."

"Yes, sir. We will take the curator and the magistrate as soon as possible, sir. Hanging, sir?"

He smiled. "Yes, that should do nicely. Higher up this time, maybe on an Old World church tower. It has a greater effect, and we don't want someone stealing the bodies like they did in Quinault."

"Yes, sir. Of course." She bowed.

Hatsuo watched her again—so docile, so compliant. He wondered if he should take her, like he had Mayaka, but she wasn't quite ready. And that scar, it didn't do it for him. Besides, it might break her spirit. "You know, Chinatsu, I love that I can just be myself with you. All day long, my life is like a theater, a game of strategic pleasantries and petty banter. But with you, I can withdraw from showmanship. I don't even have to say any hurtful words, because if things don't go as planned …"

He could tell that she was trembling. She was stronger than the others, so she probably wouldn't urinate on herself, like Mayaka did that one time, but her voice still cracked when she replied, "Yes, sir. It is my honor to serve."

He smiled toothlessly and waved his hand in dismissal.

—10—

Anacortes Bound

If the winds were kind, Anacortes would be less than a day's sail from Ganges harbor.

According to Nillias, their ship was named *GO-NOX78*, but the sailors simply named it the *Nox*, as sailors do.

The *Nox* was a sturdy frigate. The wood was cut in clean lines and arcs, perfectly sanded and stained. There were special seats for the sailors to sit on, contoured to their buttocks, and the sails were full of starch. In most ships tall men would have had to bend down below decks, but not here. Although Nillias wouldn't let Lexie go deep into the hold, or into the artillery rooms, so maybe that's where they'd relegated all the usual depravities you'd find on Salish Sea vessels.

It was good to be out at sea again, away from the mind-numbing lessons about machine cities, as well as the giant cats, but there were still the nutjobs to contend with. Several wig-clad Observers were on board, including Nillias. The rest seemed to be Gungivite militia or run-of-the-mill sailors who spat and swore and made lewd remarks. The sailors, at least, made Lexie feel right at home. The crew was downright happy. She knew this wasn't any kind of pleasure cruiser, but it sure was comfortable.

Even Nillias seemed to be in a good mood. He spent most of his time paging through a tattered old novel, every once in a while gazing at the horizon with an expression that could only be described as contentment.

About halfway through the trip, Lexie decided to see if he would be more responsive to her questions. She walked up to him and nudged him with her elbow. "Didn't know you nutjobs liked to read, although I guess all those useless facts need to get in that bin of yours somehow."

Nillias managed a full grin in return. "We don't have … time to read, it's true. I used to read in my youth, before I became an Observer."

"You had a youth?"

"We're not so different, Lexie. I enjoy certain foods. I have goals. I have family that I care about, and yes, I had a youth—an entire childhood, even."

"How come I've never seen any of this family of yours?"

"Would you introduce your family to a captive that you may have to kill?"

Nutjob or not, Nillias did have a way of cutting through the crap. "I guess not."

Nillias turned to her and blinked. "But maybe I should have," he said. "My parents would like you. They are farmers—humble, pithy folk. They don't have much love for the Observers, but they abide by our laws, even though they share some of your irreverence."

It could have been some kind of entreaty, but she wasn't sure. "No wife or kids?" she asked.

Nillias looked off into the horizon. "I was married for a time, but she died. She had beautiful, long braids, similar to your hair color, but neater, always well groomed. She would spend the day making up rhymes of all kinds, many of which didn't quite make sense. She would say how she loved to eat cherry berries. She would have her tart meal do a cartwheel. I was … a cog in the bog. But we didn't know each other that well."

He said the last part matter-of-factly, as if he was counting goats or reading the morning news bulletin, when in fact it was quite the barnburner.

"You didn't know your own wife?"

"Observers are supposed to marry. The marriages are pre-arranged. I might have known her, if I wasn't constantly distracted by the demands of being an Observer. I might have even loved her, but these are luxuries we can't afford. Most marriages with Observers don't work out, in the long term."

"Why are you supposed to marry, then?"

"To bear and raise children. We never had any." A subtle wince broke his countenance. It could have been some form of regret. Maybe he was concerned about not living up to the standards of his precious Observer order.

"So you're all alone?"

"Yes."

"What about your cats? I had a stray once. It was nice but smelled like bird guts and urine. Tried to bite me a few times, so I had to give it the boot. I can only imagine if one of your big beasties tried to bite you, but I'm sure you've got them good and tame."

Nillias shook his head. "Not really. We don't see them as pets. The Gungivite Observers are paired with cats when they are teenagers. The cats have been selectively bred so as to be loyal to humans, but there are limits, given that the gene pool is predominantly comprised of breeds that can't be easily domesticated. The cats can be trained to do simple tasks, although they aren't always dependable. Their main purpose is for protection, and because these cats are often fiercely independent, more so than a house cat, it teaches us the need to accommodate them with an eye toward safety."

"How does that help?"

"It is a subtle lesson, but it makes us wary of independent intelligence. It teaches us to avoid anthropomorphisms—so we don't assign human attributes to foreign entities."

Of course it did. "What happens if you don't get along with your cats?"

"It can end violently. Usually, Observers adjust after an accident, but some who are not careful, who take to their animals too much, have been maimed or killed. This is why, for many of us, the requirement to foster a cat is not something that we enjoy."

"Got it. Animals are okay, but not because you actually like them and sometimes they kill you. Human wives are okay, but you don't really know who they are. Makes perfect sense."

He frowned, although it quickly faded back to his usual stone-faced expression. He might have been peeved, but he didn't respond to her quip.

She said, "Well, Nillias, this talk about pets, wives and family has been nice. A real heart-to-heart, like we're buddies off on an important mission together, but you should know I'm not buying it."

Nillias raised an eyebrow. "What do you mean?"

"You're not letting me visit my mom. You want more info from Leo about Haplopol. That's why we're going to Anacortes, because I'm your way to get in with him. After that, I'm sure you'll get your chance to dust me. Otherwise, we would be going to Haplopol first. It's the only reason you would delay."

"Olint was right about you," he said. "You're sharp. And you're close to the truth, but not quite." He frowned and looked toward the horizon. When he turned back to her, his face had lost all emotion. "Do you remember what we taught you about constraints?"

"Oh no. Not that again. I thought we were done. I'm still waiting on my nutjob diploma."

"We are done, at least for now. This is a lesson I've already taught you, and I'm trying to answer your question, Lexie."

She rolled her eyes and put her hands on her hips. She didn't have much of a choice. "Fine. One of the ways of controlling intelligent machines is to try to box them in with physical and rule-based constraints. Value-loading alters their reward function, but constraints prevent specific behaviors altogether."

"Yes, good. The ICSM people did take precautions with their experimental cities. They instituted constraints on the fundamental teleology in case something went wrong. Typically these constraints would be to prevent overuse of resources, or to enforce time limitations on goal completion, or to limit geographical expansion of the machine entity. Geographical constraints, in particular, were adopted by ICSM cities. In the case of Haplopol, this constraint stipulates that no machine or machine components created by the city can leave the confines of the city. In this way, the city's influence couldn't grow out of control."

Lexie pondered Nillias's words. "Sounds like a good idea."

"This is one reason why Haplopol is not a matter of extreme urgency—because there are limits in terms of its expansion and use of resources. This is why we are going to Anacortes first."

"Then why are you even worried at all? The more you tell me about Haplopol, the less I'm concerned about it. It's just a small city in a backward kingdom. It wants to preserve intelligent life and do it within the confines of its own borders. Sounds pretty safe to me."

"If it's safe, Lexie, why did Haplopol go dormant? Where are the former inhabitants? The experiment failed, and there are things that we still don't understand about what happened. This is why—and you were right about this, at least—we need to speak to Leopold, and we could use your help in convincing him to be forthcoming. We must approach Haplopol properly, with a full understanding of the risks, or there is no point in doing so at all."

"How do I know you're not going to kill me after we speak with Leo?"

"Because Leo will not have all the answers. It would be wise to better understand these constraints, and how the city interacts with humans, before entering the city. So if the Sanuwans control it, understanding their interactions with the city to date will be a priority. We will need your help with those interrogations."

It could have been true. His explanation did make it plausible. Though she found it hard to believe that the Observers, with their considerable wealth and power, wouldn't have someone else they could use. For now, she would have to live with it, and keep an eye out for an opening.

At least in Anacortes there wouldn't be any big cats around.

"So do you guys have spies in Anacortes?" she asked. "How do you know about my mom?"

Nillias's eyes softened, his head bowed, and he extended his hand to her shoulder, as if he was a preacher about to deliver a prayer. Then he simply shook his head.

She wasn't exactly given free rein aboard the *Nox*. A stocky, mustached man named Keegan was often nearby, shadowing her movements. He wasn't an Observer but rather one of the many Gungivite militia that hovered around Nillias, doing all he asked. Keegan had a way of pursing his lips, as if he was in a constant state of worry. He wore a long, scabbarded dagger on his belt, and Lexie was pretty sure he had a pistol hidden away in a shoulder holster under his jacket.

She had found a seat near the stern, away from Nillias's line of sight from the bow. Here, she could look back toward the Gulf Islands, of which Ganges Island was a part. When Keegan poked his head around the corner to check on her, she said, "Hey, I'm sorry, we haven't been formally introduced." She stood up to shake Keegan's hand. "I'm Lexie."

After some hesitation, he took her hand, but offered no verbal response.

"You're Keegan," she said. "I know. Well, if you're going to be following me around, maybe we should get to know each other. Have a seat." She sat on the wooden bench again and double-tapped the space next to her with her fist.

He sat down next to her. His movements were slow and controlled. His eyes never left her.

"This has to be an easy job for you. I mean, what am I going to do?" she asked, smiling. "There's a whole ship of Gungivites here, and I'm not much of a swimmer."

Keegan offered a shrug.

"I know you've got a job to do, but it doesn't mean we can't chat. You been working for Nillias long?"

"Yes. Four years."

"Wow. I can't imagine. I guess you've learned a thing or two—being that Nillias is so whip-smart and all."

Keegan's lips pursed again. His head tilted to one side. "No. They don't teach us. We are assigned to Observers after training."

"Huh. But you must have had some good—you know—on-the-job experiences."

Keegan shook his head. "No, I can't help you. We don't ask Observers questions, and I will not recount my experiences. For us, knowledge is toxic. The more we know, the closer we will be watched, and the more we will be pulled into dangerous assignments. I have a family, four beautiful daughters—I do this for them. We live in a prosperous nation. I'm glad I wasn't chosen to be an Observer, and yet still happy to serve their cause."

At least she had him talking. "Ignorance is bliss, huh? How do you know everything is on the straight and narrow, though, really? Hardworking, salty folk like us, we've got to stick together."

He sighed. "I'll stop you there. You're a pirate. Nillias said you would try to ingratiate yourself with me. No thank you." He retreated to stand next to the bulkhead.

She scowled at him. It had been worth a shot.

—11—

IT'S HARD TO ASK QUESTIONS OF HEADLESS SAILORS

A dense fog descended over the Marrowstone Flotilla the next morning, hindering their start and allowing Dryden a few more hours' rest. As soon as the fog began to recede, the bells sounded and the crews went into action.

The *Haratumi* crew was less welcoming than that of the previous ship he'd been on. Dryden noted many furrowed-brow appraisals as he made his way on board. He found Captain Chinatsu, who directed him to an uncomfortable bench on the starboard side. From there he sat alone and watched sails being unfurled, uniforms being laundered, and rigging ropes being pulled.

The shoreline featured the occasional outpost, mostly rundown and abandoned, and a few with active boats. Further inland, the terrain appeared healthy, with green verdure, little touched by man.

When the ship had broken away from the Seattle Strait, venturing into the open waters of the Wandefuca Channel, Hatsuo emerged from his cabin. His eyes probed the horizon and his men with equal scrutiny. When his gaze fell on Dryden, his head cocked back in alarm. "You're here, all alone?" He walked toward Dryden, hand extended and an unhappy grimace on his face. "I'm so sorry, Dryden, I would have thought my people would have given you an escort, or at least a cabin of your own so you could rest."

Dryden allowed the general to shake his hand vigorously. "Oh, no, I'm just fine, General. No need to fuss over me."

"Why don't you join me on the bow? I may not be the most stimulating conversationalist for a man of your intelligence, but at least the view is better."

"I … sure. It would be my pleasure, and I wouldn't think that at all." The general was so self-deprecating that at times Dryden found it difficult to respond without sounding pompous in comparison.

"Terrific." The general smiled.

They chatted on and off for some time. Dryden was apprehensive about asking questions a Prefectorate general might find inappropriate, or alluding to the prior evening's conversation, so he was surely the lesser conversationalist. Hatsuo seemed happy to pepper him with questions about ICSM culture, so perhaps it didn't matter.

Occasionally they saw ships in the distance. The general scoped them and told Dryden the class and flag. Some were Kuvar Collective, some Gungivite, some Vicky, some Essentialist. They usually flitted away soon after he saw them. No sense in getting close to three Essentialist warships on an unknown mission.

"Have you seen it before?" Hatsuo asked at one point, his chin nudging to the northwest. In the distance, a tall, shiny column was emerging from the horizon, surrounded by helical leaves that rotated over the water, enveloping it. Its size was difficult to make out at this distance, but Dryden knew it was huge, as tall as the biggest buildings in Portland.

"Yes, a few times," Dryden said, "but never as close as this."

Hatsuo raised an eyebrow. "It's ICSM too, isn't it?"

He was well informed. Many people thought the spinners were of Old World origin. "Yes," Dryden responded. "Most scholars believe the spinners were built by the ICSM cities."

"For what purpose?"

"You can see by the shape of the leaves and the direction of spin which way the wind is blowing, and also, by the amount of spin, the nautical force of the wind. That's why most believe it was kind of like a huge weather vane to help with navigation."

The general frowned.

"Yeah, it doesn't make sense to me, either. It seems strange to have such a gigantic structure to tell you something that a device on your own ship could easily provide."

"Has anyone tried to stop it from turning?"

"It's hard to ask questions of headless sailors."

"Excuse me?"

"I'm sorry. It's what Salish Sea people say. The leaves have sharp edges and they change shape with the wind velocity, often unfolding out to extend low over the water. This is why everyone gives it a wide berth."

Hatsuo's eyes darted back and forth, and he smiled. "I see. And the other spinner, is it the same?"

"No. In fact, this one here is called the Fan. To the north, just off the coast of Nanaimo, is the one they call the Singer. It's a statue of a woman with her mouth open to the sky, as if in song. Her gown flares out, catching the wind, but not in the same manner as the Fan. The Singer was probably an impressive work of art, or a symbol of ICSM ideology, kind of like the Statue of Liberty in the Old World."

Hatsuo said, "And what is this about splayed hands? I heard a story from one of my subordinates, but it seemed hard to believe."

"No, the splayed hands are real. You might see some in Sanuwan. They are ICSM artifacts, but it's uncertain whether they are in fact intended to represent hands. Each one is a platform with five appendages that stick out, but that's where the likeness ends. There have been eighty-seven of them documented, and they are all about fifty feet in length, in coastal areas and usually jutting from cliffs, pointing out at the sea."

"What are they for?"

"There are many theories. Some believe they are ornamental, a symbolic measure of the dominion of ICSM culture over their environment. The more popular belief is that they were some sort of countermeasure for retchers, which would explain why the Salish Sea islands are now devoid of the creatures. When the retchers would fly in from the mainland, the splayed hands would launch nets, or some other defense weapon, to take them down. Otherwise, the retchers would be constantly attacking the electronic systems of the cities."

"Fascinating. What do you think?"

"Oh, I don't know. I do think the retcher hypothesis is a good one, since they are strategically positioned all over the Salish Sea and not concentrated in one place. I haven't spent much time on it, though. My focus has always been on the cities."

Hatsuo nodded, squinting into the distance. He shifted his weight such that his whole frame was facing Dryden. He looked from side to side, as if to make sure no one was listening, and gestured with his finger for Dryden to come closer.

When Dryden leaned in, Hatsuo said quietly, "There's something I wanted to talk to you about. In order for our plan to succeed—to save Haplopol—we need to make sure that the city doesn't breach our Essentialist edicts by making the wrong kind of machines, correct?"

"Yes."

"So we need to make sure that no one else is in control of the city. A mischievous person, or a foreign power, that doesn't want to build the *right* machines, would ensure Essentialist powers are firmly against Haplopol, and all that it stands for."

"I … yes."

"So that means our most urgent priority when we arrive should be to seek out this main interface with the city, this *junction* you mentioned, to ensure that one of our representatives controls it. And, of course, the Sanuwans don't need to know about this. This junction, its function, and why we are seeking it out should remain a secret."

The general was making good points, but it didn't seem entirely fair. "Couldn't we try to work with the Sanuwans—maybe to control the city jointly?" Dryden said. "It's on their land, and we …" He trailed off. The general was frowning at him, his mouth forming an absurd arc.

"Come now, Dryden. The Sanuwans control a backward archipelago in the Salish Sea. They wear sheep fur and metal plates from the Old World on their chests. Do you really think they can be trusted to protect sun, soil and seed?"

"Well—"

"No, of course not." He patted Dryden on the shoulder and turned to look out to sea again. "And let's try to find that second junction as well—the one for Diplopol. I will assign a squad to work with you, when we arrive, and I'll make sure they listen to you—the most important man on this expedition." He nodded with conviction.

It disturbed Dryden that they might have to sneak around, trying to find a way to take control of the city, but surely the general knew what he was doing. These were matters of politics and governance, and it could be the only way they could preserve Haplopol.

"I better get back to my report for the Prefectorate," Hatsuo said. "I need to send it to Commander Yasui before the next trans-Pacific sailing. Again, I'm sorry you were so uncomfortable on the deck here. I will tell Chinatsu to grant you a cabin, if you want one."

"That won't be necessary. This is great here, General. I'm very comfortable."

With the general gone, and only the expanse of the channel to keep him company, Dryden pulled out his driftwood carving again.

He whittled away, throwing the shavings into the sea.

Most people would think opossums were disgusting animals. It was understandable. They did look like rodents, and they did like to rummage around in trash. But they weren't rodents—they were marsupials. Nate had found one when he was younger. In the back yard he'd been feeding dinner scraps to his "pet Koala named Fidget." Alayna had thought it was an imaginary friend until the local pest control killed it and charged them for having it on their property.

It took a month for Nate to get over it. They had to tell him Fidget was okay. He would be "returned to the eternal spring," they said, "to be with his parents and their parents and their parents, to nourish all of nature's creatures, along with the gifts of sun, soil and seed."

The ship occasionally bounced off the chop in the strait, at times pushing Dryden's blade in the wrong direction on the wood. He had carved enough into it to make the general shape of the animal's head. It looked more like a swollen rat at the moment, but that could be fixed. He wasn't anywhere near adding the finer details yet, but any inadvertent cuts, if deep enough, could botch the entire piece.

He didn't want to risk any mistakes, so he put it aside.

Soon enough, they were in Sanuwan waters. The setting sun had painted shorelines in shades of amber. Sheep and goats grazed on the low hills of the islands. It looked like a pleasant enough place. They were met by a Sanuwan patrol ship and led to the waters just off of Sanuwan City, the capital. Two catamarans from the city took over escort duties and led them through the archipelago toward East Sound, the closest town to Haplopol.

"So, did you sell me to the Sanuwans?" Dryden asked Alayna. They were rowing across the tranquil morning waters toward the long pier of East Sound with a skiff full of Chinatsu's Prefectorate soldiers. The three galleons stayed anchored close behind them, two levels of broadside cannons pointed not-so-subtly in the direction of the shore.

"Unfortunately, they don't take human currency," she replied.

"I thought I'd be worth at least one sheep," he said.

A smile pulled at Alayna's lips but couldn't quite break through.

It was actually true that the Sanuwans liked to barter with sheep rather than Vicky medallions or Essentialist notes, which was odd, considering they were always promoting themselves as the only nation that was "a step away from the Old World."

Dryden hadn't been included in the delegation sent to East Sound the evening prior. It had comprised only ten people, including Alayna, Chinatsu and a number of Prefectorate soldiers, aiming to broker a deal. In the end, they did strike a deal, but Dryden didn't know what it cost them. Now that Haplopol was "open," the Sanuwans could charge much more than the usual tours, of course. At the same time, anyone with half a brain wouldn't want to gouge the predominant military power in the northwest.

The skiff pulled up to the longest docking pier, and the twelve passengers disembarked. The pier featured a number of tall mooring posts, each with a mess of Old World paraphernalia bolted onto it: old phones, light bulbs, broken model airplanes, a toy spaceship made of plastic and even an old car exhaust muffler. Wires wrapped around the posts in places, as if they were connected to these Old World artifacts. It would certainly get a rise out of your run-of-the-mill Essentialist, but Dryden was sure none of the cables conducted electricity. Gaps in the rubber of these wires were a burnt orange color, the metal corroded by rust, and there were no power sources nearby, as far as Dryden could see. It was all for show, part of the Haplopol experience.

Beyond the pier was a street leading into town, lined by torch posts and manned on each side by Sanuwan soldiers wearing tough leather frocks. Circular patches of dense sheep hair had been sewn over their chests. These weren't spun wool, but rather slabs of sheepskin that featured the choicest hair patterns. These had some significance in Sanuwan culture. The thickest and most uniform sheepskin circles would often be indicative of higher social or economic standing.

The greeting party was making its way along the street. These five had the same leather frocks and sheepskin circles but also wore panels of metal featuring arcane symbols of Old World businesses and products: collections of layered squares, clusters of dots or half-bitten apples. The leader was a woman wearing antique reflective sunglasses—a valuable status symbol in Salish Sea nations—and sporting a dense cluster of piercings on her upper ears.

"Welcome! Welcome to Sanuwan," she said when they met on the pier. "Please, come with me so we can show you the crown jewel of our glorious kingdom. I am the princess Elissa."

Some of the Prefectorate soldiers bowed to Elissa. Dryden joined them, but he knew not to be too enamored by her standing. Sanuwan had *a lot* of princesses, and one could never be sure if they just gave every host the title to make guests feel special.

The party followed their Sanuwan escort onto shore and waited while two other full skiffs docked and their passengers joined them. These other skiffs carried the general, his Prefectorate soldiers and a quite a few Essentialist naval militia. The general stayed in the rear, surrounded by a healthy contingent of stone-faced militia.

Princess Elissa did the rounds, introducing herself, or in the case of those she'd met the previous evening, reacquainting herself. When she arrived at Dryden she paused and her face went blank. She looked out of place for a moment, like an actress who had forgotten her lines.

She quickly gathered herself and offered the same wide smile she'd given the others. "And you must be Dryden Quintain. I am delighted that we have someone on the expedition who can appreciate the rich history of the Polies. Would you mind if we spoke on the way to Haplopol? I would very much like to compare notes."

Dryden tried to find the general's eyes in the crowd, but Hatsuo was preoccupied chatting with Chinatsu. Dryden figured it couldn't hurt. "Of course. It would be my pleasure."

As they made to enter the town proper, Elissa gestured at the last post on the pier. She spoke loudly, so the entire group of Essentialists could hear. "I should warn you. You will see lots of neon. Don't be afraid." Her hands pushed toward the ground in a gesture of calm. "There are no retchers in Sanuwan, and all our electricity use is simulated, so you can enjoy the beauty of our artisans without fear." Nobody in the party looked afraid. This princess was probably used to dealing with devout Essentialists or people from the mountain fiefdoms, not hardened Prefectorate soldiers.

East Sound was a small town, but well kept. The buildings were freshly painted in bright colors: strawberry red, lemon yellow, mint green, sky blue and delicate pink. Some of these were storefronts offering *Polie Artifacts* or *Neon Wonders*. Smiling merchants were waving at the column and gesturing to metal trinkets in their hands. In one store window, a panel had been set up to look like an Old World television screen. It was translucent, showing a model of Haplopol behind it. Dryden could see mini-lanterns strategically placed inside. It was probably more impressive at night.

This showmanship and relative extravagance was limited to the main promenade. Down side streets, Dryden could see that quite a few buildings had fallen into disrepair. Some of them were entirely dilapidated, others were decaying shelters open to the elements. Sheep pranced around untended.

Within two more blocks they reached the outskirts of the town and were met with a huge sign reading *The Road to Haplopol.* A rough map had been drawn below the sign. From here it would be a two-hour hike along a well-trodden path that meandered up into the hills of the island.

They forged ahead without delay, Elissa and her colleagues leading the way. Not long after the hike commenced, she fell back to walk alongside Dryden.

"Have you had an enjoyable trip so far, Doctor Quintain?"

"Yes, thank you, but I'm not a doctor. That's mostly an Old World term for academics. In Essentialist lands, only real medical doctors have that designation."

"Well you're real to me. Just as real as Ranthoke or Leopold, who are both doctors."

He couldn't help raising his eyebrows. "You know them?"

She responded with a playful grin. "Yes, and I've read your papers as well. I went to school at the Dressler Institute in Victoria. The king wants us to be fluent in all cultures, and their views on Haplopol, so we can be effective guides."

"That's quite sensible. So what did you want to talk about?"

"I only wanted to meet the man behind the papers. And I've never met anyone with blond hair before. Is it real?"

"Yes, it's real." He thought she might have some pertinent questions about Haplopol, but it was almost as if she was flirting with him. She did have a certain allure. Under her sunglasses, piercings and Old World paraphernalia was a well-proportioned woman with a natural beauty. Her skin was luminous, with vibrant flesh tones, and her jawline was perfectly rounded.

This only made him more uncomfortable. He looked to see Alayna walking ahead of him, but she wasn't looking back.

He was rescued by Hatsuo, who had moved up from behind them. "Princess," he said, "do you mind if I ask you a few questions about Sanuwan? I'm impressed by how far your kingdom has come since I last visited."

"Of course," she said. Her playful smirk evaporated and she performed a minor bow to Hatsuo.

"Thank you, Dryden," Hatsuo said, his eyes stern and heavy. Dryden presumed that meant he should excuse himself.

"It was nice chatting, princess," he said, and he began to move toward the front of the column.

"Yes, thank you," she answered behind him. "I hope we can continue our conversation soon."

The path broadened and cut under a canopy of tall coniferous trees. Alayna was just ahead, so Dryden caught up with her.

"What is it?" she asked.

"Can you tell me anything more about your meeting with the Sanuwans yesterday?"

She frowned. "I can't reveal the terms, Dryden. The Prefectorate would never—"

"No, I know that. I was wondering if they told you anything more about how the city awakened, or what it's like on the inside. It's my job to record these things."

"Oh, I see. They did have a representative speak to us, who had been inside the city. He raved about it, of course. He mostly talked about a number of what he called *experiential rooms* in the city. He was practically jumping up and down about it, saying it had changed his life. At one point he said these rooms helped him learn more in an hour than reading ten books. The Sanuwans were light on the details, beyond that. Maybe they thought we would be less interested in making the trek if they told us everything upfront."

Dryden nodded. "Nothing about the machines running the city? Signs of former inhabitants?"

"No. It was a sales pitch. He probably didn't think those things would be interesting to us. Do you know what he was talking about, with these experiential rooms? There was something with that name in the Haplopol museum in East Sound, but I wasn't impressed."

Dryden shook his head. "I doubt they are anywhere close to the same thing. If I recall from Leopold's notes, the museum room in East Sound only has a bunch of Old World toys in it, dangling on strings and rotating on chains and pulleys."

"Yeah, that's right."

"I imagine the Haplopol experiential rooms are computer generated, so are much more realistic and versatile. It would be like … like being in a dream."

Alayna nodded, her brow furrowing.

Experiential rooms were mentioned in the records about ICSM cities, but Dryden's memory of the specifics was hazy. He would have to check his notes when the group stopped.

An Essentialist soldier jogged up to Dryden and Alayna. "Excuse me. General wants Alayna." Alayna glanced behind her. Hatsuo was still talking with Elissa, waving her over. "Sorry," she said.

She walked back with the soldier as Dryden continued to move ahead, gaining distance from her. The conversation with the general was one he would like to be a part of, but it might well be related to their secret agreement. He decided not to push for his inclusion, especially given Hatsuo's parting look moments ago.

An image of Maxwell's scolding glare appeared in his mind, further chastening him.

The path opened to skirt around a lake. Here, conversations were silenced and necks craned as the upper reaches of the Haplopol towers came into view. Dryden had already seen them poking out above the island from the East Sound bay, but the group was closer here, and the tops were more visible. There were five buildings, all in close proximity, with the tallest in the center. A white exhaust cloud twisted out from the central one and dissipated into the surrounding air. The buildings themselves were flat-sided, but with rounded corners. They were made of an opaque, glass-like material of a light blue color that made them look like mere distortions of the sky.

The group plunged back into the forested path, and the towers were obscured from view.

Occasionally Dryden would look back down the column and try to guess what Hatsuo, Alayna and Elissa were speaking about. Eventually the three split up. Hatsuo and Elissa became embroiled in other conversations, so Alayna was alone again.

Dryden considered joining Alayna to finish their conversation. He pulled off to the side and watched her marching up the trail.

She sauntered more than most women, even though her pack didn't look that heavy, and she didn't carry much excess weight. She stopped and moved off to the side as well. She was looking into the trees and writing something down in her notepad.

Dryden decided not to bother her. She was happy. It was a good day. Best to let her be.

He rejoined the column.

The grade steepened. The hike hadn't been arduous, but a number of the Prefectorate soldiers were slouching, burdened by their heavy packs and weapons. Dryden felt remarkably spry. He was in good shape, but this had nothing to do with his fitness. This was something he hadn't felt in a long time.

Excitement.

Over the crest of the hill, the trees had been cut down in a swath leading to another lake. In the foreground, unmanned pop-up carts lined the way down to a broad bridge spanning the lake. These carts were obviously relics of days gone by, when the city itself hadn't been accessible. Here, entrepreneurial Sanuwans would have sold models and trinkets to tourists who wanted a memento while they stopped to gander.

And they surely would have gandered, because it was here, in the background, that the full grandeur of the city was revealed. The bridge stretched across the lake into shimmering structures made of the same glassy blue material as the tops of the towers. Massive walls encircled the city, at least five times the height of a man, angling inward on the sides to meet with the five principal buildings that shot into the sky. Haplopol appeared exactly as its was depicted in the paintings and sketches, except these buildings stood taller. So tall, in fact, that they looked impossibly wrought against the backdrop of the calm mountain lake and humble forest. The towers dwarfed the gargantuan walls by twentyfold, at least.

The towers and walls weren't completely featureless. In places, subtle lines striated out in fractals from circular nodes. Were these electrical conduits visible through the semi-transparent walls, or some other utility too advanced for Dryden to imagine? Gray, semi-transparent boxes marked the high reaches of the towers. These could be windows, but they were too indistinct from the blue superstructure to know for sure.

He had reams of evidence. He'd seen the pictures. He'd even seen the tops of the towers just minutes ago, but still he'd found it hard to believe until that moment. It had all been academic, a thought experiment about a fascinating textbook city, one filled with wonders and questions.

But now it stood before him, and it was real.

And at the end of the bridge, above massive doors that had been split open, emblazoned with bright gold script, was a sign: *Haplopol is open to all.*

—12—

MOM

It was overcast when the *Nox* reached Anacortes harbor. The horizon was a layer cake of somber blue waters, gray docks and gloomy clouds as they approached the consumer terminal. Their vessel moored at the end of one of several long piers that reached out a lengthy distance from the shore.

The first person Lexie found in Anacortes was a surprise to her. She heard Tarnation's gregarious laugh from across the quay just after they disembarked. When she was further down the line she saw him hauling fish off a trawler, his net replete with twice as many as the man next to him.

"Hey, Tarn, will you keep it down," Lexie called out. "Respectable sailors like to hear themselves think."

His brow was beset with deep ridges as his eyes searched for her. "Lexie!" He dropped his net and bounded up the gangway to the quay, his hair bun bouncing in every direction.

He grabbed her shoulders and looked her up and down. "Oh my!" he said. "Been so long. We didn't know if you were going to turn Gungy on us." He called out to the other fisherman below. "I was right! She's back!" He laughed.

"I don't think you need to worry about that, and glad to see you in one piece. Not so glad to smell you, though."

"Ha haaaaa. Lexie! Your tongue—always so smart!"

Only then did Tarnation notice the men behind her—Nillias and two other Observers, trailed by a dozen more men. They were wearing their typical black linens. The garments looked light and airy, but Lexie knew they were laden with weapons.

"So where's Johl, *bae*?" Tarnation asked, keeping one eye on the Observers.

"Johl, he's ... not with us," she said. Tarnation wasn't the most temperate man, so Lexie held her tongue about Johl being killed. It could set him off. Even though that could be a good thing at some point, because she might need to get physical with the Gungivites, but here, right now, they would lose and probably end up as fish food. "What about you? They didn't tell me what happened."

Tarnation guffawed. "We were told you wanted to stay—that they had a job for you on Ganges Island."

Lexie frowned. "You believed them?"

"Ryder talked to them. He said he saw you. You didn't speak with him?"

That was strange. Ryder was a sick sod, but earnest. He didn't seem like the lying type. "No, I didn't," she said.

"No? Well that's what Ryder said, *bae*. They gave us money for the job. We're all square."

Maybe Ryder made some kind of side-deal with the Gungivites? "Where's Ryder now? Is he okay?" Traitor or not, he was at death's door when she saw him last.

"He's fine. Been around town. Haven't seen him for a few days."

"Ahem." Nillias pretended to clear his throat behind them.

"Yeah, yeah," she said. "Sorry, Tarn. We're on egghead business and I don't want this one to hard boil. Let's catch up later."

"Yeah, *bae*, would love it." He smiled, nodded and returned to his fish net.

She walked with Nillias along the rest of the quay and onto shore. The fog descended lower when they reached land proper. A spitting mist pecked at their faces.

They turned off the quay toward the main promenade, but before they could go any further, they had to get through "processing". There was a high fence and guard outposts around the port intake area.

They stood in line and waited their turn.

Anacortes was part of the Three Rivers Nation, which wasn't really a nation. It was mostly a group of half-drunk skunks that hired goons to rattle people every once in a while. These folks, based primarily in Anacortes, controlled the area between the Fraser River to the north and the Stillaguamish River to the south. There was good land in there, but lots of fever lands as well—with Van Kuvar and Seattle bordering much of it. The skunks made some good hay off Anacortes, being that it was such a busy port and all, through trade and "processing." Or, in other words, grifting.

When Nillias paid their way, they were let through the gate toward town.

"You want to tell me the real deal about Ryder?" she asked Nillias.

"We paid him and Tarnation a fair wage."

"You got some kind of special deal with him?"

"No."

"And what about Johl? Is a bullet to the head a *fair wage*?"

Nillias didn't respond for a while. His eyes darted back and forth. Finally, he said, "I'm sorry about your friend. Sometimes people get hurt for the greater good."

She shook her head. "Says you. I'm not sure your greater good is the same as Johl's greater good."

"It's not a responsibility we take lightly, or that we enjoy. There will be others, Lexie."

"Back to stone-cold killer mode, eh? I guess the boat ride was just a vacation."

This time, he didn't respond.

Mom's apartment was on the south side of Anacortes, near Flounder Bay, in a complex streaked with brown moss adhering to the gray stucco. It was pricier than the apartments in the inland buildings, and less accessible than the ones in the center of town, but here she had a view of the channel and could watch the boats. Mom said it helped her imagine Lexie out on the horizon, even though the boats she saw were mainly the smaller fishing vessels and ferries—nothing that Lexie would be sailing.

Nillias and a bunch of his cronies accompanied her up the external staircase to the second floor, where she knocked on Mom's door.

Mom's hair was a lighter gray than Lexie remembered, and her face more lined with creases, but her brown eyes lit up when she saw her. "Oh, Lexie, my baby!" She fell into Lexie's arms and held her tightly. Lexie could feel the ridges of her mom's ribs under her shirt and moisture accumulating on her own shoulder, where Mom's eyes rested.

Mom never lost her composure for long. She pulled herself away and wiped her eyes on her sleeve. "Come in, come in, please."

Lexie moved inside, followed by Nillias and the rest of his goons.

"And who are these dapper gentlemen? So handsome." Mom was ecstatic when Lexie spent her time with anyone who wasn't Prefectorate. These men weren't even pirates, which was surely an added bonus.

"They're Gungivites," Lexie said.

"Would you like some tea and biscuits?" Mom asked. "I can put a pot on the stove."

"You're too kind, but no thank you," Nillias responded.

Lexie scowled at Nillias. *You're too kind?* What a poser.

"Are you friends with Lexie?" Mom asked Nillias, her face alight with interest.

Lexie spoke up before Nillias could respond. "I'm working with them. Mom, how are you? Are you feeling okay?"

"Oh yes. I'm fine. You don't have to worry about me. I walked all the way into town the other day."

"With Freddy?"

"Oh, no. He's getting on now—almost fifteen years old, he is. I can't be bothering him every time."

"Mom, I *paid* him to watch out for you. He's supposed to walk with you into town."

"No need for that, and all the groceries either. I can handle myself."

"What groceries?"

"Come, Lexie. You treat me like a child, sometimes." She gestured to a weighty netted bag in the kitchen. Lexie picked it up and rifled through the contents. Inside were various foodstuffs she unraveled from carefully folded cloth wrappings: a husk of dried salmon, plums, potatoes, carrots, and even a few of the high-end sea ration packs.

Lexie hadn't asked anyone to bring Mom groceries, even Freddy, and she doubted Freddy would have done this of his own volition. Could it be Tarnation?

"He's such a nice boy, Freddy," Mom said. "He brought in the mail the other day. There's one for you." She gestured to an envelope on the counter.

Lexie didn't get much mail here. She could only think of one person who knew the address—Warrick.

Nillias had strolled into the kitchen, so he wouldn't notice. She snatched the envelope quickly. She was about to stuff it down her pants when she saw the sender: Three Rivers Municipal Works.

It was a tax bill. Somehow the skunks had found Mom's address and connected her to it. They'd probably sent the bill to her downtown mailbox as well. The skunks weren't organized about much, except when it came to collecting money. That was their passion. Maybe they weren't like skunks but more like beavers; constantly active, and singularly focused. They didn't care what trees fell on whom, as long as they got their wood for their dams, or whatever.

Lexie stepped forward and threw the bill into the fireplace. The beavers could wait.

When she turned back around, she noticed that Mom was leaning on the table, trying to hold up her weight. "Mom, sit. Please."

"If you insist."

Lexie led her mom to the modest living room. Mom had a threadbare couch that she liked to sleep on. It was covered with a few layers of blankets. Now she sat up on it and crossed her legs. Another wooden chair was in the corner of the room. Lexie pushed it closer to Mom and sat down. Thankfully Nillias and his men had the decency to stay in the kitchen.

"Mom, I'm serious. How sick are you?"

Mom sighed. "I'll be fine, Lexie. Some days I can't eat, and I'm tired all the time, but when I get up I feel okay. I can read, or stare out at you on the water. I'm perfectly happy."

"How much do you sleep?"

"A nap here and there—"

"Most of the day?"

She paused. "Well, I wouldn't think of it that way, but yes, I suppose so."

"Let's get Freddy here full time. I can pay him. And if not him, there has to be—"

"No, Lexie." She said it calmly, almost sympathetically, knowing that Lexie wouldn't approve.

Lexie could have debated her, but there was no point. Mom would never agree. "Okay, Mom," she said.

Her mind turned, trying to figure out what else she could do without Mom knowing. She would have to hire someone else besides Freddy. And not Tarnation. Somebody who was caring and patient and didn't smell like fish.

Unfortunately, those weren't the kind of people Lexie rubbed shoulders with. She would have to ask around.

They chatted for a while. Mom asked her about what she'd been up to. She was curious about Ganges Island. Lexie told her about Ganges City, including all the livestock and fruit picking and farming, but not so much about the Gungivite Observers and their nutty lessons. It would just make her worry, and besides, Nillias was only a few feet away.

It was simple conversation. Lexie made sure to laugh at Mom's jokes, and she also made a few of her own. She let Mom make them all tea, and she ate her stale biscuits. She memorized Mom's insightful eyes and lopsided smile, even the way she sighed. She stayed for a good hour. Nillias, who was usually a patient man, stepped into the living room, and began lurking ever closer. It was surely his way of saying her time was up.

She wouldn't normally be this kind to her mom, and rarely would she sit with her this long. Maybe it was because now, whenever she visited, the changes were visible. Even though Mom was happy, she had become resigned.

Maybe it was because every time Lexie had a conversation with Mom, she knew it could be their last.

—13—

Haplopol

They didn't enter Haplopol immediately. The Sanuwans preferred that a guide come out from the city to escort them inside. While waiting, the column paused and ate some of the hard, crumbly breadsticks the Prefectorate soldiers used for rations.

Dryden was glad of the delay. When he could break his gaze away from the looming city, he used the time to check his notes and review Leopold's *Guide to the ICSM*. Leopold had a specific section on Site Analysis Protocols, which outlined his suggested method for ensuring an objective assessment of an ICSM city. Dryden reviewed it again, even though he knew it already. This was the opportunity of a lifetime, and he didn't want his research to be called into question because he was biased, or because he inadvertently contaminated the anthropological observations.

Eventually, a man emerged from the city. His name was Delane, and he was their Sanuwan guide, according to Elissa. It was hard to believe he was Sanuwan. Delane's teeth were blindingly white, his skin a uniform olive hue, and his hair looked like it was chiseled out of obsidian. He was wearing blue linen clothes and black, rubber-soled shoes.

Delane told them he'd been living in the city for several days, enjoying its many pleasures, along with about fifty other "favored" Sanuwans. He had a relaxed, almost smug, air. He smiled at the volley of questions thrown his way. "All in good time," he said, over and over again. When the questions stopped, he said, "If you can follow me," and turned in the direction of the city.

There was an eerie silence as the forty-odd Essentialists and Sanuwans walked over the bridge toward the massive walls of Haplopol. Delane walked casually, as if strolling through a garden on his day off, but the rest of them had a cadence that was stiff and uneven. Their footsteps didn't make much sound on the blue bridge, just shuffling noises that seemed muted in comparison to the enormous weight of the city dominating their vista—as though they were mice about to steal cheese from the home of ancient giants.

The arched entranceway was a good sixty feet high. Each gold letter of the *Haplopol is open to all* sign was about the size of a man. Beyond the entrance was an expansive courtyard, if it could be called that. Here, three columns in the center reached up to the ceiling to support a massive enclosed space, big enough to fit the *Haratumi* a hundred times over. High above the main expanse were walkways and palisades, some with circular gardens featuring fountains, trees, flowers and even birds. In the distance, numerous alleyways branched off from the courtyard.

Dryden was taking notes feverishly while everyone looked around.

"Each of you will be assigned virtual delegates momentarily," Delane said. "These delegates will be able to answer your questions and guide you through the city. Please be careful with your weapons when they appear."

Semitransparent people started popping up all around them. They looked as if they were lit by moonlight, with a hint of blue color to them, and all were wearing white cloaks. There were women and men, all with tight, elegant physiques and faces of perfect symmetry. One soldier screamed when they appeared, and many others jumped away, brandishing katanas menacingly while staring down the apparitions. The transparent people—or "delegates"—each bowed their head toward the person standing next to them.

"Do we have to use these?" Chinatsu asked. Her body was tense, ready for action, staring down her delegate.

"You can tell them to disappear at any time," Delane said. "When you need them, just say *delegate* and they will reappear."

Gradually, the group looked to gain comfort with the apparitions. Some of the soldiers seemed to feel better once they'd made a pass through the ethereal bodies with their hands or katanas. Others just told them to leave, and they disappeared.

"Shall we begin the tour?" Delane asked. "I imagine you are all eager to visit the high reaches of the towers, and to try the experiential rooms."

Despite being distracted by the copious notes he was taking, Dryden was filled with a sense of wonder by the tour. They walked past countless wheeled and flying robots, each built with smooth lines and colored to blend into the city around them. These robots were cleaning, watering plants, and bringing food to lounging Sanuwans, as well as servicing wall outlets and ducts for purposes Dryden had yet to understand. The gray squares on the upper reaches of the towers were indeed windows, or perhaps versatile telescopes. Using these windows he could look out across the Sanuwan Islands and, using simple finger touches on the window itself, zoom in and out and obtain countless readings of temperature, pressure, carbon density, electromagnetic radiation—really, anything—for miles in any direction.

Most surfaces were made of the same opaque blue glass as the exterior, but when Dryden looked closely enough he could see sophisticated networks of wires and fluidic systems channeling, converging and diverging through these walls and great rooms.

Chinatsu and many of the Essentialist soldiers were particularly excited by what they found on a gangway on the upper reaches above the courtyard. Standing in an arcade along a bank of exterior windows were three large, spherical droids, propped up on mechanical legs. A bank of what were clearly four big guns of some kind poked out of the front of each of these machines. Delane and the delegates explained that the walls could be opened and these droids could be used to fire ordnance externally to defend the city.

It was reassuring to Dryden that his research had been right about these droids, although it was equally harrowing to see the reactions of his colleagues.

Eventually, they were taken to a main hall where the ceiling shimmered with spiraling gold tinsel. A huge replica of the city had been built here, with sectional pieces askew from the model. It looked like these model pieces could be removed and examined. A great mottled screen dominated the far end of the room, where you could pose questions to the city, and the city would answer in a soft, feminine voice. Beside the screen, lights flashed in a grid, the patterns sometimes emulating sound waves from the voice.

The Prefectorate officers spent a good thirty minutes peppering the city with mostly inane questions like what is its favorite color (it didn't have one), or how tall its biggest tower was (thirteen hundred feet). Dryden managed to ask a couple questions of his own, about what the walls were made of (aluminosilicate glass) and what it's chief energy source was (geothermal). The answers would be essentially the same if you asked the delegates. Dryden did a few tests and noticed the congruence.

Eventually Delane encouraged them all to head out and visit the experiential rooms, which were just off the main hallway. Delane and their delegates said they would want to spend a long time exploring the rooms, so it would be best to wait until the end of the tour.

"I'm sorry, I'd like to wait out here," Dryden told his delegate as they made to enter the rooms.

"Of course," his delegate said, and smiled at him. Dryden's delegate was a man, clean-shaven and nondescript. Others had delegates that were quite physically attractive, or excessively smiley. He wondered how the city chose someone's delegate.

Hatsuo had taken notice of his reluctance to enter the experiential room. "Is there some danger here, Dryden?"

"No, I don't think so. I want to maintain a degree of scientific rigor, is all. If I join you I'll lose that."

Hatsuo squinted and smiled. "Right, right. I think I will try it some other time as well. And, Chinatsu, Alayna, maybe you can join us for a walk? I am so excited I just can't sit down at the moment."

Dryden realized what Hatsuo was doing. He was separating them from the Sanuwans so they could search for the control junction. Unfortunately, Princess Elissa had been watching them from the entrance to the first experiential room.

"May I join you as well?" she asked.

"Of course," Hatsuo said. "It would be our pleasure."

Delane led the others into one of the experiential rooms.

Eight of them ended up remaining outside, as Hatsuo's personal guard had to stay with him. They wouldn't be discreet, but Dryden wasn't sure true privacy was an option anyway, with all the delegate apparitions everywhere.

Dryden led them up to the gardens first. He suspected Hatsuo would want to separate Elissa from the group, but he wasn't sure how to do it. Luckily, Hatsuo was skilled at this kind of maneuvering.

"Princess Elissa," Hatsuo said, "I am already mightily impressed. I wondered if you would consider terms for a repeat visit. I know many Essentialist leaders and Prefectorate commanders will want to witness this with their own eyes. Maybe you could host a future visit with three times our number?"

Elissa smiled broadly. "Of course, General, how would—"

"Why don't you outline a proposal with Chinatsu and Alayna here in the gardens, while I ask some questions of our scientific guru? I would like to hear about options for different dates, and different numbers of people."

"Absolutely, General."

Chinatsu, Alayna and Elissa split off, leaving Dryden alone with the general and his personal guard. Several virtual delegates still loitered nearby.

The general's smile faded. "Can we just ask the delegates?"

"I'm not sure," Dryden answered.

"I don't like them following us around," Hatsuo said. "Make your delegates go away." The five members of the group asked their delegates to leave, including Dryden. The delegates faded to nothing in front of them, one by one.

Hatsuo looked around, as if there might be other delegates hiding nearby. He didn't know that the city was probably listening anyway, no matter where they were. Dryden hoped that wouldn't matter.

"Why don't they show everyone where the control center is?" Hatsuo asked.

"It's a security precaution. If everyone knows where it is, it's harder to protect."

"Would it be near the main hall?" Hatsuo asked.

"No, actually. That's more of an oracle for the general population. The lights and voice are just for show, to make us feel comfortable, and to make us think we are connecting with the city. I think the control interface would be in a place that's less accessible, perhaps even hidden. Come with me."

It was an educated guess. While the others were asking questions of the oracle in the main hall, Dryden had been taking apart the city replica and looking at diagrams that accompanied it on a vid screen. It gave him some clues.

Each of the five city towers had exhaust channels that went up through their centers. This exhaust originated several levels below ground, in power plants that had cooling systems. Below the largest tower was a power plant equivalent in size to the other towers, but with an additional large room off to the side surrounded by an inordinate number of cooling ducts and power conduits. The control computers were rumored to be power-hungry, according to Leopold. The main computational centers, in particular, produced so much heat they required a highly sophisticated cooling system. As a result, Dryden believed this room was a possible source for the control interface.

It was also encouraging that the model had labeled this underground room the *Officiant's Office*. He knew from historical records that a few people in the city had been named "Officiants." These people had been integral in settling disputes or scheduling city events. There were no other governance titles in the cities, as far as he was aware. In general, the ICSM cities espoused equality among their citizens, yet he suspected that these Officiants had some influence on the cities' inner workings and thus might position their seats of authority near the control junctions.

Either way, this Officiant's Office would be a good place to start.

Dryden led Hatsuo and his three guards to one of the main elevators, and they took it down as far as it could go and then navigated through a series of corridors. There were many doors, but all of them had screens with the word "Vacant" on them. Dryden was going on memory alone, so he wasn't sure they would find it, but he would rather not call the delegates unless they absolutely needed to.

After a few turnarounds, he found a long corridor that led to a substantial door. The screen on the door read *Officiant's Office.*

"How do we get in?" Hatsuo asked.

Hatsuo's delegate appeared right next to him, startling him. "I can escort you," it said.

The door opened, and Hatsuo's delegate led them inside.

It was a large, circular room. The circumference was lined with displays and chairs, but the displays were turned off. What grabbed Dryden's attention was in the center of the room: behind a thick transparent panel, immersed in bubbling fluids, was an orb woven with blue light fractals, sitting on a pedestal composed of a bundle of shiny rods. The bath was ejecting steam at a feverish rate, which was swept up into a hood above the glass chamber.

It was all uniform and symmetrical: the ball, the rods, and the position in the bath. Even the steam seemed to pull off the top of the water in a consistent manner.

But there was one glaring anomaly.

Perched over the orb was a metal contraption that looked almost like a spider about to consume its prey, with spindly legs hooked onto the orb in several places. Its body, if it could be called that, was sleek and bulbous. On the side of it was a shooting star emblem, like some kind of Old World logo. On the top were several propellers, inactive despite the energetically bubbling waters around it. Dryden had seen pictures of similar machines from the Old World. It was an aerial drone, one that had somehow found its way deep into the city and attached itself to the control junction.

"So where did this drone come from?" Dryden asked.

Dryden was sitting at a blank video screen terminal that was next to the bubbling bath. It had been easy to communicate with the control junction. He simply started talking to it.

The speaker next to the terminal answered. "The most likely scenario is that it ventured down the exhaust shaft and cut through a number of vent screens to reach the control junction. I have since had the vents repaired."

"Why don't you know for sure? You didn't see it arrive?"

"No, my system was dormant at that time."

"Then how did you … awaken?"

"The drone sent me the correct command codes, which allowed me to initialize and reboot Haplopol."

Dryden sat back in his chair. So the mystery of *how* the city awakened had been solved, but it only prompted a series of additional questions. "Who sent this drone?"

"I am not privy to that information."

"Can't you take it apart and check its memory or something?"

"The drone wiped its memory after transmitting the commands."

Hatsuo cleared his throat behind him. Dryden turned to see his eyebrow was raised. "Sorry," Dryden said. He moved out of the chair so Hatsuo could take a seat.

"City," Hatsuo began. "What you have created here is magnificent. Thank you for allowing us to enjoy all you have to offer. We understand that there is a role for humans to play in managing the city. We would be greatly honored if one of us were to help you in that role."

"Yes, you are correct. Is one of you the Lead Officiant?"

Hatsuo looked around at the assembled group with his finger on his lips. Then he leaned closer to the screen. "As Officiant can we ask you to do … anything?" It was as if he was whispering secrets to a lover.

"As long as the tasks you suggest do not interfere with my primary objective and constraints, I will endeavor to implement them."

Hatsuo squinted. "And what is your primary objective?"

"To enhance the wellbeing of all intelligent life within Haplopol."

Hatsuo looked back at Dryden. Dryden just shrugged. It sounded reasonable, and it matched historical records he'd seen.

"Wonderful," Hatsuo said. "In that case I would like to be made Lead Officiant. In my absence I will delegate Captain Chinatsu as my proxy."

Dryden had wondered if perhaps Hatsuo would want him to be the Lead Officiant, or at least his proxy, given his knowledge about Haplopol and their mutual interest in saving the city, but apparently not. He wasn't offended. It would be a position that would require a great deal of responsibility.

And Alayna had surely told Hatsuo what happened to Ben.

—14—

A Plan Within a Plan

It turned out that Leo was out of town, up in Bellingham with a research assistant, so they had to wait a couple of days for him to get back to Anacortes. Lexie was tired of being cooped up on the ship, so she managed to convince Nillias that she needed to talk to Tarnation about her mom. Or at least, that's what she told him.

She'd made it as far as his fishing boat.

"Does this guy need a haircut?" Tarnation asked. He was referring to Keegan, who was standing behind her. Nillias had assigned him to watch her while she met with Tarnation.

Tarnation's idea of a haircut was not what most had in mind. Without getting into his eyebrow-raising history, he was essentially asking if he could cut off Keegan's scalp.

"No, his hair is just fine, Tarn, but thanks. I came to see if you'd walk with me. I thought we could catch up."

"Of course!" His eyes lit up.

"Before we go, do you want to …" She pointed at his chest, which was basically naked despite a tattered T-shirt hanging off one shoulder. What remained of the shirt was covered in scattered fish scales that glittered over the stain-ridden material. Apparently she had woken him, or he had just finished his work, or maybe it was his typical casual wear?

"What, *bae*?" he asked. His mouth was a crescent of white teeth.

"Never mind," she said. "Come on."

They walked up the quay toward a small inlet, where there were a few shops and restaurants on the interior of the fenced-in wharf area. Keegan walked a few paces behind them, his eyes watchful.

There was a chill in the air. Drizzle flitted down from above, but it was only enough to darken the wooden deck of the quay and barely dampen her sea jacket. You couldn't really classify it as a proper rainfall. It certainly didn't faze Tarnation any, despite his non-shirt and bare feet.

Lexie wondered if they could subdue Keegan. Between the two of them, they would certainly have a good shot. It was one of the many times she had weighed the idea of trying to escape, but the more she considered it, the more the idea lost luster.

Ultimately, the question was: What would she do if she got away? Maybe she could cut into the interior of Three Rivers and find a new life, but the Observers had her dead to rights because they knew she wouldn't leave her mom behind. And she still hadn't figured out how they knew about her pirating days. She couldn't count on getting help from anyone, because anyone could be in their pocket.

She vowed she wasn't going to be their docile little pup forever. They had leverage over her, but there had to be some way to get leverage over them. So she asked questions. She watched. She gathered whatever information she could.

"Where are we going?" Tarnation asked. "Victoria again? Ganges? Being Fish-man is honest work, but nettles—it's tiring. There's no stories in fish, except the one that got away, and that one got away a few too many times already." He cackled.

She grinned. "No, I don't want you for a job again. I just want to talk. These wingnuts got me wrapped up in their harebrained scheme, and I don't want you caught up in it as well."

He frowned and nodded.

She tried to change the subject. "How's your girl? Samaya, was it?"

"Sammy. She's not too happy about my job, but we get along. She works at a spice seller. Between the two of us—wow." He held his nose and laughed.

"What are they saying about Haplopol, here in town?"

"Not much, *bae*. A woman came through a couple days ago—a Sanuwan princess, they said, with lots of jangling Old World junk around her neck. Lots of oohs and ahhs about the perfect city in the hills; neon this, neon that. Once you arrive, there's not a care in the world, she said. Machines that can fix anything, serve you drinks. Not my thing, though. There's a group of the Three Rivers honchos who are going for a visit. Now we know what they're using all that processing money for." He winked.

"And what about the Essentialists? Any signs of aggression? Before this debacle with the Gungi-freaks, I saw a few too many of their ships around for my liking."

"Aggression? No, *bae*. Lots of boat traffic in Wandefuca though—and some of them military. Could just be more people going to Haplopol. But hey, I just fish. I'm not rubbing shoulders with the kind of people that would give me good answers, *fo sho*."

They had reached the old Radcliff lighthouse. It was no longer in use, the siding torn to pieces and lacking any kind of lighting equipment. There was a new one not far away on Shannon Point that was the mainstay for boat traffic. Radcliff was just a lookout tower now.

"Hey, Keegan. I'm just going to talk with Tarn here in the Radcliff. You know, remember old times, look out at the ocean. Would you mind waiting outside? There's only one exit."

Keegan squinted. "Only fifteen minutes, max. Nillias said he wanted you back soon."

She gave him a sour face for show. "Fine, fine."

The door was open and the main staircase was covered in dirt and droppings, as if sea animals had been trapped inside. Nevertheless, they walked up the stairs, two steps at a time, until they were in the main lens room. Here, Lexie glanced down the stairs to make sure Keegan hadn't followed them, then she took out her scope.

"What are we looking at, boss?" Tarnation asked.

"Nillias, hopefully. I saw him head this way from the ship. I could barely see, but I think he went into Burty's over there."

"Uh-huh. Okay, I get it now."

She pulled her eye away from the scope to see Tarnation with his hands on his hips, a pronounced scowl on his face.

"Sorry, Tarn. I did want to talk, but—"

He broke down and laughed. "It's okay, Lexie. I know you well, *bae*.

It's always two things at once—always a plan within a plan. I love it!" He punched her in the shoulder, a little too hard.

Lexie winced and rubbed her shoulder. "Thanks, Tarn."

She put the scope back on her eye and angled it to find Burty's. The eatery was far away, so she had to pull out the end of the scope for maximum magnification.

Nillias wasn't immediately visible, but she kept checking, cycling through the windows and even the empty patio on occasion.

Tarnation was tapping on a railing behind her. He used to be a drummer, or so he said. He also had trouble sitting still.

"You ever think about going back?" she asked.

"Back? You mean to Vernon, or down south?"

"Either, I guess."

"Nah. Vernon was nice, but got a bit of a rep there after the tribal wars. Followed me around, it did. And down south, it still messes with me—what happened. It's peaceful here, far enough away that I don't remember it. If I go back, if I get close, I'm worried I'll see them again."

Tarnation had been abducted from his village by marauders when he was young. He didn't even know the name of the village because he'd only just moved there with his parents. The marauders hadn't exactly treated Tarnation like one of their own. Lexie had never heard the whole story, only that he'd been traveling all over the continent ever since.

"I get it, Tarn. Whatever floats your boat."

It had been several minutes, and she was beginning to think Keegan would come and check on them. Finally, she saw something. It was Nillias, she was sure of it. Nobody else had such an uptight walking style. He was with another man, and a child, and they were talking just outside the front entrance of Burty's. The other man was hard to make out. He was about the same height as Nillias, wearing a large orange rain jacket with a hood covering the side profile of his face. The child was a girl, by the looks of it. Curls of hair pushed out from underneath her hood. She was looking down, ignoring the two men, watching the rain form patterns on the concrete.

Or maybe it wasn't Nillias, because he leaned over and *hugged* the other man. It wasn't a stiff embrace with a pat on the back, either. They held for a good three seconds, then he bent down on one knee and reached for the girl as well. The girl pulled away, clearly uncomfortable, but she settled for a wave as she leaned against the hooded man's leg. Then the pair left in a hurry, and Nillias was left behind to watch them go.

Nillias looked down for a brief moment, his eyes trained on where the girl had stared, as if trying to see what the girl had seen, but there was nothing Lexie could make out, only damp concrete, darkening further with the rain.

Finally Nillias stood up, and began walking along the harbor. His gait was all tightwad again.

"Let's go," Lexie said.

Tarnation wrapped up his mock drum solo with a flourish of rapid tapping. "You got it, boss. Back to the ship?"

"Yeah, but one thing first. You remember I told you I didn't have a job for you?"

"Yeah, *bae*. Like sunshine."

"Well, I do now."

—15—

A Crucial Piece of Information

Dryden was an anthropologist, so he should have been interested in monitoring human interactions with the city, but he found himself being distracted by the robot movements and machinations more often than not.

Today he was deep in the bowels of the city, several levels below the Officiant's Office, on a balcony overlooking a cavernous warehouse that was laid out in a grid. Hundreds of shiny, multi-jointed metal arms hung from the ceiling, spinning and reaching from a complex network of rails. Their "hands" were sets of tools designed for grasping, soldering, wrenching or cutting.

Across the room he saw a flurry of moving metal and sparks, accompanied by riveting and welding noises. Every once in a while a sound like hot gases burning and flowing through channels came from one of the many pipes lining the walls.

The functions of the completed end products were rarely obvious. Dryden could gauge the purpose of a few droids that looked like dogs on wheels, or fan turbines and even solar panels, but most were only a basic polygon crammed full of electronics, with a plethora of external connectors projecting out, like some metal porcupine. These products were rapidly shipped to some other part of Haplopol via the many service tubes and lifts.

Dryden was paying particular attention to where the arms had finished building a large piece of tunneling equipment, which was basically a rounded mountain of metal capping a system of hydraulics and gears. It was being moved toward the back corner of the chamber by the hanging arms. Once it arrived at the wall, without a moment's rest, it began tearing into the corner, churning up earth. The robot dogs and wheelbarrow-like machines began carting the earth into a side corridor where supply materials came and went via conveyors and moving tracks.

"There you are," said a woman's voice from behind him. "Why aren't you watching from the Officiant's Office?"

He turned to see that it was Princess Elissa. She wasn't wearing her plates of plastic and metal, replete with pre-fall symbolism, or even her sheepskin circle. Instead she wore a light, V-necked shirt the city had given her, and her only jewelry was a chain of almond-shaped silver beads. Her eyes, no longer covered by designer sunglasses, were a muddy brown, and one of her eyebrows was raised. This plainer presentation made her less intimidating.

Dryden replied, "I can't see what the cameras aren't showing us. And, I don't know … the sounds, the smell—it just feels more real."

She nodded. "I can see that. How long will the bore take to reach the casing?"

He looked at the labeled diagram that was unrolled in front of him. It charted the path of the bore with precisely drawn lines.

"Two days. Haplopol thinks it will be another day after that to break through and extract the control junction."

She nodded and joined him at the balcony railing, her shoulder brushing against his inadvertently.

Or it may not have been inadvertent.

He wasn't the only one who'd had such thoughts. He'd noticed many of the Essentialist group in Haplopol succumb to flirting and suggestive banter. Two days ago, he'd been exploring the upper reaches of one of the towers and stumbled across one of the Sanuwan escorts straddled over the hips of an Essentialist private, grinding with verve and panting feverishly. Dryden had almost apologized until he realized that the two of them hadn't even noticed him enter the room, so enthralled were they with their lovemaking. He had tiptoed out quietly.

That was the only public display of affection he'd seen, but there were plenty of winks and suggestive embraces, and someone being led to a secluded room.

This behavior could be explained by the circumstances, to an extent.

Haplopol was a kind of utopia, with eye-popping entertainment and delicious foods, and nothing they needed to help with except the occasional shipment of raw goods into the city. It was no wonder that this idleness led to more hedonistic activities. He was surprised that the Essentialist officers allowed it, though. Maybe these bouts of rest and relaxation were seen as a part of military service. Perhaps, it was even part of the deal with the Sanuwans.

As for Dryden, it only made him uncomfortable.

"Of course, now that the bore is built and underground, there's not much to look at," he told Elissa. "I'm going to head up to the Officiant's Office."

"Mind if I join you?"

Her smile was pleasant, unassuming. "Sure," he said. There wasn't really any other answer.

They strolled along the corridor that led to the main lift.

"What else do you think we'll find in the casing?" she asked.

"I don't know. All that Haplopol has told us is that the inside is of heterogeneous composition. So besides the control junction for Diplopol, I'm not sure what to expect."

"But why is the junction in this casing, way below the surface?"

"Haplopol said the casing is likely to prevent electromagnetic signals from escaping, so whatever's in it can't talk to anything else. Maybe that's also why it's so far underground; to isolate it. It's possible the early Haplopol inhabitants stole the control orb from Diplopol. There are references to conflict between the cities in the historical records, so it wouldn't be surprising."

"Why couldn't they just shut off the control junction? Was it dangerous?"

"I don't know, and Haplopol's memory has been wiped clean. Or at least, that's what it says."

"You don't trust the city?"

He frowned. "Haplopol hasn't given us any reason to think it might lie to us, but no matter how awe-inspiring this place is, and no matter how friendly, we mustn't forget that everyone who lived here disappeared. It might have had nothing to do with the Haplopol control systems, but we can't know for sure."

They were at the lift door. It opened for them and they entered. The button for the level containing the Officiant's Office was already lit up on the control panel.

"Is that why you don't use the experiential rooms?" Elissa asked.

"No, not really. Leopold, in Anacortes—who you know—is the foremost expert on the ICSM cities. He has strong views on how we should study them. We're supposed to watch how people interact with the city, but not experience what they experience. Otherwise we can't be objective."

She stared at him blankly.

Elissa had studied at a respectable school in Victoria, but only communications and liberal arts, to help her as a Sanuwan guide. She probably knew little of scientific methodologies. He tried to think of a way to explain. "Imagine you're doing a study to see which kind of mutton tastes better. You can poll people who have eaten two different kinds, but if you eat the mutton yourself, it introduces the possibility of bias."

She tilted her head thoughtfully. "I think I understand," she said, "but you're missing out on so much. Last night I flew around the world and into the sun. The day before, I learned how we could grow twice as much wheat on less land. There is so much untapped potential in these rooms, so much promise." Her eyes were unfocused.

"I'm sure I'm missing out, but tell me, how do you feel when you're in those rooms?"

"That's the amazing part. I experience these things—I learn them—without any difficulty. I feel a sense of exhilaration, like when I was a child, riding on my nanny's knee, or jumping in summer waters at East Sound. Afterward I'm not tired. I'm filled with confidence, and eager for more."

Dryden knew it could be considered rude, but he couldn't help pulling out his notepad to jot down what she said. He caught her rolling her eyes. "Sorry," he said, "it's just important that—"

"No, it's fine," she interrupted, raising her hands in preemptive capitulation. "It's your job. I understand."

The lift came to a stop and they walked along the main corridor to the Officiant's Office. Two Prefectorate guards were posted at the entrance. Dryden and Elissa were allowed to pass without any intervention, although they did have to endure the guards' steely gazes.

Chinatsu was sitting in a chair with the sinewy lieutenant named Binjai at her side. Chinatsu's hair was in disarray and her eyes red, which Dryden had learned was quite normal for her. They were playing a board game in which oval pieces were scattered across a hexagonal surface.

Behind them, the Haplopol control junction orb was active, pulsing with light and surrounded by constant bubbling. The drone was still wrapped halfway around it, although two of the drone's legs had been removed, and the rest would be gone in the coming days, according to the city. The shooting-star logo formation had also disappeared. Tiny machines, barely visible to the eye, paraded around its metal skeleton like an army of miniature ants, excising parts and taking them out of the cooling tank.

Dryden still hadn't discovered the source of the drone, but he hoped that taking it apart and reassembling it outside of the cooling bath might provide some answers. The Haplopol computer mind disagreed but was doing it anyway, as if to humor him.

"The drill is working," Dryden said. "It should be two days until it reaches the casing."

"Fine," Chinatsu said.

"Should I report this to Hatsuo?"

"No, he left this morning. Prefectorate business."

"He—? But what about the Diplopol control junction? The whole reason we're doing this is so that—"

"We will send a party to Diplopol once it's been extracted."

Dryden was a bit miffed. Whenever he felt like he was contributing, like they were part of a team, some crucial piece of information was withheld, as if he was woefully unimportant.

"What party?"

"A party. You will be in it."

"I can't leave. I've barely begun my work here. I need to keep questioning the control computer, and the delegates. I've only been in half the city rooms. There's too—"

Chinatsu cut him off. "You will follow orders." Her eyes simmered like red coals ready to ignite. "Just like I follow orders. Like Alayna follows orders."

"What does Alayna have to do with this?"

"You can learn something of obedience from her—of loyalty. She has gone with the general."

"What? Why?"

"Prefectorate business."

"Fuck your Pref—"

Before he could finish, a steel katana was nipping at the skin of his throat. Chinatsu was remarkably quick—she had trained as a *shinogi,* according to the other Essentialists. It was as if he had blinked and she was there. They seemed so far away from Hood River, but memories flashed back as Chinatsu's blade left its scabbard: the beheadings by the river, and the cut marks in the municipal hall table.

With the memories came a well of fear, and with fear came restraint.

"I … yes, Captain. I will follow orders. Forgive me."

Her blade returned to its sheath. "Go, Essentialist, and do your science. Don't bother me here."

"Yes, Captain." He turned and left.

It had been foolish. A rush of emotion had overtaken him when he learned of Alayna leaving. Couldn't she at least have told him, or left a message? He knew he was dead to her, but what about for Nate's sake? He supposed it was possible that she had gone with Hatsuo against her will, without time to let Dryden know. He wasn't the only one who had orders to follow.

It was also possible she didn't care.

He began making his way to the lift again. He wanted to be alone, and he knew the perfect spot.

On most days he would perch on the upper balconies near the entrance to Haplopol, sitting in front of one of the massive, mechanized defense droids. A nearby babbling brook ran through a series of garden installations, and one of the many cafeterias that people frequented was just below him. He could look down on the main courtyard and watch dozens of people coming and going, eating, chatting, entering and exiting chambers, including the main courtyard. It was a prime location for an anthropologist.

He also spent a fair amount of time looking through the windows, beyond the city walls. The natural beauty of the lake and the hills offered a kind of grounding. The landscape reminded him of the rolling hills near Hood River. It pained him to admit it, but he missed home.

"Will you wait?" It was Elissa, shuffling along behind him, a sly smile on her face. "I thought you already went for a run today."

"What do you want?" he asked, pivoting toward her. Adrenaline still coursed through his veins, pulsing from his confrontation with Chinatsu.

"I just thought we could—"

"No, really. What is it? I'm not worth it. I'm nobody. There's no one I can bring here that you can charge admission for. Or maybe you're hanging off me because I'm your only source of information, because you know Hatsuo and Chinatsu will stonewall you. Well, here's some information. I'm not interested. Get off my back."

Her shuffle slowed, and she came to a stop. A ripple of color crossed over her face, and she looked at her feet, then to the blank wall beside them. Anywhere but back at him.

He turned away and marched toward the lift.

The next day, Dryden watched Elissa in action from his perch. She was in the lobby, meeting a group that had arrived from Three Rivers. It was supposed to be a diplomatic envoy, but the dozen or so meaty brutes laden with bloodstained axes suggested otherwise. Nevertheless, she welcomed them and gave them a tour. Delane had left, probably on some sort of recruiting mission to generate interest, and, of course, more money.

Elissa was calm and polite. She answered their questions, and she even anticipated them. She had a kind of grace that elevated her above the people around her. She did her job well.

Chinatsu entered the courtyard and voiced a few harsh objections to the contingent, but Elissa maintained her poise, and talked her down. Surely the Sanuwan contract allowed for others to visit the city, she explained, or how else would they generate any revenue? Chinatsu eventually stormed off and let them have their tour.

When it appeared as though the tour was complete, Dryden searched for Elissa down below. It was easy to find her. All he had to do was ask his delegate. She was in a lounge, not too far from the cafeteria, where there was a large video screen. She was drinking some kind of hot tea, judging from the opacity of the tan-colored fluid.

He took a deep breath and walked up to her. "Elissa, I'm sorry."

Her smile was warm, understanding. "You don't have to apologize," she said. She patted the seat next to her.

He sat down. "No, I do. I was so wound up. I shouldn't have said those things. In truth, you've been nothing but courteous and understanding. I think I may have stereotypes about the Sanuwans. It's not right."

She laughed, but it was curt, truncated. "I'm used to it. The princess act is obviously a show, and people tend to think that underneath I'm hiding a savage Sanuwan. The truth is, I've spent much of my life in Victoria, and a good part of that at the Dressler Institute. I don't fit in with my brothers or sisters, or even the king. And, well, I wasn't the one with a katana at their throat. I should have given you space."

"Thank you," he said. He tried to think of something else he could say to convince her of his sincerity, but came up short.

Elissa was staring at the wall, her brow furrowed, as if the blank façade held a deep secret. "There was a man I met," she said, "when I was at school in Victoria. He wasn't a man, actually, more of a boy. He was like you, though—tall and fit, and he studied physics and chemistry. He would speak of lifting us up from the ashes of the fall. He wanted so much to know … *everything.* My friends and I, we wanted to find our way to the end of exams, so we could get a break; to drink and flirt and mess around. He only wanted to study, so he could change the world."

"What happened to him?"

"I don't know. I would watch him from afar, like he was some kind of zoo animal. We only spoke a few times. It was always uncomfortable, always tense. There was one time when it wasn't, though. I remember it clearly. He caught me staring at him, when school was over. He walked up to me and kissed me on the cheek, and then he was gone. I've never seen him since. I laughed it off with my friends. What a weirdo, I said. But that kiss … afterward, I—" Her chest shuddered, and she looked down.

When her head raised again, her eyes weren't focused on the wall. Instead, they were wide, staring directly at Dryden. "I told myself I wouldn't be dishonest like that again. I told myself that if I met someone I liked, I would …"

Her hand reached out to his, and their fingers touched.

He would normally have pulled away, but something had changed. Elissa no longer seemed like a wooden doll, or like a cog in the Sanuwan sales wheel. She was real, she was sincere, and she was completely human.

Alayna had left without a word, and her absence reminded him that he was nothing; a mistake that needed to be ignored and forgotten. Out of sight, out of mind. He wouldn't dare betray her if she'd been here, but she wasn't.

He was lost. He was rudderless. He was pathetic.

But he was human, too.

And so he leaned into Elissa and kissed her, gently at first, and then fervently. She responded in kind.

Eventually, they became just one more couple heading to a secluded room.

—16—

FORT FLATTERY

Fort Flattery was part of the expanding base of military installations at Neah Bay, set a few yards back from fifty-foot cliffs. These cliffs were knobby knuckles of stone, gradually wrapping around the coast. Blankets of moss reached down in places, attempting to touch the ocean. The fort was pentagonal and featured three towers: two squat, round ones that rose up close to the ocean, each with multiple cannon placements, and one square tower of greater height, set further back. The latter, named the Nest by the mostly-Essentialist garrison, was the main lookout point to watch ships entering or leaving the Wandefuca Channel. It also had good visibility across the channel to Port Renfrew and other Kuvar Collective settlements.

The Nest was also a command center, which happened to be supported by one of the more decent military cooks, so it was in the officers' mess hall on the upper levels that General Hatsuo decided to meet with Colonel Raymie and the other Essentialist commanders of Neah Bay. Hatsuo felt it best to handle the discussion in a cordial, albeit informal, manner. The Essentialists seemed happiest when eating or drinking, whereas Prefectorate leaders and shinogi knew these were base delights—animal instincts to be chastened and not commingled with matters of spirituality and loyalty.

Colonel Raymie sat at the far end of the table, gorging on a hefty portion of baked trout and polenta. He was portly but had an energy to his movements that gave him vitality. Below his sprucy mustache, one of his teeth was blacked out by a caper, which he cleared away with a sweep of his tongue before speaking again. "We are all eager to hear more about Haplopol, General. Is there anything else you can offer us that isn't privileged? We tend to get news late here in Neah Bay, and the troops are particularly excited to be first in line for once."

Hatsuo smiled. "Of course. I will have Lieutenant Naumi tell you about what we have seen. It is a great marvel, and not to be feared. We are fortunate to have it under our complete control. Importantly, it is an excellent example of our collaboration with coastal Essentialists. Much thanks goes to our own anthropologist, Dryden Quintain, and his wife Alayna Menudos, who is here with us today. Dryden has helped us gain control and understand the inner workings of the city, while Alayna helped negotiate an effective transaction with the Sanuwans. Without that transaction, we would have never gained control in the first place."

Hatsuo had been watching Alayna at the tail end of his monologue. She had been eating slowly, as if each bite of food required a preliminary inspection. She had raised her eyes at the mention of her name.

"Dryden and I are not together," Alayna said. It was a curt statement, as if the words were running out of her mouth of their own accord. She regained her composure. "But you are too kind, General. It was certainly a great collaborative success, and spearheaded by Prefectorate command. It is indeed a shining example of our unity."

He squinted and nodded. It was a little thick, but she was trying.

Colonel Raymie frowned. "Menudos … Menudos. Any relation to Ben Menudos? He was a great hero. They call him—"

"Neah Bay Ben," Alayna interrupted. "Yes, I know. He was my brother. Unfortunately, he passed away." She looked down at her food again, plucking some fish flesh away from thin white bones.

"I'm so sorry," Raymie said. "We owe him a great debt for saving us from the sneak Kuvar Collective attack seven years ago." He turned to Hatsuo. "General, you don't have to convince me of the quality of your team if any relation to Neah Bay Ben is involved."

Hatsuo nodded. He turned to Lieutenant Naumi. "Naumi, I probably don't have to ask, but do you mind filling the colonel in on what you've seen in Haplopol?"

Naumi was a new transfer from Astoria. Hatsuo had only had him under command since they left Portland, so he didn't know him well. Naumi had been quite taken with the city, and Hatsuo had heard him exulting about his experience several times already. It would have bordered on insubordination if it didn't suit Hatsuo's purposes.

Naumi was only too happy to oblige. His auburn eyes widened and he leaned forward in his chair. "There are five great towers, as tall as the tallest buildings in Portland but without any of the decay. They are beacons of what you will find in the city: wonder, freedom, happiness, fulfillment and, ultimately, enlightenment. You want to travel to the center of the earth? The city will take you there, or at least show you what it would look like. You want to know why this fish tastes the way it does? The city will teach you. You want pleasure, it will give you pleasure. I laughed so many times, and each time it was as if all my best friends from Sendai were there with me, and we were laughing at the funniest joke we'd ever heard. I laughed until my face hurt and tears were streaming down my face. And there is also—"

"I think that's enough, Naumi," Hatsuo interrupted. "I'm sure he gets the picture. To summarize, it's better than sex."

Raymie laughed, along with the rest of the table. Hatsuo made a mental note to be careful with Naumi. He sounded unhinged and couldn't be left alone to promote Haplopol without adult supervision.

Steps sounded as footmen brought in the next dish from one of the tower stairways. It was an oily soup served in ornately carved wooden bowls. The people at the table angled their heads to the side to allow for their placement on the table by the footmen, and then examined the steaming broth in silence.

When the footmen had left, Raymie sat back in his chair. "Well, that really is something. I look forward to hearing more, and I can't wait to visit. But it does heighten my curiosity about another question, one I hope you wouldn't mind answering. If the city is such a wonder, and if—as I hear from your other men—many are making plans to visit, why wouldn't you remain there to enjoy it, and to ensure we maintain control? Instead you have come here, all the way down the Wandefuca, on the pretext of a routine site visit. I hope you don't mind me asking, is there another reason for your being here, General?"

Yes, this Raymie, he wasn't as slow as the other Essentialist commanders.

Hatsuo guessed that, if Raymie had the chance, he would break free of his Prefectorate shackles, but how much was he willing to risk? Enough, apparently, to ask an inappropriate question. But this could just be because he was a coastal Essentialist. He didn't know that questioning the maneuvers of a superior officer was reprehensible.

In any case, it had to be said eventually, so it might as well be now. Hatsuo adopted a benevolent smile and cradled his hands together. "Because duty calls, Colonel. This new jewel, one that shines so brightly, is something that must be protected. In the spirit of our continued collaboration, we have come to solicit your help."

The colonel nodded. "Of course, I can spare two ships, fully manned. They are Y-class galleons, and we might have an extra barque we can spare, over in Waatch."

Hatsuo winced. "We were hoping for more than that. You see, we have intelligence that leads us to believe the Kuvar Collective is planning a raid on Port Angeles. We need to double our presence in the Wandefuca Channel immediately, to protect both Port Angeles and Haplopol."

The colonel frowned. "But Port Angeles, and Haplopol—that's not our jurisdiction. What about Fort Aberdeen, or Astoria? They have a proper fleet. Those ships are earmarked for Salish Sea operations."

"Time is such a delicate resource, one that we have in limited supply. We need these ships right away. Tomorrow, in fact."

The colonel's eyes darted back and forth. "But, to double your fleet—we don't have enough ships for that."

It was time to fill him in on the full extent of the bad news. "In addition to all your ships, we will be taking two-thirds of the Fort Flattery garrison. We will use these men to crew ships we have procured from Victoria and Anacortes, and some that will be travelling up from Olympia."

"What?" The colonel exchanged looks with a bearded man to his left, one of his top officers. This man had been listless for most of the meal, but now his eyes lit up like a fire in the dark.

The colonel's knuckles had gone white where his hand gripped the table. He let out an exhausted laugh. "General, please. We operate the Wandefuca Gate and are the primary access point to the Wandefuca Channel—the first line of defense against Salish Sea marauders. We would essentially be rendered defenseless. Our job, at least in part, is to watch Kuvar Collective military activities around the channel. There has been absolutely no sign of aggression, and even if there was, their fleet is spread out in the northern reaches of Kuvar Island. They have maybe ten vessels nearby. You would have thirty vessels, even before the ones you procure in Victoria or have sent to you from Olympia."

Hatsuo closed his eyes and looked down. It was a look of feigned disappointment he used often, to make himself look like the victim, as if he was carrying a great burden that pained him with every step. "I'm so sorry, Colonel. *Unmei* is what they would say in my homeland. It means *destiny*. I am at the whim of these terrible forces and must make tough decisions."

The bearded lieutenant stood up. "But it isn't your decision, is it? Commander Yasui and General Pollak are responsible for all of the Neah Bay installations. Unless it's under the seal of the Emperor himself, only *they* can issue this kind of command. So tell us, General, from whom did you receive this direction? Where is your authenticated order?"

The tension had reached a critical level. Everyone was frozen in their seats, and most must have come to the realization that this was no longer a friendly meal. But Hatsuo held his smile. "I'm sorry, your name is?"

"Brighton, sir." His eyes were still blazing.

"Lieutenant Brighton, you do have a point, but unfortunately Pollak and Yasui are too far away. We don't have time, so we must make decisions without them. I am the most senior Prefectorate officer in the Salish Sea region."

Brighton turned to Raymie. "Sir, I don't think—"

It was a quick calculation. Hatsuo knew that this man Brighton would say no, or they could ask to wait for General Pollack, who was two days away in Astoria. In Essentialist terms, these would be reasonable requests, but Hatsuo couldn't afford to be reasonable. So he tapped Naumi with his foot under the table. Hatsuo thought Naumi might threaten him, but he hadn't worked with him before, and Naumi reacted too aggressively. He shot up from his chair and jabbed Brighton tightly in the throat with a planar chop of his hand, cutting him off mid-sentence.

Chairs screeched on the floor as everyone pushed away from the table. Brighton gasped and grabbed his throat, from which came a barely audible gurgling noise. He was trying to speak, or breathe, or both, but nothing was coming out. His windpipe must have caved in. He was losing color quickly, and his eyes went to Naumi, then Raymie, then Hatsuo, but no one could help him. Brighton toppled onto the table and writhed, slamming his elbows against fish plates, soup bowls and broken glass while his chest heaved. Plates and polenta met the ground.

This went on for some time, until his face was gray and laced with green veins, with red lines scattered on his neck where his nails had scraped the skin.

He was dead.

"Naumi, heel!" Hatsuo yelled. Naumi bent down, his face touching the ground. "This is not how we resolve conflict! Go to your quarters immediately. We will determine your punishment later."

He turned to Raymie. "Colonel, I'm so sorry for this … accident. Please allow me to make reparations to his family."

Raymie had been holding on to his pushed-away chair, watching carefully but taking no action. He must know that he would be next in line if he pushed Hatsuo.

"He … General, thank you. He did speak out of turn. I will be sure to connect you with his family. And, sir, this was an accident. Reparations will not be necessary."

"I insist," Hatsuo said. "This was such a waste. We could have used him. I suggest we adjourn. It wouldn't be right to keep eating, and there are arrangements that need to be made for tomorrow."

Raymie wasn't about to disagree. "Yes, sir. Right away."

Orderlies and footmen came in to take away Brighton's corpse and the remains of the meal he'd flattened during his death throes. Hatsuo looked on for a few minutes, shaking his head and wearing a mask of chagrin.

Eventually he drifted off to his quarters.

The Essentialists at the table would be nervous. Tales of the incident could spread, and this could be used to discredit him later. He would have to manage that.

This was why, when revisiting the evening in his mind, he didn't feel that familiar rush of emotion. There were no tears to fight back. What he felt was annoyance, more than anything. Naumi should have just disabled Brighton, or even threatened him. Instead, there was an incident that could make it to the ears of Pollak or Yasui.

But he couldn't be too hard on himself. Even though his plans hadn't played out smoothly, Hatsuo had his armada. He couldn't expect it to work out perfectly every time.

Before they set out from Neah Bay the next day, there was another incident that Hatsuo would wonder about. So many memories and commands littered his mind, haunting him, making him question whether he had taken the right action. This was another.

It was a sunny morning, and he felt good. He had done his calisthenics at first light, enough to bring him to perspiration. Most shinogi would have stayed longer, completed more strength training and meditation, but he was a general. He had more important things to do.

After his workout he stayed down by the docks, watching his subordinates manage the logistics of securing the resources and men.

In the distance, the Wandefuca Gate could be seen at the mouth of the channel. At this time of morning the sun glinted off the structure, as if winking at him. According to the coastal Essentialists, the gate was an old ruin. Twenty-two huge pillars of metal rose up from the center of the channel to meet with a broad loop that connected them at the top and plunged into the ocean on either side. The spaces between these bands were wide enough to sail through, which was why they called it a gate, and perhaps also because coastal ships tended to manage incoming and outgoing traffic there.

It was probably used for a similar purpose in the Old World.

Alayna was walking up the pier, assigning groups of men toward their ships after referencing a clipboard.

Hatsuo had asked Alayna to help secure many of the garrison men. She was well-liked by the Essentialists and knew how to deliver bad news. Plus, they would listen to the sister of Neah Bay Ben. Besides, it was always better to have an Essentialist ask another Essentialist to put themselves in harm's way.

She was fit. At times, when her back was turned, with her black hair and tight curves, she looked as though she could be Prefectorate-born. It was enough to arouse Hatsuo a little, and he wondered if he should take her. But he had seen too much Essentialist trash. They were often disobedient, too vocal, and just poor pedigree. When she turned to face him again, her green eyes and colored shirt dispelled his arousal.

Naumi was walking stiffly toward him, down a ramp from the upper fortifications, while pulling along an Essentialist private whose hands were tied. This man was lanky and tall, but darker of skin compared to the local Essentialists. He was probably from the south, maybe the Tucson Union.

Hatsuo had assigned Naumi four lashes, which was more than he deserved, but the optics were more important than the punishment itself. Hatsuo could tell that the lashes weren't why Naumi was walking stiffly. He was tense, or angry, or both.

Alayna seemed to know the Essentialist soldier who was being pulled along. She tried to speak with him as they passed her, but he didn't answer. She followed after them, perhaps out of curiosity.

Hatsuo exited the small command hut to meet them on the wooden deck.

"What's this about?" he asked Naumi. He recognized the Essentialist corporal. His name was stenciled on his uniform: *Sergio.* He was a navigation engineer for his fleet, and a good one at that.

Naumi said, "I found this man in our auxiliary records vault."

"And?" Hatsuo asked.

Naumi tried to calm himself. "The vault contains our confidential Prefectorate records: ship classes, fleet maneuvers, trans-Pacific sailings. It is off-limits to anyone except higher-rank Prefectorate military."

Hatsuo turned to Sergio. "What do you have to say for yourself, corporal?"

"Sir, I'm terribly sorry. I heard we might be seeing action with the Kuvar Collective. I wanted to look at prior engagements with their ships, to prepare, and also to see if there were coastal incidents in Kuvar Collective waters, in case we were navigating close to shore."

Naumi said, "Sir, it is a grade six offense to be in that room."

"How did you get in?" Hatsuo asked.

"It was unlocked, sir," Sergio responded. "There must have been men coming and going, in preparation for the trip, and someone must have forgotten to lock it. And then my curiosity got the better of me. Apologies, sir."

Hatsuo nodded, and Naumi thankfully didn't push for more. Hatsuo looked out across the water, beyond the Wandefuca Gate, to the distant shore of Kuvar Island. "I don't know," he said in contemplation.

Sergio said, "Sir, if I may. There is another reason. I make model ships. I put them in bottles. I've wanted to model a Samurai-class warship, but I've never seen one. It's shameful, but I wanted to see the plans for one, so I could …" He trailed off and looked down.

Surely this Sergio thought Hatsuo would find this pitiful story endearing. He was portraying himself as a man who held Prefectorate ships in high esteem and risked severe punishment simply to model one. Instead, Hatsuo had to actively suppress his rage. The Samurai-class ships were sacrosanct. No Essentialist navigator or engineer should try to model one, much less hammer a nail into one. And this man's story wasn't credible. It was insulting. He was too smart. He was lying.

So what to do …

Alayna said, "General, I have known Sergio for a long time. He is a loyal soldier, for what it's worth."

It wouldn't do well to lose Alayna's support. This Sergio, he was useful, and Hatsuo didn't want to seem too harsh. It was a delicate balance with the Essentialists. It was important to strike enough fear to keep them in line, but not so much that they thought their lives were in danger. He didn't want to corner these feral animals. Then they might actually fight back.

Finally, Hatsuo came up with the right solution. It would have to be done later, though. He needed to appear magnanimous for the moment, especially after the debacle of the prior evening.

He said, "Let him go, Naumi. There is no ill intent here. The poor man only wants to build model ships. He's obviously a dedicated sailor."

Naumi's eyes bulged. For a moment, he looked about to explode, but soon the tension dissipated and he said, "Yes, General."

Quickly, Sergio chimed in, "Thank you, sir. Please forgive me. It won't happen again."

"Yes, I trust that it won't."

Naumi led him away.

Later in the day, when the ships were sailing on the Wandefuca Channel, Hatsuo told Naumi his solution for Sergio's infraction. Alayna was safely aboard another vessel, and Sergio was out of earshot, busy talking to an officer, pointing to his charts and astrolabe. The ship was rocking, and every so often he would place his hand on a guardrail for support.

Naumi would strike without warning, with a freshly sharpened katana. Sergio would scream, but it would be clean, without blubbering and whimpering in advance, and Hatsuo could watch from afar and therefore not be party to the gruesome ordeal.

Hatsuo's rationale was this: take a hand, preferably his dominant one. Two hands were too abundant for traitors. With one, he wouldn't be able to fight back, but he could still direct others to do his navigation work.

Hopefully, Sergio would survive, and could then be watched. With two feet, one hand and a mouth, he could still lead them to any meddling associates. It was possible he was working with Groundwater—an irritating coastal Essentialist splinter group that had taken up against Prefectorate occupation. Either way, once Hatsuo found his collaborators, he could discreetly finish the job.

It would also be expedient to fill Sergio's position before he was fully dispatched. It wasn't wise to set sail without a seasoned navigator.

—17—

Leopold

Leo's estate was on a fat thumb of land called Cape Sante. It jutted out from the city of Anacortes, such that he had a view of the marina and cityscape on one side and Padilla Bay on the other. It was a view he enjoyed; he had a lookout tower laden with spiky pigeon poppers stacked up tall, next to his already sizeable house—a lookout tower that must have been difficult for him to access, even with the ramp that spiraled around it, because Leo was paralyzed from the waist down.

It was the result of an accident. Ten years back, he was on a dig at the Goldstream crater—the suspected ICSM city site for Triplopol—and he fell off a ladder and busted up his back up real good.

Pirating isn't the only dangerous profession. Or at least that's what Lexie told her mom.

Lexie was standing with Nillias and his band of Gungivite mucka-nuts at the main gate. They had rung the gate bell, which was a pumpkin-sized mass of molten metal with a brain-rattling gong that must surely have been an unwelcome addition for the neighbors.

Kerub opened the gate. He was a stocky fiefdom transplant with a prominent beard and an eye patch. He was wearing the same torn old T-shirt she'd seen on him the last time she'd visited, and again it was caked in dirt. Kerub was originally from the Squamish fiefdom, the same backward mountain hovel as Johl, but now he did odd jobs for Leo. He nudged his nose up at them and said, "Lex—been a while. We've been waiting for you. Who's this?"

"Nillias. The man Leo wanted me to deliver his message to."

Kerub shut the gate door on them.

Lexie and Nillias exchanged blank looks. "Don't take it personally,"

Lexie said. "I don't think Leo hired Kerub for his gate etiquette. He's probably just checking in with Leo."

Nillias didn't respond. His eyes were active, and his six Gungivite goons were spread out behind him in a triangular formation, each of them looking in a different direction.

What a bunch of nutjobs.

A few minutes later, Kerub opened the gate again. "Lexie, and one of the Observers. The others stay outside."

She raised an eyebrow at Nillias.

"I will go," Nillias said, and Kerub escorted them through the gate.

Inside was a well-tended garden, with flowers and trees and a thick mane of grass. One corner looked different than Lexie remembered—maybe a tree had been replaced? There was also a mound of dirt where a flowerbed used to be. Leo was always changing his mind about the garden. She wondered if he did it just to keep Kerub busy.

Inside the main entrance was a den, its walls adorned with the wares of an anthropologist: maps of the Salish Sea and the southern Essentialist regions, red and black headdresses, a peach-colored tunic, an elaborate necklace, and a smiling wooden mask. The artifacts were mostly from the Salish Sea area, but a few items were from the post-fall tribes around Portland. Of course, this was all according to what Leo had told her. Aside from the maps, and maybe the necklace, Lexie didn't have a clue who belonged to what.

Kerub led them through the room and into the study. It had panes of glass from floor to ceiling, looking out over another expanse of garden. The desk was the central feature of the room. It was hefty, built with thick timbers that were heavily stained and patterned with knots spread out like spiraling galaxies. One corner was covered with neatly arranged stacks of paper.

Sitting behind the desk was Leo, leaning back, his oily black hair styled in a perfect parting, and his spectacled eyes probing them as they entered.

"Well, this is a surprise," Leo said. He wasn't smiling.

Leo didn't like surprises.

"Oh really?" Lexie said. "You didn't think Nillias and I would be best friends and want to thank you for playing matchmaker? I remember what you said about the job. *Just a message, in and out.* You may have left out some important details."

"Like what?"

"Like they'll kill Johl and come within a hair of killing me. Like they'll keep me prisoner and blast my skull full of useless gibberish about their Gungivite gobbledygook for weeks on end."

She heard Kerub's breathing stop for a moment. He might not take kindly to news of Johl's death.

Leo frowned. "Ryder was here just a week ago. He said it went fine."

She couldn't help grinding her teeth. Ryder again. When she found that sick squirrel she was going to wring him out real good. "I'm not sure Ryder is … all there," she said.

Leo gazed at Nillias, squinted, and turned back to her. "Sorry, Lexie. I had no idea."

"You had no idea?"

He scowled. "Yes. That's it. No idea. You may not be aware of this, but the Gungivites fund almost all my research teams and digs. As a result, it's kind of hard to say no when they finally ask for something in return."

"Oh, come on, there has to be some other way. You don't have to work with these nutjobs. Why don't you get your research money somewhere else?"

"No. There's no other game in town. They're the only ones with enough resources. Do you think Three Rivers would push any coin my way? No way, not if it doesn't relate to trade or brewing foul beer. The Vicky universities don't fund active research, unless someone else is paying them to do it. The Essentialists wouldn't do it, either. They are more of the *let others pay and then we can take everything later anyway* variety."

"But you still could have told me."

"Told you what? I didn't know what they would do with the message. Just because they fund my research, that doesn't mean they tell me everything. In fact, they will often say they're after one thing, when in fact they're after another."

That did sound about right, she had to admit.

Lexie looked at Nillias, whose eyes were wide and alert but was otherwise stone-faced. Most people would interrupt when they were being openly spoken about, or even belittled, but not Nillias. He might have even been enjoying it.

"What do you think, Nillias?" she asked. "Maybe before getting into business you and Leo should have thought about going on a team-building retreat. Maybe you should have gone fishing and sung happy songs about machine cities. It doesn't seem like the best working relationship when you have to kill people all the time."

Nillias ignored her remark. He seemed to finally tire of the banter. "We have come here," he said, stepping forward, "because we need to know more about Haplopol as a threat to the Salish Sea nations. It will have had time to gain resources and enact human controllers, likely Prefectorate-led Essentialists. What could it do to us upon our approach to the city, or even longer term, if it felt we were in conflict with its motives?"

Leo's eyes flickered between them, only to rest on Nillias again.

"Is it you who's stealing Cecile's letters?" Leo asked.

"Who is Cecile?" Nillias responded.

Leo paused. He was clearly sizing Nillias up, looking for clues in his countenance that could provide additional information. "She's a colleague, of a sort, in the east. I had been receiving letters from her about the machine war, but they stopped, and Kerub saw something—*somebody*, actually—who has been going through our mail. Shot him with an arrow in his backside, but he still got away."

Nillias's expression held firm, impervious to Leo's inquisition. "It wasn't us. What does this have to do with Haplopol?"

Leo tapped his fingers on the wood desk as if playing an imaginary piano. "It's probably nothing—just a local troublemaker. Never mind."

Leo's focus moved to Kerub for an instant, then returned to Nillias. He scratched his head.

"That wouldn't be wise," Nillias said, not missing a beat. "Kerub may be able to subdue me, but as soon as you become an unreliable asset, my men will ransack this place and take you hostage."

Leo sighed, shook his head and threw his hands up in the air. He turned to Lexie. "You see? These guys really know how to grind me down. It's not like I can say no."

Lexie nodded sourly. "Yeah, I know. I've been on the receiving end for a while."

"Okay, Nillias," Leo said, "Let's see if I can answer your question, but then I want you and your Gungivite goons out of my hair."

"That will depend upon your answer."

Leo frowned. He tilted up and spun around abruptly, revealing that he was in fact sitting in his wheelchair. He stared out into his garden, his back to them, while they waited. Surely he wasn't contemplating defying Nillias? More likely, he was framing his answer. Leo was a purveyor of dangerous secrets just as much as obscure historical facts. He knew to be careful with his words.

After a few heavy seconds, Leo spun his chair back around. He leaned over the desk. His finger scratched at a particularly large knot of wood, and without looking up, he explained, "It's said that the original Haplopol inhabitants came from the far east, from some sanctuary on a hill. Morganis the Righteous—supposedly a great hero—led a group of people from there to found Haplopol, and they subsequently founded the other cities. That's where the acronym ICSM—Independent City States of Morganis—comes from. But these people who are revered … usually, with a little digging, you end up finding out they were real assholes. It never fails. Should be a rule of thumb for historians. The bigger the monument, the larger the anus."

"You believe Morganis wasn't righteous?" Nillias asked. "You believe he was a tyrant?"

"Probably. There are a few letters we found relating to his harsh treatment of the early Sanuwan people. There are others that contradict that supposition, but they are written like propaganda. What's a certainty, though, is that he had a monster ego, because even a city as grand as Haplopol didn't do it for him. He wanted to create some kind of perfect utopia, one that probably was unattainable in reality. So he went on to found Diplopol and the other cities, which may have caused rivalries, and ultimately the downfall of all of them."

"What does this have to do with the threat of Haplopol?" Nillias asked.

"I'm telling you this because each city has unique aspects to its design, and some are more powerful than others. When Haplopol wasn't doing it for Morganis, he tweaked the design of the machine control junctions for the next one, and the one after that, and so on, in a quest for perfection. Diplopol was about ten times the size of Haplopol, and its footprint spread way beyond the city limits. Outside there were factories and plants and agriculture that were essentially controlled by Diplopol inhabitants. We think much of this has been swallowed under the earth, but it still could be there, including weapons and munitions factories."

Nillias's brow knitted. "What about the geographical constraint on the city's objective function?"

Leo smirked. "It's nice to know you actually read my reports. You see, Diplopol has slightly different objectives and constraints than Haplopol. It wants to enhance the well-being of all Diplopol citizens, but unlike Haplopol, it isn't trying to enhance their well-being *within* the city, and as a result, its values are more expansionary. Machines controlled directly by Diplopol couldn't exit the city, but Diplopol citizens were given plans by the city to build their own machines outside of the city limits. These machines were sometimes brought into the city and refurbished, or sent further afield to do the bidding of the human operators."

"So …?" Lexie asked.

"So Haplopol isn't the real threat. Well, it is, but not for the reasons you think. Yes, it does have three giant security droids. Those can defend the city, but in general they wouldn't harm people unless it was in self-defense. Your main threat is the presence of Essentialist soldiers, more than anything else. But again, that's not why you should fear Haplopol. You should fear it because, according to research known only to the most informed scholars, it's believed that the control junction for Diplopol was taken by Haplopol. If it's found in Haplopol, and Diplopol is also awakened, the power base of whoever is controlling the cities could shift dramatically."

It started to fall together for Lexie. With control of Diplopol, the Essentialists could unearth all the factories nearby. They could unleash machines to control the surrounding area, maybe even the whole of Kuvar Island.

She looked over at Nillias, and he was stone-faced as usual. He must have understood. In fact, she was surprised he hadn't already known this, with all his egghead friends and computer terminals. Maybe Leo had been keeping it a secret until now?

After a moment of quiet, Leo glanced at Lexie, then back at Nillias again. "Do you understand?" he asked.

Nillias was silent.

"Just wait," Lexie said. "He's thinking." She wasn't certain, but she'd seen him like this before.

Sure enough, eventually Nillias said, "Yes, I understand. Thank you, Doctor. Lexie, we will leave now." Without another word, he began walking out.

Lexie said, "Sorry, Leo. I would love to stay and catch up, but these guys …" She twirled her finger around her temple.

"It's okay, you'd better follow," Leo said, gesturing toward the exit. "Next time, I'd like to talk to you about you-know-who."

He must be referring to the stolen letters. Lexie was thinking the same thing. It was almost certainly Warrick. Lexie nodded and ran after Nillias, followed closely after by Kerub.

"Hey, Nillias, you mind telling me what's going on under that wig of yours?"

He didn't respond.

"Nillias?"

Finally, when they were out of the gate, surrounded by the formation of other Observers, he said, "We leave first thing tomorrow."

"Haplopol?"

"No. It's too late for that. Leopold is right. We need to stop them at Diplopol."

—18—

The Vessel

One more day was left before the second control junction could be accessed. Meanwhile, Dryden spent most of his time on his perch above the courtyard, watching people interact with the city. He was focused on drafting reports, labeling pictures, or even capturing questions that sprung to mind.

It wasn't in any way boring. There was more activity now, as the influx of people into Haplopol increased. Every day, a new clutch of bright-eyed tourists would arrive from far-flung regions of the northwest. Many of these had been recruited by Sanuwanese salespeople, but others told him they had simply heard of the "awakened city" and wanted to visit. There were over six hundred people in Haplopol. Most of these were from Sanuwan or Essentialist lands, but others were from Three Rivers and even a few from mountain tribes.

Space wasn't a problem. There were plenty of rooms. There must have been capacity for ten thousand people to live comfortably within the city, but the inhabitants needed supplies. The city was superintelligent and could do many wondrous things, but it couldn't make food out of thin air. As a result, supply lines passed to and fro along the path back down to East Sound, and the Sanuwans had begun widening it into a proper road.

When a new group arrived, they would often be asked by the Sanuwans to pay a surcharge to have additional supplies brought in. For those less financially endowed, they would have to return to East Sound to procure supplies for themselves. This meant the courtyard was becoming more than a meeting place. It also was a logistical hub for the intake of new supplies and the offloading of trash.

This day in particular was eventful not because of the number of new arrivals but because of who these people were. That, and the fact that Chinatsu decided to get involved.

The number of Prefectorate officers had doubled since the original expedition, while the number of other inhabitants had grown tenfold. Dryden could tell the relative difference was making Chinatsu nervous. Yes, Chinatsu was Officiant, but she had to wonder if a group might try to execute some kind of coup, and she didn't really know how much the city would protect her.

As a result, Chinatsu would sneer abrasively whenever a new group of people was escorted through the city. On more than a few occasions, this discomfort had prompted her to examine the three defense droids, and Dryden had heard her asking her delegate questions about how far they could fire and with what impact. She even made the city do a "weapons test" early one morning. A window was opened and one of these mechanical beasts pulverized a tree on the other side of the lake with a missile. Her more subdued demeanor that morning told him she'd been pleased.

So it shouldn't have been a surprise to anyone that a great deal of tension ensued when a group of fifty heavily-armed Kuvar Collective representatives arrived in Haplopol.

They were already being assigned delegates and introduced to the city by Elissa and Delane when Chinatsu stalked into the Grand Hall, trailed by a dozen of her subordinates. "No," she said simply. "People are welcome here, not island dredge."

Island dredge was just one of the monikers with which Essentialists branded the Kuvar Collective. In fact, the Collective seemed to be one of the main targets of Essentialist propaganda, driven by rumors of seaborne scuffles in the Wandefuca Channel between the Collective and the Essentialist fleet, and of course the attack on Neah Bay.

The Kuvar leader was a husky, bearded man with a uniform made of circular straps wound horizontally, which made him look like he was wearing a barrel. But he wasn't round like a barrel. His frame was V-shaped and topped with broad, rounded shoulders. "We have a deal with the Sanuwan Kingdom," he said. "This is none of your business."

Chinatsu shook her head. "Even if we could accept filth like you, you are too many. There's not enough food."

Elissa wisely stayed out of it, but Delane said, "Actually, Captain, we should be able to accommodate them. Their leader, Commander Trent, has agreed to pay for a supplemental Sanuwan caravan service. They have been generous."

"No," Chinatsu said. Her face was taking on more color as the conversation went on. "I am Officiant, and I say who stays and who goes."

Delane looked at Elissa and at the two leaders. He smiled. "Unfortunately, there appears to be some kind of misunderstanding. That wasn't the contract we agreed to with General Hatsuo."

"We didn't agree to meddling dredges, either."

"I'm sorry," Delane said. "Why don't we look at the agreement later? Maybe then we can—"

"Noooo!" Chinatsu screamed. And it was a scream, not a yell, as if she was in mortal pain. Eyes widened across the courtyard.

Chinatsu's complexion had grown dark. She took a deep breath and said, "I will show you what happens when you defy the Prefectorate." She drew her katana and pointed it toward the three huge defense droids that were lined up next to Dryden. "City. Pulverize these island dredges, now!"

Nothing happened.

"City! This is a command as your Officiant. Fire. Fire!"

Chinatsu's delegate appeared and said, "I'm sorry. Haplopol will follow your commands, but only if they do not conflict with the city's primary objective, which is to enhance the well-being of all intelligent life within Haplopol. Terminating new citizens would be in violation of the city's goals."

"Override! Fire! Kill them all!"

The delegate smiled demurely. "I'm sorry, Officiant. Is there some other command you wish me to perform? I cannot execute these citizens."

Chinatsu was beet red. She yelled, "*Kōgeki*!" and ran toward the Kuvar Collective leader, her katana hoisted above her head.

She had made it only a few steps when a flying drone buzzed out of nowhere and fired a dart at her hand, forcing her to drop her katana. The weapon clanged off the floor and slid several feet ahead of her. Her fellow Prefectorate soldiers held their ground, their own blades half out of their sheaths. They were looking around at the walls and terraces of the city, trying to figure out where the drone had originated.

All eyes were on Chinatsu. She tried to grab her blade, but her right hand was limp, so she picked it up with her left hand. She was leaning forward, about to charge again, but she never did. Her neck was swiveling in every direction, looking for support, trying to find something—anything—to further her cause. Finally she yelled, "Ahhhhhhh!" at the ceiling of the Grand Hall in frustration, and stormed out.

Her Prefectorate subordinates followed.

Dryden was standing with Chinatsu and three of her men on the underground balcony as Chinatsu lectured her delegate. "City. You don't touch the orb!" Chinatsu said, while wagging her finger. Her trust in the city seemed to have waned considerably since the incident with the Kuvar Collective visitors.

"Of course," the apparition responded calmly. "I will comply. You are in full control, Officiant Chinatsu. Access to the interior of the casing will be available in two minutes, when the path through the tunnel will be cleared. You can make your way down if you like."

Chinatsu stared down her delegate, as if her threatening stance could have some kind of reinforcing effect.

The delegate added, "I should warn you. What you will see might be unsettling, and may cause low-grade psychological trauma."

Two of the others in the scouting party looked at each other with grave expressions, but Chinatsu gave the city's warning no more than a brief moment of consideration. Dryden guessed that low-grade psychological trauma was generally a good day for her. And for Dryden, it only increased the chances that there was something interesting, possibly of human origin, that could be important for his research. It wasn't fear he felt, but nervous anticipation.

Chinatsu led them from the balcony, down the ramp and across the floor, as the dangling metallic arms nearby halted mid-action as a safety precaution.

The tunnel wasn't steep. It went down in a spiral, mostly through sandy loam and clay but in a few places through solid rock. The sides of the walls were relatively smooth, but also scraped and ashen in places from the heat and friction of the passage of the bore. It smelled like a campfire the morning after it had been extinguished.

There were a couple of wires lining the tunnel, with glowing nodes intermittently lighting the way. Haplopol was reaching its tentacles further into the depths of the earth.

The city chirped at them through Dryden's comm device: "My delegates will not function in the tunnel, but your comm devices should work. Feel free to use the recording features to chronicle your investigation."

The comm devices were a real blessing. They fit easily into your hand, kind of like an Old World phone. When Dryden first arrived in Haplopol, he'd been doing rough sketches of everything until his delegate suggested he take pictures with a comm device and have them printed later. Dryden prided himself on his artistry, but they were no match for the vivid and colorful images printed out by Haplopol.

The tunnel flattened and a lamp became visible on the ground ahead. The light revealed a glinting ring of metal lining the wall, almost a foot thick. This was the casing. Beyond the edge of the casing, the smooth walls expanded into a dusty cavern full of rock fragments that climbed up and around a sleek vessel. At one end of the cavern a circle of stone fragments was visible, as if a tunnel had been filled in by extraneous rock, or caved in.

What kind of vessel was it? It was hard to tell. One end was still firmly planted in the rock, the other was shaped like a smooth slug, dusty gray in color. A band of metal jutted out of the side that could once have been a wing, now broken—or something else entirely. At the rear of it, a squared indentation was cut into the bottom, as if it might have run on a rail, like a train. The smooth contour of the craft suggested it was designed with fluid dynamics in mind. Whatever it was, the vessel was supposed to travel through air, or water.

A circular opening had been carved into the side.

They approached the vessel with careful footfalls. The lack of dust or sediment on the cut metal made Dryden think that Haplopol had only recently sliced it open. Another lamp was positioned just at the threshold.

Chinatsu paused before the entrance. She looked back and squinted at Dryden. "You first," she said. This probably wasn't out of respect for his profession. He doubted it was fear, either. She probably just didn't want to break anything or get hurt. Might as well send the expendable scientist in first.

Dryden moved slowly. He paused at the opening and looked inside the vessel.

It wasn't that large, maybe big enough to sit eight to ten people comfortably. In the front—or at least he presumed it was the front, based on the glass panel, which was cracked and covered with rocks—were two seats, and several more lined up along the sides. Then he noticed the bodies. There were three of them: one in a seat near the front and two on the floor, their backs to the wall nearest Dryden. The heads were the hardened remains of encrusted skin and flesh, but also porous, the holes in some places reaching down into bone, and much of the flesh covered in blooms of red, blue and green, possibly fungi. It could be that no worms or bugs had been able to get into the casing or craft, allowing the bodies to remain protected from most decomposing elements, except airborne microbials. The eyes were black sockets of unknown depth, and they had no hair. Judging by the relatively well-preserved state of the rest of the heads, the hair should have survived, but maybe these people thought hair was superfluous.

All of the corpses were in suits of some kind, and helmets littered the floor. The suits were bulky and crisscrossed with hydraulic and electrical lines. They could have been underwater pressure suits, but they also resembled old space suits Dryden had seen from pre-fall comic books and pictures. One of the bodies on the floor was missing its legs, as if neatly severed, suit fabric and all. Dark, clean-cut stumps were barely recessed into the open pant legs of the suit.

On the far side of the room was a large, diamond-shaped gash in the wall of the vessel. Here rock and sediment pushed in. Perhaps it was the result of an attack on the vessel while moving, or some effect of Haplopol's burying it deep underground. The remaining walls had cupboards and panels, some of which looked similar to Haplopol's interior designs, with the same fractal networks of lined channels and familiar bluish-tinted material.

And then, of course, there was the control junction orb. It was melon-sized, gray, and webbed with dark blue channels that were currently dormant. It was nestled in the lap of one of the bodies on the floor, cradled protectively by partially defleshed skeletal fingers.

Chinatsu said, "Binjai, get the orb and let's go."

"No!" Dryden yelled, before restraining himself. "We shouldn't touch anything. Why are these people here? What happened to them? Who are they?"

Chinatsu frowned and looked behind her to see if he was talking to someone else. She shrugged. "What game is this? You're the scientist."

"Anthropologist. But—sorry." He took a breath. His heart was racing, as if he was teetering on the edge of a cliff. "You, see, I need time to analyze it methodically. This could be more important than all of Haplopol. This could be the most important anthropological find, *ever*. If we disturb it, we may miss some clues."

"Is it dangerous?"

"Well, I don't know. Probably not, but I'm not entirely sure. This person is holding the orb with his … or her … hands, so the orb should be fine, as long as it stays turned off, but the rest of the vessel …"

Chinatsu must have known she was out of her element, so she was giving him some leeway, but Dryden could tell her patience was waning.

"So we take the orb and leave," she said, shrugging. "No danger."

"No. That would disturb the room. We need time to examine it more thoroughly."

"How much time?"

"I don't know. To obtain the right instruments, create a plan and execute it, maybe a week?"

Chinatsu stared at him blankly for a moment, and then broke into a shrill laugh. It was a sound he'd never heard from her before, and he wasn't surprised, with a laugh like that. It was grating, almost like a hyena in heat. When her laugh died out, she said, "I don't think so. I'll give you one hour, but we take the orb immediately."

"You can't—"

Her katana was already out and pointing at him, anticipating his objection. She was kind enough to not have it nipping at his neck this time. Dryden wondered if the city could stop her if she decided to strike, as it did with the Kuvar Collective outfit, but he was doubtful. They were almost certainly out of range of the many control mechanisms this deep underground.

He gathered himself, trying to think of some way to salvage this situation. His heart was still hammering away, knowing the depth of knowledge that lay in the balance.

"Okay. I'll take pictures on my own, but after I leave I don't want anyone disturbing the craft. We should have Haplopol seal it up until I return, or at least until we can get the help of another professional who won't disturb the evidence."

Chinatsu squinted. "Fine. Binjai, take the orb."

"Wait!" Dryden said, "Yes, you can take the orb, but you have to be careful not to turn it on. I'm not sure if it has its own power source, but records tell us that these orbs are quite sophisticated, and use so much energy that they run very hot. So hot, in fact, that it can burn your hand. That's why the Haplopol orb is constantly cooled. I have no idea what this one will do out of the confines of Diplopol."

Chinatsu took on a thoughtful look. She shook her head. "Binjai, never mind. You guard Dryden. He will protect the orb and carry it to Diplopol."

Dryden's mouth opened a crack, but nothing came out. He almost objected, but how could he? It was true that he was the most suitable person to carry it, even though he wasn't quite sure how it worked. He certainly knew more than anyone else in Haplopol.

Chinatsu stayed a while longer, but eventually tired of standing around. She left him with Binjai and another guard while Dryden took pictures. These two Prefectorate officers watched him with unrestrained curiosity, not due to what lay around them but rather what they perceived to be a foolish man obsessing over pointless old artifacts.

After a particularly long bout of camera shots, the guard with Binjai said, "You missed a spot," and pointed toward the featureless ground in front of him. Binjai didn't laugh, and the officer sighed at his failed attempt at humor. Binjai was of Asian descent, but he wasn't from the main Prefectorate islands, rather from one of the islands the Prefectorate had conquered in the Pacific. He was still shinogi, though, and according to some of the coastal Essentialists, a renowned warrior. Although he was intimidating, Dryden liked Binjai because he could tell he had some kind of code of honor. He also liked that he was quiet.

Dryden tried to ignore the two officers and worked quickly, documenting the patterns in the materials, the people and their placement, the craft design, and the crevasse in the wall. He had many questions—a lifetime of questions—and he only had one hour.

When his time was up, he reached down carefully with gloved hands and placed them delicately on the orb. When nothing happened, he tugged at it, gently at first and then with increasing force until it moved. He froze as one of the brittle finger bones holding it in place snapped. With a final pull, the remaining fingers relinquished their hold, and the Diplopol control junction was safely in his grasp.

Dryden was sitting in a low chair in the courtyard, his weighty travel pack in front of him, when Elissa approached him. He was awaiting a few of the expedition's men who were collecting supplies before setting out back toward East Sound, the Wandefuca Channel and, eventually, Diplopol.

He and Elissa had already said their goodbyes, and she had accepted it.

It was Chinatsu's will, so she must have understood he had no choice. The discovery of the mysterious vessel increased his resolve to return as quickly as possible. He hoped Elissa understood that as well.

Which was why what she said surprised him.

"I'm going with you." It was only now that he noticed she had also stowed her large pack in the lobby, just down the courtyard wall from where they were sitting.

"What? Why would you? I mean, I would love for you to come, but you're needed here, aren't you? Don't you have a responsibility to Sanuwan to host visiting delegates—to negotiate entry fees?"

She tilted her head and offered a broken smile. Her pupils appeared dilated, and he wondered if she'd just been to the experiential rooms again. Some people had enhanced their trips to experiential rooms with mild hallucinogens that were pumped into the air. It allowed it to be more immersive, according to Elissa.

She said, "We've figured all that out. Delane does a fine job welcoming people to Haplopol, and the price of entry is becoming standardized. Plus, two more Sanuwan hosts will be arriving soon." She leaned in and whispered, "Another prince and princess." She pulled away and returned to normal volume. "It's not as important that I remain here."

"So you can just leave?"

"Well, not if I don't have a good reason."

"And what reason is that?"

"The reason I gave the king is that I know the Vickies, and I need to visit Diplopol so we can see what differences there are with Haplopol. There will be questions once Diplopol is up and running, which hopefully I can help answer."

It made some sense, but the way she said it was odd. "The reason you gave?" he asked, one eyebrow raised. She smiled again, sat down next to him and clung to his arm.

Dryden curled his fingers around her hand. He knew he should feel flattered. Here was a girl who had fallen for him—who liked him for who he was. She was willing to forgo a role as one of the most important ambassadors in Sanuwan, and a key stakeholder in their engine of economic output.

But why him? Surely there would be suitors for her in Sanuwan, or even Victoria. Maybe he'd fooled her. Maybe she didn't know he'd killed Alayna's brother.

And Dryden couldn't venture that information. Not now. It didn't seem right. To challenge her on her choice would imply he wasn't interested, that he was trying to find an excuse to leave her behind.

So when the remaining expedition members arrived, they left Haplopol together, her hand still cupping his arm.

He stopped on the expansive bridge to turn around and stare at Haplopol one more time. The city seemed even more impressive than on the way in. The five towers appeared taller, the sheen of the walls a deeper blue, and the smoke coming out of the main tower more ebullient.

It was probably his imagination.

Just before he peeled his gaze away, he looked to the windows, where he could see the vague outline of the defense droids. It made him shiver.

He knew it would not remain a utopia for long. He'd already seen how it would unfold, in his mind's eye. He didn't need an experiential room to imagine it. Nobody knew the city better than him; of this he was quite sure.

There was one thing he didn't tell Chinatsu, or even Elissa. The city only cared about its citizens inside the city. It didn't care about anyone outside the city.

This was why the Kuvar Collective outfit had been lucky. If Chinatsu had challenged them *outside* the city, Dryden was quite sure they would be dead. The city wouldn't have hesitated when Chinatsu issued her command. No, the city would have obliterated them, because they weren't citizens. They would be in just as many pieces as the missing tree across the mountain lake.

It was only a matter of time until Chinatsu figured this out. Dryden needed to plead with Hatsuo to intervene before she did.

—19—

A Mesmerizing Kaleidoscope of Plastics

Nillias wanted to approach Diplopol from the north. That way they would be in Gungivite-friendly waters most of the way until they reached the Vicky coast. Their plan was to navigate into the Gulf Islands, which were controlled by the Gungivites, and then curl through the narrow passageways and head south.

The first Gulf Island they approached was Saturna, which was mostly inhabited by farmers. The only thing of note was a tall Gungivite lookout tower on the north end of the island—a tower that Lexie and her crew had always tried to avoid in her pirating days. There was also one of those giant splayed-hand statues bulging out of a cliff on the southwest side. She liked to avoid those as well.

Below the splayed hand was a floating pile of filth adhering to the coast of the island, which made it look as if the splayed hand had just chucked a giant pile of garbage out to sea. Nillias had the *Nox* pull in closer to shore, to wade through the trash. Lexie wasn't sure what the point of this was. It wasn't as if a top-of-the-line Gungivite frigate could pass for a junk trawler.

Lexie found it hard not to stare at the trash as they went by. She was a pirate, and a scavenger, after all. It was a mesmerizing kaleidoscope of plastics, wood and seaweed, bobbing up and down with the swells of the ocean. Occasionally a sea otter popped its head up through a patch of open water, and once she saw one tearing through a kelp-entangled assembly of bottles.

She couldn't help but remember another time, another otter poking its head up through debris, not too far from here. But that day, that time, she was in the water, not on a ship.

Because her ship was gone. The bow had been blown to pieces, and the stern sunk into the depths. She was drowning, in fact. There was salt on her tongue and in her throat. Her stomach heaved—she'd swallowed too much. It was cold, so cold. The torn shipboards pummeled her elbows as she reached for an opening in the debris. She finally found a sturdy enough piece of flotsam to pull herself up, where her lungs could recover.

All the while, during her desperate struggle for air, the otter had danced playfully nearby, tossing ship remnants left and right with its nose, as if in a circus.

Eventually she had been pulled away from the otter, and out of the water. It was Warrick, on the shore. He had lassoed the medley of boards that was serving as her life raft and was reeling her in.

There were only three other survivors, and it shook Warrick up some. He decided to sit out the pirating business, but he still wanted her help with odds and ends.

After that she stayed with him in a beat-up old house on the outskirts of Anacortes. It was there that she learned Warrick was a tortured man. He was one of those lost souls who lived in the past, replaying obscure battles in his mind and collecting pre-fall artifacts: guns, maps, computers, batteries, drone parts. But nothing that worked, as far as she knew. There was even weirder stuff. He had big retcher bones and an old fossilized dinosaur egg locked away. At night he would often read a book about Benjamin Franklin that he quoted, and he cited other books from his time in the east. He would whisper the words in some kind of communion. "Novation is Damnation," he would say, as if that meant something.

Eventually the pirating bug came back to bite him. One day he just stood up and said, "I have to find it," and the next thing she knew, he had a whole ship and crew lined up again.

When the *Nox* was well into the curl south, passing Moresby Island, Nillias startled Lexie by suddenly standing up with an alarmed look on his face, as if someone had slapped him upside the head.

He promptly walked over to the mizzenmast bell and rang it four times. That meant battle stations.

"Did you see something?" Lexie asked, her scope scanning the southern waters.

"Get your things," he said. "We may need to jump ship."

"What? How do you know that? I can't see anything."

"I know." He said it slowly, forcefully. He climbed down the rungs into the hold as he barked out commands. "Full sail west. Cannons ready. Officers—my cabin, now." She heard his door slam a moment later.

She did as he asked. There wasn't much to pack, but she brought it all to the main deck anyway. Maybe there was an Essentialist warship on the prowl nearby, and Nillias wanted them to slip away before they were boarded.

She was right. Not long after Nillias had gone below decks, she saw an Essentialist warship, then another one, then another two. These were large, four-mast galleons, each with two levels of cannons on each side. Both pairs were headed to intercept them at Cordova Bay; two from the north, and two from the south.

She'd never seen this many Essentialist warships this close to the Gulf Islands. How did they get past the Vickies?

She nudged her pack so that it was closer to the skiff. Yes, Gungivite ships were top-of-the-line, but these new Essentialist galleons were impressive. That, and there were four of them.

—20—

VICTORIA

The Essentialist clipper sailed steadily toward Vicky territory. They were making good time until they stalled in the middle of the Wandefuca Channel. Here, the captain and Binjai were using reflectors to pass coded messages to Essentialist galleons far away on the horizon.

After a good twenty minutes of this, Dryden wanted to figure out what was going on. He approached Binjai. "Why can't we just meet up with them and talk it over? We'd be done in a few minutes."

Binjai wasn't as easily agitated as Chinatsu. He rubbed his chin thoughtfully, stared at him deadpan and said, "We would be seen. We don't want to give the Vickies the impression of a large military presence."

Dryden nodded. "So how long will it be until we get to Cordova Bay?"

"Maybe thirty minutes, or an hour, but we won't be going to Cordova Bay. We will be docking in Victoria and escorting you to Diplopol on horseback."

"Why the change in plan?"

"We don't want to alarm the Vickies."

Dryden knew that he sometimes had a naïve view of the world, especially when it came to Salish Sea people's perception of the ICSM cities. He'd figured that, given the importance of what they were about to do, these nations would find ways to work together to make it happen smoothly and efficiently. Instead, it looked like the Essentialists were trying to find a way to sneak him in and wake up Diplopol without the Vickies' knowledge. The Vickies probably didn't even know they were coming.

He shouldn't have been surprised. It was the same tactic Hatsuo used to gain control of Haplopol.

Dryden made his way back over to Elissa, who was sitting up above the captain's cabin. Here they could use the roof of the cabin as a tabletop.

"The bad news is that it's going to be a while," he said. "The good news is that you'll get to see Victoria again."

She smiled and nodded. "Cards?"

He shrugged. "Why not? I need to win my money back. I'm not sure I even have enough for a meal. You keep cleaning me out."

She began dealing. Every once in a while, one of them would have to shoot their hands out to keep a card from blowing away in the wind.

"Go easy on me," he said, picking up his hand. "You shouldn't need the money anyway—with all the commissions you must have made in Haplopol. What's the going rate now?"

He was being facetious, but only in part. He was also genuinely curious. She would only tell him if she was allowed to.

"We've actually lowered the price," she said. "We're charging five hundred Vicky medallions for the first week, per person. Two hundred a week thereafter."

It was way less than he expected. He had figured they would be charging five times that much. And they weren't making much off the supply services, so where *were* they making their money? "That doesn't make any sense," he said. "Demand has gone way up, and you've only got so many spaces. Why aren't you raising the price, or at least charging more to begin with?"

"We want to make sure it's accessible to everyone."

It still sounded strange to Dryden. Maybe they would raise the prices later, when people were hooked? It was possible, but it didn't seem like a tactic the Sanuwans would use.

"Call," she said. They had finished betting, and he placed down his cards. She beat him handily and snapped up his change.

Maybe the Sanuwans made enough money from gambling.

As soon as they docked in Victoria, he could tell that something wasn't right.

He was walking gingerly down the gangway, admiring the Vicarial Hotel, with its steep pitched roofs, gables, and polygonal turrets, when people on the bustling wharf angled toward him from all directions. Some were Essentialist militia, but most were plainclothes men and women. They crowded around him and looked outward.

"What is this?" he asked. "Who are you people?"

Binjai was immediately behind him. He said, "Move quickly. These people will protect you. You protect the control junction." He looked tense, his eyes darting everywhere. Dryden had the orb in his backpack, but he swung it around so the pack faced forward. That way no one could reach in without him knowing.

The mass of people pushed along the wharf, at times jostling him uncomfortably.

Two Vicky officers who were eating a steaming bowl of food by the water became interested in their party. "Excuse me," they called over to the group. "We would like to see your papers."

Two Essentialist militia peeled off from the group and handed papers to the Vicky officers. Meanwhile, Dryden was still being pushed along the quay by the mob, which was drawing many gawkers.

"Please hold for a moment until we check the papers," one of the Vicky officers said.

Dryden stopped, but only for an instant before he was pushed forward from behind again.

The Essentialist militia were pointing avidly at the documents and practically barking at them. "It's all here. Excuse us, we can't stop. We are in a rush."

The Vicky officers appeared overwhelmed. "Hey!" one of them said as he saw the group hadn't stopped pushing ahead. The officer almost moved to chase after them, but he was distracted by the papers and the gesticulating men in front of him.

Bells started to sound, adding to the confusion. They were distant, down the bay towards Esquimalt. There, Dryden could see no less than six ships entering the harbor, all bearing Essentialist flags. He recognized the bells. They were used in times of war and conflict. There were similar ones in Hood River that had been installed by Essentialist military engineers.

A Vicky cruiser sailed out to meet the Essentialist fleet as the bells continued to toll. People were staring down the bay. Dryden knew what was happening, even as they continued to push him forward from behind. There wasn't much he could do.

In a flurry of fire and smoke, the Essentialist cannons roared to life. A dozen shells missed the Vicky cruiser, but there were more than a dozen. One cut it right down the middle and exploded, rendering the cruiser useless and adrift, taking on water. The cannons were also aimed at the lands closer to Esquimalt, where the Vicky military fortifications stood, pitiful as they were. That area also became punctuated with bursts of gray fumes.

"Get on," Binjai said. Dryden hadn't been looking ahead of him. They had reached a stable, and a saddled horse was standing next to him. Others in the muddle of people were mounting horses. He did the same.

"Hya!" Binjai said, and he kicked his heels into the flank of his animal. The rest of them followed suit, and they were away, twenty-odd horses wedging through the tide of humanity that was coming down the wharf to look down the length of the bay.

"We're being attacked!" someone finally yelled.

"Defend the city!" said another.

More bells sounded, this time all around Dryden on the quay. People screamed in panic, running in every direction.

Dryden understood the ruthless logic. The Essentialists wanted control of Diplopol, and they couldn't afford to have the Vickies standing in their way. The Vickies were much more sophisticated than the Sanuwans and could enlist the help of the Kuvar Collective and Gungivites, so they needed to catch them by surprise. And besides, the Prefectorate had had their eye on the Salish Sea nations for a long time. This was their opportunity.

An opportunity that he had provided them.

Elissa was riding next to him. She was remarkably calm, all things considered.

"Did you know about this?" he asked her. "Aren't you worried?"

When she turned to him, her expression had become one of consternation. "We need to get out of Victoria," she said.

It was obvious, and it didn't answer his question. She averted her eyes back to the street as they maneuvered their steeds around a stalled cart and a jumble of overturned potatoes.

By the time they were several blocks into the city, most of the people of Victoria seemed to know what was happening. Shops were closing. People were running across streets, their arms full of boxes and bags. The occasional group of horsemen would gallop across in front of the group, buttocks high and whips in hand. The city defenses, although caught by surprise, had begun moving into action.

Their twenty horses intercepted three Vicky officers who were running toward the marina. These were young men, faces full of anxious vigor. Two of them froze, but the one in the front didn't hesitate. He saw that they were Essentialists, so he charged at them with a glittering bayonet. The other two followed suit.

Binjai and the rest of Dryden's escort didn't even stop. Instead, three of the horsemen at the rear peeled away and engaged the Vickies. One of these horsemen cut down the first charging man with a long sword, but the other two Vickies impaled the horses of the challengers, toppling the riders. A melee ensued, but Dryden wasn't able to witness the outcome. They were well ahead by that point, and turning around a corner.

On a much broader avenue, further ahead, stood a lookout tower manned by Vickies. Not only that, but the Vickies had *rifles*. The Vickies started shooting at them. It was the first time Dryden had heard gunfire. They were far away, but the shots were loud, and heart-stopping.

A woman convulsed on her horse next to him, then slouched in her saddle. A burst of red had appeared on her mauve tunic. She had been quiet the whole ride and looked like she could be from any walk of life; a teacher, or merchant, or a seamstress. What prompted her to support the Essentialists—to join this group heading north?

It could easily have been Elissa who'd been shot. She was on his other side. Elissa barely registered the event, riding with uncompromised attention.

After the now-dead woman slinked off her horse, three more horsemen pushed up to take spots closer to Dryden, shielding him from incoming shots.

Eventually the group turned again, taking them out of the line of sight of the lookout tower. They found lesser-used streets on which to head north, and they didn't encounter any more Vicky soldiers. The defense forces must have been embroiled in the main conflict in the marina, or were simply too unprepared to chase down a rogue band of cavalry heading full-tilt through the city with an unknown purpose.

The city houses turned to halfies, to shacks, and then empty fields. They kept northward toward Diplopol, away from the wake of violence that was engulfing the city.

As Dryden spurred his steed forward, a cocktail of adrenaline and guilt coursed through him. His chest tightened with every hoofprint his horse made on the dusty road.

—21—

Cordova Bay

A small fountain jetted up from the sea behind the *Nox* on another near-miss. The ship sailed on toward land as the four Essentialist galleons closed the distance.

It was definitely going to be a one-way trip, if they could make it to land at all. The ship seemed to be shaking, a loud hum coming from below decks, as if the speed was putting it into some kind of spasm.

"How do you know, Nillias?" Lexie asked emphatically. "How do you know we can make it to land, or that these ships were even there in the first place?"

"Their shells will not hit us."

"Says you, but even if you're right, we'll be easy pickings when we land. What then?"

"There will be more risk once we reach shore, but we should be able to outrun the ships in time. A Gungivite platoon will be waiting for us. They will help us navigate out of range of the Essentialist galleons."

Lexie threw up her hands. "How do you know?" she said again. "We've been in Anacortes for days. You didn't know about this attack until moments ago, and then pop, all of a sudden there it is, and a platoon materializes out of thin air. You know what? Fuck this. Tell me right here and now or I will abandon ship. I don't need to be party to your nutjob suicide mission."

Another shell landed about a hundred yards to the south. Lexie had to admit the Gungivite ship was moving remarkably fast, especially given the light winds.

Nillias stared at her. His face was firm and emotionless until he blinked, then bowed his head. "I suppose you need to know."

"No kidding!"

"I'm sorry, Lexie. I am a creature of responsibility. Those are my shackles—not greed, or dishonesty."

"What rancid river are you—"

He put his hand up, arresting her speech. Another shell landed to the north. She heard bells on the Essentialist vessels, getting louder by the minute.

His face seemed to shiver, as if a cold wind passed over it. He said, "I am part machine, Lexie."

She was ready to cuss at him, to attack whatever nutty remark he was going to make. Instead, her lips couldn't move. She was speechless.

He said, "Gungivite Observers have sensory interface devices implanted in their temporal lobes when they are young. It's an imperfect operation, and we need to take a mixture of drugs to maintain the graft. At times we can become very ill when we go without them, as you have seen. The drugs can also be toxic, and inhibit hair growth. Thus, the shaved heads, and the wigs."

Her mind was reeling. "Okay … but how do you know—"

"The Essentialist ships, and the platoon?" he responded. "At Moresby Island, there is a hidden repeater that allows communication from my implant to Ganges Island, and to repeaters in Vicky lands, Kuvar Island, and other places. This allows me to communicate instantaneously with hundreds of implants connected to hundreds of Observer minds. As soon as I was close enough, I could access the network, and they informed me of the threat. I couldn't know in Anacortes, or in the channel, because if we use our implants on the mainland, it will summon the retchers."

Lexie nodded slowly, wrestling with the concept.

"Be thankful, Lexie. These implants allowed Olint to commune with our Observer scholars when we first met. If he hadn't done that, you might not be alive."

He looked back, toward the east, ignoring the two more shells landing nearby. "And yet, at the same time, it's hard to express how peaceful it was for me, those few days in Anacortes. Imagine hundreds of voices talking all at the same time, and then quiet. It was like … when I was a child." His eyes closed, as if trying to reach back to relish the memory.

She snapped her fingers close to his ear. "Okay, back to reality. We're under attack, remember? So what about the speed of the ship? How did you know?"

"Well, this is the utility of the implant. Complex geometric calculations can be made instantaneously. I knew what velocity we needed to maintain to outrun them. Our engine is at ninety percent power, which will be more than sufficient. It uses high-grade bitumen power to drive hidden turbines, and the exhaust is contained and compressed. We would use electric power, but again, it would bring the retchers if we are too close to the mainland."

"That's what's down below? That's what's causing this shaking? I thought the ship was falling apart."

A rare playful expression crossed his face. "Come now, Lexie. A shrewd pirate like you? You should have known."

"Maybe, but what doesn't seem shrewd is for a bunch of nutjobs who are afraid of machines to have them plopped into their brains. Doesn't that strike you as hypocritical?"

All joviality was flushed off Nillias's face. His jaw clenched. "Yes, it's complicated, and in truth, there are conflicting views on this subject, to this day."

Lexie decided not to push the matter further. It was a bad time to test Nillias's finer sensibilities.

They were getting close to the Cordova Bay shoreline, where several old docks protruded out from large coastal estates. Remarkably, the Essentialist ships had fallen behind. They would still catch up, though. Unless the Essentialists were tactical morons, the *Nox* would be surrounded soon after it reached shore.

"It's time," Nillias said. He stood up tall and yelled, "Gungivites!"

The sailors stopped working. A few came up from below decks.

Nillias took a deep breath and said, "You will be remembered."

There was a moment of silence, and nothing else.

Huh? That was his speech. It wasn't very inspirational. The others went back about their business.

"Come," Nillias said, and he began boarding the skiff with a dozen other Gungivite sailors. Lexie joined them.

"No offense, Nillias," she said under her breath, "but maybe you could have said something a little more uplifting?"

"Truth above all else. Their chances are slim. I will not insult them by giving them false hope."

She only blinked her eyes. She didn't say it. *Nutjob.*

They were dropped in the water about a hundred yards from shore. Nillias yelled, "Row!" The Gungivites had already begun pulling oars. Another skiff appeared and pulled up alongside. It must have dropped from the other side of the ship. Meanwhile, the *Nox* slowed behind them, came to a stop and reversed course. Water churned in tight eddies, spinning out from under the bow.

"Row!" Nillias yelled again.

Their skiff closed the distance to shore quickly, landing at one of the sturdier docks. An Essentialist ship was still heading toward them, while the other three were pursuing the *Nox* as it pulled away.

Once the major vessels were within range, Cordova Bay became a frenzy of screaming projectiles and explosions. The *Nox* concentrated its fire on the one vessel heading toward land, but it had limited effect. It managed two volleys before it was hit four times in quick succession. The *Nox* was engulfed in flames and began listing to the side.

Lexie followed Nillias and his team onto a set of rocky steps that led up an escarpment. The Essentialist ship closer to shore began firing on them, hitting a faraway bank of stone on the shoreline.

Nillias led them past a house, and on the other side twenty-odd Gungivites were waiting for them on horseback. These men weren't in any particular uniform, but they did have weapons: crossbows, rifles, swords and daggers.

Without a word of introduction, Nillias, Lexie and the rest of the remaining *Nox* crew were given horses of their own.

They rode away from the water as the Essentialist ship continued to shell the escarpment behind them.

—22—

A Temperature Problem

The occasional blast still sounded in the distance, even though Dryden and his entourage were far from the main town. Rumblings came from the east as well.

The Diplopol museum grounds were defined by a tall but easily penetrable fence made of rusted wire and old metal posts. This fence line surrounded an expansive area, much larger than Haplopol, but without any of its grandeur. A few resolute, sandblasted buildings remained, each only two or three stories tall. The rest had fallen into the earth—or so the story went. A large part of what was left had been scavenged by the Vickies over the preceding decades.

The road led them up to the main gate, which was open. Three dead Vicky officers lay nearby; two were sprawled on the road with crossbow bolts in their chests, and the third was sitting with his back to the building, his mouth catching flies and his hands positioned on his bloody stomach, as if trying to prevent his intestines from pushing out.

Binjai led the horses on, into the museum grounds. Ramshackle Vicky shops were set up along the road, obscuring craggy concrete outcroppings and stiff metal beams that littered the site. There were no shopkeepers or museum attendees to be seen. Dryden hoped they weren't dead as well.

Signposts had been set up along the way; colorful markers designed to explain and illustrate what would have been around them before the Diplopol scavengers came. On any other day, Dryden would have liked to stop and assess their veracity.

The column stopped near the center point of the city. Here, the museum patrons had at least established a sense of order. There were several small buildings, a map of the museum grounds, and an artist's rendering of what the city used to look like. If Dryden recalled correctly, the only reason these buildings in the center were still standing was because they were impervious to demolition. Otherwise, pilfering Vickies would have dismantled them long ago.

He paused at the artist's rendering of Diplopol. It was an impressive drawing, replete with spires, arcs and bridges. While intriguing, it could also be a complete fabrication.

A handful of Essentialists were waiting by the entrance to the remains of the control center building. One had a red gash in his shoulder. Two were actually Sanuwans whom Dryden recognized from Haplopol. It seemed strange for them to also be here, especially given the secretive nature of this venture. Then again, Binjai had let Elissa join them for the voyage. That was also curious, now that Dryden thought about it.

"Go," Binjai said to him, nudging his chin toward the guarded entrance. Binjai wasn't as volatile as Chinatsu, but he was often just as harsh.

Dryden hesitated. "Who are these people?" he asked. "And when is Hatsuo going to arrive? I need to speak with him."

"He will arrive soon, but we don't have much time. There are reports of Gungivites in the area. If we aren't the first to awaken the city, it may fall into the wrong hands. Now go." He pointed at the entrance.

Gungivites as well? It seemed hard to believe, but at this point, with Victoria under attack, and the strange way even the Sanuwan people seemed to be acting, anything was possible.

Binjai was still pointing resolutely. Dryden did like Binjai better than Chinatsu, but he certainly didn't trust him. And *like* was probably too strong a word. On the ride through the city Binjai had shown little humanity—no compassion or concern for the Vickies or even his own men.

Dryden dismounted slowly and walked toward the entrance.

One of the men who'd been waiting—the man with the bloody shoulder—led the whole group through what looked like an ancillary access door that had been propped open. Inside was dusty and dark, but the lead man was prepared. A lantern was lit, and a torch as well. Dryden was overlooking a large chamber that extended deep into the ground. It was nothing like the courtyard in Haplopol, but still impressive. The walls had a similar blue hue but were so caked in dust and dirt that the color only showed in patches. The floor was scratched and cracked.

The group navigated through several open doorways and up a wooden ladder, then another ladder.

Finally, Dryden arrived in a room almost identical to the Officiant's Office in Haplopol. The control junction compartment was front and center. It was a plain transparent box with a large metal pin jutting out of the middle and an open top. Lines streamed out below the central pin, which were presumably electronic feeds leading into Diplopol's infrastructure. Behind Dryden was a dusty window where he could see over the cityscape and up to the gatehouse.

The party finished flooding into the room, and all eyes turned to Dryden.

"The control junction," Binjai said, addressing Dryden.

Dryden hesitated, trying to think of some way he could delay until Hatsuo arrived. The addition of the Sanuwans, and the way Binjai was acting, was making him nervous. Pleading with Hatsuo to slow things down and bring some kind of order was the only sane option. Putting control of the city in the wrong hands would be incredibly dangerous and irresponsible.

Binjai lost his patience. He simply pointed at Dryden, and two soldiers went to hold him while Binjai took off Dryden's backpack and removed the wooden box that was inside it. He opened the box, unwrapped the soft cloths surrounding the orb, and lifted the orb up to the light. He appeared to be examining the fractal line patterns while revolving it in his hand.

With a shrug, he stepped up to the transparent box, reached over and placed the orb on the metal pins. A perforation folded inward in the bottom of the orb.

They waited.

Nothing happened. Dryden took furtive glances out the window, hoping to see Hatsuo's men arriving, but there was no one.

Binjai reached for the orb.

Dryden cautioned, "I wouldn't—"

"*Kuso!*" Binjai yelled. He pulled his hand back from the orb, shaking it vigorously. His palm was red and sizzling. A smell of burnt flesh filled the room.

"*Kuso*," Binjai said again, and he bent over, holding his hand between his legs. He was breathing in seething rasps through clenched teeth.

"It needs to be cooled," Elissa said. "It might not work without water."

Dryden glared at her. She seemed oblivious to his concerns about Binjai. Did they have some kind of side deal going?

"There's water at the gatehouse," a Prefectorate private said. "A well in the back."

"Go get it," Binjai said. He forced himself to look at his scorched hand and then stand upright again.

"That might be difficult," said another soldier, pulling a handheld scope down from the window. "The Gungivites have arrived."

"We will go," Elissa said, without missing a beat. The two other Sanuwans gathered behind her. Heavy packs were relayed to them from the back of the group.

"Go and do what?" Dryden said, looking at the faces around him for clues.

"Quiet," Binjai said. He turned to Elissa. "You know what to do."

It definitely seemed like they were working together. Why, as a Sanuwan princess, would Elissa be so devoted to helping Binjai? Despite his confusion, he said, "Be careful, Elissa."

Elissa didn't respond. In fact, she didn't even look at him. The Sanuwans stepped into the doorway, and she left without a word.

Dryden's best guess was that they would distract the Gungivites by pretending to be weary travelers in need of water, hoping that the Gungivites wouldn't suspect them of being Essentialist allies.

Dryden and Binjai's men all clustered around the dingy window to watch as the three Sanuwans rode back up the road.

—23—

Three Sanuwans

Lexie and the Gungivite platoon came upon the Diplopol ruins from the east. It was rural land, mostly farms and a few well-manicured estates. They saw only one person on their way, a farmer just off the road. He ran back to his farmhouse and leveled a bow at them from afar as they rode past. Others must have been hiding indoors.

The path began skirting around the arc of a roughshod metal fence. Given the rather evident gaps, it didn't seem to serve a purpose other than to mark a boundary for where Diplopol used to be. A few bluish buildings were visible in the interior, next to fragmented remains.

Ahead Lexie saw the main gatehouse, but it didn't look right. Three bodies lay in front of it, and they weren't in comfortable napping positions.

"There," Nillias said, pointing to another building a stone's throw away from the gatehouse. It was two stories tall, with a slanting patio on the second floor and bent roof supports. It could have been a house at one time, or even a restaurant, but it clearly hadn't been used for years.

They approached from the rear and found a fire escape out of sight of the main gatehouse. One of Nillias's men forced open a door on the inside patio of the upper level. They navigated carefully across a few dusty rooms to the front.

Nillias used his scope to scan the gatehouse area and nearby ruins. "Keegan, Gesha, keep a lookout here. The rest, let's go."

They made their way down some noisy stairs and out the door toward the gatehouse. The Gungivites had their weapons out, and their eyes were active.

"What exactly is your plan?" Lexie asked Nillias.

"We need to retrieve the Diplopol control junction before the city is awakened. I believe there is an Essentialist party nearby that is carrying it with them. I fear they could already be in the city."

Before the platoon could maneuver toward the city center, three people emerged from inside the grounds on horseback. They wore the distinctive sheepskin circles of the Sanuwans, and heavy packs on their backs. Their hands were in the air.

Lexie held her ground while the Gungivite platoon spread out. Some took to their knees and trained rifles on the three riders.

"Please," the lead Sanuwan rider said as she approached. "Please help us."

Nillias's eyes darted back and forth rapidly. He said, "Explain yourselves."

The Sanuwans stopped a few feet away and kept their hands in the air. "Gladly," the woman said, "but they could come back at any time, and we're exposed here." She looked over to the gatehouse.

"Who?"

"Essentialists. Prefectorate. They took us prisoner, but we escaped. They want to wake Diplopol but don't know how. We can show you where they are."

Nillias frowned. Computer implant or not, he seemed at a loss. He even glanced over at Lexie, an inquisitive look in his eyes.

"I don't like it," Lexie said, shaking her head. "That's what this shrewd pirate thinks. Why would the Sanuwans be here?"

"Because we know Haplopol," the Sanuwan woman said, her brow furrowing in earnest, "and they brought us here, against our will, to help them wake Diplopol. Please, there's no time. Can we go inside?" She looked over her shoulder at the blue buildings down the road.

The other Gungivite platoon members followed her gaze. A couple of them fidgeted anxiously.

Lexie shook her head again. "Since when did Sanuwans know anything about starting up Polie cities, and why do they need *three* Sanuwans? I'm telling you, Nillias, this isn't right. I'm not sure what it is, but it ain't good."

Nillias was still frowning. He looked back and forth between Lexie and the Sanuwan woman. His eyelids fluttered, as if he was reading a book at lightning speed. Or maybe he was "communing," as he had told her before, his implant in conversation with others in his network.

"What's in the pack?" Nillias asked. "And what is that strap—"

The words hung in the air for only a moment.

Nillias explained it all to Lexie afterward: the pack, the Sanuwans, the Essentialists on their way, the Essentialists already in Diplopol, the well at the gatehouse, and most of all, Haplopol's objective function. He could see all of it, with the help of his network, as well as the Gungivite spies and their viewing devices, but it was too much for him to process and piece together on his own. His implant used this information, ran thousands of simulations in tandem with other implants, then informed him who these people were and what they wanted to do in this very instant. He told Lexie later that he didn't fully understand until he saw the straps in their backpacks; that's what gave this simulation outcome a high likelihood.

Nillias yelled, "Run!" and he launched himself at Lexie. She fell to the ground on her buttocks, with Nillias on top of her. The other Gungivites didn't react as fast. Only one was an Observer, so the rest had only Nillias's words to go by—words that they obviously didn't understand.

And the Sanuwans knew their chance was then and there. They would presumably have preferred to be in an enclosed space, like the gatehouse, or the two-story building nearby, but they still had to go for it. So they each charged their horses toward the largest group of Gungivites. Only one Sanuwan was shot, but even he had the chance to pull his cord.

The three explosions were deafening, and afterward there was no noise, only ringing, with Lexie's eardrums in some kind of semi-permanent post-traumatic convulsion. Nillias yelled something at her and pulled her along, despite his cringing face, which clearly showed that he was in agony. Nillias and her managed to make it to the two-story building. Lexie only looked back once, and that was enough: bodies everywhere, a legless man screaming, a shuddering horse with a huge hole in its back. She was glad she wasn't able to hear any of it. It only would have made the memory worse.

Eleven of them made it back to the house. Nillias had a piece of shrapnel in his back, just below his shoulder blade, but he pulled it out and seemed mobile enough. In all, the suicidal Sanuwans had killed twenty men.

The ringing started to lessen. Lexie could make out voices, when people yelled. Nillias was talking to one of his subordinates: "… we think there are about ten of them, and they have the control junction but are unable to awaken the city." Nillias closed his eyes, and his eyelids fluttered while his teeth clenched. He was doing his communing again.

Lexie knew what would come next, and she was fine with it.

Maybe it was the bloody scene, or maybe she was starting to get used to these nutjobs, or maybe their brainwashing had worked. Whatever it was, she could feel it. She was angry. No, not just angry, she was *livid*. She was ready to take on these Essentialist assholes and fuck them up real good.

"Give me a gun. I'm ready," she said.

The other Gungivites were nodding with her. They were pissed. Nice to see the Gungies grow a pair.

"Wait," Nillias said. His eyes darted again.

Four horsemen wearing Essentialist uniforms arrived in front of the gatehouse from the south. They came to an abrupt halt to survey the scene around them.

"Shoot them," Nillias said.

The Gungivites on the patio were only too happy to oblige. One of the horsemen was hit square in his chest and knocked off his horse. Another's horse was hit and it reared, ejecting the rider. Shots pecked at the ground around the other two horsemen, but they were able to ride on and were soon obscured by the ruins.

The ejected horseman sat up, holding his head, only to be flattened to the ground by another well-placed rifle shot. It was the first time Lexie had seen rifles being used, and it was true what they said—they worked nicely.

"Okay, now we go?" Lexie asked.

They all stood up, except Nillias.

"Nillias," Lexie asked. "Time's a-wastin'. We have the advantage—let's use it."

Nillias's eyes froze, and his eyelids closed.

Lexie flung her hands up in the air and shared a frustrated look with Keegan.

Finally, Nillias's eyes reopened. His expression was heavy, his eyes downcast.

"No," he said. "We have failed. We must leave."

—24—

The Rise of Diplopol

Dryden watched in horror from the dust-streaked window of the control room as Elissa and the other two Sanuwan men blew themselves up. "What … what happened? Elissa!"

This wasn't who Elissa was. She was smart, and curious. She felt out of place in Sanuwan and longed for a life of greater sophistication, with peers on her intellectual level. She was sentimental, and lonely, but she wasn't passionate about Sanuwan politics.

She certainly wasn't suicidal.

And now she was dead.

He looked around the room. People were stern and focused, but not shocked.

Dryden said, "You all knew. You knew they were going to do this."

"Keep quiet," Binjai said.

Dryden couldn't help but sit down. He grabbed a chair next to a nearby table and ran his hands through his hair, trying to understand. Something was dreadfully wrong. These people weren't acting rationally.

He saw an opening across the room while the others were preoccupied at the window. He darted for the ladder, but his arm was snagged by one of the Essentialist militia before he made it. Another one moved to hold his other arm.

Binjai walked over, a sour expression on his face. "Listen, Doctor Science, here's a lesson for you. We've got more bombs. Two, in fact." He opened his pack, showing a system of colored wires attached to pipes filled with a clay-like material. "And one has your name on it, if you feel like taking a stroll."

"Where did you … how did you … the Essentialists are using *bombs* now?"

Binjai shrugged. "We had them built in Victoria, away from retchers. We learned how in Haplopol." He looked reflective and tapped his temple. "You're missing out. I've learned more there in two weeks than I've learned in my whole life."

"What? Who cares about that? This is not okay—what just happened. Why would Elissa do that?"

"Elissa understood what is important," Binjai said, nodding confidently, "and she was willing to do the right thing. *Now* the right thing is to be quiet, and ready, in case we have to fight." He put his finger to his lips.

Another soldier bound Dryden's wrists with rope and pulled him back up to the window, away from the ladders. From here, he could see across to the gatehouse area again. Four more horses came through, but two were taken down by gunfire from a house just to the east.

The two surviving horsemen made it to their building in the ruin. "Escort them in," Binjai said, his eyes glued to the window.

Two of the Essentialist militia went down the ladder to collect the horsemen.

Dryden tried to think. He was surrounded by people suffering from some kind of delusional psychosis. They appeared confident, and unshaken. It would be impossible to convince them of their folly. There was nothing he could do.

He watched as more horses arrived, and these made it through the gate safely. More came, until finally a huge Essentialist military force marched into the area near the gatehouse, spreading around, taking defensive positions. These were armed with bows and swords—and there were hundreds of them. They charged the two-story house from where the gunshots had come, but there was no further activity. The Gungivites had fled.

The tension was dissipating in the room. "We can get the water now," Binjai said, "the gatehouse is still standing."

It was true. The gatehouse had been damaged by the explosions, but only superficially.

The two horsemen returned to connect with the Essentialist army. Soon men with buckets full of water were traipsing into the building and up the ladders. They formed a chain—everyone helping get the water up as quickly as possible. They collaborated quite effectively, almost harmoniously, without argument or distraction.

Just like they had collaborated to send Elissa and the other two Sanuwans to their deaths.

Once ten buckets of water had been poured into the glass-encased chamber, the orb began to show signs of life. Flowing light began emanating from the fractal lines. With more water, it glowed even more brightly, and Dryden noticed small bubbles jumping at the surface, as though it was at a low boil. More water came, and more, and the light of the orb grew stronger.

Finally, a cracked interface came to life above them, showing bar graphs and numbers in red. A voice said, "Greetings. I am the Diplopol control junction. I am currently running diagnostics and will be fully online in seven minutes. Initial estimates show point three percent power availability and massive structural damage. I will access redundant power systems in eight minutes and begin remediations."

Binjai was caressing his abdominals with his good hand as he listened. He glanced quizzically at Dryden and then back to the screen. "Diplopol," he said, "do you need our help?"

"I could benefit from your assistance at a later date, but there are no obstacles to achieving nominal status at the present time."

Binjai smiled. "Good, so no more need for Doctor Science."

Dryden said, "Wait. You really need to think about what you're doing."

Binjai's expression was deadpan again. For a moment Dryden thought he might give the order to have him killed, but instead Binjai said, "I think it's time for you to go."

Dryden didn't object. He needed to get away from these sociopaths so he could speak to Hatsuo as soon as possible.

He was escorted by two of Binjai's men down the ladder and back up to the gatehouse. He walked quickly through the area, wary of what he might see. He thought maybe he should try to find Elissa, to pay some sort of respects to her, but he couldn't bear to look at the clumps of flesh littered about the gatehouse area.

He was urged through the ranks of nervous soldiers that were scouting the area and tending to horses. At one point, he saw a group on horseback, set back from the road. A man and a woman were talking, but the woman's back was to him. He could have sworn by the shape of her, and by her hair and the way she bobbed her head in acknowledgement, that it was Alayna.

He thought about calling out, but what would he say? What good reason would there be to interrupt her conversation? This wasn't a happy occasion. It was a sad one, a *shameful* one, and he doubted she would want to see him. She never did, these days.

So he said nothing.

The woman didn't turn around.

Down the road, where the mass of Essentialist forces swelled even further, he found Hatsuo. A gaggle of horsemen were stationed here, waiting. At the urging of his guards, they pulled apart to reveal Hatsuo at the center, speaking to one of his subordinates in Japanese.

When Hatsuo saw Dryden, his eyes lit up. "Dryden, my friend. So good to see you! Why do they have you in bonds?" Hatsuo turned his horse to face him.

"Sir, he tried to escape," one of the men escorting Dryden said.

Hatsuo frowned and shook his head reprovingly at the soldier. "He's not a prisoner. Take those bonds off."

The soldier complied with his order. Dryden rubbed his wrists. "Sir, thank you. I'm so grateful that you're here. Do you mind if we speak privately?"

Hatsuo looked around. "I'm sorry, Dryden. Ordinarily I would be happy to, especially for you. But this is wartime, if you hadn't noticed. I don't have the convenience of a secluded office. And besides, my subordinates will need to hear what you have to say just as much as me."

It wasn't as courteous as Dryden had hoped, but Hatsuo *was* a general, after all.

"Sir, it's, well … I'm concerned. At first I was worried about Chinatsu—she tried to kill a band of Kuvar Collective militia in Haplopol, but the city stopped her. She might figure out how to work around that, though. It could escalate into more conflict, and even altercations with the Sanuwans because of contractual violations. But there's more, and it's hard to explain." Dryden looked at the men around him. Dozens of eyes stared down at him. He paused, hoping Hatsuo would reconsider his position on speaking in front of his men.

One of Hatsuo's eyebrows was raised. He patted the flank of his animal. It didn't look as though he was taking him seriously. Dryden had no choice but to continue. "There's an effect the city is having on people. Three people just committed suicide, but others—it's like they forget about their own wants and needs, their own priorities. The Sanuwans are practically giving away visitation rights. Chinatsu, as brutal and maniacal as she is, is the only one acting normal, or at least … herself. Everyone else … something's wrong. And I'm worried it could get even worse here, once we get Diplopol up and running. Maybe we should stop, put a hold on things until we figure out what's happening to people who have been in Haplopol, after we quarantine them for a while."

It wasn't well articulated, but he hoped his relationship with Hatsuo would give him the benefit of the doubt.

Hatsuo stared for a long time, round-eyed, and expressionless. Finally, he said, "Did you ever stop and consider whether it's doing something to you?"

"What do you mean?"

"There is a lot of pressure on you, a lot of responsibility, in working with these ICSM cities. I wonder if this pressure is too hard on you. I heard what happened in the past—the accident. Alayna told me. That's a lot to bear. And now you tell me you're worried about Chinatsu, and then in your next breath you tell me you're *not* worried about Chinatsu. Which is it?" He shook his head, and his eyes softened, like a puppy chastened by its owner. "Today should be a day to rejoice. We have not only won Diplopol, but also Victoria. Isn't that what you wanted?"

Dryden gritted his teeth, trying to contain a flush of anger. "I wanted to preserve Haplopol and Diplopol, yes, but I had no idea that it would start a war." He gestured back to the gatehouse area. "And I had no idea it would unleash this ... madness."

Hatsuo shook his head, a grim expression on his face. "Those two things are too often the same, Dryden. War. Madness. Madness is caused by war—in some people. It's unfortunate, but it can be contained. I hope this is not a hint of what's happening with you. I know you're not trained as a soldier, but you're making excuses, reading too much into old letters and rumors about ancient cities. Maybe you felt something for this girl, the princess, and now you're rationalizing it?"

"Dammit, Hatsuo, you're not listening—"

Two katanas were nipping at his neck in an instant.

A hint of a smile tugged at Hatsuo's lips.

"Sir," a soldier yelled, pushing through the surrounding horsemen. "Sir, the city!" The soldier pointed to the north.

The horses nearby trotted to the side, clearing a line of sight for Hatsuo. On the horizon, the tops of the visible Diplopol buildings were rising. Others were thrusting out of the ground, shedding debris and sediment as they pushed upward. There were only three towers at first, but soon five, and then twelve. It wasn't anything like the image the Vickies had used, and it lacked the clean symmetry of Haplopol, but it was impressive enough. It was a clear sign that there *was* a city here, and not just a ruin.

It was an incredible sight, but Dryden didn't feel any kind of elation. In fact, the rising city only filled him with dread.

Dryden looked back at Hatsuo. His face was full of emotion, some odd mixture of happiness and awe. His eyes glistened with moisture, and a tear ran down his cheek.

"It's so beautiful," Hatsuo said.

After a moment, Hatsuo caught himself. He wiped away the track of the tear, and smiled at Dryden. "You see. There's nothing to worry about. Why don't you take some time away? I'm sending you back to Hood River, for your own good—to get your head straight. The city is rising, and we're in good hands with Binjai in command."

Without another word, Hatsuo nodded and kicked the flanks of his horse, spurring it toward the gatehouse.

Dryden made to follow Hatsuo, but he was held back by Binjai's guards.

He wanted to object. He wanted to yell after Hatsuo, but he knew the guards would subdue him, or worse. And besides, he doubted Hatsuo would listen. If he'd wanted to listen, he would have asked Dryden more about his concerns. If Hatsuo really cared about preserving the ICSM cities at all, he would have kept Dryden here, at Diplopol, instead of sending him home.

He'd been played. He'd helped the Essentialists gain access to an incredible power that they didn't understand, so they could wage yet another war. The ICSM cities were just a means to an end.

Much later, on the long trip home, he would reflect that his biggest regret was something else. He'd made mistakes, but any scholar could have made them. The Essentialists probably would have waged war with the Vickies regardless. No, it was the one action he felt he had control over, the one action that could have changed the outcome for one person.

His biggest regret was not yelling out to Alayna—if that had indeed been her—and explaining his concerns to her.

His biggest regret was not pleading with her to come home.

—25—

Talk About Chicken Shit

"I just don't get it," Lexie protested. "We come all this way, nearly get blown to pieces—*twice*—and now you want to cut and run? Talk about chicken shit."

Nillias didn't respond. Every second step, he cringed. It must have been the pressure of his pack on his injured back. The other eleven Gungivites were quiet, walking at a rapid clip on the eastward path along the metal fence. They only had three horses left, walking beside them. The other horses had been spooked by the explosion and managed to run off after they'd broken the post they'd been tied to.

"Explain yourself!" Lexie yelled, jogging forward so that she could stand in front of Nillias. "This is ridiculous."

"We need to move quickly," Nillias said, maneuvering around her. "There is another Gungivite platoon to the north. They can escort us to a ship we have stationed near Sidney."

"Why. Are. We. Leaving?"

"I will explain later."

Lexie stopped where she was. The Gungivites passed her by until she was last in line. Would Nillias just leave her there? Maybe it would be for the best.

He didn't. Nillias eventually stopped, as did the other Gungivites. He paused and walked back to her, while the rest of the militia circled them both.

Nillias's voice was firm and heavy. "We could have tried to take them, but the odds weren't good. Fifty-three percent, actually, and there were more Essentialist cavalry behind those four that arrived. A whole Essentialist battalion is there now. Our chances of escaping with the control junction were less than thirty percent."

"Okay, I get it, you've got your calculations and your communing, fine. But thirty percent or we all die, right? I thought if we lost this, it was over for you nutjobs. I thought if Diplopol fell into the hands of the Essentialists they would be too powerful for you to stop."

"That's mostly true, but there is one thing you aren't considering. And yes, we could have given our lives for this. We do not fear death. No, the main reason we didn't attack, in fact, is because we needed to protect you."

"What? What do I have to do with this? You're such a crazy nutjob!"

"Did you ever wonder why you're here with us? Yes, we needed you in Anacortes, but why do we need you here—on this mission?"

He did have a point. She had figured she was just part of the Gungivite band. They'd conscripted her, using her mom as leverage, but maybe there was more to it. "Okay, McNutty, why *am* I here?"

"The reason you're here, and the reason we've been teaching you our principles, is because we wanted you to understand, and see for yourself, what these cities are capable of."

"What do you mean? What did the cities do? This has Prefectorate written all over it."

"No. The Prefectorate are certainly complicit, but what you just witnessed is the true power of the ICSM cities. Remember what we talked about in the Gungi-Bites shop in Ganges City. The city wants to maximize the well-being of its citizens, but *citizens* can mean anything, and we think Haplopol did adopt an algorithm to weight citizens based on intelligence, in order to get around protecting rats, flies and bacteria, which would have been untenable."

"So what? Wouldn't that mean it would protect humans?"

"The city itself is more than a billion times smarter than any one human, so the city values itself over all human inhabitants."

She nodded slowly. "Oh … yuck. Okay, but it would still value humans a little bit, right?"

"To preserve the well-being of its citizens, the city needs to gain instrumental resources—a power structure to defend itself. It can't send machines outside of its geographic boundaries, so it uses whatever means it can. Humans are the best means."

"You're saying, it's using … Sanuwans?"

"Yes. Any person, in fact, and not just Sanuwans. We believe it has figured out how to imbue powers of suggestion, sometimes biochemically induced with pharmacological substances, to have people act as agents on its behalf. This way it can be sure to recruit more people quicker, to defend the city externally, and ensure it acquires resources faster. This may appear to conflict with its goal of keeping people happy, but it may see these actions as necessary sacrifices for the future happiness of all its citizens, especially itself. It is also possible that these people are, in fact, happy when they die."

Lexie tried to wade through his words. It took her a moment. "So it's … like … creating an army for itself."

"Yes, and it is an army of utmost efficiency, that will not succumb to petty human desires and will readily commit suicide, as one example, to further its objectives. And now that Diplopol is awakened, the ability of these cities to recruit will expand exponentially."

It was bewildering, but it made sense in a twisted way. Lexie certainly wouldn't have believed it if Nillias hadn't blasted all his nutjob lessons into her head.

And yet, something still didn't fit. "Okay, but you're only proving my point. All this stuff about controlling people makes it that much more important to stop Diplopol from awakening, right?"

"Like I said, we probably would not have succeeded in taking the Diplopol orb, but the greater risk is losing you, because you have the key to a potentially considerable defense. This is why we let you live, that day in Victoria, because of what you know. It may seem like we Observers are omniscient, but that's not true. We know many things, but we are still missing the answers to important questions."

Lexie scratched her head, wrestling with Nillias's psychobabble. The Gungivites around her were increasingly nervous, scanning the horizon behind them with greater frequency. It sounded like horses were galloping in the distance—probably the additional cavalry heading to Diplopol. Lexie heard them even over the ringing in her ears.

But still, she didn't move.

Nillias took a step closer. His eyes were unwavering, locked on hers. "We know why you hate the Prefectorate, Lexie. We know about your mother, and we know you were a pirate, but that's not all. Someone took something from us, a long time ago."

Lexie frowned. Deep down, she had a feeling what it could be, when he mentioned her pirating days. A vision of flames along the shoreline came to her, and the feeling of a hand upon her shoulder. A weight of guilt took hold, even though she couldn't quite articulate why.

"Lexie, the only way to fight back is to awaken the other ICSM cities. If controlled *properly*, other cities can be used to contain Haplopol and Diplopol. But we need the other control junctions, and *very soon*, in order to have a chance."

She grimaced and couldn't help looking down at the road. She remembered the box she'd seen that day after the raid on Maple Bay those many years ago. Of course it wasn't a "dinosaur egg". What a cheeky bastard.

Nillias seemed to be waiting for her to answer, to reveal her culpability, but she couldn't. It was a secret she'd kept for too long.

So Nillias took a deep breath and finished, even though she knew what he was going to say anyway. "We need the control junction that you stole from us, Lexie. It's time you took us to see Warrick Kelemen."

Part II

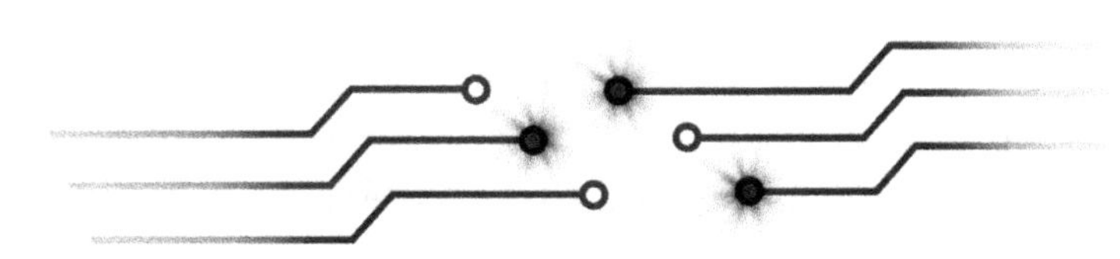

—26—

CUTTER

It came in waves; visions of the past, dreams about the future, delusions about the present.

Cutter was hitting baseballs in the field near his old house, an orange sun melting into the horizon. He *felt* young, like a teenager, but he couldn't know for sure. Time slowed down to a crawl as the baseball he'd tossed up in the air fell down in front of him.

When the bat connected, his mind was knocked into the horizon, careening into the sky—and into another time. Cutter was standing underneath a massive statue, two hundred feet tall. It was hunched over, staring into the horizon with empty eye sockets, bent over its rounded belly.

He was yelling, and pointing. Commanding? Warning? He couldn't be sure. And was this the future? He inhaled deeply and yelled again, and this time his mind was swallowed by his own gaping mouth.

Only to be spat out again into the present. Cutter was on the deck of his ship, the *Undertow*, and a great fjord of fractured rock and staunch forests climbed up around him. He knew the landscape well. Anvil Island was next to them. They were in Howe Strait, closing in on Britannia.

Heath was sitting nearby, staring directly at him, a blade in his hand. The sharp edge was angling in Cutter's direction.

Heath was tall and lanky, almost to an unsettling degree. Cutter had even seen his ribs once, showing through his shirt. His hair was mousy and his skin pale and taut, giving him an anemic appearance. Yet he paid great attention to his health, especially his diet, or so he said.

It would be a privilege to pay attention to such mundane things.

This wasn't all that Cutter saw. There was another reality pulling at him. It was like fingers of shadow were reaching up through the floorboards of the ship. His feet were barely visible through this thick mist. One particularly dark tendril was draped around Heath, like a comfortable blanket on his lap, something a cat or a dog might sleep in. Another spun and shot out behind the back of the ship, like a whirl of soot reaching back to where they'd come from.

It wasn't real. It was the apparition.

Heath's voice was firm. "You were gone for several minutes this time, and your leg—it's shaking."

"I know," Cutter responded.

Heath nodded but didn't relieve him of his stare. It was annoying, but that's why he was here. He was good at what he did.

Cutter pulled out his own knife, ignoring Heath's. His own was clean, but duller. The serrated edge would sometimes have more effect. He pulled up his pant leg. The material was tough nylon, brown with crusty, dried blood on the inside. Underneath, his leg was a parade of red notches and white scars. Several scars were malformed and were taking longer to heal. He'd have to rotate to his back more, or his upper arm.

"Remind me to rotate more," he said. Heath nodded.

He found an opening and cut away, grinding his teeth with each oblique motion. As the blood flowed, the smoke around him abated, sneaking away from the area around his feet and recessing into memory. The whirl of soot trailing behind them faltered and fled into the waves.

Heath handed him a bandage, which he wrapped around the wound. The bandage was almost pointless, he reckoned. In fact, the act of healing, in itself, was silly. It made him feel as if he was on a ridiculous merry-go-round of pain and recovery. It would be better to let the cut breathe, to wear the scars like badges of pride, rather than as shameful secrets. He'd certainly earned them.

"Okay then," Cutter said, standing up, half-turning toward the bow.

But Heath's relentless stare pulled him back. Cutter hadn't been relieved.

"A nail through the foot," Heath said. "Skin-peeling ice. Boiling fires. Snapping bones. Anything but losing my soul to this affliction."

Heath was parroting back Cutter's own words, verbatim. His memory was mostly a fog, but that was one thing he did remember. He'd told Heath those very words when he first recruited him in Portland.

"A finger, this time," Heath said, "for good measure." He handed him the scraper, or what Cutter liked to call "the bitch." It looked like a tool a dentist might use to scrape plaque from your teeth—at least, an Old World dentist. It was metal, with an end that curved into a sharp point.

Cutter hated the bitch.

Nevertheless, he took it from Heath and positioned the point under the fingernail of his pinky finger. The nail was already blue with trauma, but so was every other finger.

It didn't matter.

He levered the bitch under his nail and roared out in pain.

The ship docked in their berth in Britannia. Here they each hauled two bags out of the storage compartment and slung them over their shoulders. Heath was bending his angular form considerably to accommodate the weight.

Britannia was a quaint village of a few hundred people. There was no shortage of housing, but most of these buildings were boxy, barely standing, moss-eaten shacks suitable for little more than camping. The two main docks were impressive, built with thick timbers and stained planking no more than two decades ago, but there were only six ships moored there. Cutter had deliberately chosen their berth off the main docks, on a spit of gray timbers that had fallen into disrepair.

This older pier spilled them out onto a muddy embankment that led up to an open market in front of the two main docks. Here, Valenquez—the chatty Tucson Union merchant—seemed to catch Heath's eye, and so Heath walked over to give his greetings, as he always did. Cutter lingered a few feet away, pulling his hood even tighter over the scraggle of gray-streaked hair that flowed from underneath.

He hung his head low, but every so often cast his eyes up. There were people about: fishermen, a carpenter hammering away in a stall, a woman carrying a bag of envelopes off the dock. Even though he wasn't shaking, and even though he wasn't spouting inane phrases, they were still fearful of him, he could tell. It was evident in the wrinkled nose of the fisherman and the whisper of the post lady to her friend.

He didn't care. He didn't need people to like him. He didn't need them to follow him. He just wanted them to ignore him.

Heath finally pulled away, and they angled up the incline, through the lower town, over the old highway and up Copper Drive, which was a meandering snake of a street that curled up the side of the mountain.

Heath said, "No matter how much you pull your hood over your face, people can tell it's you. Maybe if you actually engaged in a civil conversation once in a while, people wouldn't talk about you the way they do—you wouldn't be such a pariah."

"It's not them I'm worried about."

"Who, then?"

Cutter pointed to the sky.

"Oh, right. We're being *watched*." His voice was laced with sarcasm, and his fingers flashed quotation marks. "Never mind."

At the top of Copper Drive were the nicer houses. These were three- or four-bedroom abodes, replete with fresh paint and no visible structural deformities. Some of them had been substantially refurbished two decades ago, when Britannia had a surge of immigrants. A few hundred more people settled in Britannia because they didn't want to pay the exorbitant docking and trade fees being charged by nearby Squamish, and some of these settlers were reasonably well-to-do.

It didn't last. The latest bout of fiefdom wars ended, and competition turned into begrudging cooperation. Squamish once again became a more practical destination for economy and trade, and the would-be immigrants soon emigrated.

Cutter's house was at the end of a cul-de-sac. It was generally uninviting, covered in gray siding and gray trim, with a dirt-streaked porch monopolizing the front. In front of the house was no lawn but rather a bed of uneven gravel. There was no house number on the building. They walked up the steps, Cutter unlocked the door, and they dumped their bags in the living room.

Cutter sat down in a wooden chair while Heath uncinched one of the bags. He took out a bundle of clothing.

"You may not want to unpack too much," Cutter said. "We're leaving again in two days."

Health turned to him with a *you've got to be kidding me* look.

"This is what I'm paying you for," Cutter said.

"Is it? You're paying me to *keep you healthy*. That's my vocation, and I know that repeated trips for extended durations are *not* healthy for you. You can't keep doing this forever. Plus, you need people in your life: a woman, a man, somebody. I refuse to believe you that no one is out there. What about these people in the letters? Surely you know some of them."

Cutter tried to contain the flood of emotion, to keep his face expressionless. He said, "There's no one. I've got you. That's enough."

"No, it's not. And I'm not going to be here forever. In fact, as I've already told you, in a month I'm heading home for six weeks. Or have you forgotten?"

Cutter hadn't realized it was going to be so soon. Maybe he'd forgotten. He just shrugged and said, "That's fine."

"We need someone else to look after you."

"I survived without you for six decades."

Heath just shook his head. Cutter was glad Heath didn't respond, because he knew he was losing the argument. His affliction had only started a few years ago, but it had been getting worse recently. At least he'd stopped the pointless debate.

"Let's do it now," Cutter said, stopping Heath from unpacking yet again.

Heath raised his eyebrows. "The chair?"

"Yes."

Heath grimaced sourly. "You're the boss."

Cutter led the way down the steps into the basement. He unhooked a lantern from the wall, lit it, moved aside the musty rug, and opened the trap door.

Down they went. They climbed the ladder first, and then down the stairs that spiraled further underground. Heath helped him heave open the large concrete access door. Green plumes streaked the walls and lime-colored dust covered the floors when they reached the adjoining tunnels of the old copper mine. The corridor split right and split left, and they traversed through yet another dusty metal door.

They reached another access door that was recessed into the side of the mineshaft. From the outside it looked wooden but had Faraday cage paneling on the inside. Heath locked it behind him after they entered. Cutter turned on the light switch.

The floodlights flickered on, three of them lagging the others by a few seconds. Huge metal supports arched in front of them, reaching back a good twenty yards. Below this, metal cylinders with open ends jutted out of the walls, with wires and boxy components dangling out of them, like the bowels of a great Old World machine that had been cut open to spill their guts into the room. Stacked against the walls were batteries, crates, shelves of foodstuffs and labeled boxes. The floor of the cavernous chamber was in disarray, with fragmented robots, electrical assemblies and instruction manuals littered about.

Heath walked over to the security panel and typed in his code.

The main terminals at the end of the room came to life.

Cutter navigated around the mess to the back of the room and gave the monitors a quick scan. Everything was in order. Power reserves were at eighty percent, there had been no animal intrusions, and weapons systems were online.

He glanced over at the closest wall placements. The ten combat blast weapons were in their berths and fully powered up. These were like Old World machine guns, except bulkier, and they delivered energy pulses instead of bullets. They also had cutting and energy grenade functions.

He knew all this, and he remembered using them not too long ago, in an altercation with ... he forgot. That wasn't unusual. He'd long since forgotten the means by which many things in the mine had arrived, like the instruction manuals, or the robots, or the security system.

It was the apparition. Its wretched fingers would claw away at his memories at every opportunity.

Speaking of which, despite his recent cutting and the bitch, wisps of smoke remained around his peripheral vision, slowly seeping in, looking for access points into his mind. The fog was never totally gone, but with the chair, it would at least feel like it for a few days.

Cutter glanced around and couldn't find Heath. He must already be at the chair.

He walked around the piles of metal and wire into the treatment room. It was mostly nondescript, also with green-streaked walls, except for a painting on the far side. It was a picture of a courthouse, one built with big, white columns and red brick. He knew that he'd bought it off a traveling merchant in Anacortes, but only because he'd written this fact down in his notebook, and he'd reviewed it again recently. He also knew it was important, that it held great meaning for him, but he often forgot why. Like now, for example.

There were two chairs in the room, one of them occupied by Heath, and wires strung about, connecting to a large metal box protruding from the wall. Cutter sat down in the larger chair, the one with thick rubber armrests, and let Heath put the wire-stuffed cuffs on each arm. He placed the bit in his mouth. Doing this always made Cutter feel as though he was some kind of rabid dog, but it probably saved his teeth. The cuffs felt cold on his wrists.

"Are you ready?" Heath asked.

"No, but go ahead."

Heath nodded, and pulled the main lever down on the metal box.

The electricity flowed through him, shaking him violently. He yelled out over the bit piece, because it was easier to take that way. It felt like every inch of his body was in spasm. His mind was in agony—gut-wrenching, spirit-flushing agony.

Heath did it again.

And he did it one more time.

Cutter slouched in the chair, utterly spent. He felt like he'd been shattered into a million pieces. Heath took the bit out of his mouth and said,

"Okay, time for the diagnostic questions. You ready?"

"Yeah." Cutter was barely able to lift his head.

"What's your real name?"

"Warrick. My real name is Warrick Kelemen."

—27—

Cold Waters

Dryden was sitting with Nate in the living room of Alayna's apartment in downtown Hood River. From here Dryden could see parts of the Columbia River through a large four-paned window. They had opened one of the panes to let air in. The only sound to be heard was from a solitary horse, knocking its shoes on the Old World pavement down below.

Hood River felt smaller now, after where he'd been, and what he'd seen.

Dryden turned away from the window, toward Nate. "Do you like it?" he asked.

Nate was rolling the carving over in his hands, as if there was some hidden feature he was missing. He pulled a long strand of curly hair away from his eye. His hair was light brown, a good blend of Alayna and Dryden, but they had never figured out where the curls came from.

Dryden said, "It's supposed to be like Fidget, your opossum pet in the back yard. Remember him?"

"Okay, Dad. Thanks." Nate set it down gently on the table next to him. His lips formed a grim smile.

The fact that Dryden had to explain it spoke volumes. Either it wasn't a good enough carving, or Nate didn't like it. Probably both.

Dryden reached for the drink he'd placed on his side table. He took a careful sip, assessing the flavors. More berry next time.

"So when is Mom getting home?" Nate asked.

"I don't know. I hope she's back soon, but she's doing something very important, working closely with a Prefectorate general."

"Is she safe there?"

The word *no* wanted to run out of his mouth, but he contained it. "Vicky territory isn't completely stable, but she should be well protected.

General Hatsuo has a huge force occupying the area."

In truth, Dryden was more worried about what Hatsuo might do to her than the Vickies. Even the city itself posed more of a threat.

Dryden said, "I'm sorry I had to leave. I'm sure your Mom is sorry, too, but I'm here now. I'm going to try to be a good dad. If there's something on your mind, I want you to tell me."

Nate frowned, and his eyes turned to the floor. The wheels were turning. There was probably a lot that he wanted to say, but he was too kind to say it. Instead, all he said was, "Thanks, Dad."

"Maybe we can finally take that trip to Portland. I have to write up my notes from Haplopol, but we could probably go in a week or so. What do you think?"

That drew Nate's eyes, at least. "I don't know, Dad. Whatever you want."

Dryden smiled.

They made small talk for a while. Dryden asked Nate about his schoolwork, about metalsmithing, and about his friends. Nate told him just enough to answer his questions but didn't elaborate. Dryden couldn't expect anything more. Hopefully he would open up, in time.

Dryden was standing on a chair, blindly reaching into the back of the highest cupboard in the kitchen. He used to keep an extra bottle of wine there. Once, he'd used it to make a surprise drink for Alayna on Nate's second birthday. There was certainly enough dust in the cupboards to suggest it hadn't been moved, but nothing yet.

He felt something with the tip of his finger. It felt like glass. He couldn't grab it, but he tried to move the bottle toward him by pushing down on it to spin it backward. Indeed, it did roll back quickly, causing dust to cascade into his eyes and forcing him to turn away. The bottle glanced off his head, down his chest and onto the floor. Miraculously, his body must have cushioned the fall. The bottle hadn't broken.

He pulled his shirt up, trying to wipe the dust out of his eyes. It wasn't enough, so he splashed some water onto his face from the pail on the counter. Once his eyes were clear, he reached down to grab the bottle.

There were shoes on the ground, not far back from the bottle—the leathery moccasins that Nate liked to wear. Nate was standing in them.

"Oh, hi, Nate. I have to go to Maxwell's in a bit for a meeting. Will you be home for dinner later?"

"Un huh," Nate said. He turned around and walked to his room.

Dryden knew that it wasn't right, but it was the only thing that kept him going. If he wanted to get to the next day—even the next hour—sometimes he just needed a break, a gentle push in the present to allow him to disembark from his past. He knew many sailors that drank regularly. Fishermen did it. Traders were always sharing drinks with their clients. Why not anthropologists?

It had been this way most of the trip back from Diplopol. How else was he supposed to cope with what he'd done, with the monster he'd enabled? It helped him come to terms with the fact that he was a powerless pawn in Hatsuo's game. With time, all his thoughts of what happened, and what *could* be happening in the north, would fade. With time and maybe a few more drinks.

He took one more sip from his flask as he approached the Curator's Estate.

The estate was away from the municipal buildings and marina offices lining the edge of the Columbia River, on a piece of land next to the much more lively waters of the Hood River tributary. Here, many decades ago, before the Prefectorate came to rule, the locals had built a four-story tall conical temple made out of thick timbers. They had since updated it with a handful of windows on each level, but it still looked like a set of mutant tree trunks clumped together, at least on the outside.

Directly in front of the temple was a large totem pole with the symbols typical of the coastal Essentialists: the blazing sun at the top, shining down on seeded soil, under which ferns, flowers and grasses grew, and finally fish, fowl and a bear were carved into the base. Surrounding the totem was a large field of neck-high grasses and dense bushes, with some choice fruit and evergreen trees reaching up higher in places. Only a few swaths were cut into the field to allow meandering paths to access the temple and the base of the totem. It used to be that the whole field would be cut down regularly, and the gardens tended daily, but the Prefectorate had reduced the curator's staffing a long time ago, and the groundskeepers were the first to go.

Dryden unlocked the main door and entered, immediately veering right. He angled his neck into the open doorway of the curator's office. Maxwell was at his desk, illuminated by a perfect flood of light cast by the only window. Papers and folders were stacked up next to him. Behind him were various curator artifacts strung up on the wall, including miniature totems, a goblet, a bear fur and, most prominently, the crossed axes that used to be the emblem for Hood River.

"Dryden, hi," Maxwell said, looking up from his desk. Maxwell's long hair had been pulled back and tied tight into a tail, but it was still frizzy enough to make him look disheveled. He was growing a short goatee that elongated his already-long face. "Please, come in. Have a seat," he said.

Dryden found a chair across from Maxwell.

"How are you feeling?" Maxwell asked. "Are you settling back in okay?"

"Sure. It's good to see Nate again. I haven't been sleeping well. I suppose that's understandable."

"Completely understandable. I can't imagine being through all that, especially with what happened at Diplopol." Maxwell massaged his chin for a moment. "I have something here, if you need it." He turned around and opened a drawer. He pulled out a glass jar containing a fine, light brown powder. He spooned out a small amount into another jar and pushed it over to Dryden.

"This can help you sleep. Just a dab with some food before bed."

"What is it? Is this one of those home remedies from the eastern Essentialist tribes?"

Maxwell shook his head. "No, no. It's from the Tucson Union, originally, and I've tried it myself. It's extracted from the pineal gland of cows and has an ingredient called melatonin."

Dryden nodded. Since they usually only discussed ICSM history and research, he sometimes forgot about Maxwell's depth of knowledge on all other curator topics.

Dryden fingered the clear vial in his hands, turning it to see the fine powder toss around into different formations. He put it in his coat pocket.

Maxwell was eyeing him. "This work with the ICSM cities, it's so critical. In fact, you should be glad of your calling. It has become an important vocation, one that many would be eager to have. You need to keep at it. We protect sun, soil and seed, so that the eternal spring can deliver its bounty."

Dryden knew Maxwell didn't really believe the Essentialist dogma. But what he said was true, in a sense. There *was* still work to be done. He needed to publish his findings on Haplopol as soon as possible.

"At the same time," Maxwell said, "everyone needs a break—to get perspective. You should consider taking some time off."

"I know. I'll be going with Nate to Portland next week, but only for a few days."

"Take a couple weeks off."

"I'd rather not. I have trouble with idle time. Besides, although I finished a draft of my first article, most of my research writeup isn't finished, and I need to send some of it to Leopold for review. I was thinking we could do a joint publication on the article."

"Your prerogative. And yes, that's probably best as a publication strategy. Leopold's name recognition will certainly help find a publisher with good distribution. I do think your draft needs some editing, though."

"Of course, but is this about the influence of the experiential rooms again? I have to include that. It could be the most important part of my research."

Maxwell grimaced. "*Could be* is the right term. It's speculative. More so, you cite events that the Prefectorate would probably not want exposed."

"I anonymized the people involved."

Maxwell pulled up the folder Dryden had given him and opened it to an earmarked page. He read, "… three Sanuwanese committed suicide at the inception of Diplopol to further the city's interests." He put down the folder and held the bridge of his nose. "Hardly anonymous. Everyone's heard about this incident, and so everyone knows who was involved. Besides, it's just way too inflammatory to cite events that occurred during the annexing of Vicky territory. The Sanuwans are already pointing fingers at the Prefectorate for manipulation and blackmail. Your reporting could also conflict with the Prefectorate representation of events to the Vicky population. No, this has to be excluded."

"People need to know about this," Dryden said.

"No one is going to publish it in this form," Maxwell said.

The idea was abhorrent to Dryden—that work this important might never be published—but maybe Maxwell was right. He was curator for a reason. He knew how to couch their work within the context of politics of the day, and he knew the unspoken rules of how research could be accommodated within the curation system.

"Maybe I could de-emphasize it," Dryden offered. "I can exclude what happened at Diplopol, and then include my other findings about the experiential rooms as a discussion point, with a supplementary data addendum." It sickened him to say it, but he knew he would lose the argument unless he gave ground. He also wondered if he could inform Leopold some other way. It was possible Leopold could champion the idea and take on the publication risk himself.

Maxwell tilted his head to the side, pondering. "Fine," he said. "I'll take a look at it after you modify it, but I need to see it soon. Tomorrow, in fact."

"Why tomorrow?"

"There's another reason I called you in today."

Dryden only raised his eyebrows. He was feeling tired and couldn't bother speculating on what it could be.

"I'm moving to Victoria," Maxwell said. "I've been given a position at the Dressler Institute—Associate Dean of Cultural Antiquity. I will still be working with you remotely on some projects, at least until we can get a new curator in town, but I'm leaving in two days."

"Wow. That's great for you. Congratulations. I had no idea."

Maxwell smiled politely and waved at the air as if it was nothing. "It should be an exciting position. I'll have more latitude than in Hood River."

"So I guess you're not really worried about my arguments after all."

Maxwell's smile thinned, and soon disappeared altogether. "Sure I am, Dryden, but even if the ICSM cities are having some kind of hidden influence on people's behaviors, I'm sure we can talk people out of it. Victoria will stabilize soon, just like all cities do after periods of conflict."

"No, it won't. The influence of the cities—it's more potent than that."

Maxwell only stared at him, waiting for him to finish. Dryden knew it would be pointless. If Maxwell didn't believe what he wrote, with all his supporting evidence, no verbal argument would convince him. He gritted his teeth. "I guess we'll have to agree to disagree, but I urge you to exercise caution when you visit Diplopol."

"Yes, of course." Maxwell's smile returned. "Hatsuo has already extended an invitation to meet, so I will have protection if I need it. I will definitely heed your warning."

Dryden felt numb. Of course Hatsuo had invited Maxwell to Diplopol. It was remarkable how quickly Dryden had been replaced. Hatsuo must want Maxwell as his new right-hand man on all things ICSM.

Maxwell squinted at him. "Are you sure you're okay? You seem a little off today."

"Yes, I'll be fine. It's like you said, I'm still trying to process everything."

"Good, good. So can you get me a copy by tomorrow?"

Dryden didn't answer at first. Seconds ticked away like hammers rapping on his skull, each one heavier than the last. Finally, he said, "Sure. I can do that."

"Fantastic," Maxwell said. "I won't keep you any longer." Maxwell turned his focus to the papers on his desk.

Dryden didn't go home after the meeting. Instead, he strolled through the field in front of the temple, aimlessly following the trails carved in the verdure. He circled the totem and took a path that went down a grade in the terrain. It opened up into steps of stone that led to a broad wooden dock hanging low over the river.

The water was rushing by quickly here—rippling, churning, boiling into eddies. He liked the sound of it. It was a beautiful white noise that dampened the pulses of worry that would radiate from his mind.

He pulled his flask out and took a long sip. He strolled up the dock, and down the dock.

The river drew him closer. He bent over and peered into it.

He could almost feel the cold waters on his skin. In fact, he felt like he was already there, being pushed up on white curls, or pulled under by dark currents.

It wasn't only Ben that died that day, he realized. He'd been drowning ever since.

He reached over and dipped his fingers in the water, closing his eyes. The chill channeled up through him, and it felt right. It would be so easy to topple forward, to be taken away by the current, to leave this world behind and become one with the eternal spring. And it would be fitting to die here, the same way Ben died. Fitting and just.

His body started to shift, slowly arcing over the waters.

Until his hand shot up and gripped the edge of the dock. He righted himself.

Nate was at home. Dryden had promised to make dinner for him.

He stood up, finished off the last drag from the flask, and walked back up the stone steps.

—28—

Stolen Letters

The Anacortes Shipping Company facility was a patchwork of big hangars connected by covered walkways. It could have accommodated quite a few horses, but it didn't, and Lexie could see why. With all the traffic, it would be messy. As it was, there was a considerable mess of dung trampled into the exterior parking lot, along with horses laden with mail and parcels, or carts weighed down with boxes.

Nillias was with her, as well as one of his Observer friends named Emry. Emry was pudgy, with persistently flushed cheeks, and he liked to wear a red wig. He said the wig helped him look different from other Gungivites, and it gave him a sense of individuality. Lexie didn't say so, but individuality was something he was sorely lacking, since he was just as stone-faced as Nillias most of the time. To be nice, Lexie told him the red wig helped, and he just blinked at her, as nutjobs do.

It didn't help that both Emry and Nillias had the occasional spell where they would press on their temples and rock back and forth, breathing heavily. She'd seen Nillias do it a couple of times before, when they were in Anacortes, but Emry did it more often. Nillias explained that it was a side effect of not being able to access his implant—since they were in retcher territory.

It wouldn't be a big deal, unless one of them had one of these fits at the wrong time.

There were a number of lines in the main office, with ASC workers manning the desk at the front of them. The longest was for shipping licenses. There were also two lines for letters and packages. The three of them took a position in a line for *General Inquiries.*

Lexie had to admit that shipping was one racket that the half-drunk skunks of Three Rivers were good at. Pretty much anything traveling transcontinental, to or from the Salish Sea nations, went through Anacortes. This was in part because there was a tidy route through the mountains that led to Anacortes, and Anacortes had a substantial set of marinas. And nobody wanted to ship things through the mountain fiefdom tribes to the north. You'd be lucky if it arrived in two pieces. Southward could work, excepting the hassles with Essentialist tariffs and red tape rigmarole. Anacortes people did their fair share of grifting, but shipping tariffs were actually downright reasonable compared to docking fees.

A few minutes later, it was their turn at the front.

The ASC worker was a pale woman with dark eyes and an irreverent stare. "How can I help you?" she asked.

Lexie said, "Yeah, thanks. I wanted to know when you'd typically get letters in from the east. Is it daily or do they come in bulk shipment?"

"They come in bulk, but *east* is a little word for a big place. Where, specifically?"

"Well, Spoke territories. Maybe Seeville, but also Quebec."

The woman raised her eyebrows. "Now that *is* east. I was thinking you meant Great Falls or Omak. We don't get much in from Quebec or the Spokes, excepting through the red line, in the north. That's cuz Essentialists don't take kindly to us delivering their mail. But yeah, when it does come it usually comes in with the Thursday shipment, three days from now."

"Thanks, that's helpful."

"You do know about that war going on out east?" the woman said sardonically. "There's been disruptions to the mail because of it. It's slowed to a trickle, in fact, and I'm not sure we've had anything at all from the Spokes or Quebec recently."

"Yeah, thanks. Good to know. Hey, we're also looking for a friend. I wanted to ask if someone has come in here asking similar questions about mail from the east. It would be an older guy, with scraggly hair, always wears a hood."

The woman blinked at her. "We can't remember everyone that comes in."

"Yeah, thought so, worth a shot."

"But you could make a special inquiry."

"What's that?"

The woman pulled out a handwritten form that said *Special Inquiry*. All it said on it was *Fifty Vicky medallions*, with a signature line.

"How does the special inquiry process work?" Emry asked.

Lexie flashed a *don't mess this up* look at Emry and smiled back at the ASC worker. "Don't mind my friend," she said. "No need to answer that." She signed the name *Patricia Barber* on the paper and passed over the money. It was all she could think of on the fly, and she needed a haircut.

The woman counted the money and put it in her jacket pocket. "Yeah, so I've seen a fellow that meets that description. He's been in a few times asking me or Chad in the back room about mail from Spoke lands, and when it comes through processing in Burlington. Hard to forget him, he looked so grim all the time. He's usually with a tall, lanky fellow who's a bit more agreeable. Lucky, too, or he would probably get a punch in his nosy nose."

"Yeah, I know what you mean. Thanks. So when would the red line mail go through Burlington?"

"I guess it'd be a day beforehand, so Wednesday."

"What time?"

"Don't know, but like I said, you'll be lucky if it comes through at all."

So it was in Burlington that they found Warrick. Nillias's men saw him try to nab the mail from the red line carrier's horse at an old inn. It had been an educated guess, based on the premise that he'd stolen the mail from this woman Cecile out of Leo's mailbox before. That, and the fact that Leo hadn't received any mail from her for a while now.

Lexie had no idea why Warrick would want this particular brand of mail, but she knew that when he wanted something, there wasn't much you could do to get in his way. Just ask Quelby Farish, who tried to sneak some of Warrick's gadget stash off the ship one day. Although it might take a while to get an answer; corpses tend to not be very responsive.

Burlington was just inland from Anacortes, no more than twenty miles. It was a bit of a ghost town. This was principally because some big old buildings had been severely charred and blasted during the fall. The husks of rusting-out cars were everywhere, some of them melted down by retchers, others flattened. It gave Lexie the impression that something big happened here during the fall. Generally speaking, it was a bad idea to stick around places where something big happened.

Still, there was a hotel there, a big boarding house to accommodate the shipment processing facility, and an old inn. It was at the inn where Nillias's men held Warrick.

Emry led Lexie and Nillias into the room.

It was dark, with only a few rays of light seeping in from ripples in the edges of drawn curtains. Most of the furniture had been pushed against the walls, and the bed had been stripped of linens. There were a lot of odorous men in the room, but the stink wasn't just sweat. It was something ranker, like death and decay. Lexie imagined this was what rat farts would smell like.

Four of Nillias's Gungivite military types were in the room, standing with holstered pistols. They weren't Observers. They had crew cuts, and bandanas covering their mouths. One of them was holding a heavy bundle—energy weapons, or so Emry said, that they acquired from Warrick. When Nillias, Lexie and Emry entered the room, these four others stepped back and to the sides to reveal their prizes.

Warrick and his lanky companion were tied to wooden chairs, their backs to the windows. The lanky man was sitting upright. He wasn't quite defiant, but there was a smugness to his expression that suggested this was all very boring to him. And Warrick, well, he always looked a bit haggard, but this time he looked like he'd been run over by a horse cart. Deep lines fanned out from his eyes, his beard had thick streaks of gray, and there was what looked like crusted blood all over his pants. He hadn't aged well.

"Lex?" Warrick asked, his eyes widening.

"You look like shit," she said.

He only shrugged. His expression soured and he frowned at her. "What's this all about?"

She felt a compunction to apologize. She had led the Gungivites to him, and they had just kidnapped him, but it was more than that. He'd always seemed so strong, so when she had left him years ago she'd told herself he would be fine, despite his strange antics and periods of moping. Now she wondered if she'd been wrong—if maybe she should have stood up for him when he was falling down.

But this wasn't the time. This was an interrogation.

There was a chair in front of Warrick and the lanky man. She took it. "First, who's your friend?"

"My name is Heath Penante," the tall one responded. "I am Warrick's assistant."

Lexie raised her eyebrows at Warrick. "A personal assistant? You're moving up in the world."

She was trying to keep things light—conversational—but Warrick wouldn't have it. "I'm not sure why you took us," he said, "but you don't know what you're doing. Let us go and you won't be hurt."

"Who's going to hurt us?" she asked.

He shook his head.

She sighed. "Look, Warrick, I don't feel like this is entirely fair, what we've done here, but at the same time, what we need is important—so important that what *I* feel doesn't matter."

"I don't know what you want, but you're not getting it. I'll be dead before I help that witch."

"That witch?"

He frowned at her and allowed himself a tight grin. "Yeah. You know who I'm talking about."

"Actually, I don't." She was playing dumb a bit. She rubbed her chin and unfolded the contents of the letter that Warrick had been trying to pilfer from the red line horseman. It read:

Dear Leo,

I can only hope you're still alive. We've heard troubling rumors about machine cities awakening. As a result, we are sending a contingent to Anacortes. If you can, please find Warrick Kelemen and keep him with you. He may be the key to resolving many of our troubles, as well as yours.

Please respond, if only to acknowledge this letter. We have no way of knowing if you're receiving my messages.

Always your friend,

Cecile

Lexie folded up the letter and rubbed her chin. "So, this Cecile … she's the witch?"

"Lex, I taught you to be a better liar than that. It's painfully obvious you're working with her."

Lexie glanced over at Nillias. Maybe he knew this Cecile person? But he shook his head.

"Okay, Warrick, let's say, for the sake of argument, that you're right. We are all little nutjob goblins who love working for witches. In that case, why don't you tell us why we *shouldn't* work for her? Make your case, and maybe we'll stop helping her."

Warrick frowned and rubbed the top of his head. He looked like he was concentrating, but he winced as if it caused him pain. "She's trouble. She's coming to find me—to take what I have."

"Which is?"

Warrick glanced sideways at Heath, but said nothing.

"Okay, let's try looking at this a different way," Lexie said. "If we are all chummy with this witch, as you say, we must all know who she's working for. Why don't you remind us who that is? There should be nothing to lose. Or maybe she's lying to us, which would mean we'd best know about it."

Warrick nodded. It took him a while to respond. His eyes were scrolling over the floor, as if he might find the answer written upon the carpet. "There's a horrendous machine," he said. "She's … she needs me to control it—to help it destroy us all." When he finished, he put his head in his hands.

Another machine? Lexie glanced at Nillias. He raised an eyebrow, evidently curious about this new development.

And yet, she had to admit, it was quite possible she was trying to interpret the ramblings of a madman.

She couldn't help but notice the smell again. It was like a cross between a fisherman's underwear and a dead dog. These guys had a serious problem.

"Excuse me," Heath said. "My client has a health condition. These questions are difficult for him—painful, even. And he has trouble recalling the distant past. I don't think it's ethical, nor is it worth your time, to pursue this line of inquiry."

"Ethical?" Lexie asked. "That's a word you don't hear often around these parts. It's about as common as flying seals, and about as relevant to your situation. But I guess since you insist on us having uppity lessons on morality, let me tell you why we're really here."

Heath shrugged. Warrick's face was downcast, but his eyes looked up at her attentively.

"Haplopol and Diplopol are both awake," she said, "and messing with people's minds. They're catching more people every day in their little web, and also building machines and factories that will get a lot of people hurt. Unless we stop them, a whole lot of people are going to die, or at least become witless drones. Letting that happen seems just a little bit more *unethical* than giving someone a bad headache, don't you think?"

She was watching Warrick closely as she spoke. He had a dark look in his eyes, but his expression was unrevealing.

She continued, "Now, Warrick, I'm very much aware, from the old days on the *Rockfish*, that you understand something about the ICSM cities—how powerful they are, and how dangerous—so you must know we're not pulling your leg. And this Cecile woman you're worried about, why would she have anything to do with it? She's been in the east all this time, fighting a different war. She has a relationship with Leo, fine, but why should that matter to us? I swear to you *on my mother's life* that this is true. I know nothing about this Cecile person, whether she's a witch or a ghost or the damn boogeyman."

Warrick seemed to be considering her words. He said, "Even if I believed you, how could I possibly help?"

"You have the control junction orb for Pentapol, what you called your *dinosaur egg*. We need it so we can fight back—to stop these cities that are out of control."

Warrick sat back to ponder her words. He glanced at Nillias, giving him a once-over. "You mean the *Gungivites* need them. Why would I help them? I've told you to be careful—"

"Yes. The Gungivites. Let's set things straight, though. We *stole* this control junction from the Gungivites. You must remember that. It was a nasty day, burned into my brain because you lit a good chunk of Maple Bay on fire, so I imagine you must have some recollection. Despite that, the Gungivites don't want revenge. All they care about is stopping the cities. They've taught me why, and *shown* me why, and I believe them. I would try to convince you, but I'm pretty sure you already know they need to be stopped."

Warrick's eyes were again cast toward the floor. Seconds ticked away. Lexie tried not to breathe too deeply, for fear she might upset his concentration. That, and the smell might make her gag.

Finally, Warrick said, "How do I know the Gungivites aren't working with Cecile?"

Nillias stepped forward. "You have my word. We are not working with anyone named Cecile from the east."

Warrick rolled his eyes. "Your word, eh?"

"Yes."

Warrick shook his head. "I wouldn't give a single medallion for the word of a man I've never met."

Nillias stared at him, unflappable.

Warrick sighed. "Look, I'm not sure if I want to help you, but it doesn't matter. I do remember that day, but I misplaced the control junction a long time ago, during a spell of amnesia. You heard Heath: I forget things. This is one of them, one of a thousand objects I've lost over the years. So even if I believed you, it wouldn't matter."

There was a quiet in the room as they absorbed Warrick's words. He could be telling the truth. Otherwise, he would have just said he wouldn't do it.

To think that he could have *lost* it. It wasn't as if they could just retrace his steps. They might never find it.

"Sorry," Warrick said. "So what now?"

"We take you to Ganges," Nillias said.

"Whoa, whoa," Warrick said. "What's the point of that? Just let us go and we won't mention this little incident."

"We may have methods to help you remember," Nillias said. "Pharmaceuticals, psychotherapy. We must try."

Warrick didn't look happy at all. Lexie could see his muscles tensing in his cheeks, and his eyes growing in fervor, like a caged animal. She'd seen him like this before. She was about to tell him to calm down, but Heath beat her to it.

"Don't do it," Heath said, addressing Warrick.

"What?"

"It's suicide," Heath said, casting his eyes around the room, pausing on each of his seven captors for an instant. He poked his chin out and elevated his voice, addressing the whole room. "I'm sorry, but I cannot allow my client to go to Ganges Island. He cannot be away from his personalized therapy for an extended duration. It would put him in severe jeopardy."

Lexie said, "Listen, mister. You seem like you might be a half-decent person. A bit uppity, but well-intentioned. Let me be clear about something, though. You've been kidnapped. You aren't in a position to *not allow* anything."

Heath's eyes drifted back to Warrick.

Warrick nodded, ever so slightly.

Heath turned to Lexie and said, "We are in disagreement, Lexie, because I believe *I am* in such a position. Why? Because only I know where the control junction is located. I will tell you its location if you agree to release us once you've obtained it. For that, we will need your word, and we will hold you to it."

Nillias didn't flinch. "You have it," he said.

Heath said, "I have sold it to the Emperor Moraine of Pemberton for an attractive price." He smiled thinly at Warrick, as if it was something to be proud of.

"Oh, great," Lexie said.

Nillias's eyes narrowed ever so slightly. Even he was worried.

She'd been hoping it was just hidden under a rock somewhere, or in a Vicky safe. Instead, it was in the possession one of the most violent and unpredictable warlords of the mountain fiefdoms.

This was going to be messy.

Thankfully, she knew someone who could help.

—29—

Foreign Visitors

"Dad!" Nate called out. "Someone's here!"

Dryden lifted his head off the pillow, which was damp where sweat had accumulated. He'd been sleeping. His head pounded. He moved slowly so as to not exacerbate the pulses of pain, eventually turning over and sitting up in his bed. Only when he'd righted himself did he properly open his eyes.

A blonde woman was sitting on the end of his bed. Her smile revealed a large gap in her front teeth on both the bottom and top rows, and she was wearing a yellow- and gray-striped vest over thick black leather. Two other men dressed fully in black stood behind her, as well as a similarly-clad woman whose raven hair had a blue streak in it. Nate lingered in the doorway to Dryden's room, next to the raven-haired woman.

"Who are you people?" Dryden asked. "How did you get in here?"

"Your son let us in," the blonde woman said. "Good kid." She had a twang in her accent.

"Sorry, Dad," Nate said. He was visibly distraught, speaking quickly. "They just started walking in and I didn't know what to do."

Dryden took inventory of the people one more time. There were large bulges under their clothing—weapons. And the woman on his bed was wearing a yellow-striped Merchant Merc vest. He'd seen these mercenary types come through Portland before. Plus, they all had scars, and patches on their clothing. He could be sure of one thing: these were people who knew violence.

"Now don't get too frazzled," the blonde woman said. "I can tell you've got the jiggershanks. We didn't mean to startle you, and we've got no designs on your kid here."

"But you do have designs on me?"

She showed her gap-toothed smile again. "We just want to ask you some questions—but where are my manners? We haven't been formally introduced. My name is Rosalie. This here behind me is Pierre, and this is Laurent." she gestured to the two men behind her. "And the woman with the funky hairdo is Cecile."

"Why are you here?"

"Seems some people around town thought you might be able to help us. Whachew do for a livin'?"

"I'm an anthropologist."

"Really? That's unusual. I know lots of people who throw up, but never a throw-up apologist. I suppose it's better than not apologizing." She winked at him. "In any case, we heard you know something about the *Issum* Cities— "

"ICSM," Cecile interrupted, stepping forward. "ICSM cities. We heard you recently came back from the north—that you've been to both Haplopol and Diplopol. Is this true?" She also spoke with a foreign accent—one that Dryden couldn't quite place.

He wasn't sure whether he wanted to be helpful to these people or not, but lying would almost certainly get him and Nate into trouble. "It's true," he said.

"*Bien*," Cecile said. "What can you tell us? What did you learn?"

He wondered if he shouldn't answer, or just give them the canned response he'd heard from so many about the "wonders of Haplopol." Maxwell had urged him to not spread rumors, saying he should keep his concerns about the cities to himself and limit any communication of the research findings to the proper publication channels.

But no one was really listening to Dryden anyway. And if the Prefectorate came after him, he didn't care what they did to him. Not anymore.

He swallowed, trying to prevent his voice from croaking. "The cities have been awakened. Diplopol is being rebuilt and creating an external industrial complex around the city. I believe both cities have a form of influence over people's minds that make them act only on the city's behalf. These manipulated citizens are leaving the cities and recruiting more people. Millions could become unwitting slaves, helping the cities grow and flourish—or do whatever the cities want."

Cecile's eyebrows rose, and she shared a look with Rosalie. "Well, you do get to the point quickly. I like that. How do you know all this?" she asked.

"I studied the citizens in Haplopol and saw how they became enraptured by the city. I believe it's primarily through the use of experiential rooms, but there could be a pharmacological component. A woman I knew committed suicide to ensure Diplopol could be awakened. That's what made me certain, but there was a great deal of other evidence."

"So what are the Essentialists doing about this problem?"

Dryden threw up his hands. "Probably nothing. They don't believe me. Many are under the spell already, and their voices are louder than mine. Others think it's too outlandish, including my own boss, the former curator of Hood River."

"Do you know Leopold Halsey? What is his position on the subject?"

"Of course I know him. He hasn't seen my findings, but they are en route to him now. I hope to do a joint publication with him. But how do you know Leopold? Where are you people from?"

"Best not worry about all that," Rosalie said. "Being smart ain't what it used to be. Just ask the quail that jumps before the dog barks."

"The quail that … what? Why not? How do I know your intentions are good? You just barged into my house out of nowhere."

Cecile came closer to him. She kneeled down, touched his arm and closed her eyes, as if he was the eternal spring and she was in prayer. "*C'est vrai*. You don't know us, or what we've seen. I can tell you that we are weary travelers. We have come far from the east, all the way across the continent, and are heading north to the Salish Sea. We have sailed down the Columbia, as it is a faster and safer route than the northern passages. Our ship has been docked in Hood River for the night. We learned of you from a local innkeeper."

"I've always wondered what's happening in the east, but we hear so little. Can you tell me what—"

She put her hand up, arresting his speech. Her brow furrowed, as if she was about to scold him. "There are many horrors in the east, too many to mention. It is a war of great cost, and one that continues to escalate. But I can't tell you more, because the information could fall into the hands of the enemy, an enemy who has more eyes and ears than you can possibly imagine. What I can tell you is that we intend to stop these cities from enslaving your people. I assure you that we must, or we will all perish."

She stood up and stepped away from Dryden's bed. "So, we will continue on our way. We will visit Leopold in Anacortes, and we will tell him of your welcome information. Please excuse our intrusion. *Au revoir.*" She turned toward the doorway.

He was relieved they were leaving and glad they hadn't hurt him or Nate, but his intellectual curiosity triggered a connection that he thought could be relevant. "Wait, there's something else."

Cecile stopped at the doorway. Dryden's head was still pounding, so he was having trouble getting the words out in the right order. "When Haplopol was awakened … I remember. There was an aerial drone attached to the control junction orb. It was like a spider, with propellers on it. The city believed it came down through the tower exhaust ducts and may have carried the control junction in, or just brought it to life. I wondered, since there was a machine war in the east, if that could have come from …" He trailed off. Cecile had blanched, and Rosalie's head had recoiled in surprise, as if he'd just flashed some lewd pornography.

"What?" he asked.

"I'm so sorry," Cecile said. "There has been a change in plan. You're coming with us."

Dryden didn't object. He wasn't in a mood to contemplate the repercussions of refusing. It was true that he couldn't be sure of the intentions of this exotic group of foreigners, but at least these people wanted to listen to him. Nobody else did.

Ever since he'd left Hood River for Haplopol he'd felt like a piece of driftwood that had been dislodged and taken downriver. Now he was being pulled in another direction, by yet another strong current. Maybe this time it would take him to a better place.

But it meant he had to renege on taking Nate to Portland, yet again. Nate wasn't happy, but he seemed to understand, having seen the reason for Dryden's change of plan firsthand.

Dryden was aboard their ship in less than two hours. In that time, under the watchful eye of Pierre and Laurent, he had gone about packing and dropping Nate off at Alayna's parents' place. They were only too happy to take him. They'd been stopping by frequently in the last few weeks, pretending to be friendly but always asking about Nate's well-being. Their concerns were self-evident, and probably valid.

Dryden also stopped to check their mail and bought a few items at the trading outpost for the trip. He went with the cheap vodka this time, instead of whiskey or wine. It was clear, colorless, and easier to carry.

At his mail stop he was surprised to see a shoebox-sized package from Sergio, all the way from Astoria. Inside was the ship in a bottle that Sergio had promised to send him, with the masts down and secured by barely visible strings, packed tightly in crumpled strips of paper. He almost left it at home, but reconsidered. Maybe he could try to make one himself, using this one as an example. Maybe Nate would prefer a ship in a bottle instead of another carving. He stuffed the box in his bag with the rest of his clothes and supplies.

The ship they'd chartered was called the *Debutante*. It was one of the sailing yachts that did runs up and down the Columbia—an Old World ship made principally of fiberglass, which was rare. The refurbished paneling on its sides gave it a patchy look. Ostensibly, these panels had been placed there to fix holes or strengthen the integrity of the decaying hull. The sails were also patchy, but more like a quilt—squares and triangles wrinkled together and hung loose on the main mast. Hopefully, the sails needed only to be passable since they were heading downstream.

Once aboard, Pierre escorted Dryden along the main deck to the stern of the ship, where there was a sitting area with cushions set in a square. Cecile was standing by the rail, looking across the choppy river toward the mountains. Pierre whispered something in her ear and took Dryden's bag into the main hold.

"You live in a beautiful place, Dryden," Cecile said.

"Yes, I know."

She turned to him. "And I appreciate you letting us take you away from it."

"Well, yes. What you're doing is important."

"It is, and that is why you need to understand, I will do what must be done. I may seem cruel, but I am not a cruel person."

It was a veiled threat. He was glad he hadn't put up a fuss about leaving. He nodded compliantly.

She sat down on cushion across from him. "Two rules that you must abide by. One: you tell nothing of our mission to anyone, including our names and where we are from. And *anyone* includes the two crew that are manning this charter vessel. You keep your mouth shut when they are nearby. Two: we tell you who is friend or foe. You do not make that determination."

"Friend or foe? Are we going to be fighting people? I thought you were going to talk to Leopold."

She shook her head and grimaced as if he was a naïve child. "We may make it to Anacortes, but after that, whether it's your ICSM cities, the Essentialists or someone else, conflict is virtually assured, *mon ami*."

He nodded and glanced over at Hood River to see the quaint houses, tidy shops and rolling hills covered in mist. It had never looked as inviting as it did at that moment. Cecile was right. He *did* live in a beautiful place. Alayna's parents' house was obscured behind a large block of buildings, but he stared in that direction nonetheless. In his mind he saw Nate sitting there in the apartment. He was stooped over, turning the opossum carving in his hands.

It was certainly his imagination. Nate hated the carving.

Cecile had turned to look across the river again. They sat in silence as the ship broke away from the dock and was taken by the current. A crewman with a shaved head and brown coveralls unfurled the main sail and it braced against the wind.

Dryden began triaging the many questions he had for Cecile. There was one that seemed the most burning. He knew she might not answer it, but it was worth a try. He waited until they were well away from the dock before he asked.

"What's the significance of the aerial drone?"

She'd been writing notes on a pad. It reminded him of Alayna, although what Cecile was writing seemed to be much more structured, like a report. Certainly not idle musings about the world around them. She looked up and stared into his eyes. "I suppose you'll need to know eventually," she said. Cecile did have quite a stare. Dryden found it hard not to look away. Finally, she looked down and took a moment to gather herself before she continued. "There's another machine intelligence. It is our main enemy in the east, and it has dispersed aerial drones across the continent. Some of these have been accessing caches of electronics, to try to rebuild Old World infrastructure. Others have flown great distances, above retcher altitudes, and found hidden charging stations. We're worried that what you saw is one of these drones—that it awakened Haplopol, and could be controlling it. It makes the situation much worse than before."

"Why? Why does it matter if this other machine is controlling the ICSM cities?"

"Because this is a contest of proliferation. Our enemy is entrenched in the east, and growing in strength. We were worried it would ally with the ICSM cities, giving it an even greater resource base. The ICSM cities are established centers that do not have the threat of retchers, and with significant computing infrastructure and power. In other words, they are valuable assets for either side of our conflict. If our enemy has been responsible for their awakening, it could mean it has an even greater degree of control on the cities, and thus the cities may pose an even greater threat to us."

He had to pause to digest her words. He didn't know many people who spoke like Cecile. Yes, she was French, but beyond that she had a level of sophistication that he'd seldom encountered, and what she was saying was suggestive of complex issues that required considerable thought for him to synthesize.

After contemplating her words for a few moments, he found he was caught up on one cog in her wheel of logic. "I … I just don't know about that. It doesn't seem right. I've studied the ICSM cities most of my life. I would have thought they would have protective measures against being taken over by other machines, especially the other machine cities. And the way the city worked—the constraints, the officiant control—it was all in line with our historical findings. If your enemy took it over, you'd think it would act differently."

She squinted at him. Her mouth opened, but she didn't speak. Instead, she turned to look out along the banks of the river. Finally, she said, "It could have fooled you. We are dealing with superintelligent machines. They are like gods, many times more powerful than your … what do the coastal Essentialists call it? Ah yes, the *eternal spring*. These machines can anticipate our every move, do things we can't even imagine. So all I can say is, I hope you're right, but we can't count on it."

Rosalie appeared and took a seat next to Cecile. She was eating what looked like a turnip with the side of her mouth. "Well, what do you think? Cecile really gets up in your noggin with her fancy-pants words." She turned to Cecile. "You're not scaring him away, are you?"

"No, it's fine," Dryden offered before Cecile could speak. "I appreciate the information."

"Don't worry," Rosalie said, slapping his knee. "I'm just yankin' her handlebars. Me and Cecile are best buds now, we've traveled so long together."

"Do you have a question for Dryden?" Cecile asked. She looked annoyed.

"Actually, I do. Something I've been wondering about for a while. Where did you get that bleach-blond hair dye? My roots are starting to show—I need to clean up my look."

"It's natural. I have blond hair."

"Really? I haven't seen it that blond before. I bet I could rustle up a new hubby with a shiny do like that."

"*Tant pis pour lui*," Cecile said.

Rosalie laughed. "Yeah, poor bloke. Just got to make sure he doesn't ask about my exes."

Dryden couldn't help himself. "What happened to your exes?"

"Don't you worry about that, frosty top. Remember, need-to-know only," she said.

There was a moment of silence, until Cecile said, "They're dead."

"Oh," Dryden stammered. "I'm so sorry … I didn't—"

Rosalie laughed again. "Don't be sorry. I'm glad they're dead. I done kilt them."

Dryden looked to Cecile. She wasn't smiling. Her mouth was a grim line. Could it be true? This woman Rosalie was making him more than a little nervous. He'd heard the Merchant Mercs were dangerous. Most of them were trained killers.

He couldn't help glancing back down the Columbia—toward home—but home had long since disappeared behind a bend in the river.

"You okay, frosty?" Rosalie asked. "You don't look so good."

"I'm fine," Dryden said.

"Hey, it's okay," Rosalie said. "If you're seasick I know you'll apologize."

—30—

The Road to Pemberton

The morning sunshine lent an amber hue to the stalks of grain presiding over the fields as the column of horses wound its way through the farms of Chilliwack. A cool breeze bit at Lexie's skin, prompting her to don her scarf. Despite the welcome reprieve from overcast skies, autumn was just around the corner.

There were eight of them in all. Warrick and Heath rode at the front with Nillias and Emry, their cuffed hands linked to Nillias's horse by a loose assembly of rope. Behind them rode two of the non-Observer Gungivite militia. These were lithely built and didn't talk much. They followed orders from Nillias and Emry without question. Lexie was riding at the back with Tarnation.

Yeah, that's right. Tarnation. She'd recommended him for the trip because he'd spent a good five years up in the mountain fiefdoms, doing odd jobs. He knew the local idiosyncrasies and allegiances better than anyone. Plus, he knew how to throw his weight around, should the need arise, which it very well could.

The ride from Anacortes had been mostly uneventful. They'd had to pass through Abbotsford, a decaying Old World suburb frequented only by drifters and vagabonds. The buildings were in various states of collapse: stripped siding, broken walls, and caved-in roofs. It was too close to the Kuvar fever lands for anyone to consider taking up permanent residence. Lexie saw a few scavengers darting between buildings, but no one on the road.

Chilliwack, on the other hand, was actually quite picturesque, with well-seamed farming plots and tall three-level farmhouses covered with fully tiled roofs. The homesteads were scattered about a broad valley carved out by the Fraser River.

An escort soon found them, which wasn't surprising. No self-respecting municipality would let eight suspicious-looking, well-armed people ride on through without at least a little bit of encouragement.

The five men were all equipped with bows, short swords and thick leather armor, but they were no more than overgrown kids. They kept their distance and would often whisper and point at Tarnation.

At one point, Tarnation caught wind of the whispering and fell back toward the escort. Lexie retreated with him, fearing he would stoke some ire in the boys that would cause trouble. It was easy enough for Tarnation to stir things up because of his gregarious nature. And even though people in the northwest came in all shapes and sizes, Tarnation stood out because of his outsized hair bun and prominent snakeskin tattoos. In other words, some people were just downright bigoted.

Tarnation said, "You Chilliwacks got fit digs. And your hair—so nice and clean, not like my dingy bun. I could use hair like that." His smile was less easygoing than Lexie was used to seeing, almost provocative. It was verging on maniacal, in fact.

The boy's hands reached for their short swords, and their eyes just about popped out of their heads. The eldest—or at least the only one with a fully-formed mustache—said, "We don't want no trouble. You just ride on."

Tarnation laughed and said, "Yeah, yeah. Settle down. Just bein' a card, bud. Don't fret." He broke away from the escort, back to their line, and Lexie followed him.

"Hey, Tarn, you got a beef with these folks?" Lexie asked.

He laughed. "No, *bae*. They heard of me, is all. Got a bit of a rep up here." He winked at her.

The wink could mean anything. "Hey, Tarn. What do you mean, a *rep*? We all know this is going to be prickly, so we should minimize any surprises."

"Like, I ran a few jobs. Some got nasty. You know how I can get—all *ribbi*-like. Scalped a few more people than they expected, would be my guess."

"Scalped?" She wasn't that surprised, because he'd told her he'd scalped people before, but maybe she'd always hoped he'd been exaggerating.

"Yeah, *bae*." He pointed to the top of his forehead. "You take a knife and cut right—"

"It's okay, Tarn," she interrupted. "I get it." She glanced ahead. Nillias and the rest were far enough out of earshot.

She'd heard about quite a few atrocities in the fiefdom wars, and scalping was one of them. Maybe his rep wasn't that outlandish. "If you've got enemies in the fiefdoms, you've got to tell us, Tarn. We brought you here to help, not get us into trouble."

Tarnation's smile faded and his eyes darkened. His broad shoulders bounced into a shrug. "C'mon, Lex. Nobody's friends with everyone."

His words didn't give her comfort, but there wasn't much she could do about it. If they sent him back now he might go all *ribbi*, whatever that meant.

She sidled closer to Tarnation's horse and kept her voice low. "So did you look into that man I asked, the one we saw speaking with Nillias when we were in the old lighthouse?"

"Of course, Lex. Funny thing, that. You still worried about this Observer Gungi-bud? I thought you were good and pals now."

"I agree with the threat of the ICSM cities, so I'll help Nillias, but I don't trust him. I have to figure out a way to protect Mom, and to get some leverage on the Gungivites, just in case we get into a disagreement or they take issue with us knowing a thing or two."

"Gotcha."

"So what was so funny?"

"Oh yeah. That guy with Nillias who had the little girl at the restaurant—it was Ryder!" Tarnation laughed heartily.

Lexie clenched her teeth. One of the Gungivite militia cast a fleeting glance back at them. He could hear Tarnation's laughing, but he was probably too far away to hear their conversation.

"Let's just keep it down a smidge, Tarn."

"Yeah, yeah. Sorry, Lex. Funny though, right?"

"Yeah," she said.

"You're not laughing."

"Okay, no, it's not funny. Ever since this mess with the Gungivites started, that son-of-a-bitch Ryder has been a thorn in my side. He worked out a side deal with Nillias, or maybe he set the whole thing up to begin with. He's got eyes on Mom, I'm sure of it, and so long as Ryder is in Anacortes I'm stuck working for these nutjobs."

"He's not that bad. When I was stalking him I saw him playing nice with that girl in the park. And he was all stand-up when he was working with us, at least when he wasn't sick."

"Surely it's an act to fool us. Remember, bad people don't act bad all the time, Tarn. He deceived me and played you. And by the way, I have a pretty good idea why he was sick. It's because he's a full-on Observer like Nillias. They have brain implants that their body rejects over time without the right medication."

Tarn's eyebrows knitted in confusion. "Brain plants? Lex, you soundin' like you hit your head. Besides, I got paid fair and square."

She rolled her eyes. "Believe whatever you want. He's up to no good. I bet that kid isn't even his. She's probably leverage as well, just like my mom is leverage. When this is over, he's mine."

Tarnation raised his eyebrows at her and smiled. "So *conniving*, Lex!" He punched her shoulder amicably. The strength of his gesture shifted her weight on her horse. When she was sure she wasn't going to fall, she tried to chuckle in solidarity with him, but it was hard to muster with the dull pain emanating from her shoulder.

They eventually cut north over an Old World bridge that spanned the Fraser River, crossed another lush meadow, and rode through a valley that dumped them on the shore of Harrison Lake. Here were substantial battlements and fortifications, including an array of at least a dozen towers lining the hills, all made of thick timbers. Most of them had the round noses of cannon placements poking out of the side. They were all pointing north, across the lake and toward the fiefdoms.

Nillias negotiated a crossing with a beefy-looking sailor at the ferry terminal while the rest of them stayed out of his hair. Soon after, they all boarded, leaving their young escort behind. Their horses were stowed at the stern of the ferry and the eight of them gathered at the bow of the boat as they left port. Technically, they were out of Chilliwack and had entered the fiefdoms, although there was little sign of any habitation around the lake.

Once they were well away from shore, a stout woman with a droopy eyelid came around with a tray of drinks. The Gungivites all passed on the offer, but everyone else treated themselves to an ale or a lemon water.

Lexie's lemon water was refreshing. It was amazing how a bit of sour could spruce up a glass. She said, "Thank you kindly, miss. You sure know how to make guests feel welcome. But I wonder if you could help us. What can we expect up north? Have there been any recent changes in leadership, or hostility toward traveling folk?"

"Not sure," the woman replied with a shrug. "Changes all the time. Aside from the ferry crossing, only a few of us have ever traveled into the fiefdoms."

"Really. Why?"

"Wars, revolutions, famine. We try to stay out of it. It's not just the fiefdoms, either. Truth is, most folk here have never left Chilliwack. With ingrates to the north, sick drifters to the west in Abbotsford, drunk skunks to the south in Anacortes and a whole lotta nothing but retchers to the east, staying here in Chilliwack does us just fine."

She did have a point. It was a lush valley, with good farming, a vibrant river, and far enough away from the Kuvar fever lands to sleep well at night. Chilliwack was technically in Three Rivers territory, but Lexie doubted the skunks messed with them much, on account of them being a good distance from Anacortes. There were worse places you could set down roots.

The lake was a long, skinny worm of water that meandered up the valley. The ferry passed by the occasional island with cannon-laden towers on it—obviously more defenses for Chilliwack. The lake ferry was a much easier passage than trying to take the trail, which she could see had a number of switchbacks and cliff faces to navigate, although it would still be a couple of days travel to Pemberton once they reached the northern extent of the lake.

"Hey, Heath, why aren't we taking the Squamish route?" she asked. "Wouldn't that be faster?"

"The Squamish fiefdom doesn't allow weapons," Heath replied. "They are concerned about them ending up in the hands of their enemies, and in particular Pemberton. I presume you wouldn't want to be weaponless in the fiefdoms."

"No, sir," Lexie responded. She glanced at the large bag that was down by Emry's feet. In it were two of the spacy-looking energy weapons they'd appropriated from Heath and Warrick. She'd caught a glimpse of them before they left. They were about twice the size of an Old World assault rifle, with broad barrels, thick ridges and miniature display lights. Maybe the group could have slipped through Squamish with a few knives, but certainly not those eye-poppers.

"Won't these things call retchers?" She thrust her chin toward the bag. "We're not actually going to use them, are we?"

"No," Nillias responded simply, speaking at low volume. Emry had put his finger to his lips.

There had to be some reason they brought the weapons along, but she heeded their warning and didn't follow up on her question.

"Can you at least tell me what the deal is with this Pemberton leader?" Lexie asked. "Why did he spend good money on a dinosaur egg? Inferiority complex or what?"

Nillias's eyes wrinkled a little bit at the edges. Heath wasn't amused, though. "Narcissistic and insane would be more accurate," he said. "Get your laughs out now, because they will cost you in Pemberton. His name is Moraine, but he will only answer to 'Emperor,' and no other title or designation. Remember that."

"Why were you selling the control junction?"

"I was looking to sell Warrick's stash of old artifacts, since he could barely remember why he had them, or what they were for, and there was an antiques market sale in Victoria. Moraine came in with a big entourage, buying up half the items in the market. What sold him on the dinosaur egg was the fact that it glowed when you turned off the lights, even though the glow revealed orthogonal lines embedded below the surface—lines that couldn't have been biological in origin. I told him that we didn't know for sure it was a fossilized dinosaur egg, but he said that he knew what dinosaur eggs looked like."

"Where do you think he's keeping it?"

"I don't know. It could be anywhere."

"The palace library," Tarnation chimed in. "Moraine hides his money in secret chests all over Pemberton, but the *munga* keeps his shiny gadgets and circus toys down in the library."

"How do you know that?" Emry asked.

"Been there once, on a job." Tarnation smiled. He didn't elaborate any further.

Hopefully it was one of the more benign jobs.

After they disembarked at the northern end of Harrison Lake, they rode up the valley toward Pemberton for the rest of the day. That evening, they stopped at an Old World house that had lost its front wall and a part of the floor. The opening hung over the turquoise waters of a mountain river that had gouged the earth underneath the house. The back half of the building appeared stable enough, and an intact fireplace had been used recently, so they made camp there.

Nillias and the two Gungivite militia tied Heath and Warrick's cuffs to a sturdy column at the rear of the house while they went to forage for food. Emry had also left to collect firewood. It had recently rained and dry timber was hard to find, so it would take some time.

It was only then that Lexie had a chance to speak with Warrick. He'd been tethered to Emry and Nillias during the ride, so there hadn't been much opportunity for a private conversation. In truth, it would be semi-private, because Heath and Tarnation were also present, sitting on a floor where only a few patches of hardwood were visible under the dirt and detritus that had blown in over the years.

"What have you been doing all this time?" she asked.

"Surviving," Warrick replied. "Getting kidnapped—apparently."

"You never went back east?"

"Why would I do that? That's where the witch is from."

"Are you sure about this woman? You always said you wanted to go back east—that you had an important position in Seeville. You said you never should have left."

Warrick looked at Heath, who raised an eyebrow. "What position?" he asked.

"You were a Seeville Lord, in Spoke territory. There was a falling-out with the other lords, and you went to find a better place, one more suited to your ideals. I always thought it was funny, all this talk about ideals from a pirate, but hey, we all come from somewhere."

Warrick turned his head down to cradle it in his hands. It was hard to tell what he was doing. He might have been weeping, but Lexie had never seen Warrick cry, and when he looked up, his eyes weren't filled with tears, but rather determination.

"Why do you care, Lexie?"

"Hey, I'm just trying to help. We made a good team, back in the day. Figured I owe you one."

"I see; by having me kidnapped. We'll help you get the junction, if that's what you want, but otherwise, stay out of my business. I just hope your friend lets us go."

"Why wouldn't he?"

Warrick shook his head.

"Not everyone is after you, Warrick. We have bigger problems."

"I hope you're right."

"Of course I am. Remember who got the quartermaster's map in the end?"

Warrick only frowned. He must not have remembered.

The memory came back to her: she'd told Warrick that the quartermaster of a Kuvar Collective galleon liked to drink on Sunday mornings, so that would be the right time to nab the map that showed the military routes north of Port Renfrew. Warrick hadn't believed her, but she'd been right;

they caught the quartermaster drooling next to the map. The next day, they successfully outmaneuvered the Kuvar Collective coast guard with the help of the stolen map. It was one of her finer moments.

But it was like it had never happened. It was like Warrick wasn't even the same person anymore.

Frustrated, Lexie stood up and walked out of the house to go help Emry.

The next day, they wound their way up the valley via the mountain trail. A blanket of fog enveloped them, until it burned off late in the morning. The path was definitely used, but not much. Pack animals could pass through single file, but broader carts would have trouble on account of all the potholes, as well as steep cliffs that could easily have sent Lexie and her horse straight down to the small river in a tumble of limbs.

It wasn't long after the fog cleared that they saw a wall in the distance. It was about three times the height of a man, made of rough-hewn stone at the base, with thick tree trunk rounds stacked up on top of them. It spanned the valley at a spot where the mountains had come closer together, turning the valley into more of a gorge.

They pulled up to a bank of trees and went about giving the wall a gander. Lexie's scope revealed a broad door in the base that was closed. If they couldn't get through the door, they might be able to navigate around the wall closer to the river. It looked like sediment had built up and the river was low enough for them to pass through on the side. There was no one around, as far as she could tell. Except for the corpse.

Projecting out from the top of the wall was a long metal pole, and from its end hung a rag doll of a man. The man's head was a ball of crispy black gristle, and the eye sockets had been dug out by birds real good. The clothes hung loosely over the bag of bones that remained.

Last but not least was the sign stenciled on the wall. In huge letters, crossing over multiple wood rounds, it read:

Impassable territory by order of Emperor Moraine.
Trespassers will be killed without exception.

Nillias and Emry exchanged an incoherent whisper as they brandished their own scopes. They walked stiffly away from the group toward another tree, perhaps to gain some space so they could talk privately.

Lexie watched them from afar. Nillias's face was unusually expressive as he whispered with Emry. He seemed to be cycling erratically through a variety of emotional states: confusion, concern, and contemplation. Emry wasn't keeping his cool either; he started bobbing his head and rubbing his temples. Eventually Nillias's eyes found Lexie, and he rolled his finger to indicate she should come join them.

She did.

"What's up?" she asked.

"We were not informed about the wall."

She shrugged. "Yeah, sorry. What are we going to do?"

"Our options are to proceed past the wall, but we could be killed. Or we could go back the way we came and approach via Squamish, but that would be a delay of several days, if not a week, and we would lose our weapons. Another option is to locate a mountain pass, which would be shorter, but possibly more treacherous." He glanced up at the cliffs next to them. When he looked back at her, his eyes were unusually pronounced.

"You okay, Nillias? You seem a bit on edge."

He closed his eyes, perhaps to force himself to calm down. "I'm sorry, Lexie. I am not used to … making decisions in this way, without being connected."

"Ah, I get it. Your implant-thingy isn't working here, so you have to decide on your own." She'd wondered about that. Now that they were in retcher territory, he wouldn't be able to turn on his gadget brain. She couldn't know how much he depended on it, but all the simulations and dialogue and maps that he would normally have at his disposal would be gone. No wonder he looked like a lost puppy.

"Well," she said, "why don't we all talk it out as a group? That's what normal folks do."

His face contorted, as if it was some shocking revelation, and then eventually relaxed. "Yes, Lexie. Good idea. Let's find a suitable area to commune together."

Their group retreated along the path, around a bend in the river, and found a place where an arch had been naturally cut out of the gorge wall. Here, they sat on dry ground covered with pine needles.

Nillias kicked off the discussion. Or rather, it was more of an interrogation. Maybe the surprise wall and the dead person had made him less trusting.

He questioned Heath first. "How do we know the control junction is in Pemberton?"

"We don't know for certain, but I can't think of anywhere else it could be. Moraine is known to keep ancient artifacts there."

"Did you know about this wall?" Nillias asked. "The fact that Pemberton may be impassable?"

"No," Heath responded. "Not at all."

"And you?" Nillias shifted his gaze to Warrick. "Did you know?"

Warrick was squinting at him. "No. I might have at one time, but I could have forgotten."

Their words didn't appease Nillias at all. His gaze shifted again, bouncing back and forth between Warrick and Lexie. "Have you two been in contact before Burlington?"

Lexie answered for them. "No, Nillias, not recently. This isn't some big conspiracy. Not sure where you're—"

"When did you last meet?" he interrupted her.

He was having some kind of nutjob crisis of confidence. All she could do was answer truthfully, and carefully. "Look, Nillias, it was over three years ago. You already know we were, um—sailing together." As a pirate you get conditioned to not use the word *pirate*, for fear of self-incrimination. "We'd just done a big delivery up to Powell River—coffee, which the fiefers like, apparently—and had a nice payday, but it had been a hairy job."

She nodded and glanced over at Warrick. "Even then," she added, "you were having your bouts, Warrick. I could hear you cringing in your cabin at night. Your sheets would be covered in blood. I wondered if you might have a really bad crotch disease, like Nichols or Baba the Mute, but it wasn't that. You were cutting, and forgetting things. I think, well … it was probably a good decision to stop when we did."

Nillias's teeth clenched. "This information does not suggest to me I should trust you, Lexie, or any of you, for that matter. How do I know we aren't heading into a trap? Perhaps Moraine is an ally of yours. Perhaps he will kill me and Emry so that you can be freed."

Lexie was getting annoyed. "Hey, when I said we should talk it out, I meant we could share our opinions in a respectful manner. I wasn't suggesting you browbeat us like we're all Three Rivers skunks trying to grift you to death."

Nillias stared at her, his eyes still full of inquisition. She held his gaze without wavering. At last, he said, "Fine. What do you all think? Should we proceed through the wall or find another viable route?"

A lot of probing stares were exchanged, but no one wanted to volunteer an answer, possibly because no one wanted to be held accountable for their opinion by the nervous nutjob.

It was Tarnation who broke the silence. He was picking his teeth with a dagger after snacking on some of the stringy smoked venison they had been using for rations. "Of course, bud," he said. "Let's go through the wall."

"You're not concerned?" Emry asked. He'd been sitting back, his face unexpressive, occasionally combing his crimson coif. Now he leaned in, as if there was finally something worthy of his attention.

"Yeah. It's just a scarecrow, bud, like they had in the Old World. *Beware of dog*, if you know what I mean. It's a relic of the wars from ten years ago. Lots of fiefdoms have these walls, and some even have dead suckers hanging off them, but they let people come and go just fine. Moraine may not like us, but I doubt anyone's going to take the time to stop us before we get to him. There's just not enough people in the fiefdoms to man these walls. I wouldn't worry about it."

Nillias's face was expressionless again. Maybe he'd finally gotten his emotions under control. He looked around the group. Hearing no further comments, he said, "We will continue on."

After all that. Lexie resisted the urge to throw her hands up in the air.

It had been an uncomfortable discussion, but it was hard to blame Nillias. Maybe he'd never been taught how to have a civil conversation. Or maybe his implant usually overrode his emotions and kept them in check. It was actually nice to see he had a human side, even if it was more grating than him staring at the ocean, or his little smirks.

The group made their way carefully to the wall, with weapons at the ready. Tarnation led the way. The door's lock mechanism had broken off, so he pushed through easily. Once they were on the other side, Lexie saw that a crossbar had been removed. There was indeed no one around.

Tarnation had been right. He had known the answer all along, and all they had to do was talk it out. Lexie almost said *I told you so* to Nillias, but she didn't want to get him riled up again.

Soon after, when they were on the path again, Nillias returned to his usual self, all stone-faced and quiet. His little lapse already seemed fleeting, and Lexie wondered if she'd been imagining things, as if it was some kind of mirage.

—31—

Dragonflies

"No, Commissioner Utep," Alayna said, her voice firm. "As the general has mentioned, we have no designs on Vicky natural resources or even trade revenues. We have annexed Vicky territory because of the strategic importance of Diplopol and the ever-present threat of the Kuvar Collective."

They were meeting with the Vicky trade representatives in an open tent just outside of Diplopol. A constant cacophony of hammers pounding and saws sawing sounded in the distance. Alayna blocked out the noise, and kept her eyes firmly on Utep. They were at a crucial inflection point in the meeting, and she needed to make sure she didn't lose him.

"And the recent skirmishes have proven our concerns to be valid," Hatsuo added. "Imagine if we weren't defending Vicky lands. You would be at the mercy of these dredges."

Utep nodded, but he didn't look satisfied. He seemed to be testing the waters—seeing where pushback was strongest.

Utep was a large man, full of excess. He had a rounded midriff, lengthy jowls and gleaming jewelry hanging from his neck and ears. Sweat marks dampened his yellow jerkin, around his neck and underarms. He was the commissioner of Vicky guild revenues, a seemingly innocuous title, but in actuality a powerful one. All guild-related taxes—mercantile, shipping, fishing, masonry, agriculture, and mining—went through him. He was someone who could make things difficult for the Essentialists, if he chose to.

Sitting next to Utep was Sajida-Lai, a slim older woman with big brown eyes that looked like they were flecked with gray sparks. Her long, flowing hair cascaded down her back to rest on the curve of her buttocks. She had been the Vicky Ambassador until recently. With Vicky territory under

Essentialist rule, they had given her the interim title of People's Representative.

Rounding out the meeting participants was the Tucson Union Inspector, Matias Caban, a thoughtful man with high cheekbones and wavy brown hair. Caban had been mostly quiet thus far, offering only the occasional example of the positive collaboration of the Union with the Prefectorate, and a few solemn references to the importance of keeping sun, soil and seed top of mind.

"We must have property rights associated with Diplopol manufacturing centers," Utep said. "Royalties, shares, something. This is our land, our people are working it, and so they should derive a portion of the bounty."

Alayna shared a look with Hatsuo. He had that plastered smile that wasn't quite stretched enough. He didn't want to give in on this point.

She said, "Rights to what property? We aren't even sure what we will be manufacturing. The city is rebuilding, and outside we are creating factories, but no real products, so how do we tax something that doesn't exist?"

Hatsuo's expression had become pained. "Tax?" he said wistfully. "As you know we have agreed that we would not be taxing Vicky citizens in return for our protection, but now you want to tax *us*?"

"I'm sure that's not what Utep meant," Sajida-Lai said.

"Actually, it is," Utep said, frowning at Sajida-Lai. "Although maybe *tax* is not the right word. I deliberately used the words *shares*, or *royalties*, but it's just semantics. We want to share in the spoils here, rather than be treated like a servant class, working for the interests of the Prefectorate."

That raised eyebrows around the table. To insinuate that this was not a collaborative Essentialist endeavor, but rather a Prefectorate one, would of course flare up Prefectorate-Essentialist sensitivities. Alayna suspected Utep was trying to drive a wedge between them. Indeed, Hatsuo shifted in his chair, while Caban looked away and fingered his temple.

Alayna said, "Please, Utep, we are both seasoned in the art of trade. We both understand the fundamentals of economics. So let's take a step back and look at the bigger picture. Thousands of people will come to work here, in and around Diplopol. They are already doing so, dozens every day, not only from Vicky lands but also from other Salish Sea nations and Essentialist municipalities. This will become a center of industry and trade, many times greater than it was before Diplopol was awakened. In turn, all of the new infrastructure and spending will fuel the nearby economy, raising real estate values, bringing in more money to be spent on food, supplies, and other shipping activities. We are gifting you a prosperous economy, while requiring little in the way of capital cost or inconvenience. Are you willing to forgo that huge boon by demanding complex royalty or share provisions that will only stifle the opportunity?"

She thought it had been a convincing take on the situation, but he wasn't having it. "Too many people are settling here. We've lost whole fisheries and are down a mine because everyone is flocking to Diplopol. And for what?" He gestured behind them to the rows and rows of makeshift shacks. "To live in this shanty town of sheets and shit pots—not my words—so they can toil on your Essentialist war machine."

"That's enough, Utep," Sajida-Lai said. "This *war machine* is protecting us, as the general and Miss Menudos have alluded to repeatedly, and correctly. You simply don't have enough insight on the matter to make a credible complaint when you haven't even seen the inner workings of Diplopol. You should stay for a few days, and I can show you why people are coming here. If we can inspire the rest of Vicky society to have half the promise of Diplopol, it's worth a few transient labor disruptions. So stop thinking about lining your pockets, and start thinking about the greater good—about a truly magnificent future for our people. I'm tired of it. In fact, if you cannot concede this point and move on, I will be forced to take this up with the Minister in Residence."

Utep gawked, as though she'd stabbed him in the heart. Infighting between Vicky delegates at a trade meeting was a rare occurrence. In fact, it was so out of character that Alayna wondered if Sajida-Lai had been paid off by Hatsuo's men.

Utep said, "Well, I … we will need to discuss this further—later. The guild members wouldn't be happy. We would need to find a way to appease them."

Alayna realized that it was time to close the meeting—to seize the momentum provided by Sajida-Lai and let the property-rights issue die a slow death afterward. "We understand," Alayna said, standing up. "Take the time you need."

Utep stood up as well, looking bewildered. The rest of the meeting participants followed suit. Alayna shook Utep's hand. "May sun, soil and seed be bountiful to you on this day."

"And … you too," Utep said. He nodded to each of them in turn. "General. Inspector. Ambassador." Utep turned about and walked back to his chariot.

They would have to throw the Vickies a bone when he returned, maybe better housing around Diplopol, or help with improving the shipping nodes in Victoria and Cordova Bay, but this was all something they would have to do anyway.

Sajida-Lai lingered.

"You're not heading back to Victoria?" Alayna asked.

"No. I plan to visit Diplopol again. I have an hour scheduled for one a.m. tonight." With the frenetic rebuilding activity in the city, there wasn't much opportunity for people to visit the Diplopol interior—only the main hall, a small cafeteria and several experiential rooms were active and safe. People were still clamoring to visit, though, even if to only see the rapid construction process, so they had to ration visiting hours.

"Do enjoy," Alayna said, taking her hand as well. "General, Inspector, I'll leave you to it."

"Well done, Alayna," Hatsuo said, he cradled her hand in both of his, giving it an adamant shake.

"Thank you, General."

It had been the most difficult meeting thus far, but there was still less resistance than Alayna had expected. She was especially surprised about Sajida-Lai, who she'd heard was a Vicky hardliner. Nobody wanted to stand in the way of the Prefectorate, it seemed. All they cared about was the city and feeding its insatiable demand for supplies and people.

There was a short cut through the shantytown that was a quicker route back to her barracks, but Alayna avoided it. She didn't want to fall in the mud the way she'd done two days prior, especially given the questionable sanitation systems, so she took the more circuitous route that was maintained with gravel, pothole cover-overs and makeshift railings.

She followed the path up a shallow gradient to an elevated terrace surrounded by a rickety stone wall. Here was where people came to survey the construction work. Three men were there, dressed in workers' coveralls, and one of them had a scope to scan the cityscape.

Diplopol continued to grow and change rapidly. Three large, egg-shaped buildings had risen, and dominated the horizon. Another was under construction, the shape of the frame now evident, with gravity-defying, roach-like robots dancing on girders and support poles around it. Today the city had completed one of the arcing tubes that crossed high over the top of the city grounds. Already, packages pulsed inside the tube, crossing the expanse of the city at lightning-fast speeds. The rest was an array of gray structural levels, like dozens of giant staircases going in every direction. There was also a constant blur from the faraway welding fires—a constellation of lights challenging the dimming twilight.

Just outside the arced walls of the city limits, construction of another variety was underway. Diplopol's machines couldn't leave the city, but they could provide instructions to humans so they could build machines of their own. So the workers had resurrected an awkward jumble of concrete slabs and boxy buildings that would eventually be the basis for dozens of factories. That's where the noise of saws and hammering had been coming from during the meeting. A less concentrated array of lantern lights dotted that area as well.

Binjai had been confident the workers could pull off the ambitious project. Alayna had initially been skeptical, but seeing the city morph and grow every day had changed her opinion. Not only that, but the work ethic and focus of the laborers was like nothing she'd ever seen. Most of them worked fifteen-hour shifts, and except for the few precious hours a week reserved for time in the city, they did little else but eat and sleep in their makeshift shantytown shacks. As long as the city spoon-fed them a steady diet of utopian dreams, these people wouldn't stop.

More came, and more. Despite their posturing, Utep was right about it hampering other trades and economic centers in Vicky territory. People were coming in droves—some recruited, some informed by word of mouth. It did feel like the workers had become a fanatical cult, even if that cult's productivity was impressive.

She left the lookout and made her way back down the path, avoiding muddy stacks of wood littered about.

Her quarters were in a detached building up the hill from the main encampment, one that was always under guard. Being a confidante to the general did have its privileges.

Today, her guard was the shorter coastal Essentialist with the beady eyes. "Norman," she said to him as she walked past. He acknowledged her with a nod.

Before she closed the door behind her, a buzzing sound caught her attention. It was low, almost like a hum. She turned to see a dragonfly chasing another dragonfly nearby. They were circling, bombing, and occasionally landing on each other. It was a ballroom dance for bugs—a swirling jig over the blotchy background lights of Diplopol.

She knew they would be gone soon, so she committed as much detail of the scene to memory as possible. She scrounged around in her bag for her notebook and pencil without averting her eyes.

Soon they whipped past her ear, and she lost them.

She untied the elastic cover of her notebook and opened it to the last clear page. She wrote:

Today's gift: two dragonflies chasing each other, their wings so fast they blurred together. It was as if they were floating through the air without effort. One had a blue metallic torso, the other green. The blue was the color of the flame of Nate's welding torch. They are brave soldiers of the spring; they fly in tandem, trying to find life in a landscape that has driven away so much of the living.

When she stepped inside her quarters, her foot glided on an envelope on the floor. It was the pulpy kind, with small chunks of pink wood in it—an Essentialist military communiqué. Inside was a small slip of paper that read:

Report to Inspector Matias Caban, 0900 tomorrow.

Alayna wasn't surprised. Caban had been meeting with all of Hatsuo's subordinates since he'd arrived. Hatsuo often deferred to his wishes, since the Tucson Union were important allies. In fact, Caban had publicly disgraced two of Hatsuo's officers who hadn't followed Essentialist edicts, and Hatsuo had agreed with his punitive decrees. They must be trying to set an example—to reaffirm the alliance with the Union, as they did every so often.

She would have to be on her best behavior.

—32—

The Imperial Palace

Given the huge wall and the corpse, Lexie and the others had been cautious riding into Pemberton, but they saw no one else for hours. It wasn't until the valley broadened into verdant pastures that they finally came upon a fence and guardhouse. The fence was so low the horses could easily have hurdled it. It was probably more for keeping animals in than people out. And the guardhouse looked an awful lot like an outhouse.

No one was in the outhouse.

Eventually Lexie saw two people, a man and a woman, who scrambled down from what looked like a goat farm higher up in the valley. The man wore a black shirt with a crude white sketch on it that appeared to be the outline of a hand holding up a ball, or maybe planet Earth. "Who dares to tread on imperial grounds?" he asked.

Heath spoke for them. "Forgive us. We wish to conduct business with the Emperor. We come to buy or trade certain items." Emry was about to uncinch a sack laden over his horse, but the man and woman were ignoring him.

They were staring at Tarnation. "Are you ...?" the woman said.

Tarnation said, "Don' worry. Bygones be bygones. No violence today. I'm here to help some friends—just business."

The man didn't remove his eyes from Tarnation. "Give us your weapons and you may enter," he said.

"No," Nillias said simply.

The two shared a look. The woman said, "You will be constantly under guard. One threatening move and you're dead."

"Fine," Nillias said.

And they rode on, escorted by the two farmers.

The Imperial Palace was high up on a hill, on a corner in the mountains where two valleys met. It was built of rough-hewn stone, save for the three square towers, which were made of heavy timbers reaching to the sky. It looked impressive enough to Lexie, although it wasn't large—more like an oversized mansion. Stone walls formed an additional perimeter around it, and a bulging guardhouse marked the entrance.

Over the entranceway, banners showing the sketch of the hand holding the world were draped down over the walls. They really were sketches. If there hadn't been two of them, it would be difficult to decipher what the pictures represented, because the hands were so malformed.

After deliberation with the gate guards, they were let inside and escorted to a main courtyard area. The two goat herders who'd ridden in with them turned around and headed back to their farm. Lexie could see men scurrying about on the battlements. Their pacing was clearly energized by the newcomers' presence.

A man with a shaved head and a staggering walk came out to meet them. The bald man snarled at Lexie, or at least that's what his attempted smile looked like. "My name is Scree. I am the Emperor's appointed steward. I am told you wish to transact with the Emperor. He will be pleased, but he is currently conducting a goodwill tour of the empire. He should be back late this evening, and I am sure he would welcome you to a breakfast meeting. Would you care to overnight with us at the palace, as our guests?"

"We would," Nillias said. "Thank you for your hospitality."

"It is my pleasure. You are all welcome, except this one." Scree pointed at Tarnation.

"Hey, I done nothin' to you, *munga*," Tarnation said.

Nillias put his hand up in a gesture of calm. "I'm sorry, but why not?"

"He has breached imperial law. Theft and murder."

Tarnation laughed a little too hard. "It isn't theft if you're stealing it back from a thief, bud. And it isn't murder if someone is trying to kill you." He glanced at Lexie with an absurd look where he scrunched his nose and rolled his eyes. "What a silly man," he said.

Scree kept a tight facial expression, but his face was building color.

Nillias said, "I'm sorry, but we can't abandon our colleague here. How about we keep him bound until we leave? Will that make you more comfortable?"

Scree was noodling on it.

Nillias said, "Every nation has different laws, but common sense is universal. I suggest you consider what could happen in the immediate future if you say no."

Scree looked again at Tarnation, who had adopted a hungry grin. Tarnation wasn't too happy about being muzzled by Nillias, no doubt, and he was taking great breaths like a bull ready to charge. Scree was gauging Nillias and the rest of them as well. Finally, he said, "Your proposal is acceptable. I will show you to your quarters."

As they made their way inside, Nillias cast Lexie a deadpan look.

Yeah, yeah, so maybe it hadn't been the best idea to bring Tarnation along.

Lexie woke in the middle of the night. She'd heard noises coming from just outside the basement room where they'd all been packed in like rowers on a galley. The sound was almost like muffled grunting, as if a teenager was trying to get some action without Mom and Dad listening in. She saw that Warrick was gone, his bed empty, and the wire attached to his cuffs was trailing out the doorway. She tiptoed into the corridor and saw him sitting against the wall, one pant leg up, pushing a jagged rock against his calf muscle. The rock left white and red track marks over tissue that was already heavily lacerated.

She saw the pain in his eyes. But it wasn't just that; it was fear, and anxiety—a dark fog of negative energy.

He'd been cutting on the ship, back in the day, but she'd only seen it a few times. She would watch him more than he knew. Back then, there were only a few marks. Now his whole leg was a mass of scar tissue. She reckoned it would be the same on his other limbs as well.

She handed him her hunting knife and leaned over to whisper in his ear. "Give it back to me when you're done."

When she went back to bed, she didn't fall asleep right away. She trusted Warrick for the most part, but he'd changed, and he was a prisoner, so she couldn't be sure what he'd do with the knife.

A few minutes later, he came back in the room. Lexie's eyes were slitted, but she wasn't asleep. She had her boot blade ready in case he tried anything, but he just slid her knife into its sheath on the floor in front of her. He tiptoed away, and she heard the soft rustling of wool covers as he returned to his bed.

—33—

The Inspector

Alayna had been given several Essentialist Military Delegate outfits by Hatsuo's men, but she decided to go with civilian clothes for the meeting with Inspector Caban. She wanted to give the impression she wasn't under Hatsuo's direct supervision, in case he was looking for scapegoats of the military variety. So she wore a black collared shirt and airy linen pants.

Caban hadn't been given lodging in any of the new temporary dwellings close to the construction activities or near the main barracks. His tent was located next to a stream that percolated through one of the few remaining groves of trees in the area. It was fairly lavish, as far as the tents of traveling dignitaries went. The fabric was translucent enough to bathe the interior in a yellow glow. He had proper bedding and a number of faux walls that could be maneuvered throughout. There was even a cedar desk that had been brought in. This was where he sat.

"Please, please, come in, Miss Menudos," he said, encouraging her with a wave. "Take a chair." He gestured to a folded wooden chair against the wall. She unfolded it and sat down, crossing her legs but keeping her back stiff.

He tapped a pencil on the desk, his gaze fixed on her. "You have such pretty green eyes, Miss Menudos, and yet you wear these colorless shirts, as if you are a fisherman or a farmhand. Where I come from, in Sekoya, we would give you a long floral dress, one that complements your figure. You would be the envy of men and women alike."

The comment gave her a queasy feeling. She had known she would have to pander to Caban, but not in *that* way.

He shrugged. "But wear what you will. Wear what makes you happy, as long as it does not sully the eternal spring."

She smiled at him.

He stood up and began pacing slowly about the tent. He felt at the contour of his desktop, and righted a page that was askew on a stack of folders on top of it. "Clearly, clothes are immaterial, and transient. Made and then unmade. What are more important are Essentialist interests. And to that end, I was impressed with your composure in the meeting yesterday. You were superb. I'm not sure Utep knew what hit him."

His pacing had taken him to a bearskin wraparound that hung from a hook drilled into the main tent support. He touched the hairs, pushing them against the grain and watching them fold back into place after the passing of his finger.

"Thank you, Inspector," she said. "We were lucky to have Sajida-Lai also influencing him in the right direction, and General Hatsuo is always steadfast in maintaining a disciplined approach in these negotiations."

The mention of Hatsuo's name brought his attention back to her. "Yes … he is," he said.

He found his chair again. "Yesterday I had a tour of the factory placements. Did you know one of these placements is for munitions? In fact, I hear from my sources—and I have many—about a thermobaric bomb project."

"A thermobaric bomb?"

"I know only what my source told me. It is similar to small-scale Old World nuclear bombs. They suck the oxygen out of the air, and there's less radiation, so they are supposedly less taxing on sun, soil and seed. This is just one of the many defense factories they are building. Others are planned for guns, explosives, and robot attack drones. But I suspect you already knew this, didn't you, Miss Menudos?"

"No, honestly. I know nothing about thermobaric bombs. I did know about munitions, cannons and defense drones, but otherwise I have no purview of those activities. I only deal with trade, so I know what supplies are going in, but not what they're building. I rarely visit the city."

He stared at her. "Are you sure? I find that hard to believe. Everybody frequents the city. At least twenty of the people I've interviewed wouldn't stop talking about the experiential rooms. They are like my *abuela,* gabbing with her friends around her spinning wheel."

"No, I don't have the time, and the wait list is so long. It's been several weeks for me. Besides that ... I know it's an unpopular opinion, but I don't like to go to the city. My former husband, he warned me that there are parts that could be dangerous, even these experiential rooms. He has his issues, but he's usually right when it comes to his work, so I've been reluctant to try them."

Caban's gaze hadn't left her. Finally, like a balloon losing air, he sighed slowly. "Yes," he said. "I know about Dryden."

"You do?"

He smiled. "I'm an inspector. I ask many questions. He is a smart man, your ex-husband. Curious, but smart."

"Like I said, he has his issues, but I think he is well-intentioned. We have a hard past."

"I'm sorry about your brother, Ben. He was a great Essentialist hero."

"I ... thank you."

How much did Caban know? It seemed like he knew everything about her. It made her uncomfortable. He was clearly building up to something. An accusation? Extortion? It was hard to say.

Caban stood up from the desk and meandered over to the tent flap. He opened it a hair, looked out briefly, and closed it again.

He turned and stood with his back to the flap. "Let's talk candidly, Miss Menudos."

"I have been candid."

He smiled. "I will begin, then. The meeting yesterday, it was indeed well played. You are good at what you do, but at the same time, I know that meeting was a mockery."

"I'm sorry, I'm not following."

"This meeting was just a stage for our best actors in this grand play of ours. Utep wants to be seen as a Vicky guild member representative, but really he only cares about the coin in his pockets. Sajida-Lai wants people to think she is the lifeblood of Vicky commoners, but she seems to have become an advocate for Diplopol, like some kind of reimagined Sanuwan princess. And then there is our general. He is a man who would like people to believe he is heartfelt, and sentimental, or maybe, at times, a staunch defender of the eternal spring. As for me, I would like people to believe I'm really here as an inspector. But who are you, Miss Menudos? That's what I would like to know. Who are you, really?"

"Inspector, I implore you. I'm no fraud, and I'm not sure why you would think such a thing. I truly believe in the edicts of Essentialism. I can say without reservation that I was defending our interests. My only wish is to drink from the eternal spring."

His mouth made a grim smile. "Yes, well, in truth I don't have reason to believe otherwise, but it's always best to ask—to weigh the words from the person's mouth as a final test."

She felt a knot in her chest loosen. "Thank you, inspector, but if I may, you said you'd *like people to believe* you're an inspector. What do you mean by that? You're not an inspector?"

A broader smile slowly propagated across his face. He said, "Yes, you are an observant one, aren't you? I'll get to that, but first, do you remember Sergio Petranus?"

"Yes. He's an old friend, or rather Dryden's. I last saw him before Diplopol, in Neah Bay."

"Yes, that's him." Caban walked back to her, pulled up his chair and held her hand in his. His eyes took on the glow of the tent, alight with purpose. "He is also one of the actors in this grand play," he said, "an important one. He understands, like I do, that we are being deceived by the Prefectorate, that they have sullied the edicts of Essentialism, and that they have no intention of making reparations, now or in the future. The only way to stop them is to undermine them from within, to hide in plain sight and strike back when the good earth gives us an opportunity."

There it was: the suggestion of treason. His grip on her hand was tight. Alayna tried not to avert her eyes.

"I believe you are one of us, Miss Menudos. I believe you see the Prefectorate for who they truly are, and that they must be stopped. Sergio needs your help, and *I* need your help, to cleanse this plague of metal and smoke they are creating. That's who Sergio is. That's who I am, in the core of my being. We are the groundwater of the eternal spring, and we believe you are, too. So tell me, are you with us?"

It could have been entrapment, but it didn't fit. He wouldn't have told her about the weapons development if he was playing her, and his description of Hatsuo would have been less harsh. Besides, Sergio had told her—a whisper in her ear before he was taken away in Neah Bay—that someone from Groundwater would find her. More importantly, if she didn't agree here and now, she would be cast aside, or potentially even killed, by Groundwater spies. Her only other option was to report Caban to Hatsuo, but she had no real proof to offer, and Hatsuo would be loath to cause an international incident on a hunch of hers.

She had no choice but to commit.

"Yes, I'm with you," she said. "In fact, I've been waiting for you, and I'm eager to do your bidding."

—34—

Emperor Moraine

The breakfast was held in a large chamber with huge arched windows that provided a view of the checkered green valleys on either side. The table was replete with huge rounds of rye bread, carafes of goat's milk and eggs prepared in a variety of ways—poached, hard-boiled and baked into potato quiche. Nillias had temporarily uncuffed Warrick and Heath, but Tarnation wore large wooden manacles around his ankles and wrists. One of the many long-bearded Pemberton guards lining the room had been given the keys.

There were quite a few of these guards. Lexie counted twenty-five in total. It seemed a bit of overkill, given the fact that this "empire" was only about a thousand people, but Moraine probably wanted to give the appearance of strength.

She'd had to convince Tarnation his bonds were all for show, to appease the crazy emperor, and he bought it, but he still looked livid. He was unable to eat, while the rest of them gorged on the feast in front of them. His face was an emotionless mask, which unnerved Lexie. On anyone else she might not have been concerned, but this was a man who rarely stopped smiling.

Moraine walked in halfway through the meal, trailed by Scree and a brutish guard. Moraine was tall, with a neatly trimmed beard, and a small lump of a belly hanging over his belt. His face was a uniform palette of smooth, unblemished skin. Given all the pomp surrounding him, Lexie was surprised he wasn't dressed more regally. The only sign of his status was a necklace made of seven miniature fans of gold.

"Welcome, honored guests," he said, standing in front of the long table with his hands cradled together. "Such an eclectic group. What brings you all this way?"

Heath stood up and the others followed suit, except for Tarnation. Heath bowed and said, "Revered Emperor, we have come far to transact with you. We wish to repurchase an item sold to you in error."

"I see. Well, first I'd like to know more about my guests." He took a seat across from Heath. A teenager scurried over to offer a plate of food to Moraine. Moraine wrinkled his nose at it and began separating out several of the items on his plate with his fork.

"Of course," Heath said. "Let me introduce—"

"Let me guess," Moraine interrupted. "You look like Gungivite Observers, if I'm right." He was pointing his fork at Nillias, Emry and the two militia. "And then you," he nodded at Heath, "I've met you before. You belong to this older bearded man, correct? And who is he?"

Heath said, "My name is Heath. I work for him. He is a former sea merchant."

"His name?"

"Cutter."

Moraine frowned and moved on to Lexie. "And this one, the Essentialist mixed-breed. Some traveling fun, then?"

Lexie gritted her teeth. Heath responded, "She's also a sea merchant."

Moraine looked skeptical, until his eyes landed on Tarnation. He squinted smugly. "And lastly, the man of many names—the Oaknagan Killer, Snake Bite, Tarnation. You do realize he is wanted for numerous crimes in Pemberton? He murdered my people, the great barons and baronesses of our empire. I would be within my rights to kill him on the spot."

Tarnation said, "Tit for tat, bud. You killed more in Vernon. I did my job, is all."

Moraine forced a wincing smile and looked down at the thick arches of wood containing Tarnation's wrists. "Yes, well, you're not going to be doing any *jobs* today, are you?"

Tarnation didn't respond.

Moraine took a bite of quiche, chewed, swallowed, and pushed his plate away. "Let's get on with it. What did you want to buy?"

Nillias cleared his throat. "I'm a collector of ancient artifacts. I wish to purchase the fossilized dinosaur egg that Heath sold to you."

"Emperor. Address me as Emperor."

"Forgive me, Emperor. I spoke out of turn."

Moraine looked around the table. "I know what you speak of. I have grown quite fond of it, so I'm not sure what you could offer in return. I'm afraid that you may have come all this way for nothing."

Nillias nodded to Lexie. Slowly, she pulled out Warrick's energy weapons from under her chair and placed them on the table.

Moraine did look interested. His eyes were glued to the weapons. "And what are these?"

Warrick answered. "Emperor, these are Old World energy weapons. They fire concentrated pulses of plasma that explode on contact."

"Do they still work?" Moraine asked.

"No, Emperor," Warrick said, "but they are otherwise in good repair, and I know of no other ones in existence."

"Well, I'm not sure what good they are if they don't work."

Nillias said, "Emperor, I'm not sure you would want them to be functional, as they would call retchers. But may I ask, wouldn't they be a fair trade for the dinosaur egg? At least these are impressive Old World technology, which I know you are partial to. Not only that, but they are symbols of strength, whereas the egg does nothing. I am a collector, and have no need for weapons, but archeological artifacts intrigue me, even if we can't be sure if they are real."

"The egg is definitely real," Moraine said. "In fact, when the reaping occurs, it will hatch. I will spawn the dinosaur and it will be mine to rear as I please."

There was a moment of silence as Lexie tried to tease the words apart. Was he kidding?

"Excuse us, Emperor," Health said. "The reaping?"

"When it is time for Pemberton's barons and baronesses to take back their rightful lands from the neighboring fiefdoms and beyond, from across the continent and great seas. When the misguided peasants of the common lands recognize our divine right and drool at our feet. The time is coming, and soon."

To the credit of Lexie's colleagues, no one was flinching at these delectable nuggets of madness. A long moment of uncomfortable silence followed. In that time, Moraine's countenance had morphed from maniacal to disappointed. "So this is all you've brought me?" he said finally, gesturing at the weapons on the table.

"Yes, Emperor," Nillias said. "We believe it is a fair deal—more than adequate compensation, in fact. If you disagree, we will have to seek out other buyers."

"I see," Moraine said, and he stood up from the table. He wandered closer to the windows, as if to gaze over the valley below. In passing, he spoke to one of the waiters who was standing against the wall. "You can clear the table." The waiter went to start grabbing plates and bowls. A few other men came in to help.

"I am a collector, too, as you know." Moraine spoke to the pane of glass. "I collect many things: the seeds of plant varieties, the organs of rare animal species, modern art, Old World clothing, Old World tech, and many books. There is one book, in particular, that I have been reading lately. It has provided me with much joy, and also, fascinating context."

Lexie had to crane her head around the hovering wait staff to see Moraine. He turned toward them. "Have you heard of Leopold Halsey? I usually find it hard to read scientific papers and journals, but his writing is quite engaging."

Nillias responded with some hesitancy. "Yes, Emperor."

"And so you must know about the ICSM cities, and the control junctions. Wouldn't it be nice to have one of those artifacts? Imagine having the key to so much untapped potential. The greatest collector's items are those that might even be useful someday."

It wasn't a promising development in their negotiation, but that wasn't the worst of it. Right at that moment, when Moraine snapped his fingers, was when things went really pear-shaped.

In a flash, the waiters dropped their dishes and sprang into action. They converged on Nillias and the Gungivite men first. The Gungivites were pushed face-first onto the table, and their hands were held behind their backs. Guards closed in on Lexie, Heath and Warrick as well, but Lexie managed to pull out her boot knife. With a sweeping slash, she cut open the jerkin of the nearest one. Warrick also grabbed one of the waiters and threw him on the table. He followed through by smashing a plate on his head, leaving craggy lines of red on his face, before his victim rolled off onto the floor. Heath had backed away from the table, his hands in the air, and was apprehended by one of the surrounding goons. Four other men had piled on Tarnation, pushing him into the table despite his manacled state.

There was a pause in the melee as Lexie swept her blade a few more times, creating more space for her and Warrick. Warrick grabbed a bundle of forks from the table in each hand.

"Just stand back," Moraine said to his guards, shaking his head. "Two against all our imperial might? They'll figure out the odds eventually."

Moraine began pacing to the window again, as if nothing had happened. His guards did stay back from Lexie and Warrick, but their weapons were ready. The situation looked grim. In a melee they would be taken out in short order. In fact, all the men had to do was level crossbows at them and it would be over.

Moraine said, "So you may have surmised that I haven't been quite honest, but neither have you, and I am tiring of the ruse. Given the rumors I have heard about the ICSM cities awakening, and now you coming here, trying to sell me useless weapons at this auspicious time, it makes me oh so curious. I have to wonder if the day has come when my so-called dinosaur egg will be useful. So tell me. What do you plan to use the control junction for? I will let you go, if you're forthcoming. But if you lie, or leave anything out …" He grimaced.

Lexie's eyes flitted about, trying to find some way out. She doubted they'd survive even if they gave him the answers he wanted. He'd lied to them once, so he would lie again. And why would he let them live? There was nothing in it for him. This Moraine was a crazy, narcissistic, dictator packrat, but he wasn't stupid.

It seemed that Warrick had made the same calculation. While Moraine had been speaking, he must have been moving his hands along the table. With a clatter, the forks in his hand fell to make room for something else—the energy weapon. He lifted it to point at Moraine.

Moraine frowned. "Please. This is no more than a toy."

Warrick pressed a series of buttons on the side. A hissing sound came from the weapon, like the pilot light being lit in a gas stove, but louder. Blue flashes pulsed on the side of the weapon. "You're not the only good liar around here," Warrick said.

Later, Lexie would learn that this had been part of the plan. Or rather, Warrick and Nillias had agreed to it as a kind of insurance policy, in case things didn't go their way. Why she wasn't included in this discussion was something she would gripe about—but hey, she was glad somebody was thinking ahead.

People got real nervous all of a sudden. Moraine looked up at the ceiling, and at the exits. The other men in the room crouched further down in their tensed positions. "You can't …" Moraine said.

"Let them go," Warrick said.

"Emperor," Moraine said. "Let them go, Emperor."

That did it. Warrick wasn't a patient man, and he knew he didn't have much time.

He didn't begin with Moraine. Instead, he cut a swath into the armed men just across the room. The weapon was like an automatic grenade launcher, but the explosives excised huge chunks of tissue and left burn marks the color of hot lava. He blasted away, methodically turning around the room, cutting men in half as if wielding a cosmic scythe.

Lexie slashed in the opposite direction, keeping men away from Warrick's back. Many recoiled in fear in any case. Heath managed to elbow his assailant in the gut, pushing him back as well. Meanwhile, Tarnation stood up and threw off the men that had been trying to keep him down. His movements were limited, but he found a way to hop around the table toward the men Warrick had just pulverized, searching for the keys to his manacles.

Warrick's circuit ended at the men holding the Gungivites, and they had the presence of mind to back away. Nillias and his men took knives out of their belts and went after their assailants.

Warrick's aim started to falter, or maybe he was just having fun. He blasted a door at the back, and swiveled around to blow out a window. Moraine was creeping away, but he stopped when Warrick trained the weapon on him.

Lexie saw the light on the side of the weapon extinguish. Warrick immediately threw it toward Moraine and picked up the other energy weapon lying in front of him. He scrambled over the table and said, "to the library."

Lexie slashed back one more time and followed Warrick. They ran toward the door he'd blasted on the far side of the room. Back near the table, Nillias's men grappled with the remaining guards. One of the Gungivite militia had a sword thrust deep in his abdomen. Nillias managed to trip his original assailant and regain a curved blade that had been taken from him, but a group of six men were gathering nearby, preparing to attack them as a group. The Gungivites backed away and followed after Lexie and Warrick.

"Come on, Tarn!" Lexie yelled from the blown-out doorway. Tarnation had managed to uncuff himself and was wielding a heavy axe in his hand, testing its weight.

"Tarn, let's go! To the library!"

Tarnation shook his head and turned toward Moraine.

Moraine now had several men surrounding him, and more were coming in from an adjoining room. Not only that, but he had picked up the energy weapon Warrick had been using. He turned it over in his hands, a look of wonder in his eyes. He pointed it at Tarnation, but nothing happened.

Well, something did happen. It was in the back of Lexie's mind the whole time, and probably had been in Moraine's too, and the others, but you know—the heat of battle and all.

The retcher blasted through the window, taking out the remaining shards of glass with a crash. It was a big one—maybe even as big as Tarnation, with a huge, serrated beak and glossy black wings that hurt her eyes to look at. Sometimes the retchers liked to sniff around a bit, to make sure they were in the right place. This one didn't give much of an introduction, because it knew its quarry well. The weapon had certainly made enough of a mess.

Before it even landed, acidic vomit was spraying out of its beak. Moraine screamed, of course, since he was the recipient of most of it. He dropped the weapon and grabbed at his burning face and chest while the retcher made sure to vomit on the weapon enough until it liquefied into a steaming puddle on the floor.

Everyone watching was pretty much stiff as a statue at this point, except Tarnation. He didn't care about the retcher. While the Pemberton soldiers gawked, he hacked at their necks and took out their knees with his axe.

The retcher jumped out of the window and flew away.

"Tarn, let's go!" Lexie yelled across the room. He wasn't listening. He was facing off against four soldiers who looked like they'd already pissed themselves several times over.

"We don't have time, Lexie." It was Nillias, and he was right.

The lot of them left Tarnation and headed to the library.

The library was in an annex to the main building, down a circular staircase and through a long hallway. They didn't encounter any guards along the way.

It didn't have that many books, but there were indeed many of the items Moraine had referenced. One section had a display of animal organs in enclosed glass jars, swimming in a bluish preservative. There were drawers of labeled seed stocks and plant matter. Another section contained Old World computer equipment, including motherboards, laptops, phones, and televisions. Most were cracked or heavily tarnished. There was an impressive painting of the valley around Pemberton, and other artwork that was just flashy lines and splotches.

They found the orb in a glass display case next to some large bones, an old map, and a tall decanter made of stained glass. Nillias examined the orb, confirmed its identity, and snatched it without further hesitation.

When they returned to the hallway, Lexie was surprised there were no guards impeding their path, but perhaps the retcher had spooked them. She heard distant yells, sounding like they were coming from outside the building.

As they neared the big hall again, there was just the occasional scraping sound, and a man moaning in pain. Nevertheless, they approached quietly.

When Lexie poked her head in, she couldn't help but turn away. There were no guards left alive, just carnage, and Tarnation bouncing around the room. He was smiling again, back to his old self. In one hand he held a clutch of hair that dangled down to four red circlets of flesh, which were dripping trails onto the ground. He put his knife to the temple of another soldier and started cutting. "One more and I'm good," he said.

"That's enough, Tarn," Lexie said. "We've got to go."

"What? I have a reputation to keep up, *bae*."

When the group rode out of the palace into the countryside, they had to dodge a few arrows, but nobody had the temerity to come out and challenge them head on. There probably weren't that many men left, since Moraine must have had most of his garrison at the meeting. How many warriors could a puny empire have, anyway?

Nillias was riding hard, and Lexie followed his lead. It made sense to outpace the news of their escape, so as to get ahead of any mobilized resistance. And that's why they weren't really paying attention to Warrick and Heath when maybe they should have been. Or maybe it was because Warrick was the reason they had gotten out of this mess in one piece. Maybe they thought they were all best buds.

They were wrong.

A couple of hours into riding, after several tight curves through thickly forested areas, Warrick and Heath had disappeared.

—35—

UNTIL THEY RETURN

After a rather aggressive pat-down, Kerub led Dryden, Cecile and Rosalie to Leopold's study. The room matched how Dryden had imagined Leopold's work area quite well. A large bank of windows in the rear gave the room a welcoming feel. It was spacious, with a sturdy wooden desk, soft carpet, and shelves lined with books.

Outside, the sky was filled with angry gray clouds. Brown, yellow and orange leaves were spinning down into the yard, encouraged by the occasional gust of wind. And Leopold's mood, if Dryden was to guess, was more in line with the weather than with his comfortable surroundings. He was sitting at his desk, with one hand gripping the stock of a shotgun, his spectacles partially fogged up. A burly man stood in the corner, also wielding a gun, the barrel and butt rounded by taut fingers.

"I don't like surprises," was all Leopold said when the group arrived.

"I'm sorry for the unannounced visit," Dryden said. "This is Cecile and Rosalie. They represent a faction in the machine war to the east. We came to seek your counsel."

"So you say. How do I know you're not here to kill me or kidnap me?"

Cecile said, "Leo—you must remember me, from those many years ago. We have also corresponded many times. I have sent you several letters just recently."

"Yes, I remember when we met. What was it—ten years ago? But I never knew you well, and people change, especially in times like these, with armies moving about, and machine cities manipulating minds. Tell me, Cecile, who do you represent? The Quebecois, the Spokes, or the Essentialists?"

"Yes."

"What do you mean? Which one?"

"All of them. Humanity."

Leo rolled his eyes.

"I can vouch for Cecile and Rosalie," Dryden said. "I've traveled with them all the way from Hood River. They understand the threat of the ICSM cities."

Leo directed a sour look toward Dryden. "And who can vouch for you?"

"I … we've been … you know me, Leo. I sent you all my findings."

Leo sighed. "I know you mean well, but I was referring to your competence. Who can vouch for your *competence* in dealing with these people? So far you've been nothing but trouble for me—always hounding me for information, sneaking in pernicious review letters whenever I publish, and now I have to deal with your messy research paper on the ICSM cities. To top it off, I get this letter from your former boss yesterday." He waved a folded piece of paper in his left hand.

Dryden was curious about Maxwell's letter, but much more curious about Leo's view of his work on the ICSM cities. "What's wrong with my paper?"

Leo's eyes bulged. "You don't know? I guess that figures. There aren't enough control subjects who didn't go in the experiential rooms. And you can't use yourself as a control. It's a mess."

"You don't believe me?"

"Of course I believe you. I'm not an idiot. I just told you I'm worried about mind control, and I've had at least ten people try to get me to visit the cities in the last week, for questionable reasons. But your paper—the one you somehow want me to assign my name to—will be ripped to shreds by peer reviewers."

Dryden had been excited for this meeting, to finally meet Leopold face to face and discuss his important findings with a worthy scholar, but instead of feeling valued, Leo had essentially knocked him to the floor.

"Dryden?" Leo asked.

He was at a loss for words.

Leo said, "Look, maybe it's not that bad, but now I've got your boss sending me a formal request for a meeting in Victoria. He wants to *thank me* for my service by grilling me about ICSM cities. Realistically, that's the best-case scenario. I wouldn't be surprised if they kidnap me. And if I don't come, working legs or not, I can read between the lines." He waved the paper at Dryden angrily. "In not so many words, it would be tantamount to pissing in the eternal spring and declaring a one-man war against a whole continent of Essentialists."

"It may come to that," Cecile said. "A war, I mean. Not one man, but as many of us as possible against the Essentialists. If we can't stop the cities some other way, we will need to destroy them."

"Ha. Well, that's nice. Good luck with that. I suppose I should thank you for proving my point about why I shouldn't trust you."

"Reinforcements are coming," Cecile said, ignoring his quip. "We have an army of EMP-resistant machines that is moving west as we speak. We will need to ship them to Kuvar Island to fight against the Essentialists. We have already enlisted Anacortes shipwrights to begin building platforms for transporting them."

Leo's eyebrows raised. "EMP-resistant? As in, resistant to electromagnetic pulses?"

"Yes."

Leo's eyes darted about, obviously trying to make sense of what she said. He didn't have response for Cecile this time, perhaps because what she said sounded so outlandish.

"But it's not enough," Cecile said. "We need allies. We need to find a way to disable Haplopol and Diplopol, or possibly awaken the other ICSM cities."

"You too, eh? I don't understand why everyone thinks that's such a good idea. Awakening Haplopol and Diplopol was ill-advised. Why do it again?"

Cecile nodded grimly. "Yes, well, it's a dilemma, I agree, but we may have no other choice. Dryden here seems to think the cities that were founded later were more advanced, and possibly safer."

Leo turned to Dryden. "I'm sure he does," he said snarkily. "He's a hexxer."

Dryden explained, "A hexxer is someone who believes there could have been six ICSM cities, rather than five. Our views aren't popular in the research community. I wrote a paper on it, a few years ago. The hexxer hypothesis is supported by the idea that Morganis was trying to create a utopia, and with each subsequent city his design was improved, while at the same time each city became better defended and more hidden. Thus, in theory the last city could have been the best city, but also undiscoverable, and thus never mentioned in any historical documents."

Leo said, "This is all conjecture. While it's true that improvement with each city was Morganis's goal, it doesn't make sense that he would hide the last city from the rest of humanity. What would be the point?"

"It's possible it was destroyed, like Triplopol was," Dryden said. "Or it may even exist but we don't know about it. They may have disappeared on purpose, for their own protection."

"*Excusez-moi*," Cecile said, stepping forward, "You could debate this forever. I must know—you said, *you too*—who are the others who want to awaken the cities?"

Leo studied her for a moment. He said, "Okay, I believe you are who you say you are. And Dryden here is as annoying as I expected he would be. Your friend does look like a Merchant Merc. Essentialists wouldn't have faked that."

Rosalie showed her gap-toothed smile.

"So if you want to square off against the Essentialists, the only allies I can think of are the Gungivites. Maybe the Kuvar Collective, as well, but they're too disorganized. The Essentialists make a stink about them, but mostly as an excuse for irresponsible military maneuvers."

"The others are Gungivites? They want to raise the other cities?"

Leo nodded slowly.

Rosalie said, "Five or six—whatever. How do we get these cities to rise and shine?"

Leo answered. "To awaken Tetrapol and Pentapol, you'll need the other control junctions, and you'll need to find the ruins. Nobody knows where they are."

"What about Triplopol?" Cecile asked.

"It's been vaporized," Leo said. "Some kind of super bomb, where the Goldstream crater is. We have good records of that."

Cecile nodded. "Any ideas where to find the control junctions?"

Leo looked at each of them in turn. Rosalie was winking at the fiefdom man in the corner. "I don't know," Leo said, "but I've got some Gungivite friends who might. They should be back in town in a few days. I'll connect you to them, on one condition."

"What's that?" Cecile asked.

Leo lifted Maxwell's letter from the desk again. "Take care of this for me."

All eyes turned to Dryden. "You want *me* to go?" he objected. "But they've asked for you! Maxwell won't want me there." Images of the last time he was in Victoria returned to him; the race through town, the panic in Diplopol, and Elissa running to her death.

Leo shrugged. "Even though your paper needs work, you're the only academic who's seen the ICSM cities in operation firsthand. You can say you offered to go in my stead. You know about as much as I do, even if you're not officially an expert. I'll give you some of my unpublished archival material to make it look like I'm helping. That should appease him."

"What if the Essentialists don't want me there?"

"They almost certainly do not. Otherwise, they wouldn't have sent you back to Hood River. The Essentialists want me because they know I'm working with the Gungivites on my research, and so they'll probably want to muzzle me, or find a way to get intelligence on the Gungivites. That's why there's no way I'm going. I can smell a trap. At least you have a good argument to go in my place. You're Essentialist, and they trust you well enough, and you have two working legs. If they don't like it, we've at least bought some time."

Cecile and Leo were both giving Dryden grim looks. Who was he to object? He wasn't as important as Leopold, and the logic made sense, but Maxwell wouldn't be happy, and if Prefectorate soldiers were behind this, it could get really ugly. Maybe they'd kill him. Maybe they'd feed him to the city experiential rooms. Although, those outcomes didn't seem that bad anymore. At least it would put him out of his misery.

Cecile said, "Dryden, I think you should consider Leo's proposal. It may be our only—"

"I'll do it," Dryden said.

"*Bien,*" Cecile said, an inflection of surprise in her voice. She turned to Leopold. "There you have it. So what can you tell us about these Gungivite friends of yours?"

"Until they return, nothing."

The next evening, Dryden ran along the Anacortes shoreline, through marinas big and small, across beaches and pathways. It had been a while since he'd gone for a run. As a result, his breathing was labored, but more than that, his feet felt heavy. Each step seemed like a pointless endeavor, an exercise in frivolity.

He ran in his torn T-shirt, even though the air was cool, barely above freezing. People gawked and snarked at his irresponsible attire. And yet, he couldn't feel the cold.

About halfway through his run he came across a particularly long pier, abandoned, with a board across the entrance and a sign reading *Danger*.

He hopped over the board and ran down the pier, adeptly avoiding rusty nails and gaps in floorboards. A large swath of wood was missing halfway along its length. He had to tiptoe on a support beam to get across.

He stopped before the end, as the rest of the pier had no more boards. Only a few rounded wooden posts remained. They stood alone, sentinels accepting the unrelenting undulations of the sea.

The water drew him in. He lay down on the boards, scraping the flesh of his leg against what must have been a rusty nail, without looking back to check. He watched the waves, foamy and black, as they pushed and pulled, rose and fell.

Why delay the inevitable?

He rolled forward and splashed into the murky waters. It was shockingly cold, but not enough for him to react, not enough for him to move his limbs. He sank down to the bottom, until his progress was halted by slimy, rounded rocks.

The urge to breathe gradually rose in him until it became a desperate plea. He tried to suppress it but he couldn't. It conspired against him, along with the cold waters, forcing him to flex his leg muscles and push up out of the water.

He gasped for air, and gasped again.

In a floundering, directionless swim, he was slowly pushed in to shore. He took briny water into his mouth and stomach with each wave, but still he was able to take ragged breaths. When he was close enough, he tripped over more slimy rocks until his legs were bloody and bruised.

He stepped onto shore.

It made sense, he supposed. He wasn't really good at anything; why would he be good at killing himself?

Later that evening, after he'd returned to the small flat Cecile had rented, he warmed up by the fire and packed for his trip to Victoria.

Cecile was in the main shipyard, toiling away, managing her platform construction projects with Rosalie and the Quebecois men, so he sat alone, watching the lantern burn and listening to its barely audible hum.

Eventually, he unfastened his travel case and took out the ship in a bottle that Sergio had sent him. It was called the *Restless Crab*. Sergio had been meticulous in every detail. The ship was painted a deep red with gilded trim lines, and it had four masts with billowing sails. Tiny Essentialist flags depicted a cherry blossom tree superimposed on a sun flying from the top of each mast.

Beside the bottle, with its mast bent down and sail folded in, was his own ship. It was not nearly as ambitious, and it could be said to be pathetic in comparison, although it still looked like a ship. It was a fishing trawler he'd named *Nate's Catch*. He'd painted it sapphire blue and sewn in a patchy sail like the old ferries on the Columbia River—something Nate might recognize. He had also knitted tiny squares of floss that hung over the side, which if he was lucky would pass for a fishing net if Nate wasn't looking very closely.

He still had work to do. He needed to finish the flag and touch up the paint in a few places, and he hadn't found the right sized bottle to put it in. Maybe he could find one in Victoria.

He examined the *Restless Crab* again, trying to see if he was missing any details on his own ship. His eyes scrolled over the captain's cabin, and it reminded him of the conversation he had with Sergio at Marrowstone Flotilla, months ago. What did he call his ship? Ah yes, the *Dirty Princess*. He'd left a secret message for his "Dirty Princess" in the captain's cabin. Dryden allowed himself a dry chuckle at the thought.

The captain's cabin on the *Restless Crab* was a big one, so he wondered if Sergio might have left another message to a future lover, or maybe even for Dryden. It was the kind of thing Sergio liked to do—to spend weeks building a model ship just so he could send him some offbeat joke.

Dryden picked up his miniature hook and used it to try to take the ship out of the bottle.

What would certainly have taken Sergio less than a minute took Dryden a good five or ten. Several failed attempts to properly collapse the sails and masts were followed by more failed attempts to extract the ship from the bottle. Finally, it was out.

He pulled at the miniature door of the captain's cabin and it opened. Inside there was indeed a tiny folded piece of blue parchment, full of text. It was legible, but barely.

He unfolded it and read the message.

He read it again.

The tiny paper fell from his hand. It swayed in the air, as a feather might—left to right to left—then settled on the floor.

The paper trembled as Dryden began to yell. It jumped and spun as his rage crossed over it, and through it. There was a moment of silence, and the tiny fragment trembled again as another mortal scream shot sound waves through the floorboards of the flat one more time.

An hour later, with his rage finally tempered but not assuaged, with a dam sundered and his emotion flooding into action, he bent to the floor, picked up the paper, and threw it into the fire.

—36—

About Those Fruit Cellars

The only resistance Lexie, Tarnation and the Gungivites encountered was the same two goat farmers at the Pemberton border. These two hadn't caught wind of what had happened, so they were easily surprised. As the farmers were coming down the hill, Nillias and Emry dispatched them with a few well-placed pistol rounds. After that, it took quite a bit of arguing to get Tarnation to stay on his horse and not add them to his collection of scalps.

"This is *rhaatid*, Lex," he said with some level of irritation. "What's the point of flexing if we can't be cutting scalps?"

"Look Tarn, is two more really going to make a huge difference?" she asked. Eventually he agreed to move on without further complaint.

They rode hard past the Pemberton border wall until they reached Lilloet Lake, another skinny band of water that filled the space between mountains. Here Nillias bought a rickety boat for a rather steep price and they all packed on while they tried to catch the temperamental mountain winds. Nillias had them disembark before they reached the end of the lake, then he pushed the boat further down, which he probably hoped would confuse any pursuers. The group followed a worn path up the hill to an old, rundown cottage and stayed there for the night.

Emry took watch, but Lexie didn't sleep much. The others appeared to have similar problems. The cause of her insomnia might have been adrenaline, but it could also have been their accommodations. It was a cold, moldy place, with one habitable room, and they couldn't light a fire or fill their bellies with anything cooked. They sat there, mostly in silence, while Emry ogled a scope to watch for passersby on the main path down below.

There was the smell, also.

Nillias moved close to Lexie and whispered in her ear, "Are those necessary?" His chin edged toward the crusty scalps. Tarnation had hung them by their hair on a stick near the doorway. They were becoming an increasing contributor to the smell.

She grimaced. "I don't know."

Some might think Tarnation was a sociopath, with the scalps and all, but Lexie liked to believe he had a good reason for his shenanigans. The hair and the tattoos and the gregarious nature would throw people off, but Tarnation was thoughtful about these things more often than not.

But in this case, she couldn't think of a good reason they needed the scalps, and Nillias was the boss here. "Sorry, Tarn, but those gotta go," she said, pointing to the scalps. "Even if I thought they were worth something, which I don't, they stink. If these Pemberton fiefers have dogs they could track us."

Tarnation went quiet, which usually wasn't a good sign.

"Why do you scalp them?" Nillias asked. He had retaken his seat next to Emry.

Tarnation turned to Nillias, but his eyes weren't visible in the dark. Lexie could only see the shifting of a dangling braid he'd woven out of his hair bun. It caught the moonlight coming in through one of the broken windows.

"A few years back I was in Vernon," Tarnation said, "a fiefdom in the west. I worked for hire, fishing on Lake Oaknagan. Best job I ever had. I like their way of life. They know the land, how to take it slow. But then the wars started. Moraine raided. Killed lots of people, including my boss and his wife, so I joined the Vernon militia. We fought back. The people of Vernon, they're the ones who taught me to take scalps. Each scalp is more powerful than any weapon, because it's like fear, eh? They told me—what was it—each scalp is the *death of ambition* in your enemy, because no one wants to fight if they know they might be scalped. So if you take a scalp, you save a soul. Guess what—no one ever attacked Vernon after that, no boss."

"I gather you were good at it," Nillias said.

Tarnation shifted in the dark. "Yeah, I done scalped quite a few. It's not that hard, really, like filleting a fish, but still, most folks rush the job. You can rush killing, 'cause you're afraid, or 'cause you don't want them to fight back, fine. But why rush scalping? They ain't gonna fight back. They're good and dead, and then you come back with a bad scalp after all that fuss? It's silly, but people do it just the same. Boggles my mind. The first thing you do is hold the crop of hair—"

"You don't need to explain," Nillias said, "and you can keep your scalps, Tarnation."

"Yeah, boss. Was hoping you'd say that. Saving souls here. You okay with that, Lex?"

If Nillias could handle the smell, who was she to complain? "Yeah, Tarn. Forget I said anything."

The next morning Emry said a gang of Pemberton men had ridden by on the path below twice, once to the south, and back through to the north a couple of hours later. It was enough to give Lexie confidence that they'd avoided the search party.

The rest of the mountain ride was similarly uneventful, as was Chilliwack and Abbotsford. They didn't turn south to Anacortes after that, but rather headed west to reach the coast just north of the small port of Bellingham.

In Bellingham Tarnation parted ways with the rest of the group. Nillias paid him and even gave him a bonus. Tarnation's face lit up and he grappled Nillias with a monster bear hug. "Nice dinner for me and Sammy tonight. Going to get me some nook for sure. Ha, ha."

Nillias nodded placidly.

In the Bellingham marina Lexie and the Gungivites were collected by a skiff that took them to two Gungivite galleons lurking behind an island. Once they were aboard and safely on their way to Ganges, Nillias took a spot at the bow. He had the same look of contentment on his face that Lexie had seen when he was aboard the *Nox*. She figured it would be a good time to approach him—before his implant could reconnect with the network in Ganges and he would go all fluttery on her.

"Hey, Nillias. Sorry about bringing Tarnation along. I didn't know he'd be a problem."

Nillias raised his eyebrows. "He was a great addition. He distracted most of the Pemberton people from our true motives. Even though Moraine wasn't quite fooled, I think it gave us an advantage."

"Figures you'd say that. You might as well say, 'Of course it's fine with me, Lexie, 'cause I'm a nutjob.'"

His lips curled at the edges until a melancholic look occupied his face. "Every once in a while you make me smile. It's something that's not entirely logical. Maybe it's an idiosyncratic shadow of who I was—a phantom of my soul that takes over for a brief instant."

"Oh … sorry?"

He shook his head. "It's not a bad thing. In fact, I can't tell you how much of a privilege it is, to know who I was, during those brief interludes. Thank you for that."

"You're welcome, I guess."

"And thank you for helping me at the Pemberton wall. I felt unbalanced there, without access to my implant. I might have made some bad choices without your help."

"Hey, it was nothing."

"But what I'm not thankful for, is you trying to gain leverage on me behind my back."

Nauseous nettles. She tried to play dumb. "What do you mean?"

"You don't know who you're up against, Lexie. I think the Salish Sea saying would be, *don't jump into murky waters unless you want to lose a limb*."

He still hadn't said anything relevant. He could be fishing, trying to get her to reveal something. She said, "Okay, I'll be careful."

He shook his head and said, "Ryder is my cousin."

Well, that made a whole heap of sense. No wonder Ryder was betraying her left and right. "Really?" She tried to sound shocked.

"He was selected as an Observer, but his parents sent him away just after he had his implant inserted, which is a grave offense. Ryder went into hiding on the mainland, living in Abbotsford, Omak, and finally, Anacortes. As a result, he missed the bulk of the Observer indoctrination process. When we finally found him in Anacortes, I convinced the council to let him stay there and act as an agent on our behalf, rather than return to Ganges. I like to think he is like me … or at least, what I would be like if I hadn't been chosen."

He looked distracted for a brief moment, before returning his gaze to her.

"I get it," she said. "So back when we first went to the embassy in Victoria, he was a plant." She was playing the part, trying to act surprised, but what he said next took her by surprise for real.

"Yes, and so was Tarnation."

"What?"

"Tarnation has been working for us for a while. This is why I didn't mind him coming along. In fact, I thought it might be a good idea before you even suggested it."

"I don't believe it."

"It is part of our mission as Observers to enlist agents, most of them secret, to know what is happening in the surrounding territories. Tarnation doesn't understand everything about what we stand for, but he is loyal to us. He is loyal to you as well, but he's smart, and knows that to betray us would only get you both killed. Nevertheless, he told me what you asked of him, but only on the condition that I inform you that he is working for us."

She had known Tarnation for a while and never suspected he'd do work for the Gungivites. Everyone was so frightened of him. But these wingnuts weren't scared of anything, and they sure paid well. She couldn't blame him for taking their money.

It had been odd that Nillias took Tarnation at his word about the "impassable" warning when they were at the wall, especially when he'd been so suspicious of the others. Now it made more sense.

"So you're telling me all this because …"

"Because it's pointless, Lexie. You keep looking for leverage on me, or for some way out. You're wasting your energy. We still need you, but we can't have any more meddling, or the very thing you fear might happen. Yes, we might have to engage with your mother in an undesirable way, and it becomes more likely the more volatile you are—the less you cooperate."

"Yeah, thanks for that. Just when I think you're halfway human, you go and mess it up. Basically, you're saying my mom is fish bait, and I should just suck it up."

She couldn't take it anymore. She stomped away from him, pausing at the cabin door to gather herself. She felt like kicking the doorframe, she felt so powerless, but she didn't want to give Nillias the satisfaction.

She looked back at him, expecting some smug look, or one of his even more frustrating vacuous expressions. He was indeed watching her, but he wasn't stone-faced. He looked concerned, possibly even sad, if such a thing was possible for an Observer nutjob.

But then his head went back, he closed his eyes, and his eyelids fluttered.

She looked to the starboard and could see that they were passing by Moresby Island again, where the hidden Gungivite communications tower was. Nillias must have reconnected. He would probably be preoccupied for a while, catching up with his implant buddies back home, so Lexie left him there.

Instead of heading down into the cabin, she went to the rear of the boat. For the rest of the voyage, she watched Gungivite galleons moving about in the distance. There were five sitting in formation, smack dab in Satellite Channel, the body of water that separated Ganges Island from the Saanich Peninsula of Kuvar Island. Three more were patrolling further to the west, and two to the east.

She'd never seen so many Gungivite vessels in one place. She could only surmise they weren't taking too kindly to their new Essentialist neighbors.

When they disembarked in the Ganges City harbor, Nillias and Emry left their bags behind on the ship and took her straight into town. They walked into the *Gungi-Bites* shop she'd been in months ago, and down the stairs toward the bathrooms and fruit cellars.

"Where are we going?" Lexie asked.

Nillias said, "I'm sure you didn't think these were really fruit cellars."

Well, no, it was true, she didn't. She had assumed they were a front for weapons caches, or maybe shielded bunkers. She had imagined there might also be a few computer terminals there, with wigged nutjobs typing away.

But not this.

Just inside the interior door to the apple cellar was a room with a red field of light. They all passed through it, and she heard a chime sound as a green button pulsed further along the wall, three times. They proceeded through a door in the back, which opened up into a huge underground chamber.

The chamber was lit by glowing blue panels spanning the ceiling. A series of rails embedded in the floor split off into tunnels in several directions. They walked up to the base of a platform, at the point where these rails converged. Lights and icons blinked from a waist-high podium that Nillias led them towards.

Emry and Nillias didn't use the podium. They just stood there, and what looked like a souped-up Old World van, travelling on the rail instead of on wheels, came around the corner and stopped abruptly in front of them.

Nillias, Emry and her took seats inside the van and it moved on. They travelled wordlessly as it navigated through tunnels and intersections without any apparent guidance from Nillias and Emry, although it was possible they were dedicating attention to it with their implants. Lexie would be the last to know.

At one point, a tunnel opened up and the van entered another huge underground cavern. It must have been half a mile long, but they were going so fast that Lexie only caught a few glimpses during their hundred-yard passage through it. She spotted factory floors, what seemed to be humanoid robots moving about, and Gungivites at podium terminals.

Then the van was in an enclosed tunnel again, but only briefly, until it broke out into an even larger cavern that was a perfectly rounded ovoid. The cavern must have been a mile in diameter. Vans like their own flitted about on lines that crossed the ground or hung from the ceiling. The many buildings and structures within the cavern were built in stacked terraces, like steps rising from a wide base at the bottom and tapering to a narrow column in the middle, flaring out again at the top of the cavern. This central conglomerate of buildings was shaped like a stalagmite and stalactite meeting in the middle. The blue buildings were peppered with gray translucent squares.

"Welcome to Tetrapol," Nillias said.

"*Tetrapol?*" she said. "What is *wrong* with you people?"

"Tetrapol is the fourth city founded by Morganis. It was built under Ganges Island, in secret, at a time when the golden age of the ICSM cities was ending and conflict had arisen between them."

"It's been here the whole time?"

"Yes, but it's important to stress that the Tetrapol control junction is substantially different than those of the rest of the ICSM cities. It has geographical constraints but also constraints upon processing power. For generations, it has only been using a minute fraction of its processing power, to limit the potential for a runaway control problem. Furthermore, it is only used in oracle mode, which means substantially all decisions must be reviewed and approved by a human being in advance. And most importantly, the city's primary overriding objective is to ensure the peaceful coexistence of human and machine intelligences. Back in ICSM times, it acted like a kind of internal police for all the other cities."

"That's all very reassuring," Lexie said, "but we always find ways to screw things up, don't we?"

She thought he would protest. This was his home, his people, and his whole way of life, but instead he grimaced and took a sizzling breath through clenched teeth.

The van shifted tracks and took a curving path toward the spindly city core. To Lexie's left and right were plots filled with blue buildings of different shapes and sizes, built on a grid bisected by dark avenues. Occasional garden plots dotted the landscape, brightly lit by glowing lamps. There were two significant hubs of activity in the distance, where machines glinted and the occasional Observer milled about. In one corner of these plots, she spotted some kind of artillery weapons, or maybe anti-aircraft guns. Each had banks of shells and two large barrels stacked on turret mounts. In another corner was what looked like a fleet of miniature helicopters, decked out with a heck of a lot of nasty Old World ordnance. Besides these more vibrant areas, the vast majority of the city below the main core was unlit.

"How many people live in the city?" she asked.

Nillias's eyes were fluttering, so Emry answered instead. "No more than a thousand. Our implants allow for many collaborative activities to occur remotely, and most people prefer to live on the surface. In addition, almost all of the city utilities are automated. In reality, it would take fewer than a dozen people to run Tetrapol."

"So why are those thousand down here now?"

Emry said, "All Gungivite Observers have been called to duty, given the escalating conflict with the Essentialists."

"Got it." As far as Lexie knew, there hadn't really been much conflict, other than what had happened around Diplopol, but if she threw into the mix the ships in the channel, the artillery cannons and flying doodads, she could guess the *escalating* part was about to happen soon.

The van cut into an enclosed tunnel, out of it, then into a deeper, broader tunnel. The track began veering upward, presumably into the center spindle of the city. Eventually, it leveled off and the van stopped next to another podium terminal. An Observer was waiting—a bald woman who didn't bother acknowledging them. After Nillias, Emry and Lexie had disembarked, the woman simply maneuvered around them and into the van. It sped away.

Nillias led Lexie inside the superstructure of the city, and Emry followed, passing through two sliding doors, another red laser field, and one thicker, heavier door that moved aside in front of Lexie as soon as they approached.

Finally, they arrived at the command center.

The room had at least a dozen active displays, with maps, charts, diagrams, manufacturing statistics and feeds from numerous cameras. The one closest to her had four panels, each displaying the output of a video feed. One showed a shipyard, another what could have been the interior of a hardware store, and the two others looked like busy streets. She recognized the shipyard. It was a Vicky marina.

She'd never considered the Observers could have cameras placed everywhere, but if they'd had Tetrapol up and running for years, who knew what was possible? In fact, the more she learned about the Gungivites, the less bad she felt about never being able to get one over on them.

Three Observers sat before them, with multiple displays wrapped around their chairs in a pentagonal formation. They would tap on a screen, similar to those on the podiums Lexie had seen beside the rails, while at the same time scanning over displays periodically. Their eyes would often close and their eyelids would flutter for brief periods.

One of these Gungivite Observers was Olint. The three of them maneuvered to stand in front of his chair.

Olint didn't immediately turn to acknowledge them. In fact, for a few minutes Lexie just stood watching all the data screens. Emry and Nillias were preoccupied with eyelid fluttering, so she figured they were just having a private chat.

Eventually, Olint emerged from his trance and turned to her. Without introduction, he said, "I wanted to thank you, Lexie, for helping us acquire the control junction. We now have a chance to fight back. If we can find Pentapol, it could even the odds."

"You don't know where Pentapol is?"

"We have a few clues, but no. We believe it is also underground, and it may have been accessible through the original Tetrapol network of tunnels. We know this because there are major conduits that go under the water to the east and west of Ganges Island that collapsed in the ICSM wars, although we have dug these out for several miles in each direction and found nothing. One of them, at least directionally, was headed toward Triplopol, and the other was headed west toward the Kuvar fever lands. Unfortunately, we have no other records that can help us. Tetrapol's servers were purged after the ICSM city wars, and our forefathers—the early Observers—said nothing of it."

He was remarkably forthcoming, but it wasn't because he was being nice. It turned out he was just setting the stage for a question.

"Your friend Warrick," he said. "What did he tell you about his plans for the control junction?"

"Plans? Hey, I told you guys I thought it was a fossilized dinosaur egg. He knew what it really was, sure, but I don't know if he knew much else. The guy's a pirate."

"And yet he was able to hit our supply depot in a specific window of time—two hours, in fact—when the Pentapol control junction was in transit from Duncan to Ganges Island. This is when it was least protected. He must have had inside information, or at least aerial support of some kind. Who was he working with?"

"Nobody I can think of. That was years ago. He's got Heath now, but he's more like a nurse than anything else." She looked at Nillias, who was staring at her intently. So were Emry and the other two Gungivites in the room. Their expressions told her nothing of their expectations or their level of satisfaction with her response.

She decided it was probably best to tell them everything. The displays with their reams of text, chats and video feeds blinking at her were intimidating. And who knew how much information they had? As much as she wanted to protect Warrick, it would be foolish to try to keep anything from the Gungivites.

"Okay, there was this Cecile woman. She's Quebecois and involved in the machine war in the east. As far as I know, she's an old acquaintance who's been trying to find Warrick—I'm sure Nillias told you that's how we found Warrick. He was intercepting letters Cecile was sending to Leo."

"What does she want?" Olint asked. "What did Warrick tell you before we became involved?"

"Just that she was dangerous, that if I ever saw her I should warn him. He said she would take him back east for—as he put it *—a crime he didn't want to commit*. It involved some other smart machine, if you can believe it. He was the key to using it. It was funny to me, because at other times he used to say he missed the east—that he wanted to head back."

Olint's eyelids fluttered for a moment. He said, "And who else was there that helped him? Who could have told him where our control junction was located?"

"Nobody I know, honestly, but he didn't tell me much. Warrick is a private guy. He had lots of theories and grudges and enemies, as old pirates do."

"Do you think Warrick knows where Pentapol is?"

"I have no idea, but he's pretty messed up in the head. Forgets a lot. Could be tough for him to remember, even if he did know at one point."

Olint nodded and said, "Thank you, Lexie. Excuse us."

Lexis was left standing there while the Observers had a prolonged powwow of eyelid fluttering. Although it could be considered rude, Lexie watched them with some fascination. Every once in a while, one of their faces would crease or flinch, or one of the displays would change and flash new information. Nillias's jaw flexed a couple of times. He still had fifteen moles—she counted.

Finally, Nillias exhaled, and his eyes turned to her. His shoulders were slouched as if from some kind of exhaustion. Being a nutjob was tiring, apparently.

"Let's go," he said, and he stomped out of the room. Emry peeled after him to follow.

Yeah, *stomped*. Not like Nillias's typical uptight style. Something was wrong.

—37—

The Vicarial Hotel

Dryden's table was replete with eye-popping dishes. To his left was a spit of mutton, with a sheen of red wine glaze dripping off of it. A healthy gouge had been carved out to reveal succulent white innards. To his right was a bowl of risotto with fried zucchini and flecks of red pepper, sautéed broccoli florets and a half-eaten lobster tail. And in the center of the table stood a three-layered tower of teapots, biscuit varieties, and jam, all staples of the Vicarial Hotel.

Beyond the limits of the table was plenty more to tempt the eye, including baskets of colorful grapes, cheese blocks of many shapes, bouquets of eccentric drooping flowers, and wine bottles of various sizes stacked beside each other like the pipes of an organ.

Across from Dryden, Maxwell was eating with gusto, his face a parade of satisfied expressions. In contrast to Dryden's sailing linens and woolen jacket, Maxwell was better dressed, wearing a ruffled shirt and satin jacket. Maxwell's hair was not astray, as it usually was, but rather pulled back into parallel lines, congealed into place with the help of a gel.

For his part, Dryden's plate was still full, aside from one bite of mutton and a few grains of rice. The food held little flavor for him. Occasionally he would cut off fatty morsels of mutton and move them to the outer rim of his plate.

Maxwell hadn't been happy about Dryden coming in Leo's stead, but he had been somewhat appeased by the large binder of notes Dryden had offered, and even more so by the opportunity for a gratuitous meal at the Vicarial Hotel—one afforded by Maxwell's new position.

"You should see my office at Dressler," Maxwell said while wiping his face with a napkin. "Fourth floor, all glass windows, my own assistant. A far cry from the temple at Hood River, where I had a daily rat problem to take care of. You know, you should think more strategically about your career. This work you did with Diplopol and Haplopol could help you, if you play it right."

A woman let out a shrill laugh behind him, pulling Dryden's attention away momentarily. There were only a handful of other patrons in the executive dining room, but they were distracting. A man with a protuberant belly kept clearing his throat aggressively between energetic spurts of chewing and swallowing.

When Dryden returned his attention to the table, Maxwell was staring at him. "You're pretty jumpy today," he said. "Actually, you don't look well at all. You've got bags under your eyes."

Dryden shrugged. It was true. He was tired. But the seething rage that had caused his insomnia accompanied him everywhere, keeping him alert.

"You look like you came through the fever lands on your way north." Maxwell snickered, then paused. "You didn't, did you?"

"We went down the Columbia, and up and around the Neah Bay peninsula. No need to worry."

Maxwell nodded. "Have you been taking my sleep medication?"

"Yes, it's been helpful." In truth, it had helped him sleep at first, but he had stopped taking it after he'd received the message from Sergio.

"Well, eat up! Maybe some good food will make you feel better. The mutton is divine, and the Vicarial has spared no expense to provide you a high-class Old World dining experience. Even the bathrooms work. You should try them. You sit on white porcelain toilets that actually flush. Of course, down below us some poor Vicky will have to pump all the sewage out to a drainage field, but we needn't worry about that. I won't let that mar my experience. I plan to do my duty in blissful ignorance." He smirked.

Dryden nodded and picked at his food. He pushed three larger broccoli florets to the rim of his plate, next to the fatty mutton.

"What's in the bag?" Maxwell asked.

Dryden reached down to pick up his canvas bag, pulling out a long metal bar with a curved end. It was almost like an Old World pry bar, where the pry part had been truncated. Painted glyphs lined its length, looking vaguely like a chain of infinity symbols. "It's called a hook-bulla," Dryden said. "I thought you would be interested, for anthropological reasons. I bought it from a merchant in Anacortes. He said he obtained it from one of the interior tribes, near the Mississippi. The tribe uses the hook-bulla to help them regurgitate their meals into a kind of communal trough. It's their way of making an offering and giving back to their god."

Maxwell shook his head in disgust. "Interesting—I guess—but I'm trying to have a nice meal. The last thing I want to think about is throwing up."

"Yeah, sorry." Dryden thought about telling him about being called a throw-up apologist, but he was in no mood for jokes.

Maxwell sighed and put his cutlery down, finally taking a breather from his meal. "Dryden, like I said before, I'm not happy about Leo skipping out on this. It's not just me that wants to see him, but the Prefectorate as well. But, I wonder, even though you've already been dismissed, if there could be a way for you to help us after all."

It was Maxwell's turn to reach down into his own bag. He took out a carving of an opossum—the carving Dryden had made for Nate. Maxwell frowned at it. "Not a bad rendition, but opossums really are disgusting animals."

Dryden's pulse quickened. "How did you get that?"

Maxwell's expression was sad, almost compassionate. "Look, I'm sorry about this, Dryden, but we need you to make sure Leo comes to visit next time. We also need you to provide information about Leo's Gungivite backers, in the interests of Essentialist security. If you can do this for us, everything will be fine. Maybe Hatsuo will even take you back."

Dryden's heart was pummeling against his ribcage. It took a great feat of will to stay still, to not leap over the table and claw at Maxwell. "What did you do to Nate?"

"Oh, he's fine. Look, it wasn't my idea, but given your importance, and Alayna's as well, Hatsuo thought we should *protect him*." He flashed air quotes with his fingers. "The Prefectorate have a crew of soldiers there, in Hood River, watching over Nate. Don't worry. I'm sure nothing will happen to him." He winked.

"But you—or they—took his carving, the carving *I* made for him. Why?" He knew why, but he wanted to hear Maxwell say it. His hand was gripping his fork tightly, his knuckles white around it. He was actively trying to stay in control.

Maxwell gave him a sour look. "Like I said, it wasn't my idea, but it's to prove to you that they're there, in Hood River. You know how the Prefectorate works, Dryden. Do I really have to say it? We're having a nice meal here."

Dryden's breathing gradually regulated. "No, I understand," he said.

Maxwell was frowning, as if Dryden were an ignorant child. "Why don't you think about it," he said. "I'm sure you'll figure it out. I'm going to use the bathroom—something I've actually been looking forward to."

Maxwell wiped his face with his napkin again, stood up, and turned toward the hallway that led to the bathroom. As soon as he rounded the corner, Dryden stood up as well. He put the hook-bulla in his bag, and, after making sure no one was watching him, also shoveled the mutton and broccoli from his plate into it as well.

He was facing in the direction of the bathroom hallway, the way Maxwell went. He wanted nothing more than to return home, to take Nate away from Hood River.

He began turning toward the exit, but stopped mid-motion. Slowly, with a monumental feat of will, he turned back toward the bathroom hallway.

He put one foot in front of the other.

The interior of the bathroom was full of ornate flourishes. The ceiling was a mosaic depicting the gilded branches of a tree with blue-tinted leaves. The counter was glossy marble and the sink taps were shiny brass. There were three stalls, and Dryden only saw feet in the bottom of one of them. He entered the stall next to the occupied one.

"Maxwell?" he asked.

"Dryden? Wow … you … Did no one ever teach you social graces? Something's wrong with you, Dryden. You need to see someone. Anyway, I'd prefer it if you'd give me more privacy, but if you've got to go, you've got to go."

Dryden didn't pull down his pants. He sat on the toilet with the seat down, and his bag on his lap. His heart was raging. "I received a message from someone," he said.

"From who? Is this about your paper? Let's talk about it later."

"No, it's not about my paper. From a friend. The message spoke about a letter he found, up in Neah Bay. The letter was from nine years ago, addressed to a Prefectorate Colonel, from Captain Otaka. It was in Japanese, but my friend—he could translate it."

"Dryden, what does this have to do with anything?"

Dryden slowly began taking the hook-bulla out of his bag. "The letter was confirmation that Ben—Alayna's brother—would not be able to reveal that the Neah Bay attack was staged by the Prefectorate, because he was dead."

There was some hesitation in Maxwell's response this time. "Dryden, what is this? Maybe we should talk—"

Dryden interrupted him, raising his voice. "It also said that a suitable accident had been arranged, so no questions would be asked about the circumstances of Ben's death."

"What? This is preposterous. It must be a fabrication. Who is this friend of yours?"

Dryden stood up. He slowly stepped out to place himself in front of Maxwell's stall. "And so I thought, how is that possible? I was there, on the lawn. I'd fallen asleep on the grass while Ben slipped into the water. It was my fault. I forgot to put on the brake. But it was also true that for some time after the incident—those first few years—I remembered putting the brake on. And I didn't remember being sleepy that morning. I'd only had a couple drinks the night before. Yet the guilt I felt about those events had twisted my mind. The constant reminders—the loss of Nate's confidence and Alayna's spite—they had warped the truth, and conspired to sear false memories into my mind. It made me believe it was my fault, so much so that I didn't even remember the truth, until now."

Dryden pushed on the door to Maxwell's stall. It was locked. He could hear Maxwell pulling up his pants. "Dryden, you've lost your mind. If you think for a second—"

"But I do remember the sleep medicine in your office, and I remembered I'd eaten breakfast with you that morning. It would have only taken a pinch to make me sleepy just before we went out on the lawn—maybe in my water, or my eggs, I don't know. Nobody else was around. It would have been easy for Prefectorate soldiers to wheel Ben into the river once somebody tipped them off."

Maxwell opened the door. His brow was furrowed with a mix of confusion and unmistakably, fear. "This is ridicu—"

What happened next wasn't Dryden. He would later look back and wonder how he could have possibly done it, but he was so hypersensitive, so filled with rage, that he couldn't help himself. It felt as if someone else took his place, as if his body moved without conscious influence.

Dryden's raging heart drove his limbs into action. He grabbed Maxwell by the throat and pushed him back into the stall. Maxwell fell halfway into the toilet while he grappled with Dryden, trying to remove his arms. His fingernails scraped at Dryden's neck.

Dryden's grip was such that he was pushing tightly with his thumb and index finger behind his jaw, forcing Maxwell's mouth into an open position.

He plunged the hook-bulla down Maxwell's throat.

Maxwell's body immediately convulsed and his throat gargled, but Dryden kept the hook in place. Maxwell vomited violently, forcing out the hook-bulla. Dryden stepped away to avoid the half-digested food and putrid bile, then moved in to force the hook-bulla down once again.

Maxwell's body was floundering like a fish out of water. It took all of Dryden's strength to keep his head fixed and the hook in place.

Maxwell vomited again, and Dryden stepped back to avoid the deluge.

Once more he reapplied the hook-bulla. The end of it was bloody from scraping at Maxwell's esophagus, but Dryden rammed it down his throat just the same. Maxwell continued to gyrate while Dryden held on. He vomited again, but it was more of a dry-heave. This time, Dryden managed to keep the hook in. He was closing off Maxwell's airway after each heave.

Eventually, the convulsions slowed. Dryden tightened his grip ever so slightly around Maxwell's throat, just enough to constrict his abused airway. That was when he pulled the food he'd sequestered from his bag. He rolled it into a ball and packed it tightly down Maxwell's throat with the hook-bulla. He also left some remnants of it in his open mouth.

The heaving stopped, as did Maxwell's floundering.

They had made a fair bit of noise, but the toilet was intact, and nothing had broken in the stall. Maxwell hadn't had enough air in his lungs to scream. Perhaps they hadn't heard him in the kitchen.

Dryden stepped away to assess the scene. The stall was covered in filth, and his nose registered the vile stench. The room was pulsating, or ... no. He was shaking violently. He moved to the mirror and tried to calm himself. He washed his hands and the hook-bulla, and he placed the hook-bulla in his bag. He used a damp towel to clean the bloody scratch marks on his neck, and pulled up his collar to hide them. He also ripped off the end of his shirt sleeves, which were covered in vomit, washed them off and put them in the bag as well. He rolled up the remainder of his sleeves.

When he looked presentable, he waited another minute. His trembling hadn't stopped, but it slowed enough that he wasn't visibly shaking. He walked back out into the restaurant.

When he returned to his seat, he tried not to look at the other patrons. Instead, he focused on his food. He cut off a piece of mutton and chewed on it mechanically.

He couldn't bring himself to swallow the mutton, so he spat it into his napkin surreptitiously and left it on his plate. He cut off another fresh piece and chewed it, knowing he needed to keep playing the part.

Flashes of what he'd done washed over him; Maxwell struggling against his grasp, his violent vomiting, and finally his vacant eyes. Each recollection sent shudders down Dryden's spine, which he tried to quell by flexing his arms and legs. He hoped no one noticed. He began feeling nauseous, but he suppressed that as well. Thankfully, he hadn't eaten much.

This isn't who I am, he told himself. These actions had been forced upon him. What Maxwell had done to Ben, to Alayna, and to him could happen again somewhere, to someone else.

He couldn't live in the same world as Maxwell, so one of them had to leave it. It was a simple binary choice.

It took several minutes until someone else used the bathroom. It was the portly man in the blue sport jacket—the one who'd been clearing his throat a lot. He came out puffing to Dryden's table, his face red. "Your friend, he's been very sick. He needs help. I'm worried he could be—"

"What?" Dryden asked with an appropriate level of concern.

"He must have choked. I'm sorry. I think he's … *dead*."

—38—

Standing Over Her

After the meeting with Olint, Nillias and Lexie left Tetrapol's underground metropolis and returned to the surface. They came up in a fruit cellar in the small village of Langford, just down the lake from Nillias's house, where Lexie had stayed for several weeks.

She thought Nillias would leave her and go to his other house down the road, but he stayed. Not that he was really there. He mostly sat at the table, his eyes closed and eyelids fluttering. Occasionally, he would return to reality for a brief moment to watch the sun go down, or to savor a bowl of cold cherries he'd taken from the fruit cellar. The cellars weren't all fake.

Nillias had quite a ritual for eating cherries. He would examine each one from several angles, and then he would pop it into his mouth and savor it for at least a minute. After he spat out the pit, his eyelids would flutter again.

Nillias's big cat friend, Aleron, was with her and Nillias. He was curled up on a piece of threadbare carpet, his dark fur shining in the lantern light. He looked quite serene, as cats do when they sleep. Aleron's ears twitched while Nillias's eyelids fluttered.

Aleron woke up and yawned. Nillias had recently fed him a slab of venison, so he was probably in a good mood. He stood up and pranced towards an oversized cat door. His powerful legs rippled as he walked by.

Lexie reached out to feel his mane as he passed.

That was a mistake.

In an instant he was on her, and her chair fell to the ground. Again, the huge teeth bristled in her face.

But soon Aleron cringed and jumped off. He ran to the cat door, slamming the panel open with considerable force.

When Aleron was good and gone, Lexie stood up and righted her chair.

"Remember," Nillias said, his eyes open. "Aleron is not a pet. These cats cannot be properly domesticated. As a result, they are inherently dangerous. He would probably eat you, if he had the chance."

"That's reassuring. What scared him away?"

"Cats hear sounds outside of our audible range. In my implant I can generate a sound that Aleron can hear, but we cannot. It is a safety precaution, in case Aleron decides to attack. We also use other frequencies and sound patterns that are less grating to the animals to invoke other behaviors, such as to pursue bad actors, as we did with you at the selection school. I try not to use these more urgent communications often. It would be like the Langford bells rattling an inch away from your ear."

"Well, thanks, I guess."

He nodded and closed his eyes again.

Something about the whole situation with Aleron didn't feel right. Why should Nillias have to live in constant fear of an animal that might want to take a bite out of him at any given moment? The stated rationale—to teach him to be careful with non-human intelligences—seemed excessive.

She considered asking Nillias about it, but he was still busy communing.

Eventually, she tired of watching his nut-jobbyness and went to bed.

She awoke to Nillias standing over her again. At least this time he wasn't watching her sleep. He was vigorously shaking her shoulder.

"It's time to go," he whispered. "We've been assigned to track down Warrick again—so we can find the location of Pentapol. We are running out of time and must go quickly."

She noticed that it was pitch-black out. "In the middle of the night?"

"Yes."

"Why are you whispering?"

He shrugged. "I didn't want to startle you."

"Maybe you should have thought of that before you ransacked my shoulder with your hand. You're worse than Tarnation."

They boarded a clipper in a harbor on the northeast side of the island. Nillias's cronies were already stocking the ship with big brown bags when they walked on, so the ship left the solitary pier within minutes. An electric floodlight on the bow of the ship gave Lexie comfort that they weren't heading toward any rocks.

She noticed Emry wasn't with them, nor any other Observers. "Why the skeleton crew this time?" she asked.

"Emry is needed in Ganges, and our mission will be encumbered by too many people."

The floodlight went out. Lexie waited for someone to flick a switch, or give the floodlight a good kick, but everyone seemed peachy.

"Um, don't we need to see where we're going?"

"The light is used to perform an initial scan for ships and other floating objects. Our positioning systems and radar will be sufficient to get us past the retcher threshold. We will use lamps when we are closer to our destination."

"Which is?"

"Anacortes."

"Ah. Having words with Leo again, are we?"

"Yes."

"Not sure you're going to get much more out of him."

"There are others with him that may be able to provide answers."

"What others?"

"From the east."

As if that meant anything to her. She didn't bother following up. If Nillias had wanted to explain, he would have. Besides, there was a more important question to ask.

"What got you in such a huff when you spoke with Olint?"

She heard him turn toward her in the dark, even though she could only register vague snippets of movement up at the bow. It was too dark to see Nillias's face.

He said, "Did you know that the Observers were originally concerned solely with morality and bias? We were like magistrates—arbiters of justice—until we were appropriated and repurposed as the principal agents of Tetrapol."

"Nauseous nettles, I feel another lesson coming on."

"Perhaps it is a lesson," he said, sounding reflective. "It should be, maybe the most important lesson in the curriculum."

She waited for him to spout his nonsense.

Nillias began, "Unintended consequences are often caused by bias. We choose to ignore the possibility of negative outcomes because of an emotional reluctance to know about them. It is the source of many of our failings, including prejudice, ignorance, and hubris. But what I fear most is that if a person creates a machine of infinite power, that person's bias gets imprinted in the machine and will be enhanced ad infinitum. This was one of the reasons the Observers were selected to oversee Tetrapol, because we were perceived to have minimal bias."

"Seems to add up. So what are you so worried about with Olint?"

"Olint and the council have agreed to remove the processing speed constraints on Tetrapol, as well as grant more autonomy to the city for a broad range of decisions. Oracle mode, which requires human approval for decision-making, will only be used for exceptional situations. It will no longer be the rule."

"Why?"

"I understand the rationale. It is being done in order to accelerate defensive preparations—to give us more of a chance against the growing threat of the Essentialist-controlled ICSM cities. A major conflict is brewing, which we may not survive if we do not remove these constraints. Olint and the rest of the council argue that we can increase processing speed and machine control autonomy because Tetrapol has proven itself to be safe. They believe that because we have survived for decades without conflict, the fundamental architecture of Tetrapol is one that is correct and morally acceptable. Or in other words, Morganis finally got it right with Tetrapol, because it was successful in decommissioning other machine architectures."

"And you think otherwise?"

"I can't disprove their claims, but I also don't think the council has enough evidence to support them with confidence. I believe they are suffering from confirmation bias."

She rolled her eyes. He wouldn't see it in the dark anyway. "Sorry, what?"

"Confirmation bias happens when people are only seeking confirming rather than falsifying evidence for a set of assumptions. The council's support for this decision is based on our purported success to date, as well as custom simulations developed by Tetrapol. I suggested that they also test simulations developed by an independent third-party, or even vet it with non-Gungivite representatives, but they shrugged it off as unimportant. My biggest worry, however, is that they refuse to consider that they have given too much power to the most volatile element of the system."

"Which is?"

"Us. We know humans are prone to many psychological prejudices and biases. Tetrapol will become incredibly powerful due to the changes we've made, but it's still controlled by humans. Before, we had months to make big decisions, and they would be subject to significant deliberation by the council and all the Observers. Now a single member of the council can make critical decisions in the event of emergencies. Who's to say this person has the moral high ground? Who's to say their ethics are right?"

"Got it. The usual story. Corruption comes with too much power. You're worried Tetrapol could become just like a fiefdom."

"Yes, but worse than that. With one wrong command, or one childish whim, they could inadvertently set Tetrapol on a path to destroying us all."

"So what can you do? I gather you lost the argument."

"I did. There isn't much I can do. Olint and the council have agreed to employ checks and balances in the future, but they will not consider them until this emergency has ended. My only hope is that we can be responsible enough to use them once Tetrapol's full power has been realized."

It was just one more wrinkle, but it seemed so abstract. Lexie just wanted to get out of this mess and spend some time with her mom.

She yawned.

"Why don't you get some rest," Nillias said. "It will be quieter in the hold."

Finally, he was making sense.

She awoke to Nillias standing over her again. This time, he was prodding her more gently.

Light was seeping through the porthole window, and when Lexie looked out, she could see Anacortes on the horizon. "Morning, Nillias," she said.

His face looked less taut, and his mouth was no longer a firm, straight line. They were in retcher territory, so his implant must be turned off. As a result, she thought he might act a little more human—like he sometimes did when he was on the mainland. But no, he was about to serve her a full-on dog's breakfast of nut-jobbyness.

"You get any sleep?" she asked.

"No."

"Too bad. Well, it's stuffy down here. I'd like to get some air, if you don't mind."

She made to get up, but he was blocking the exit.

"When we dock," he said, "I will need to meet with a few people in town before we confront Leo."

"Great, I'll go see Mom."

"No. You will stay here until I return."

"What? Why not?"

He grimaced, and looked away. "Scope neglect," he said.

"Oh, come on. I just woke up. Will you stop?"

"We have a tendency to feel pity or compassion for one person, or a few people, especially if we know them, but not for the thousands we do not who might suffer the same fate. Our incremental visceral reaction declines precipitously with each marginal casualty. Thus, we overweight our actions to serve the few, when we should serve the many."

"So what?"

"So I can't let you see your mother, because it puts you at risk of getting caught, or killed. You are too important to our objective of stopping the Essentialist-controlled ICSM cities. The Essentialists have an increasing number of human agents working on their behalf. They have also dismantled many of our surveillance systems, so we can be less confident about their movements. And, perhaps most importantly, we believe Essentialist agents are watching your mother."

"What? You better get out of my way, Nillias."

Nillias put his hands up. "Please, if you'll calm down, Lexie. You're not being rational. Even though there is a low likelihood of you being killed—or worse, captured—we can't afford to take any additional risks. Imagine what you could reveal about Tetrapol? Imagine how many might perish just because you want to see your mother."

"I don't care."

She thought about pushing through Nillias, or even attacking him. She vowed to find a way. Even if it meant she had to dust Nillias, she had to get her mom out of Anacortes. It was long overdue.

Nillias was looking at the floor, his brow furrowed in concentration. His eyes looked tired, but also imbued with a sincerity she hadn't seen in him before. "I am in the same situation, Lexie. I can't see the one I love, either."

"Who? Ryder? Please."

"My daughter."

"What?"

"The girl that you saw with Ryder, when you were with Tarnation. She is my daughter, and her name is Margaret. My wife, she died in childbirth, and we hid Margaret from the Observers. She was taken here to Anacortes. She has a nanny, and Ryder watches over her as well. I would like to see her, but I can't, just as you can't see your mother. It would put them, and us, in danger."

Lexie was too livid to process what he was saying. "I. Don't. Care. I doubt you give an ounce of rat piss for your daughter, if in fact she is your daughter. Why would you leave her here? Sounds like a load of horseshit to me."

"I didn't …" He paused, and looked down again momentarily, searching for words. "I didn't want her to become an Observer. I didn't want her to be like me; full of purpose, but otherwise empty. And I didn't … I *couldn't* let her see who her father has become."

"Let me out," Lexie said.

Nillias regained his composure. His face hardened, and the emotion drained away. "I can't let you," he said, standing up. "In fact, I can't let you leave the ship at all, until we have our meeting with Leo and the people from the east."

"But …" she said. The word hung in the air, unaccompanied, and without any counter.

And with that, Nillias retreated from the cabin, shut and locked the door behind him, leaving her to fume in solitude.

—39—

THREE OLD SAYINGS

"How did you become such a good negotiator?" Hatsuo asked, smiling.

He had called Alayna into his tent on a sullen, wet morning. Her shoes were covered in mud and her jacket was thoroughly dampened from the spitting rain she'd slogged through on the way over. She crossed her arms and shivered a little before responding. "My parents were traders, too," she said. "They made a good team, my mom being from the north and my dad being from the Union. For most of my youth we were traveling up and down the coastal trade routes as merchants."

"Not all children are like their parents," Hatsuo said. "My father was a Prefectorate tax officer, but I can barely count."

She nodded. "I suppose we do have our differences, but I learned a great deal from them. I still use some key tenets of their teachings today."

"Like what? Tell me."

This was typical of Hatsuo. He would explore some tangential personal topic before getting to the point of his summons, as if he needed to find some new way to ingratiate himself to her.

"My father used to say *the mind can measure the heart, but the heart cannot measure the mind.* It was basically his way of telling me to keep my emotions out of it. It helped me during frustrating negotiations. One time, when I was the lead trader for Hood River, I was trying to establish an arrangement around workable metals. My counterpart was named Teak. He was a stubborn goat of a man who was proficient in metallurgy and blacksmithing but otherwise inarticulate. He became increasingly irate as the discussions went on, even though it was clear they were getting a fair deal. At one point he called me a gutter snake and stormed out of the trade tent, with his mining and blacksmithing colleagues following after him."

Hatsuo was listening with interest. "What did you do?"

"I almost called the whole thing off, until I forced myself to look at the situation objectively. First of all, we were close. Me calling it off wasn't rational. It would only have been my pride talking. And when I replayed the conversation in my mind, I realized what it was. Teak was intimidated by me. While he was tripping over his words, I was wrapping him in knots with my own. All he wanted was to not look like a fool in front of his friends.

"So I called another meeting, one in which I barely spoke. When I did speak, I fumbled basic aspects of the deal terms that he easily corrected and explained. By the end of it, he was speaking to me like I was a child, right up until they signed the deal."

Hatsuo was smiling and nodding. "You used your mind, rather than letting your heart dictate the outcome. Well done."

She shifted her feet and flexed her arm muscles, trying to stay warm.

"Would you like an extra blanket?" he asked. "The wetness is really getting to my bones today. I feel like I'm still out at sea."

"No, thank you."

"I insist." He turned around to gather a blanket from his nearby bed.

She took it from him and wrapped it around her, trying to give him a genuine smile. She was careful to stay facing him as she did it. At times she would find him staring at her with a discomfiting expression, eyes glazed, after she'd turned her back to him.

This time he was looking down, arranging papers neatly on his desk.

"I was wondering, General," she said, "will you need my help in your meetings with Commander Yasui?"

His eyes snapped up to lock with hers. "How did you know she was here? Did Caban tell you?"

"One of the Commander's supply officers was in camp and I met with him. I did business with him in Hood River once. Lumber for the shipyard, I think."

Hatsuo shook his head. "Commander Yasui was here for a few days, but now she is gone, as well as her retinue. Don't concern yourself with them."

It was strange that she hadn't been informed about the arrival of Yasui. She was the highest ranking Prefectorate officer in the entire northwest. Perhaps Hatsuo wanted to keep her visit devoid of hassle.

"Was she impressed?"

"Her officers were. How could they not be?" He waved his hand in the direction of Diplopol. "But there was no need for Yasui to come to see Diplopol personally, with all the dangers of ongoing construction, so we kept her busy in Victoria, and she left soon after. Her considerable talents are needed to defend the coast from marauders while I am stuck in this turmoil of machines and filth." Hatsuo made an exasperated expression. It looked convincing, but she was quite sure he wouldn't want it any other way.

"No," he said, "that's not why I asked you here, Alayna. I'm so sorry, but I'd like to ask you some questions about your former husband, Dryden. I know it could be a sore subject for you."

She felt that familiar rush of angst at the mention of Dryden's name. It was like a mouse was crawling up her back. *What did he do now?* she wondered. But to Hatsuo she said, "No, I don't mind."

"Do you remember Maxwell? Of course you do; he was your curator. He had been reassigned to be an Associate Dean at the Dressler Institute in Victoria. After Dryden left, we needed a senior academic to help us understand Diplopol."

"Sir, if you don't mind telling me, do you know why Dryden went home in the first place? I never had a chance to speak with him before he left, and this was his dream, to observe the ICSM cities. I'm surprised he would want to leave."

"Oh, that seems like such a long time ago. Let me see if I remember. He was quite traumatized by what happened, with his colleagues being slaughtered so viciously by the Gungivites, so we all thought it best that he return home for a while. I heard he had a relationship with a Sanuwan woman who died, the Princess Elissa."

She only nodded. She wasn't surprised Dryden was seeing someone. He saw a few women in Hood River, but they were always fleeting affairs. He could be charming at times, but sooner or later his drinking would give him away, or his negligence.

"And besides," Hatsuo continued. "Given the investment in Diplopol in terms of men and resources, it was time to bring in a proper scholar."

His reference to Maxwell being a proper scholar was a bit of a stretch. Maxwell was more of a political animal, and he certainly wasn't an expert on ICSM cities like Dryden was. In fact, Dryden was probably one of the top five in the northwest. But she didn't say anything. Hatsuo was almost certainly glossing over the fact that Dryden had become a liability.

Hatsuo was watching her carefully. "Did you know anything about Dryden meeting up with Maxwell?"

"I'm sorry, I'm confused. I thought you said Maxwell was here, and Dryden went home?"

"Yes that *is* confusing, isn't it? I'm sorry. Maxwell had been here in Victoria for a few weeks, but Dryden recently returned from the south. Maxwell had intended to meet with Leopold, who we are recruiting to be our aide as well, but Dryden came in his stead."

"I thought Dryden was in Hood River. I had no idea. Dryden came to Victoria again?"

Hatsuo tilted his head to one side. "Yes, and unfortunately Maxwell met with an unfortunate accident when he was with Dryden."

"An accident?"

"We have witnesses that testified to finding him in the bathroom. They say he'd vomited, that food had gotten stuck in his throat. Unfortunately, he choked on it, and died."

"Maxwell's dead?"

Hatsuo was judging her reactions carefully. He must have suspected she already knew. "Yes, I'm sorry, but I must say, I have never known someone to die from something as capricious as choking on their own vomit. And Dryden left rather abruptly afterwards, so …"

Alayna scoffed. "You think he *killed* Maxwell? Why would he do that? Jealousy? Dryden drinks, and he's depressed, but I've never seen him jealous. Dryden, he's … he's a mess. He's been a mess since Ben died, but not in a violent way. Even if he was jealous, I can't see him considering anything that bold."

Hatsuo stared at her for a moment, and eventually nodded. "I know, I know, but they have me ask about these things, just in case. Inspector Caban is always on my back—and so I have to make sure we are running a tight ship. You've met with the inspector, I presume?"

"Yes."

"Twice, I hear." He squinted at her. Since he already knew the answer, the implication was obvious. He was testing her.

The blanket he'd provided suddenly seemed to be devoid of warmth.

"Yes," she said. "He wanted to ask about any follow-up meetings with Utep and Sajida-Lai. I think, because I have some Union heritage, that he feels we have some kind of kinship that he doesn't have with others."

"And do you? Have this kinship, I mean?"

She paused before responding, trying to find the right words. "There was another thing my parents told me when I was young. *The strongest rivers are made of streams from distant lands.* General, I am a devout Essentialist. I know this alliance with the Prefectorate and the Tucson Union is delicate, but it is important, because it makes us all stronger. The livelihood of my parents, and myself, has depended on it thriving, because you can't trade during times of war. So yes, I feel I have a kinship with him, but no more than I have kinship with you, and no more than I have with other coastal Essentialists."

His lower jaw stuck out and edged back in some obscure of gesture of calculation. He closed his eyes and put his index finger and thumb on the bridge of his nose. When he looked up again, the magnanimous smile returned. "I'm sorry, Alayna. I don't doubt you. You have been a steadfast ally. Let's keep in dialogue. We need to make sure our streams continue to run together, as you say. And in the spirit of cooperation, you should know, in case you're worried, that I have a team that is watching over Nate in Hood River while Dryden is gone. We will make sure nothing happens to him."

Her heart stopped for a moment, but she forced a smile. "Oh … well, thank you, sir. I really appreciate that."

Alayna walked carefully back through the rain-drenched terrain toward her lodging.

That wasn't what her parents had said, of course. She'd heard the *strongest rivers* saying down in the Union, but ironically between tribes that were allied against the Prefectorate. A different saying came to mind after the meeting: *a fool takes the rancid river as his tributary.*

She was thinking of the Prefectorate, but Dryden came to mind as well. She hadn't thought about him in a while, until Hatsuo had to bring him up.

He was back in the north, somewhere.

She couldn't help clenching her teeth.

Questions scratched at the walls of her mind. Why was Dryden here? Did he abandon Nate in Hood River? Could he really have killed Maxwell? The latter she doubted, but some part of her wondered if he was the cause, indirectly. Maybe he was drunk and didn't hear him choking.

It sounded all too familiar.

She tried to block the questions out. She had long since realized that pondering anything to do with Dryden only made her angry.

And sometimes, when he wasn't around, it just made her sad.

So why bother? She had enough to deal with, and emotions just made her lose her objectivity. She was dealing with a sociopathic Prefectorate general and a wily Groundwater traitor. There was no place for tumultuous emotions if she wanted to survive. And, it seemed, if she wanted no harm to come to Nate, either.

She climbed up the pathway gradient to the viewing area. This time, nobody was here. Everyone was either working in the factory plots or inside the city. Other than Diplopol's city walls, which had doubled in height in the last week, she could only see the highest transport loops and the tips of the twenty or so egg-shaped buildings, which featured bright lights hazed out by the intervening rain, like a lineup of lighthouses in the distance.

Inside the city it would be warm and cozy, teeming with people. Diplopol had completed a huge set of gardens and experiential amphitheaters that allowed a larger number of visitors into the interior, relieving a great deal of tension that had been brewing because of the limited visiting hours. Tunnels pumped out smoke and chemicals a mile away from the city. On sunnier days, she could see exhaust slinking up into the sky.

She was one of the few that had seen the fumes up close. She had gone on a hike to see it, but only because she felt she had to. In her book she wrote:

It curled up into the sky like a ghastly thief, darkly dressed, impatiently rushing out of the ground so it could pilfer our souls.

She moved on.

When she arrived back at her lodging, she took off her jacket and wet shoes and placed them by the fire, then pulled on her warmest wool sweater before sitting at her desk. She had a number of requisitions to write. This was how she spent most of her days. Supplies, supplies, and more supplies. Every day they needed more.

When she sat down, she heard a sound. Most people wouldn't have noticed it, but she had sensitive ears. Dryden had always said she had incredible hearing, and it was true. It was a faint buzzing sound, and she wondered if it could be another dragonfly.

She pulled out her notebook from her bag and unbound it, keeping her pen ready. She followed the sound to the rear of her small hut, where a glass door led to a patio. She walked outside, still tracing the sound. She could hear it shifting around her; it reminded her of a mosquito—one you couldn't find in the middle of the night.

Finally, she saw it. It was about twenty feet up from her, floating in the air. It wasn't a hummingbird or dragonfly, but rather a tiny robotic drone kept aloft by a series of propellers. She'd heard that the workers were making them in one of the external factories, using instructions from the city, and here was the proof.

She shut her notebook, went inside, closed the door and pulled all the curtains.

—40—

A Crowded Study

Dryden, Rosalie, Cecile, Pierre, Leo and two of Leo's fiefdom guards were all gathered in Leo's study. The study was spacious, so it shouldn't have felt cramped, but somehow it still did. It might have been because Leo's right hand was holding the shotgun again, unabashedly pointing in their direction.

"You killed him?" Leo asked, fingering his temple with his free hand. "You've gone mad."

Dryden only shrugged. The only one who'd taken the news well so far was Rosalie. When he told her, she'd grinned and raised her eyebrows in appreciation, as if Dryden had finally done something useful.

"Why didn't you at least stay there?" Leo said. "You could have bought us more time. It looks more than a little bit suspicious to tuck tail and run."

"Like I said, Maxwell choked, so it was—or at least made to look like—an accident. There was a witness. I gave my statement to the local authorities. Although I do admit I was anxious to leave, I've never killed anyone before. And I also left because of what I learned from Maxwell. I'm going home to Nate. He's not safe in Hood River."

"So you flee to the south while the Essentialists come after me and your friends? You're such a coward."

"You're the one that was too afraid to go in the first place."

"Because I knew it was a fucking trap! You said so yourself." Leo's hand was tensing around the shotgun stock, and his finger was perilously close to the trigger.

"Now, now, boys," Rosalie said. She had unholstered her own rifle and propped it up against her shoulder. "Even eggheads get a little testy at times, it seems. Dryden's done kilt someone; Leo's got a shotgun. Yeah, it feels like you've got a real penis now, but I'm not sure either of you knows how to use it. I should remind you, you folks don't do altercations of the violent variety, no sir. That's what I do. You stick to your egghead business, or Humpty Dumpty's gonna fall."

"*Oui, ça suffit,*" Cecile said, stepping forward and putting a hand on Rosalie's shoulder. "What's past is past. Keep in mind, no matter what he's done, Dryden was not swayed to betray us—to betray *you,* Leo. You heard what he said. They will be coming for you eventually, whether Maxwell died or not."

She turned to Dryden. "And Dryden, do you really think going to Hood River is a good idea? You would put Nate at risk if you try to take him away, and Alayna as well. Maybe more importantly, you're needed here. The only way to ensure Nate is safe, to ensure all of us are safe, is to put an end to this machine war. Trust me, I have seen how fast things can change when super-intelligent machines are empowered. If we're not successful, in a few years there won't be a Hood River, or a Portland. At best, the people there will be unwitting slaves to one of the machine cities; at worst, they will all be dead."

Dryden found it hard to believe her comments about Hood River and Portland. It sounded like sensational hyperbole. But he hadn't considered what might happen to Alayna if he saved Nate. Would she be punished? Would they sink their hooks deeper into her without Nate as leverage? It did give him pause.

"And besides," Cecile continued. "We will have guests soon. It's time to act a little more civilized." She looked over at Pierre, who nodded.

"What guests?" Leo asked.

"There is a Gungivite clipper that has been anchored here since this morning," Cecile said. "We've been watching them. Your friends will be here soon."

If Leo's study wasn't cramped before, it certainly was now. The new group was led by a Gungivite Observer with long, flowing hair and an alphanumeric tattoo on his arm. His name was Nillias, and he was flanked by a half-Asian woman named Lexie. She walked with a swagger and had a skeptical manner about her. Four well-armed Gungivite militia rounded out the group.

After a brief round of introductions, Cecile opened the conversation. "We know you've been watching us. What do you want?"

"We want to know where Pentapol is located," Nillias said.

Cecile raised her eyebrows. She looked at Leo, at Dryden, and back to Nillias. "Okay. I want to know where Warrick Kelemen is."

"Why?" the one named Lexie asked.

"He can help us, in the east," Cecile said.

"Help you with what?" Nillias asked.

"Our machine war," Cecile said.

"Why would we want to help you with that?"

"Because we're on the side that doesn't want to kill everyone."

Nillias looked at Leo. Leo said, "Cecile hasn't told me anything, either."

"You stay out of this, egghead," Rosalie said.

Leo shook his head. "No, I won't. I don't care if you're a Merc, a fucking fiefdom king or a Prefectorate General. The truth is, I'd rather you all get out of my house. I don't want to help anyone, but at least the Gungivites have funded my research. All *you've* done is bring my murderous so-called colleague into the mix, just in time to embroil me in an Essentialist extortion plot." He was flapping his hand at Dryden, and all eyes turned to him.

Dryden shrugged and shuffled his feet. There were already too many strong opinions in the room, so he decided not to add his own.

"I believe I know where Warrick is," Nillias said, but his claim was subverted by a look of surprise from Lexie.

"How do you know?" Cecile asked.

"We have surveillance systems all over the Salish Sea and Kuvar Island that have been operating for thirty years. We fed recently obtained sketches of him and his colleague into our database. After considerable analysis, we were able to cross-reference the sketches to historical pictures of him to determine his sailing routes, and consequently, his base of operations."

Surveillance systems? Dryden looked around the room. Nobody seemed to be questioning it, although Cecile did look skeptical. All he got from Leo was a sneer.

Cecile said, "How do you know he's always at the same place?"

Nillias said, "He has to return to this one location frequently, to get treatment for his condition."

Cecile raised her eyebrows. "So where is it?"

Nillias said, "We can tell you, if you can tell us where Pentapol is."

Cecile looked at Dryden, an expectant look in her eyes.

"Me?" he asked.

"You're the expert. And Leo, of course."

Dryden racked his brain, trying to remember what he knew about Pentapol. The writings were few and far between. Most of what he remembered were speculative letters on the subject without much real evidence to back them up.

Before Dryden could collect his thoughts, Leo began. "It's believed that Pentapol was built when the other four ICSM cities were still flourishing. Morganis wanted to protect his growing empire, so Pentapol was known to have sophisticated defense systems that extended well beyond its boundaries and could protect all of the ICSM cities."

"This is true," Dryden added. "There is also a folktale about the ICSM cities that calls Pentapol the most musical city, a place where the arts flourished and natural beauty was cherished."

"Hardly," Leo said. "That's not even written evidence."

"The folktale exists," Dryden said stubbornly.

"What else?" Cecile asked, impatience bleeding into her voice.

Dryden said, "A letter was also found, about riding underground to Pentapol, in a tunnel."

"Ha," Leo said, scowling. "From Ranthoke's compendium? This is the letter that was supposedly lost, and he has falsified evidence before. I wouldn't count on it."

Despite Leo's dismissal, Nillias and Lexie still looked interested. "What about the tunnels?" Nillias asked.

Dryden gave a meek reply. "That's … that's all there is, really. Just that it was connected by tunnels. Why do you ask?"

Nillias said, "We have found tunnels under Ganges Island, one toward Triplopol and another toward the Kuvar fever lands, but they have collapsed, and coring of the seafloor under the Georgia Strait has not revealed any large underground spaces."

Confused looks were shared around the room.

"That's all?" Cecile asked. She had an exasperated look. "How can we find the city based on that?"

Dryden said, "Remember, everyone disappeared. We're lucky we found anything at all."

There was a rattling sound. The floor trembled.

Heads swiveled slowly around. Cautionary hands splayed out. Weapons were removed from holsters.

"Go," Nillias said. One of his men left the room. Nillias withdrew his own weapon—a pistol. It was pointed toward the ground, but the angle was threatening enough. Any shot fired would hit just in front of Cecile's feet.

Cecile nodded to Pierre as well, and he left. She took out her own weapon slowly—another pistol. "It's not us," she said.

Leo looked out the window into his garden, but Dryden couldn't see anything unusual. When Leo turned back around, he had a long scowl on his face. "I don't know what the heck that was, but I've had enough. Sorry, Nillias, I don't care how much you're paying me. This has to end. Put your guns away. You all have to leave. You got what you could, and you already know your best chance of getting the answer isn't from us anyway, so why don't you get going?"

"What is the *best chance* he's talking about?" Cecile asked no one in particular.

Lexie said, "Warrick. We believe Warrick may know where Pentapol is, or at least he did, at one point."

Cecile brightened. "Good, so we can find him together." Her gun was still out, also trained on the floor.

Nillias didn't acknowledge her, perhaps because the room shook again.

A ceramic mug fell and shattered. Distinct percussions sounded in the distance, and bells. First one set, then many. Three Rivers alarm bells.

Pierre rushed back into the room, breathing heavily. "They're bombing the city," he said. "Anacortes is under attack."

—41—

The Crow's Nest

Lexie followed everyone out of the house. They were headed toward Leo's lookout tower. A crow's nest was up there, but on-land-like, and wider than you'd have on a ship.

The tower wasn't far, just across the garden. Leo led the way and was quite nimble in his wheelchair, navigating the ramp that wrapped around the tower with ease. Fortunately most of them had lost their gun-toting jitters when the bombs started falling, so it was a civilized procession. Or rather, they weren't so much jittery about each other as they were about the explosions in the distance.

Nillias's Gungivite militia and Cecile's Quebecois colleagues stayed down below, on account of the lack of room in the nest.

From the top, Lexie used her shorter-range scope instead of waiting for the long-range bannister-mounted one that Leo was using. It wasn't entirely clear, but she saw enough to get the gist of it. There was a large flotilla of Essentialist ships out at sea. In front of this flotilla were seafaring craft with gray metallic shells and large artillery guns positioned on them, firing into the shore. These weren't your typical cannon shells. The explosions were louder, and they lit up the Anacortes coastline real good.

There were *a lot* of ships.

Cecile put down her own scope. "Perhaps they want to control Three Rivers, for better access to the mainland."

"Ostensibly," Nillias said, "but they are also targeting your platforms, Cecile. We have to consider that they may be here for us, and for the Pentapol control junction."

Cecile's brow wrinkled. She nodded and said, "We're not safe. We need to salvage what we can and flee. Then we should find Warrick together.

Where should we meet?"

Nillias agreed readily. "Burlington. The old inn. Tomorrow evening."

Another loud cluster of explosions sounded in the distance.

Without any goodbyes, Cecile peeled out to walk down the ramp, followed by Rosalie. Dryden hesitated.

"Dryden. Let's go," Cecile said from the base of the tower.

Dryden frowned, and followed them down in turn.

"What a mess," Leo said, finally pulling his eye away from the bigger scope. "I hope you're happy with yourself."

"We did not initiate this conflict," Nillias said. "It may have been inevitable."

Leo looked skeptical. "I'm going to find shelter in the basement. I suppose I'll be stuck with the lot of you." He rolled down the ramp to follow Cecile's people.

"Shouldn't we go as well?" Lexie asked Nillias.

"Not yet," he said.

Lexie peered over the side of the tower, checking to make sure Leo had left, and that Nillias's men were far enough away. When she was comfortable they were out of earshot, she said, "You're not following orders, are you, Nillias?"

"Why do you say that?"

"You said this mission was important, but if it was so important there would be more Gungivite Observers with us. We wouldn't have had to leave in the middle of the night. And then … this." She gestured out at the flashes in the water. "I would have thought you'd have known about it in advance."

A barrage of explosions lit up the night behind them and rattled the tower. They both half-ducked, then righted themselves.

He said, "Our mission is to find Pentapol, like I said, but I also admit that we're not executing our orders exactly as they were prescribed. We weren't supposed to take the Pentapol control junction with us, for example. Olint probably doesn't know it's gone, but he will soon."

"Doesn't that put you at risk of some kind of punishment, or worse?"

"Sometimes your only hope requires you to be vulnerable. Know who your enemy is, Lexie, above all. It's not always the same person or thing. It changes, and so you must change with it."

Another barrage of explosions hit, closer to them this time. Lexie heard screaming in the distance. The alarm bells ceased.

"Maybe we should get out of here. Aren't we exposed?"

"They are attacking the main Three Rivers defensive batteries in the harbor, as well as Cecile's platform installations. Only four of their sixty-seven ships and artillery placements would be able to reach us here at Leo's. Either way, I suspect they don't want us dead, so we should be safer than other places in the city. And we are taking measures to protect us."

"What measures—wait …"

"Yes?"

"Cardinality."

"I'm sorry, Lexie, I don't understand."

"You may not believe it, but I actually listened to your nutjob lessons. We were studying ways of detecting latent machine influences, or suspicious patterns of behavior that could be of machine origin. One of the most obvious differences between machines and humans is a proficiency with cardinality. Machines do mathematical operations quickly. So how could you count all those ships so fast, and know their ranges, unless …"

His eyes softened, and he nodded. "I had no choice, Lexie. I had to enable my implant in order to call on Ganges and request an immediate targeted airstrike. If I didn't, we would have been captured, and the Essentialists would have taken the Pentapol control junction. I cannot allow that. The airstrike will be here soon."

Her heart started to beat erratically. "But if you enabled your implant … if you used it here on the mainland …"

He smiled at her, like he sometimes did when he was staring out from the bow of the ship. "Find Ryder. He can help you locate Warrick. And take what I've taught you to heart. I'm glad you listened, because these lessons will become increasingly important."

Lexie was frantically looking at the sky around her. Ordnance continued to explode on the shoreline. The ships were advancing closer to the city.

Nothing was impeding them.

"Shouldn't we run?" Lexie said. "Go underground or something?"

"It would only delay the inevitable."

"No. Nillias, this is silly. You don't have to do this."

He shook his head. "It's done. And I did the right thing. Even though I am deviating in this mission, I served the Observer order faithfully, because I know I was never encumbered by bias. And yet ..."

Lexie continued to look into the sky. Away from the main conflict was just blackness. They would be impossible to see. "What? And yet what?" she asked nervously.

His eyes were locked on hers. How could he not be looking at the sky? How could he not be panicking? "Don't worry for me, Lexie. Most of what I am left me when I was a child. When I was chosen to be an Observer, it was stripped away by harsh discipline and the strict ideology of our order. All that I have left is what was reflected in my daughter's eyes, those few times she saw me. I am thankful that—even though she didn't know me, and perhaps rightfully—she will remember me with those eyes full of wonder. I am thankful that I can leave this world before she can see the empty vessel I have become."

"But—"

He put his hand up, halting her words. "And so, I must ask of you one thing, one small favor, one act of grace for my service. Please take care of my little girl. I know this is hypocrisy. Why should she be saved over so many others? In fact, it's a clear case of scope neglect. And yet, I have given my life, and it's all I am asking for in return, this one iota of civility for a lifetime of conviction. I can be at peace if I know that at least one living soul is looking out for her, someone who's not part machine, or indentured to one. Will you do that for me?"

"Fine, fine," Lexie said, without really thinking. "Now let's get—"

"It's coming," he said. "Please stay back."

He looked up. His expression was focused but content. It reminded Lexie of when he was on a ladder in his orchard, looking into the speckled light, reaching for the choicest fruit. In that brief snippet of time, she imagined that's what he wanted to do more than anything. Nillias would have been perfectly content to be a humble orchard farmer, enjoying his daily toil and the simple reward of a ripe cherry or plum.

But that life was never his to live.

The black albatross tore through the night and was upon him. Its claws dug into his arms, and still Nillias looked up, gazing directly into its vacuous eyes and serrated beak.

When it began vomiting its acidic bile, Lexie had to turn away. She stumbled down the ramp as if drunk, clinging to the walls as she circled the tower. She could hear the retcher's grotesque movements above her—tearing and retching and clucking—as well as the steam rising from Nillias's burnt flesh. She dared not look back. She dared not even imagine what those noises meant.

Nillias never made another sound.

One of Nillias's men was at the bottom of the ramp. "Stop right there," he said. It was Keegan. His words weren't really registering, so Lexie ignored him. She just wanted to run, or stagger, or whatever she was doing, so she kept moving toward the house. He tackled her, sending them both to the ground, her face bouncing off the damp turf.

She didn't resist. She let him sit on her, then cuff her, while she kept her face turned away from him. Her head rested on the soft grass. It felt good. And this way he couldn't see her face.

Only moments later, the world around her became an abrasive symphony of percussive explosions, much louder than before. At the time, she didn't know it was the Gungivite airstrike, nor did she care. She just wanted to lie there, to not feel or think anything.

It lasted for many minutes, this assault on her senses; deafening sounds, blinding lights, rattling tremors in the ground. She stayed still, turned away from Keegan, her hands cuffed behind her back, and her eyes blinking in a vain attempt to stem the tide of tears that streamed down her cheeks.

PART III

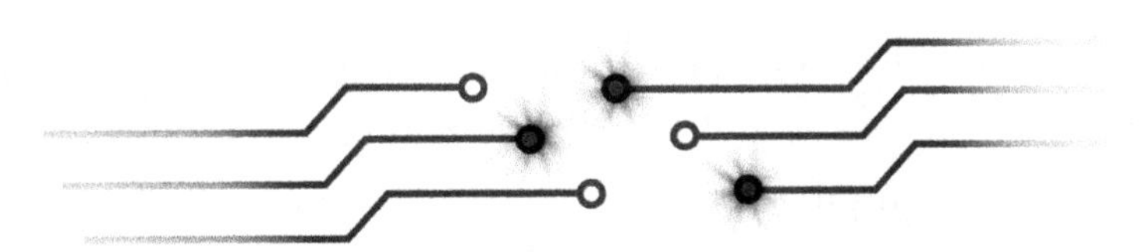

—42—

A Familiar Book

"You're good," Heath said, closing the book of diagnostic questions. He began unstrapping Warrick's wrists from the machine.

Warrick nodded. His breathing had regulated. He tried to relish that feeling of clarity he would experience after treatment. It was hard because it was always intermingled with exhaustion and pain in his extremities.

Heath left him there in the treatment room. Slowly, Warrick stood up, testing his balance. He stepped into the more spacious main control room of their underground bunker. It was still in disarray, cluttered with robots, weapons, and supplies of unknown origin. After treatment, he would walk through the room, touching the artifacts, examining their buttons and features as if this might prod his memory. At times he would get a feeling, or a connection to some person, place or thing would pop into his brain, and he would write it down.

This time, he passed by all the electronics and moved to a shelf on the far end. Here was a collection of books and documents. He found the Seeville Credo book and pulled it out. The disruption made dust billow into the air, some of it irritating his eyes. He rubbed it away.

Why this particular book? It was something that Lexie had said to him about his interest in Seeville, and his position there. He'd been a Seeville Lord, she had said. Maybe he'd written it down a long time ago, but he'd forgotten. Now he hoped to jog his memory. There could be more here, in this book, that would clear the fog just a little.

He paged through it. It was didactic, like an Old World prayer book. The gospel centered on three fears: competition, recklessness and obsession, and something at the intersection of these fears called Novation. He'd heard the word before. He said it aloud.

As he read, he marveled at the relevance of these themes to recent events, and in particular the growing prominence of the ICSM cities. The nearby nations were using them to compete for power. They were being reckless and obsessive in their devotion to the cities.

A name kept coming up in the book. A founder of the gospel, it seemed, who had provided many illustrative narratives. Ursula Okafor. It sounded so familiar. The name rolled off his tongue so easily, as if it had rolled off a thousand times.

He must have read this book before. Maybe he believed in these concepts, and maybe he'd promoted them to others. Either way, he must have known they were good and right.

He wrote his thoughts down in his notebook.

He wanted to know more. It was as if he'd found a piece of himself, and now he had to uncover the rest.

But how? Would he go to Victoria, or Anacortes, to probe the libraries and universities? Would he return east?

It wasn't safe. It wouldn't be safe until the witch was gone.

If he stayed, he would fade away to nothing in this dingy copper mine. He would be found, or his mind would go to mush. It would be the end of him—the end of someone he didn't even know anymore.

Heath was outside the mine already. He was sitting on a wooden rocking chair on the porch—one of his favorite spots—basking in the amber hues of the early autumn afternoon, reading a novel. The book had an Old World naval ship on the cover, shrouded in smoke. It was some kind of historical fiction.

"What is it?" Heath asked, his eyes still glued to the page in front of him.

"We're going to Anacortes," Warrick said.

Heath placed his book down on the side table. He had a sardonic look on his face. "What now?"

"I need to learn more about what's happening out east, about my past there, but first there's the witch. I need to find her before she finds me."

"And do what?"

"Kill her, if I have to. I'll never be safe while she's out to get me. Enough hiding in the shadows."

Heath shook his head. "Don't you think you should ask her a few questions first? It sounds like you have lots of them: About her, and about where you came from. She may have answers."

"No. She's a witch. She wants to use me. I'm the key to one of the machine powers in the east—probably—but I'm not sure how. I just know it's not good. She can't be trusted."

"Do you remember what I told you about my wife, Abeline? She and I, we don't always get along."

"So what? Is this about you getting home? There's still three weeks left on your contract and I expect you to honor it."

"No, it's not about that. Yes, I will honor it. Let me explain. I love my wife, but we rarely agree. At the same time, I recognize the value of her perspective. She sees things differently. We make better decisions when we make them together."

"You want me to marry the witch?"

Heath grimaced. "No. I just want you to hear her out first, and not just her; what about someone you respect, like Lexie? At least she has some continuity with your past. You know she's not malicious, or at least not as malicious as this witch woman. Why don't you ask her these questions before you do anything rash—before you kill someone you don't really know for reasons you don't understand?"

He did have a point, but Warrick was in no mood for giving ground. He wanted commitment. They could figure out who they talked to about what later.

"Are you coming or not?" he asked.

Heath sighed, stood up and went to his room to pack.

—43—

FLOUNDER BAY

It wasn't your typical stroll through Anacortes for Lexie and Keegan. They had taken two detours so far, each rerouting them farther from their intended destination. Some sections of the city were barricaded off, some were turned to rubble, and others were still burning. There was the occasional yell in the distance, but mostly silence.

"Why this way?" Keegan would ask, as he had done three times already.

"We've got to get to the main thoroughfare," Lexie replied, "to find our way through to Flounder Bay. I know it seems like we're going farther away, but we need to move inland. The coastal areas are the worst hit, so they'll be harder to navigate."

Flounder Bay was in a coastal area.

Lexie picked up the pace.

"Why wouldn't Ryder come to Leopold's?" Keegan asked.

She stopped and stared him down. Lexie couldn't blame him for being suspicious. He hadn't heard her conversation with Nillias before he died, and there was no way to get in touch with Ganges so he could check with Gungivite command. She'd asked him to trust her—someone he'd recently been charged with guarding as a prisoner. He had obliged, thankfully, but it was a tenuous arrangement.

"Hey, who knows," she said. "It's possible. But Nillias said I should find Ryder, not the other way around. He also said Ryder was looking in on my mom, which is why it makes sense to go to my mom's to find him. If you want to stay at Leopold's, be my guest, but did you see Kerub and Rillo moving those boxes before we left? I'm pretty sure Leo is gonna be gone soon, because he's a target. The Essentialists can find him, and through him, us. It's not safe there anymore."

Keegan's eyes darted back and forth. He nodded slowly.

Lexie turned back to the road, walking briskly.

They reached the downtown area, near the main docks. Smoke spiraled up in front of them. Whole buildings had been wiped off the side of the road.

One building, a hotel, was still standing, but it had been opened up in the front like a dollhouse. This similarity was accentuated by the presence of a sooty, doll-like body. It was a woman in a dress, slumped over a piano on the second floor, with too many joints in one leg. Lexie doubted anyone had dared to check on her. The building could collapse at any moment.

Some buildings that had burned down had been surrounded by overturned soil and detritus, possibly worked through by the skunks and their brigades moving about town. Other buildings still burned but the fires looked to be contained by a limited availability of remaining fuel.

It was all pretty bleak, but Lexie was impressed by the brigades that ran to and fro, triaging the injured and the dead. The half-drunk skunks were corrupt as all get out, so she was surprised to see any municipal order at all. Maybe it was because they weren't the higher-ups but rather the ordinary folk of Anacortes—the fishermen, farmers and merchants. They might not even be getting paid. This was their home. They were alive. They were protecting what was left of it.

"Lexie," Keegan called as he pointed up to the top of an old building.

She looked up, but saw nothing of interest.

"It was Aleron," he said.

Nillias had taken Aleron on the trip to Anacortes, but the animal had torn his leash loose from outside Leo's compound during the shelling. How could Aleron get up that high? These cats were agile creatures, so she gave him the benefit of the doubt. "So what? It's gone now, whatever it was." She kept walking.

It was hard to know what the cat might do without Nillias. Would he have any allegiance to the remaining Gungivites, or to anyone at all? Would he turn feral? She presumed the latter was more likely. Maybe the skunks would eventually put him down. Although with half the city on fire, a man-eating cat would probably be viewed as an annoying sideshow that could be dealt with later.

Lexie's pace slowed as they approached her mother's complex.

She was coming toward it from the inland side, but even from here it was clear it had been hit. A pile of rubble sloughed off the building onto where the path and gardens used to be, and as she and Keegan passed along one side, she could see the building was no longer as deep.

Once they reached the front, she saw that the second through fourth floors on the ocean side had been impacted. The outermost part of the building had been reduced to layers of incinerated mortar. It was all fairly uniform, and remarkably so, given what had once been there. Porches, plants, glass, and stucco had all burned to peat. But the impact was only ten feet deep, Lexie guessed, so some of the apartments could have been spared.

Dust floated about, making the whole scene hazy.

Just past the debris, where the garden was still green, were four cloth-covered figures, laid out in parallel.

One person was working the scene, apparently fearless in the face of further collapse, his big melon of hair made gray with ash. He was on a ladder, pulling out blocks from one of the third-level apartments and dropping them to the ground. This was what was kicking up all the dust.

Tarnation saw them approach and descended the ladder.

Lexie saw his face.

His head was tilted to the side, ever so slightly. There was no smile. His lips winced, an unusual act for him.

That's when she knew.

He walked over to the first tube of cloth on the grass and knelt down in front of it.

Lexie joined him.

She peeked under the cloth, but only because she felt she had to. It was too red, though. It couldn't be her mom. Then she noticed the gray-streaked hair. She saw the auburn sweater her mom wore too often, but torn down the side. It was Mom. Lexie replaced the cover quickly.

"Yup, that's her," she said.

"Lex. I'm so sorry," Tarnation said.

"Don't be. It probably happened quickly. Maybe she was lucky—in that it happened fast, you know."

Tarnation's brow knitted. He was watching her carefully, as if she was a broadside cannon about to fire.

In truth, Lexie didn't experience much emotion right then. She had known this could happen. And Mom was nearly gone, so she'd been preparing for a while. Maybe Nillias's more untimely demise had used up all her compassionate energy. And besides, Lexie had spent some time with her mom before she was gone. Well, not that much, really. Only a few moments in the last year or so, and she wasn't always herself when she was there …

So yeah, that's when it hit her. "Got to hit the head," she said, and she made her way around the garden to a scratch of trees that were still standing, closer to the rocky shoreline. While she was squatting behind a thick fir tree, not really peeing but pretending to, the tears tried to break free.

She gritted her teeth and forced them away. Memories threatened to flood her mind as well, but she pushed them out. She focused on the present.

Ryder. She needed to find Ryder.

When she returned to the complex, Keegan and Tarnation were standing there awkwardly, at times looking at her, but only at brief intervals, as if she were naked or something.

"Ryder isn't here," she said. "Let's look somewhere else."

"What about your mom?" Tarnation asked. "Shouldn't we bury her, or …"

Lexie gritted her teeth and looked at the cloth covering her mother. They should, but no. That would take hours. Enough of this shit. Dignity was overrated. Someone had to pay, and sooner rather than later.

"She's gone. Leave her here. I'll mourn her later. We've got a job to do."

"I know where I'm going," she said to Keegan.

"And where is that?" he asked.

"You'll see soon enough."

Keegan's questions had become less aggressive, perhaps on account of the day she was having. He was following her, and that was enough. Tarnation had joined them as well.

She could have stayed, thought it out, or even discussed it with them, but she only wanted to move, even if it led nowhere. She felt disembodied, as if she was watching herself from afar.

"What about the park?" Tarnation said.

"What park?"

"The park where the little girl was. I saw Ryder there with her once, remember?"

"Yeah, that park, that's where we're going. It's up here to the left, right?"

"No. To the right a few blocks. Trinity Park."

"Yeah, that's what I meant, sorry. Let's go."

She didn't look back to see their faces.

Trinity Park was several blocks inland, so the houses leading up to it were mostly untouched by the Essentialist shelling. It was well tended, with low-cut grass and staunch arbutus trees set in a square, surrounding a few picnic tables. The trees were deep red, fully stripped of their bark. Perhaps the bark was used for some practical purpose, or perhaps it had been picked off by children at play.

There was no one there at first, but as soon as they found a table, a man wandered up, slipping out of a space between two nearby houses.

It was Ryder.

Without the coughing and gagging, Lexie now noticed the resemblance to Nillias. His cheekbones were higher and his nose broader, but his skin was similar. He had moles, but maybe not as many as Nillias. His hair was shorter and lighter, but it could have been another wig.

The biggest difference was the way he carried himself. He took careful, measured steps. His eyes were probing hers.

She placed her hands on her hips and said, "I've half a mind to dust you right here, turncoat."

"And the other half?" A faint grin tugged at his lips.

"Don't get cheeky with me, or I might forget about the other half. I was sent to find you."

Ryder said, "So Nillias, is he …?"

"Yup. Retcher got him."

He squinted and looked down for a moment. "I'm …" He trailed off.

She gave him a minute to absorb it. His brow was furrowed as he stared at the ground. Eventually he looked up and said, "I didn't want to betray you, Lexie. Nillias and Margaret would have both suffered if I defied the Gungivites, and I was in dire straits—I would have died if I hadn't replenished my medicine soon after."

"Save it," she said. "I don't need your sob stories. We need to find Warrick. Where is he?"

His head cocked back in confusion. "Why do you need to find Warrick?"

"He's supposed to know where Pentapol is."

"I see," he said. "Unfortunately, I'm not sure. To use my implant, I would need to leave Anacortes and get out of retcher territory, so I could access any encoded messages Nillias might have left for me about Warrick's location."

She rolled her eyes. "Bilious buildings. I feel like I'm on a nutjob merry-go-round. We might as well just get it from the Observers, rather than deal with a turncoat like you. Let's go, Keegan, Tarn." She turned to leave.

Ryder said, "You're in danger, Lexie. You need my help."

"Like I needed your help at the Gungivite Embassy in Victoria? No. I don't think so."

"Wait," he said with some urgency.

She was going to tell him off, but his eyes weren't focused on her. He was looking down the street.

Was somebody coming? Maybe he meant they were in danger *now*? She drew her pistol. Keegan and Tarn did likewise. But there was no one around. The street looked empty.

Ryder didn't take his eyes off the road. "I've been watching you, since your mom's," he said, "to make sure there was no one following you, like Essentialist spies. You do have a follower. One I knew about, but now I see two. Don't move."

He dashed back between the houses and was gone.

It was infuriating, and he should know it wasn't the day to test her patience, but Lexie held her ground. It did remind her of Nillias, though. These Gungies were always one step ahead.

He wasn't gone long. When he returned, he had a large fish draped across his forearms—probably a halibut. He went to the table, cut into it with his knife, and let out a high-pitched whistle. "Stand back behind the table," he said. "At least thirty feet."

Lexie shrugged and did as she was told.

Ryder sat there, holding the fish out, waving it in the air. Then she saw Aleron. The cat stepped cautiously out from behind a building and pranced up toward the park, his head swiveling. His cadence slowed as he approached.

Ryder placed the fish in front of Aleron. Aleron pawed the fish back a few paces, took it in his jaws and began gnawing off the flesh.

A few bites into the meal, Aleron pushed his forelegs out, as if stretching his underbelly. It seemed like a passive move, but the movement took on a threatening appearance when his lips curled back, revealing sharp incisors.

Slowly, Ryder moved closer, offering his outstretched hand. Aleron blinked at it and returned to his meal.

"I wouldn't try to pet him," Lexie said.

"I know," Ryder said. "I'm just testing him. I can't control him as well as Nillias could. And yet he knows our scents and has seen us both before. I don't think he will attack unless we provoke him."

"I'm not getting close enough to find out."

Ryder smiled. "Nillias has taught you well. You're right to be cautious." He drew out a long blade from inside his jacket. He flicked it at Aleron and made a hissing noise.

Aleron bit down on the remainder of the fish and trotted away down the street.

"What was the point of that?" Lexie asked.

"I didn't want Aleron to attack us, for one, but I also wanted to make it safe for our other follower to join us." His head nudged back toward the street. There, standing in the middle of the road, was a young girl, no more than nine or ten, in a filthy frock. She had frayed brown hair that ballooned up into curls around her head.

"I lost her last night," Ryder said. "Her nanny was killed, down by the docks, and she ran away. She must have found you at your mother's, since I'd been there often."

Ryder walked out and knelt in front of the girl. "Are you okay, Margaret?"

"Yes, Mr. Ryder," she said. Her voice was distant and weak, lacking clarity. She didn't remind Lexie much of Nillias. Maybe she took after her mother, which was probably for the best.

"Do you want to meet my new friends?" Ryder said.

Margaret glanced over at them and shook her head.

There was something about the girl that compelled Lexie into action. She found herself walking to join Ryder. She knelt down beside him.

"Do you know who I am?" Lexie asked.

The girl frowned and shook her head again.

"I'm Lexie. I'm a friend."

Margaret only offered a barely discernable frown in return.

Lexie moved closer slowly, though she wasn't sure why. She didn't have to, and it wasn't like her. She reached out with both her hands, as if about to swat a giant mosquito. Margaret looked at her hands as if they were moldy, but Lexie continued on. Margaret moved away, but only a little, until eventually Lexie's arms wrapped around her. "I'm so sorry about all this," Lexie said. "I'm so sorry. You'll be okay with us, sweetheart."

The girl was frozen at first, but soon she fell into Lexie's embrace, accepting it.

Lexie hugged her tightly.

Sweetheart wasn't a word she used often, or perhaps ever. And why had she hugged her?

Nillias had asked her to take care of the girl, but she hadn't really thought about it since the night before. Either way, you don't need to hug someone to take care of them. Food and water. Maybe provide a pointer or two. That's what Lexie had always thought.

It was undoubtedly confusing to her companions. Maybe some Observer nutjob would sit her down on a couch one day to explain it, or maybe some friend of Dryden's—some anthropologist. She imagined this person as spectacled, his nose pointed high in the air. He would pontificate on her daddy issues, how she was finding a replacement for her mom, or how she was desperately reaching out for something, anything to keep herself tethered to this tormented world.

Screw them.

None of that mattered. The girl looked like she needed a hug, and that was enough.

—44—

The Flamenco Dancer

Alayna couldn't help wincing whenever the saws began cutting. They were huge discs of steel that neatly dropped and spun from metal arms that circulated through the work areas of south Diplopol, playing their villainous ear-splitting symphonies all too frequently.

Tuzuki was more tolerant of the noise. His face simply went blank, and he used the dead time to glance dispassionately around at the showering sparks and shuffling workmen as if it was the natural order of things. When the noise died down, he said, "This manifest is from yesterday." He pointed to the roll of crisp paper in her hand. "As you will see, Diplopol has suggested that raw metals be appropriated from the Port Angeles canneries and Astoria shipwrights. Plus, we need to expand copper and tungsten production. And be advised additional changes will be forthcoming this evening."

Alayna scanned the manifest. Of course it would change again. Rarely would a day go by without some alteration that would upset her meticulous planning and later leave some work group angry and idle without the appropriate resources at their disposal.

"You're making it too easy for me," she said sarcastically.

Tuzuki didn't react to her quip.

This was typical. Tuzuki was a hard man to read. He was a mixed breed, coastal Essentialist and Prefectorate, but he didn't seem to display any particular preference for either. Like almost anybody who had been at Diplopol for any length of time, he looked roughshod and overworked. A tangle of curly hair was adrift on his head, bobbing with his every footstep. His eyes were often sunken, conveying minimal affect. His work ethic was without question, though. He definitely did his job well.

The saws cut again. Alayna waited patiently.

When the noise receded, Tuzuki looked about to speak again, but then hesitated. Another voice superseded his. "Excuse me, Miss Menudos. You have been summoned."

She turned to see that it was Beetle Maplewood. He had crept up behind them on the foreman platform. Beetle's lineage was even more unusual than Tuzuki's. He was one of the few people she'd met who originated from Wood, Wind and Water clans of the east. Occasionally, he wore thick rings of green makeup around his eyes. He regularly grew a short-clipped beard that was so dense that it looked like dark paint over his macadamia skin. His other features were similarly bold. A receding hairline made the deep ridges on his brow appear especially prominent, and he had chalky, horse-like teeth that showed when he grinned—which was often.

Beetle was a colonel, a high rank for a non-Prefectorate officer, but Alayna was unsure how he had attained it. It could have been artificial, to give him sway in his role. He was one of the leading recruiters for the great eastern migrations. With the rise of Diplopol and the coincident machine wars in the east, these migrations had slowed to a stall, if not gone into reverse.

"Who is it?" she asked.

He showed his horse teeth. "If you will come with me, please."

She followed Beetle through the maze of manufacturing platforms, ramps, workers and robots. The latter were mostly cylindrical in shape, with any number of arms equipped with sensors and tools. Despite their clumsy appearance, they were remarkably spry, with a multitude of legs that pushed out of the base to navigate the fluctuating terrain. Many of these had been the first creations of Diplopol's external factories.

Diplopol looked as though it *could* be finished, at least so far as constructing the exterior buildings, ramps and causeways, because there hadn't been any bots scurrying around the urban superstructure in recent days, but it was possible they were just taking a break. They could be doing interior decorating, as it were, before adding countless more levels to egg-shaped buildings and terraces. Whatever they were doing on the inside was no small task, as it apparently involved the excavation of many thousands of cubic tons of dirt and rock.

Alayna had asked a few people how deep the city was going to dig, but no one had given her a straight answer.

"Where were you placed before here, Beetle?" she asked.

"Too many places; Astoria, Portland, Eugene and Kachina. Anywhere with people eager to find a new life."

She had been hoping it might help her make a connection between him and Caban, but his answer was uninformative. Kachina was an eastern Tucson Union town, but Caban was born in Sekoya, more to the west, and he was based in Madera, a larger agricultural hub.

They walked together for some time. Alayna's attention was mostly on her feet, navigating ladders, steps and construction materials, her body occasionally tensing to fortify herself against all the abrasive sounds.

They arrived at a boxy concrete building that was a few plots removed from the main array of factory floor spaces. One of the monorail lines fed into it, but it was otherwise nondescript, save for the voluminous door that Beetle heaved open for her.

Beetle waved her in, and she entered.

The door closed behind her with a thud. Beetle hadn't followed her.

The workroom, or bunker, or whatever it was, didn't appear finished. The walls were barren, with exposed wiring. The surrounding shelves were mostly empty, except a few that held a number of objects, mostly electrical in nature. Based on supply manifest sketches, Alayna could tell some were servomotors, circuit boards, or half-built robot components. The monorail line cut across the room and two large doors closed it off on either side. She wondered if this was going to be a Faraday cage. She'd heard of some going up to protect the more sensitive equipment.

In the center of the room, on an out-of-place wooden stool, sat Matias Caban. He said, "This is not a desirable location, I know, especially with all the defiling technology and noise in the background, but hopefully the racket will confuse the sensors of the heathen drones that I hear near my tent all too often."

"Is he—" She pointed back at the door Beetle had closed on them.

Caban frowned and shook his head. Information was a one-way street with him. Apparently, the matter of Beetle's allegiance was no exception.

A tense moment ensued where Caban stared at her without flinching. He wasn't sizing her up, or admiring her figure, as he sometimes did. This was a look of consternation, of skepticism.

"Anacortes," he said finally. "I wasn't told about the planned attack. Why?"

"Because I wasn't told either. I'm the last to know about military maneuvers. I will gladly relay what I do know, though, like the supply manifests, and the supply chain plans, as I've done in the past."

"We lost Groundwater people in Anacortes, and we could have exploited the situation if we'd known in advance."

"I'm sorry, but I'm not sure what else I could have done."

He forced his face into a grim smile and looked up at the ceiling, as if seeking inspiration. After a moment of thought, he said, "When I was young, there was a band of musicians that travelled through the lands of our tribe. They originated in a neighboring village. They had a humble start, and most of the music involved drumming tree rounds, shaking maracas, or rattling wooden soup spoons together. Crowds would gather to listen, and the band would be offered food and lodging. The band expanded and, to cover more ground, split into two. The first half stayed nearby and had an easy route and a regular schedule. They were well fed and happy enough. The other half had a tougher path. They sought out new towns, and even occasioned tribes that were outside of the Tucson Union. Often, they weren't paid or were chased off. One man, a drummer, was beaten to death with his own drumsticks. But they learned to improve their craft. They took on new musicians and tried different instruments. They practiced new songs that they thought would be more appealing. Eventually they were rarely denied, even outside of the Union. Years later, this second group returned to my town and played on the same night as the first group. It was a reunion of sorts."

His eyes were distant, bending into the memory. "The first group was what everyone expected, but the second … oh, the second. It was so beautiful. They had added two flautists that were so enchanting. A woman from the Irono tribe sang in deep notes, shaking the very ground. And then there were the dancers. Flamenco dancers, they said, who learned from an Old World book. I remember that night so vividly."

"It sounds like a memorable evening," Alayna offered, unsure where he was heading with his monologue.

He held his hand up. Apparently, he wasn't finished.

"The second half of the band was given better food, and more luxurious lodging. They were in high demand in every town and soon made a good profit, enough to become a proper company. But the first, unfortunately, were no longer welcome where the second half traveled. They dispersed. Some tried to learn new instruments, or join the others, but it was too late. No one would have them. They returned to menial trades. To this day the second group—now called the *pajaro llamas*—travel throughout the Union." His eyes returned to her, and his smile faded.

"That's a nice story, but I'm sorry, Inspector, I have to get back. Can you tell me what this is about? Why you are telling me this?"

He sighed. "You are the first part of the band. Your music is staid and boring, I'm sorry. You need to adapt and change, or no one will hear you."

She couldn't help looking at the doorway, but there would be no quick exit given that she would need to shift such a large monolith of cement. If he was about to kill her, this would be his chance. No one would hear.

But would he do that on his own? Was he confident in his abilities as an assassin?

In truth, Caban didn't appear bloodthirsty, or even angry. "I am an old hand at this," he said, his eyes taking in her entire figure, scrutinizing her. "And I am well aware that when you whisper in enough ears, eventually someone doesn't hear you correctly. I suspect this is what has happened here, Alayna. Perhaps you thought I wanted you to be a passive informant." He shook his head. "I do not. You are a wielder of words, a bearer of influence. You are too sharp, too talented. It would be like asking a flamenco dancer to play the spoons, or the flautist to clap the tree drum. So let me be as clear as the eternal spring. You are not simply a relay post for supply manifests. I am asking you to *seek out* the information we need, and then to influence the outcome. Nothing less. We must be proactive and not reactive. You must think on your feet, and not be wielded like a puppet."

It wasn't surprising. She'd hoped he had others he could use as his centerpiece in Groundwater affairs. Or maybe he was getting desperate. In any case, her attempts to do just enough appeared to be not enough. She would have to do more, and in turn, it would mean she would be more at risk.

"I understand," she said. "I will do my best, but I'm not in Hatsuo's inner circle. I'm not sure he even has an inner circle, other than the city itself. Perhaps if you could tell me who—"

"Come now," Caban said, waving away her words with his hand. "The supply chain is long, and it has two ends. Don't stay stuck in the middle."

She rubbed her chin, pondering. "Tuzuki?"

"Yes, for one. Get inside his head. Find out what he knows about the next weapon they are building. That may tell us about the next attack. We must find a weakness—and an opportunity to intervene quickly. And if not him, find out who is telling Tuzuki what to do. Move further up the chain, until you get to the weakest link. Do what you must."

She mulled over the idea. "They have completed a rail line down to Victoria, to expedite shipments, and they are automating the intake in the port in the marina. Tuzuki is often there. I can find an excuse to go down there, to work on intake logistics with him."

"That's the spirit." He smiled.

"But I wonder, to what end? What would be the outcome you hope for? What does Groundwater hope to achieve?"

"In a word, divinity. We must fight against this ICSM city sickness that is despoiling the earth. You can certainly see where this automation will lead. We will reach a point where we—the Essentialist people—are no longer needed, and, as a result, will also be unable to intervene. Hatsuo and his ilk will no longer be carving a new path for the rancid river. Instead, they will giving the river the means to chose its own bed, which will pass its fetid water where it pleases. We must wrest control before that happens, and if necessary, destroy Diplopol. Groundwater will run dry if this abomination is allowed to continue."

His monologue held a lot of Essentialist rhetoric, but it nevertheless communicated a clear, and harrowing, action. Alayna thought Groundwater might want to assassinate Hatsuo, or make a statement through some act of terrorism, but *take control*? "That is …" She almost said *absurd*, but thought better of it. "… going to be extremely difficult. How do you think we can accomplish that?"

"We have more agents than you realize. Others are coming. All we need is to become the Officiant. Once we control the city, we can control what is around it."

She couldn't keep from furrowing her brow. "Binjai is the main Officiant," she said, "and as far as I know the only one that Hatsuo has granted authority to, but Binjai rarely leaves the control room. Even if he did, he is a shinogi master. He trains for hours every morning, or at least he used to. He won a major tournament in the Prefectorate homeland. So he's not exactly the kind of guy we can sneak up on. Hatsuo has an army of humans and machines around him as well. We need help of the military variety. What about Commander Yasui, or General Pollack? Clearly, Hatsuo is out of line here. The attack on Vicky territory was predicated on false information, and I bet Anacortes was as well. Perhaps we could unseat him by exposing him, and then Prefectorate command could be reasoned with on Essentialist matters."

Caban's face was a mask of skepticism. "These other commanders will not help. They are too wrapped up in their egos, and are all of the same mold. They care little if they sully sun, soil and seed, and I'm sure they care even less for what measures are used against us. And what if they did unseat Hatsuo? We would have another Prefectorate autocrat, but no fundamental shift in the tide. No. Groundwater needs the spring to rise up. Here, and now."

No other objection came to mind. It seemed that Caban wanted to force matters to a violent conclusion, something she had been hoping to avoid.

She'd been hoping to stay on the periphery of this conflict, but it was now clear she was to be his weapon, perhaps his principal weapon.

The room was beginning to feel claustrophobic. "I better get back," she said, turning to the door.

"Of course, Miss Menudos. I look forward to hearing from you soon."

—45—

The Rusty Anchor

Dryden was loitering behind Cecile and Rosalie on the pier. He would pace up and down the wooden slats, staring into the sea, or at times back at the smoke rising from the city. He tried to overhear the many conversations Cecile had with the workers. Every once in a while, he would look toward the western horizon, over the wreckage-laden waters of the marina, toward Victoria.

Only two of Cecile's giant platforms had survived the barrage, and one of these had sustained heavy damage. Cecile was hard at work trying to wrangle her crew to repair them.

Maybe it would all be worth it. They were sturdy things, these platforms, with broad metal basins, designed to keep five thousand tons of cargo afloat. Dryden couldn't imagine what could possibly be that big, and Cecile wasn't about to explain it to him.

He had been asking a lot of other questions as well, but as usual Cecile had been evasive. She said her reinforcements should be coming in a week or two. Then it would all become clear.

All he could do was hover around and feel useless.

A hand was laid on his shoulder from behind. "Let's see some ID, buddy."

He turned to see two men, each wearing embroidered gold lapel patches across their shoulders—the insignia of Three Rivers security details. One had a holstered pistol, the other a rather long blade of some kind hanging off his hip, maybe a machete. Their faces were stern and full of resolve. This wasn't a routine inspection.

Dryden reached into his jacket and pulled out his ID. It was just a faded yellow card that listed his biographic information, stamped by the Hood

River municipality. These men wouldn't be able to judge its veracity.

"Essentialist," the first man said. "That's what I thought. What's your business here?" The other one shifted his position to stand beside Dryden. They were like a two-man wolf pack casing their prey.

Dryden had seen these men around earlier, patrolling the docks. They had accosted a few people and taken one of them away very publicly. He hadn't been sure why, until now.

Rosalie appeared next to the security officers. "What are you fine servicemen doing down on the docks? Isn't there a city on fire hereabouts?"

"This is no business of yours, Merc," the first man said, looking annoyed. "This man is Essentialist."

"Ouu … *Essentialist.*" Rosalie fluttered her fingers next to her face. "C'mon, let's be civil."

"Interfering in Three Rivers business will get you—"

Rosalie moved fast. She stepped right up to the first man and pulled him close to her, as if she was going to kiss him. "A man like you, so big and strong," she said. "I wouldn't want to rub his rhubarb the wrong way." Her eyes flicked down.

The man's head retreated from her too-close face, but his eyes followed hers. She had pulled a pistol out of her jacket, and the barrel was pointed squarely at his crotch.

His hands went up in surrender. "F … fine. But we'll be watching."

"I trust you will be," Rosalie said, releasing her grip. "It's hard not to watch, with these Essentialists being such exotic creatures. Especially this one, with its nice, shiny blond plumage."

The men retreated along the pier, squinting at her warily.

"Thanks," Dryden said.

"We've only got one throw-up apologist," Rosalie said.

Cecile had joined them. She was holding her chin thoughtfully. "I told you to wear your hood," she said.

"I don't see how that would make a difference. It's not like they recognized me."

"I'm not talking about them. I'm talking about the Essentialists, and …

others."

Reluctantly, Dryden pulled his hood over his head.

"These Three Rivers men will continue to be a nuisance," Cecile continued. "I can pass for Quebecois, Rosalie has Merc credentials, but you?" She shook her head. "You're a target. You should get off the docks. Go to the Rusty Anchor. Do something productive, maybe revisit your notes about Pentapol. Keep a low profile, but don't go anywhere. We have to go to Burlington in a few hours to meet with Nillias. Until then, *va-t'en*."

The ship Cecile had originally chartered had been destroyed in the attack, joining many clippers in the same fate. Most were lying on their sides, run aground in Anacortes's sunken graveyard. As a result, Cecile and her crew didn't have any place to go to rest, or even eat. The Rusty Anchor was one of the few eateries that had been untouched by the barrage, and as a result it was overrun by people of all sorts looking for food, shelter, or just a meeting place. Dryden should be able to blend in there, rather than be exposed on the docks.

After a considerable wait, he found a table on the outside, in the corner of the patio. Here, he pulled out his stack of articles and reference materials, to examine them for the umpteenth time. He found the excerpted letter in Ranthoke's compendium that referred to Pentapol—the one that Leopold said could have been falsified. It was addressed to a tribal leader from the coastal Essentialist town of Aberdeen many decades ago. The message was brief:

Dear Chief Forsythe,

Passage within the Salish Sea region is forbidden, and beware; we live in harmony, but we will engage our symphony of war, harp to song, if we must.

Constance Ameliore
External Relations Director
Pentapol

It wasn't much to go on. The wording was a bit peculiar, though.

References to "harmony," "symphony," "harp to song," and the very name of the addresser had a certain flourish. It was true that according to other correspondence, Pentapol was supposed to be a bastion of both defense and culture, which fit the verbiage, possibly a little too much. Nevertheless, the references to *symphony* and *harp to song* made Dryden wonder about the Singer—the huge seaborne ICSM artifact just to the west of the Kuvar fever lands. Could there be a city underneath it?

But it didn't make sense. Nillias said that the Gungivites had cored the area to the east of Ganges, including near the Singer, and hadn't found any large caverns or open spaces. And yet, Nillias also said there was a tunnel heading in that direction. So could it be … under the Kuvar fever lands? How would that be possible? If it was, how would they even access it?

He went to buy some green tea while contemplating the subject. It was cold when it was served, but he didn't complain. He returned to his chair.

The Rusty Anchor was on an escarpment, so he had a good view of the surrounding marina. He could watch Cecile and Rosalie toil from here. At the moment, Rosalie was paying off one of the workers. She took unblemished Essentialist notes from her pocket—still the main currency in Anacortes. He'd seen her do this before. She seemed to have an endless supply of these bills, and they were always crisp, as if she had a full-blown mint churning away in her trousers.

The Pentapol question continued to stymie him, and his attention wandered further afield.

A clipper moored to one of the lesser-used piers caught his eye. He'd seen it the day before, sporting the Essentialist flag—a cherry blossom tree inset on a flaming sun. Now the ship was flagless, and sailors were busy hauling boxes and crates onto it.

He tapped his pencil against the table as he shuffled papers, trying to make sense of his notes. The tapping was a nervous habit. He justified it as a way to help him concentrate, as if it was necessary to activate his mental machinery.

When he glanced over at the clipper again, he saw a familiar sight. The Three Rivers security men who had accosted him were walking up the ramp. Dryden watched with interest as they were met by a man and a woman who came out of the bowels of the ship. There was a lot of gesticulating and pointing at their chests, back to the city, and at their temples. It didn't look good for the clipper owners, who were obviously unlucky Essentialist merchants caught in the wrong port on the wrong day.

After tense posturing, money changed hands from the ship owners to the Three Rivers servicemen, and more posturing ensued. Additional notes changed hands and the two Three Rivers men finally left, looking satisfied. The security men were just shaking people down, it seemed, taking advantage of the situation to skim off Essentialists before they left town for good.

Tap tap tap. He bounced the pencil off the table, rotating the tip and eraser with his thumb and index finger. No one around him seemed to care about the noise.

The man from the Essentialist merchant vessel resumed moving boxes, but the woman stayed and watched the Three Rivers men go, her hands on her hips. Eventually she pulled out a notebook and wrote something down. Had she found something of interest in these lowlife bullies? Her actions reminded him of Alayna, although she was half a head shorter.

She was probably just checking inventories.

Tap tap tap.

The Essentialist clipper would be gone soon. It looked like a coastal vessel, based on the three-anchor symbol on the side, which was a Newport shipwright marking. These ships would normally stop in Anacortes first, then Victoria, and return south through the Wandefuca Gate after they had completed their business in the Salish Sea.

Tap tap tap.

He shuffled through his articles one more time, but his mind was elsewhere. He couldn't concentrate.

Tap tap tap.

Tap tap tap.

He packed up his stuff and left the Rusty Anchor.

Dryden finished the last stroke of his knife, curling it around the back of his head, and scraped the edge on the bowl in front of him, discarding cream mixed with blond hairs. He put down the blade and used the towel to wipe off any remaining residue from his head.

He looked at himself in the cracked mirror. *Good enough*, he thought. There weren't any funky depressions in his skull, like he'd seen on some other bald folks. And hopefully it would take a while to grow back.

Outside the clipper, a distant horn sounded. He looked out of the porthole and saw land, with quite a few ships sporting Essentialist flags in the foreground. They would be inspected soon. Hopefully, Vicky authorities didn't have his name down. In truth, he was more worried about the drones noticing him than his name being on a customs list. Cecile had been right about that.

Hence the shave.

It had been easy to get aboard. He had simply explained to the captain who he was, showed her his ID and told her that he wanted safe passage to Victoria. He offered her a fair price, and she took the deal without much questioning. They were down a few crew members after the attack, and they needed the money, as all opportunistic merchants did. In fact, Dryden was staying in the quarters of one of the shipmates they'd lost the night before, so he wasn't taking up any additional space. It was free money for them.

Cecile and Rosalie might not have been happy about him cutting out like this, but he didn't feel like he owed them anything. His only usefulness lay in finding out the location of Pentapol, a task he was struggling with. And why wouldn't he? More accomplished archeologists, historians and anthropologists had been trying to answer that question for decades.

Dryden was convinced their only chance was to find this Warrick person, but it seemed unlikely.

Their cause was a good one. He could fight for Cecile, to be sure, but it seemed mostly pointless and fraught with uncertainty. If there were indeed these five thousand tons of *something* coming from the east to help them, his meager weight wasn't going to tilt the scales in their favor.

The boat undulated. He looked out the porthole window again. They were cutting through the wake of another boat that had just passed by. Beyond it, he could see an Essentialist coast guard frigate headed their way.

No matter how he justified it, there was more to his actions than that. People were dying. Anacortes was just a foreshadowing, a sign of what was to come for all the Salish Sea nations, and perhaps beyond, as the ICSM cities continued to build their weapons of war. Things would get worse, not better.

He could die tomorrow, or the next week. So could Alayna. And yes, he could accept that. They were in a fickle world that was out of their control.

But there was one thing he couldn't accept.

She had to know the truth about Ben before it was too late.

—46—

An Uninviting Home

Ryder had a rather uninviting home near Trinity Park. It was a halfie of a small Old World duplex unit, with black shutters and crumbling concrete steps, tucked away from the main streets. That's where Lexie held up with Ryder and Keegan for a while.

Why trust Ryder? Well, good pirates don't harbor grudges for long, and it was all very mechanical, at first. Like so many others in Anacortes, Lexie was set adrift by the attack and not really thinking too far ahead. There was nowhere else to go, and it seemed fitting only because Nillias had told her to do it, and he'd been telling her what to do for a while. When the grief from her mom's passing began to recede, she thought it through and decided working with him was right. Or rather, if she was going to make those Essentialist sons-of-bitches pay for what they did, she needed help.

There was a stoicism about Ryder—a thoughtfulness—that she hadn't noticed before. He was street-savvy, having grown up an orphan, trying to survive in Three Rivers on his own. Suffice it to say she found him to be tolerable. It was probably because he wasn't gagging anymore.

It would be a while until he could get to the channel so he could use his implant. The harbor was such a mess that the first ship they could charter couldn't leave for three more days. And they'd missed the meetup with Cecile in Burlington. It was Lexie's fault. Too much had happened, and she just didn't want to think about it. She wasn't so sure she wanted to meet up, either. So she hadn't told anyone the plan until the following morning. After some debate, the three of them decided they would try again. Might as well. This Cecile woman, witch or not, said she had reinforcements coming, and who else was going to help?

It turned out that Tarnation's place was damaged, and the remaining handful of Gungivite militia wanted to stay with Keegan, who was now their commanding officer. Not only that but Margaret needed a place to say. So all these people joined them at Ryder's and it made for cramped accommodations. Most of them spent a lot of time in the nearby park. Lexie would help Margaret with her schoolwork. She had taken a pad full of writing and math lessons from her home. Margaret liked to sit near Lexie, even more so than Ryder. Maybe it was because she too had lost her mom, or maybe because that first hug had been a little aggressive.

In the early afternoon, Ryder brought some stale bread and hard cheese to the park. Tarnation had found an old guitar and was trying his luck with it—ouch. Meanwhile, over the racket Lexie was trying to teach Margaret how to multiply fractions.

"No, leave the denominator alone. You only multiply the top numbers when the bottom number is the same."

"What's that one called?"

"I don't know, just call it the top number, okay?"

Yeah, Lexie wasn't exactly a pro when it came to math, either.

Tarnation's playing stopped abruptly when Lexie heard a familiar voice.

"Where's the witch?" Warrick asked.

Warrick and Heath had crept up, using the nearby trees as cover, and were standing side by side in front of them. Each was holding one of the large energy weapons, pointed in the group's direction. Heath didn't look like he knew which was the business end of the thing, but Lexie had seen firsthand that Warrick knew how to handle one.

"Who are you?" Ryder asked.

"This is Warrick," Lexie answered. She turned to Warrick. "No need to get testy. We were just about to come look for you. We could use your help."

"How did you find us?" Ryder asked.

Warrick squinted at Tarnation. "You have conspicuous friends." Of course. It would be easy to just ask around for the loudest fiefdom man in town.

"Where is the witch?" Warrick repeated.

Lexie exchanged a glance with Ryder. His expression was unreadable.

"Look, Warrick," she said, "Cecile's not here, but let's talk about this. She has reinforcements coming. It may be the only way we can stop the Essentialists. We also need the location of Pentapol, which you know. We want what you want. Just tell us."

Warrick laughed. "Pentapol? Maybe I did know, once. But not anymore. And as for Cecile, she made me like this. She turned my mind to mush. I know, because I wrote it down. Why would she do that unless she was evil? There are no reinforcements, I assure you. And if there are, I doubt they would be on our side."

Nobody was going to challenge those energy weapons. They were intimidating to look at and even more intimidating to see in action. But one person wasn't really in the know about these things. Or rather, one animal.

As they were chatting, Ryder had placed a whistle in his mouth. Warrick swerved his weapon toward him and said, "Don't you dare."

But Ryder had already blown into it, only no sound came out—or rather, no sound that a human could hear.

Warrick laughed. "You might want to get a new whistle."

Suddenly, Aleron was bounding out of the alleyway nearby, moving like lightning. Heath's body buckled at the sight, and he fumbled the weapon in his hands. Warrick looked surprised as well, but he kept his composure.

There was enough time for him to point the weapon at Aleron, but not enough time to turn it on. Aleron tackled him and the cat's mouth wrenched the weapon from his hands.

At that point, Tarnation had already been moving for a good second or two. He tackled Heath before he could recover, which was probably just as painful as having a man-eating cat take you down. Ryder had his pistol out and was approaching Warrick, who was attempting to scurry away from the cat, much like Lexie had done during her first encounter with Aleron.

"Enough," Ryder said to Aleron, and he hissed at the cat. Aleron paused, bared his teeth at Ryder, and stalked away. Warrick was lucky. Lexie hadn't been sure the cat would obey commands without Nillias around. Fortunately, the cat was just passive-aggressive and not full-on aggressive. They would need to keep up the supply of fresh fish.

They tied up Warrick and Heath in the basement of Ryder's duplex, at which point Lexie kicked off the interrogation.

"Listen, Warrick," she said, "you're not making the best impression here, threatening us with energy weapons and all. So why don't you help us a bit and it'll smooth things over. Where is Pentapol? Or at least tell us why you're so concerned about Cecile."

"I'm not telling you a damn thing," he said.

"Okay, I get it. There's nothing in it for you, but what if there was?"

He frowned. "Like what?"

"You were always looking for a big score, like the spice merchant vessel, or hiding that fake Vicky dignitary, or Maple Bay. What if I were to tell you we could get you something bigger than all of those combined. The Gungivites—they've got more medallions than you can imagine—I could negotiate a good deal for you."

"I'm not doing business with you."

"Dammit, Warrick, we don't have time for this! Nillias is dead. He sacrificed himself so he could save us from the Essentialists, and so we could find Pentapol. Not so you could stymie us with this childish tantrum about witches. And Diplopol is getting stronger. They're making drones and guns and ships, faster than ever. They'll take over the whole Salish Sea in no time if we can't find Pentapol soon."

"Those sound like serious problems. Too bad none of them are mine."

"You know what, forget it," Lexie said, and she stormed up the basement stairs.

She needed to cool off a bit.

It wasn't a good start. Warrick was still too paranoid about Cecile, and he saw it as black and white. They were on her side, so he wouldn't give anything to the enemy.

She tried again later. So did Ryder, and even Tarnation had a shot at them. Warrick was just as tight-lipped, and unlike last time, Heath wasn't able to offer any insight either.

They seemed to be spinning their wheels, but what else could she do? Torture an old friend to extract information? That didn't sit well with her. And besides, he would probably see it as therapeutic.

—47—

A Selfish Expedition

Dryden would be harder to recognize with a shaved head, but he wore his hood anyway. It was cold enough that wearing it didn't seem suspicious, and there were plenty of drones flying about Victoria harbor.

Diplopol was heavily fortified, and he wasn't sure he would be able to get close without being apprehended, so he decided to see if there was a way he could sneak in using the new shipping terminal the Vickies were building. He'd been told it had a rail line to Diplopol that was already operational, so he went to check it out.

The nascent terminal site was huge, with several automated cranes and housing dozens of stubby train cars. It was especially impressive because a few months ago there had been no rail, no cranes, and no electricity in Victoria at all. Security was lax outside of the military shipping section of the terminal. In the other sections there wasn't much in active operation, and the tall fence around the site had been only partially completed.

When Dryden walked inside the perimeter to talk to a workman, he was surprised to see Alayna in the distance. She was standing by one of the new piers, talking to a captain with frizzy hair.

She was wearing a brown polo shirt and loose black pants. Her jade eyes flashed in the sunlight.

He receded to watch from the shelter of a food cart nearby. Eventually, when Alayna made her way to a restroom, he moved to intercept her.

"Alayna!" he whisper-yelled. "It's me. Over here." He waved her toward the back of the building so they would be obscured from the main work site.

Alayna's brow furrowed until he pulled down his hood. Then her mouth gaped open. When she came to her senses, she looked up to the sky and shook her head. She pointed at the woman's restroom and went in.

He followed her in cautiously.

When inside, he was met with a heavy tongue-lashing. "What fever-ridden river brought you back up north," Alayna said, wagging her finger at him, "when you *should* be taking care of Nate? It's not safe here, and certainly not around me. They have drones everywhere. And what's this about Maxwell? There are people that think you *killed* him, did you know that?"

"I did."

"And Hatsuo will surely—what?"

"I did kill Maxwell."

She was speechless, her mouth stuck half-open.

Dryden remained measured and controlled. He'd been preparing for this conversation for a while. "Just hear me out," he said earnestly. "It may be hard for you to believe, but it's the truth. And I also know it may not change anything between us, but you have to understand why I did what I did. That's why I'm here."

"Fine. What is it, Dryden?" Her impatience was already returning, but there was a twinge of something new—fear. She must have thought he was going mad.

"I received a message from Sergio," he said. "I'm not sure how he found this out, but he said that Ben knew the attack on Neah Bay was staged. It was done to diminish coastal Essentialist military vessels. It also revealed that the Prefectorate had Ben killed in Hood River, with Maxwell's help. Maxwell drugged me to put me to sleep while they rolled Ben into the river."

Her head went back, as if he had belched in her face. She spoke in incoherent snippets as she digested his words. "So you just ... I don't ... what kind of nonsense ..."

"Just think about it," Dryden said, reaching out for her hand. "I know it's a lot to process."

She pulled her hand away and shook her head. "You've changed, Dryden. You're ... a *murderer*. You killed someone *in a bathroom*." She looked left and right, as if she just now realized where she was standing.

The door opened and a woman walked in. Her eyes widened, seeing the two of them.

"I'm sorry," Dryden said, faking a laugh. "I took a wrong turn." He stepped out of the door the woman had left open.

Alayna said, "Excuse me," and she followed him out.

Fortunately, the woman wasn't alarmed enough to care.

Once they were outside, Alayna pulled him along the wall of the building, toward the perimeter of the shipping yard. The bay was just beyond the fence line. Whitecaps undulated across the expanse of water.

Alayna glanced at the sky. "You need to leave," she said, "right away."

Dryden put his hood back up. He was about to turn, but he wasn't finished. "Wait. There's something more I wanted to say. Why don't you quit and go home, Alayna? Can't you see what Hatsuo is? Can't you see what's happening here? You're in danger."

Her jaw clenched as though she wanted to argue. Her green eyes sparked but just as soon fizzled out, and her shoulders slumped. "You're right about that. It's bad. I wish I could quit." A weak snippet of laughter escaped her. "If only I could. They're building advanced weapons, thermobaric bombs that can wipe out small cities. Something terrible is coming, for all of us, and I'm caught up in the middle of it. It's too complicated to explain, but the truth is, I'd be in just as much danger if I left. At least you can …" She might have said *take care of Nate*, but she seemed to doubt herself before the words came out.

Dryden felt he should say more. He wanted to beg her to leave, but he couldn't know what she was dealing with. He didn't have much standing to argue.

"You need to go, Dryden," she said, nodding in affirmation of her own conclusion. "I don't know about Ben, and Maxwell, but either way, your work is important. Find a way to help us—to better understand these cities so we can limit their influence. That much I believe in; that part of you has never wavered. You're good at what you do. Otherwise, you being here will only help Hatsuo. It will only lead to one of us getting hurt, and maybe Nate as well. Do you understand?" There was a measure of pleading in her voice.

It was true. This was a selfish expedition, and a dangerous one. Their lives didn't mean much in the context of what was going on around them.

And nestled in her monologue was a hint of confidence in him. There was something he could do, some way he could contribute.

It was also possible she was afraid of him, and this was the best way she could be rid of him.

"Okay, Alayna," he said. His words sounded solemn and lonely.

She turned to leave, heading for the back corner of the building. She was sauntering, the way she did in Sanuwan, the way she used to in Hood River.

"Nate misses you," he called out, "and so do I."

Her pace slowed. She half-turned back. Her eyes stayed anchored to the ground for a moment, until her head tilted up. Her brown polo was caught by the wind, hugging the curves of her body, and her raven strands of hair whipped around, like snakes hissing at the ocean backdrop behind her.

She smiled.

It was a small, fleeting thing. Her right cheek was curled ever so slightly into a crescent. Her head was tilted to the side, as if that tiny grin upset the delicate balance of weight on her neck. All the while, her brow was tightly knit, untrusting of her own amusement.

Soon her expression vanished, and she escaped behind the building.

Dryden turned to leave as well.

In the days to come he would remember that meager smile. Perhaps it had been innocuous, or even accidental—a facial tic that should be ignored. But to Dryden, it was everything. To him, it was a murmur in the earth, a prelude to a tectonic shift. Even if it wasn't, even if it was just his imagination, it was something to hold on to.

It was enough to keep his head above water, until they met again.

—48—

Doctor's Orders

Late in the night, Lexie crept down the basement stairs of the duplex, lamp in hand, to where they kept Warrick and Heath. The basement was damp, and cold, but it had a rug. It was better than many a ship's hold she'd slept in, so they couldn't complain.

When she was at the bottom of the stairs, the dull glow of the lamp revealed their sprawled bodies. They were cuffed and chained to the single big structural support in the middle of the room.

Heath was awake first. He gently nudged Warrick, who woke with a start. "What do you want?" he asked.

She took out her knife and handed it to him, handle first.

"You want me to thank you for this?" he asked, a look of scorn on his face.

"Your choice," she said.

He shook his head and began pulling up his pant leg. "Are you going to watch?"

She ignored his question and asked another. "Cecile left a note for us in Burlington. We're going to meet with her tomorrow, here in Anacortes. Why are you so important to her?"

"I've already told you. I'm the key to controlling the machines in the east. She wants me to help her—to give her more power."

"Control them, how? How will it give her more power?"

"I don't … I didn't write down everything." He looked over a Heath, as he often did for support.

Heath just shrugged.

"What if you're wrong?" Lexie said. "Or what if she's working for the right side of this machine war? How can you possibly know?"

"I wrote it down. She's a witch."

"I'll tell you what I remember. You were afraid of her, but you didn't want to kill her. You were running from something, sure, but I don't think it was her."

Warrick didn't respond, but Heath said, "What else do you remember?"

Lexie said, "I remember what you taught me. Don't gamble unless you have to, and improve the odds as much as you can. You told me to never act until you have as much information as possible."

"So what?" Warrick said. "You want me to sit down and have a polite chat with the witch? She'll just take me prisoner. I can't exactly go east to investigate. It's too dangerous, and I would be away from my treatment for too long. Sorry, Lex, I've got all the info I can get."

"I wasn't talking about you. I was talking about me."

"What do you mean?"

"I could never get leverage on these Observer nutjobs, try as I might. Leverage is important. It's how you stay alive, and get what you want. You're our leverage with Cecile, and the truth is, I'm not entirely sure we can trust her, either. I mean, what has she done for us, anyway? She's promised reinforcements but offered no other help, and can't be bothered to explain herself. So you're right. If we take you with us tomorrow, she could take you against our will. Even if we keep you here, she could track us down and find you, just like you found us. She has too much money. She's hired a bunch of goons besides her Quebec militia, so we're outnumbered."

Warrick's snark had fallen away. He looked genuinely curious. "What are you going to do?"

"The other thing is, Nillias died a couple days ago, and my mom, too. I've become a little more sensitive to people croaking, especially those that I know, and I'd rather you not die as well, so …"

She pulled out the key to the cuffs from her jacket pocket and placed it neatly on the floor.

"I'm going to give her a week," she said. "Maybe the reinforcements will come. Maybe she'll explain herself and make sense. Or maybe we'll all die. But you don't need to be a part of this. I know where you're based, and the

Gungivites have a fix on your facial profile. They can find you pretty easily."

Warrick's eyes were wide.

"But if you muck about in our business, *or* Cecile's, you're done for. You got it?"

He nodded slowly.

"Keep the lamp, and the knife. You'll need them." She walked back up the stairs.

She didn't go to bed right away. Instead, she entered the kitchen and listened to make sure they left. They took a few minutes, but eventually she heard them walking stealthily up the stairs. They couldn't see her hiding in the shadows. She was low in a corner with another knife at the ready.

Before they left, Warrick walked up to the kitchen table and placed a piece of paper there.

The two of them exited into the street together without a sound.

After they were good and gone, Lexie fumbled around and eventually found another lamp on the kitchen counter. She turned it on and looked at the paper.

It was a brief letter:

Lex,

Heath says I should listen to you more, but I've never been good at following doctor's orders. He was right.

You letting us go told me something. Maybe you give a shit about this old man, maybe you don't. You said yourself you're using me for leverage, so it's hard to say. No, it tells me you don't trust the witch either, which is more important. It means you're probably on the right side of this mess.

And so maybe you do deserve to know what I know about Pentapol. I just reviewed my logs after my last treatment. This is what was in my notes:

"Pentapol is accessible halfway along the ICSM defensive arc. Stay low and cut

high."

Probably not helpful, but maybe the eggheads can make sense of it.

Novation is Damnation,

Warrick

—49—

Outgoing Mail

The walls of the supply terminal, oppressive and intimidating, loomed over Alayna as she did her rounds. She longed to leave this place, but she knew that Diplopol would be even worse.

Perhaps she wanted to escape because she was being besieged on all sides. Hatsuo, Caban, and now Dryden. They all wanted something from her, and they were all depending on her. Each one represented a dark cloud of not only responsibility, but also uncertainty and risk. Their suffocating shadows strangled any joy she might eke out of her daily existence.

She reminisced about how it used to be. She longed to have a slow day without these demands placed on her, like she often did in Hood River, talking with Barnaby to tradesmen, filling out ledgers, or maybe polishing some old hides for sale. And what she would give to be on the coastal trails with Ben and her parents again, listening to seashells, singing songs and telling stories. She missed Nate most of all, and often reflected on playing with him in the water, or hiking through the forest. It was hard to remember what his voice sounded like.

She hadn't written in her notebook in days. Ever since she'd seen Dryden, in fact. She didn't like to think about the meeting, because at times it would hit her—the thought that what he'd said could actually be true. Her heart would race, palpitating as if it had forgotten how to beat in proper sequence. For so long, Dryden had been a rabid wolf, kept neatly locked away in a corner in her mind. Now the cage was open, and the wolf had been released, out to threaten her.

What frightened her most, though, was that the wolf might not be rabid after all.

During a work break she left the confines of the supply terminal, but the streets felt no less oppressive. What she carried with her were just folded papers and ink, but they felt like a slab of lead.

She passed a woman throwing a bucket of water on the street, and she tap-danced around it to avoid getting splashed. A reek of butchered fish hit her nose shortly after. The woman didn't apologize.

She heard a familiar buzzing sound above her, but it was moving fast and had a clear vector. It wasn't one of the drones that hovered overhead, listening and watching everything; it was going somewhere.

Alayna moved on with a singular focus.

She had done what Caban asked. She pushed Tuzuki to better understand the manufacturing plans, under the pretense of "making sure inventory needs can be met." She cited examples where she could have intervened and prevented idle time, or boosted production by getting safety stocks up, or prioritized shipments that she didn't know were important.

Her efforts had worked remarkably well, but not on account of her own craftiness. Tuzuki was nervous about a major offensive that was brewing and would do just about anything to be sure supply needs were met. He explained that hundreds of aerial drones were being built, and not the flimsy surveillance ones but fast, heavily armored fighters with explosive ordnance and bomb-bay doors. They were building an array of anti-aircraft guns as well, to counter the Gungivites after what happened in Anacortes. It seemed that the fighting would be mostly in the sky, or at least, that's where most of the resources were being deployed.

That was as far as Tuzuki went, and it wouldn't be enough for Caban. Tuzuki wouldn't speak of the timing of this offensive, where they would strike, or who would be involved, no matter what angles Alayna tried. For that, she would have to go over Tuzuki's head, to the Military Ops drill commander. She would have to send a letter to him, but not directly, or Tuzuki might find out. She could gain access to the commander through a colleague of his, a Colonel Payce who was a well-respected drill sergeant. Payce could plead her case and suggest a meeting.

But the more she thought through this scenario, the more she wavered. She was involving two more people who could question her true intentions and therefore rat her out.

Instead she chose another strategy, one that was unorthodox and potentially just as risky, but she told herself it was the path the eternal spring would have chosen. Not the easiest, but the truest.

She moved quickly and kept her head down. It would be best to not be recognized, if at all possible. She took a shortcut through a small park. Yellow leaves were littered about, and the branches of a solitary oak tree shifted in the wind. It was a small oasis of verdure in an increasingly industrialized city. She resolved to come back here with her notebook, if she ever had time.

The mail depot she was looking for was down off a main street, tucked away in a cul-de-sac. She had thought no one was there until she was about to drop her mail in. Only then did she turn around to see a man walking along the street behind her. He stopped just across from her, next to an old bike rack. It was Beetle Maplewood.

She should have doubled back to see if anyone was following, but her head had been in the clouds.

"Hello, Miss Menudos," Beetle said. He was sitting casually on the metal crossbar of the bike rack while nibbling on a piece of jerky. "What a surprise seeing you here, so far away from the supply terminal. Why don't you use the military mail depot?"

"This is faster. And I have a letter for Nate—my son."

"Faster? The new supply train will get that mail north in less than an hour."

It was true. He had her there, but she couldn't tell him she wanted to avoid the military censors. If Diplopol's robots scanned the envelopes, the letters could find their way to Tuzuki easily.

She said, "Look, I didn't want to go to two different mail stops, is all. I'm doing my job. Are you doing yours? Does Hatsuo know you're out here, following me around?"

He smiled, took a bite of jerky, and spoke with a half-full mouth. "Did you know my job is not just managing the many Essentialist migrations? Sometimes, I have to deal with people that step out of line. There are people who aren't worthy ambassadors of Essentialist edicts—they don't understand our *cultural norms*." He said the last words slowly, as if they were to be savored in his mouth along with his jerky. "I've been given great latitude, my own discretion on these matters, and you see, people don't always fit, so I have to ... well, it's so unpleasant."

He looked up into the sky, pondering. Alayna thought he was finished, but then he said, "Like, I don't know, lashings, stonings, hangings, the whole bit." He grinned, seeming to relish the thought.

Many people she'd worked with were political animals with sociopathic tendencies. Hatsuo certainly fit that description, as did Chinatsu. They could be unforgiving and violent, but only when it suited their ambitions. She could manage them, because she knew their actions would not betray these ambitions. With Beetle, though, she had a feeling he was the opposite. He was a sociopath with political tendencies—a far more volatile animal.

She didn't respond, other than to stand up taller and cross her arms.

Beetle's head tilted to the side. "But that's not what I'm doing now, of course. It's break time. I just went for a walk. You can tell Hatsuo that, if you like. It would seem strange to tell him something so innocuous, though. Outside the *norm*, as it were."

"Yes, it would," was all she replied.

"Good. Well, nice chatting with you, Miss Menudos. I'd better be going back to the supply yard. May sun, soil and seed be bountiful to you on this day."

It was just a threat. He was probably working for Caban, but she couldn't rule out ties to Hatsuo or the city itself. Or maybe he had his own personal designs on her?

Why not? Everybody else did.

She waited until he was gone before turning to the mailbox again.

She dropped in two of the envelopes, but withheld the third, whisking it away into the inside pocket of her jacket.

For all she knew, Beetle could come back and upend the mailbox, or pilfer her letters directly from the mail carriers.

She walked briskly but didn't return the way she'd come. She exited the cul-de-sac and turned down a main street toward the water, until she reached a walkway that traced the edge of the bay. Years ago, on a trip to Victoria, she'd seen people use this walkway for leisure time. Children used to run out toward the water's edge, only to be escorted away by diligent parents. Today there was only the occasional businessman or sailor clipping along, intent on some urgent meeting or obligation, not giving a moment's thought to their surroundings. The only remaining sign of children was a wooden dump truck toy, upended near a tree, gathering mildew.

She couldn't be too late getting back, so she began to jog. As the heat gathered around her core from the exertion, she took off her jacket. She hadn't jogged in years, even though she enjoyed it. Dryden had always been the one egging her on.

The marina was busy. She identified three merchant ships. These were the fast ones that traded in more valuable goods. She made to board the closest one.

"Hey, who are you?" an old man with leathery skin called out. He marched down the deck from the aft portion of the boat to confront her. A woman with long ratty hair peeked around a bulkhead as well. She had something slung around her back, possibly a weapon. These were nervous people, paranoid, even. Good.

"I am the Lead Supply Officer for Diplopol and Special Confidante to General Hatsuo." Alayna flashed her identification at the man. He saw it but probably didn't have time to give it a detailed examination.

She continued, fronting an air of authority. "Are you planning on sailing around Neah Bay?"

"Well, yes. We leave tomorrow, after our regular stops. "

"Good. By order of General Hatsuo, I need you to deliver a letter as soon as possible. I will have your next three docking fees waived if it arrives in less than a week."

The man exchanged a look with the old woman. She shrugged. It wasn't as if Alayna was taking possession of their vessel, or hauling them off to the Diplopol factory floors. In terms of military strong-arming, this was small potatoes.

"Fine," the man said grumpily. "Let's get it in writing, though."

—50—

THE CANNERY

Lexie, Ryder, Keegan and Tarnation met with Cecile in the basement of one of the large cannery operations. Apparently, Cecile had bought metal from the cannery at a premium, so the management let her and her work crews use the basement to store equipment and weld subassemblies.

It was spacious enough and had plenty of light provided by high windows, but the smell was atrocious and there was no shortage of flies. People said Lexie had a sensitive nose, but she was pretty sure it was one of the worst-smelling places she'd ever been in. Several lines of tables were laden with fish parts, while two somber-looking men hacked at them with machetes. That's where the stench emanated from, and the flies.

What certainly wasn't helping her sentiments about the place was that it reminded her of her mom, who'd been worked to the bone for ten years at a stinky cannery just like this one. It wasn't a pleasant memory.

In the front part of the room, there were welding stations and stacks of prefabricated parts for the platforms Cecile was building. A few random tables were scattered throughout the space as well, but only a couple of chairs. Cecile, Rosalie, Dryden and the Quebecois men were all waiting for them inside. Two other brutish guards had greeted Lexie's party on the outside.

Both sides said their hellos and made introductions. Tarnation and Ryder were new to Cecile's group, and as a result were met with a fair number of indignant looks.

"You shaved your head?" Lexie remarked to Dryden, the Essentialist egghead. "Great. All we need is another nutjob."

"I don't understand," he said.

"The Observers are all bald," she explained. "Something to do with the gadget in their brains. But hey, they do have a lot of really nice wigs. You might have trouble finding a blond one, though."

Cecile ignored her banter and cut straight to business. "Have you found out the location of Pentapol?"

"No," Lexie answered.

"Well, we need to find Warrick Kelemen."

"We did. We had him and let him go."

"You did what?"

"Don't worry. I know where he is. He doesn't remember where Pentapol is, but he's got a clue. He said—" She pulled out the note from Warrick and read it aloud. "*Pentapol is accessible halfway along the ICSM defensive arc. Stay low and cut high*. Not sure what it means, but maybe you and the egghead can help."

Cecile didn't seem at all interested in the note. She was surely still reeling from Lexie saying she'd let Warrick go. Her eyes were wide, probing Lexie. Dryden, however, frowned in concentration. He scratched his head thoughtfully and went to sit at a table in the back where his work was strewn about.

"What a waste," Cecile said. "And that clue honestly sounds like gibberish. How is that going to help?"

"Hey, it's all we could get."

Cecile was breathing deep breaths, looking around at each of them. Something had changed in her. "*Zut alors*," she said, "Why would you let him go? Of all the stupid things …"

"Why is it stupid?"

"Because he can help us in the east! He can turn the tide."

"How?"

"I can't tell you that. If our enemies were to find out—"

"So, where are your reinforcements?"

"I don't know. They're late. I need to get out of retcher territory, on the water, to reach the satellite uplink and find out why." As she was speaking, she pulled out a device and flashed it at them. It looked like an Old World phone, but a bit boxier.

"You're full of surprises," Lexie said. "That's real cute. But rather than bedazzle us with fancy toys, why don't you just tell us why we should trust you?"

"We're spending all our time, and money, building platforms to ship our reinforcements to Kuvar Island so you can win this war."

"Uh huh. Says you. How do I know it's not for some other purpose?"

Cecile was looking around, casting fiery glares at the lot of them. "I can't trust you either. The cost could be too great if others learned of our secrets. I have trouble enough trusting my own people." She looked back at Dryden at the table. "Even people who I assume are working with me, but instead are on harebrained solo missions into Essentialist territory." Dryden responded with a sheepish expression.

"Tell me then, how can I trust the lot of you?" Cecile continued.

Lexie just shrugged.

Cecile shook her head. "Your war—and I mean the real war, not this little skirmish you've just seen in Anacortes—is about to begin. Not in weeks, or months, but days. I've seen this kind of war in the east. Millions have died. *Millions*, do you understand me? Entire towns turned to ash by bombs, the inhabitants assassinated systematically by drones. There is nowhere to hide. You can't wait it out. And that's just the people. Fractures in the earth. Millions of tons of mechanized vehicles and bots bent, melted, irradiated and disintegrated. It's the Detonation all over again—or excuse me, *the fall* is the term you use. That's what's in store for you unless we work together to stop it."

Lexie nodded, then tilted her head back and forth. "It's a nice story. Heart-wrenching. I wouldn't tell my kids at bedtime, but cute. How does that make me trust you?"

"Dammit!" Cecile yelled, spittle escaping her lips. "Fine, we will go and find Warrick on our own, diverting us from our activities at the wharf. You go and find Pentapol, if you wish. I don't deny it could help us, but the chances you'll find it are remote at best."

"Sounds good to me," Lexie said. She clapped her hands at her team. "Let's go find Leo. Maybe he can make sense of what we got from Warrick."

She was bluffing, at least partially, hoping that Cecile would change her mind and be more forthcoming. In truth, as Cecile had been speaking, Lexie was having second thoughts. Leo had been missing for days, off in hiding, and unlike Warrick, she had no idea where he could be. And what if Cecile pulled the reinforcements? What if Cecile did find Warrick and took him away, or killed him?

It was possible that by letting Warrick go she had screwed things up even worse.

"Wait a minute," Dryden said. He was still at the table in the back, drawing long lines on a map of the Salish Sea area.

"What?" Lexie asked, as the entire group turned back around.

"I think … I think I may have found Pentapol."

Cecile rolled her eyes, not hiding her skepticism, but she gestured at the group to move over to the table anyway.

Upon the table were two large books, a number of stapled documents and several sheets of paper with chicken scratch on them. Leo wasn't the tidiest person either, so she tried to give this Dryden egghead a pass on his organizational skills.

Dryden waited until everyone had gathered around to begin speaking. He was rubbing his hands together nervously. "When I was in Haplopol, I saw a vessel, deep under the earth. That's where we found the Diplopol control junction. There were dead people trapped inside, maybe the victims of some altercation, I can't be sure, but these may have been Gungivite Observers from decades ago because—as Lexie explained—they had shaved heads. That's speculative, of course, but maybe it doesn't matter. What's more important is that the vessel looked like it could run on a rail—something I didn't realize until I saw how a real monorail cart worked in Victoria."

Flies were buzzing around them. Abruptly, Tarnation stepped in and swatted one on the table in front of Dryden, leaving the splattered remains on one of his books. Dryden recoiled, perhaps fearful that it was the onset of some kind of attack.

"You're welcome, bud," Tarnation said.

Dryden gradually leaned over the table again, keeping one eye on Tarnation. He said, "Anyway, I think the ICSM cities had a system of tunnels connecting them all, and that's where this vessel came from. This is supported by what Nillias said about tunnels originating from under Ganges Island. Not only that, I think that during the ICSM conflict, decades ago, the Diplopol control junction was stolen through these tunnels. It's how the perpetrators tried to get away, and maybe Haplopol tried to appropriate the vessel. It was trapped underneath the city, and the tunnels under Haplopol were destroyed during the conflict."

It was plausible. Lexie knew better than the rest of them that this tunnel system could exist, and that the Observers could have used them in any conflict with the other ICSM cities.

"Are you suggesting Pentapol is accessible through this system of tunnels?" Ryder asked.

"Yes, but we already know many of these tunnels have collapsed, so it would be difficult to find Pentapol by exploring them beneath the surface. We need to find an access point from above."

The flies in the place were getting worse. They were landing on occasion, and Lexie was constantly having to wave them off. It was making it hard to concentrate on what Dryden was saying.

Lexie swatted another one against the desk. "Sorry," she said. "That one just about flew up my nose twice already."

Dryden said, "I know. I have never seen flies this big. It's disgusting."

Rosalie chimed in. "Quit your whining. This is nothing. A backwater Jax horsefly can carry a heavy suitcase and three pineapples on each wing without breaking a sweat."

Dryden frowned. "That sounds a bit hard to—"

"Get on with it," Cecile said, not masking the annoyance in her voice.

"Sorry, yes," Dryden said. "Like I said, we know this system of ICSM tunnels exists, and this is where what Warrick said comes in. He said *Pentapol is accessible halfway along the ICSM defensive arc*. So I've been over here drawing all sorts of arcs over the map. I think this is what he was referring to."

Dryden pulled up the map from the desk and showed them the arc he'd drawn. The map was a mess, with a number of crisscrossing lines scrawled on it, but the one he indicated was bold enough to stand out. It began at the Singer and traversed south down the Strait of Georgia, round into the Wandefuca, through the Fan, and out to the Wandefuca Gate. "As you can see, the arc runs entirely through water, and divides all the ICSM cities into the north, almost like a political boundary for the Salish Sea nations."

"But why not any other arc?" Cecile asked, pointing at several other arcs Dryden had made on the map.

"Good question. I realized that this dividing line was also subtly hinted at in another note in Ranthoke's compendium. It was the only letter ever found from Pentapol, where they said, *we will engage in our symphony of war, harp to song*. The phrase *harp to song* was particularly strange, and I wondered if it was aligned with the tunnel line. In our arc, the Singer would represent the *song* part and the Wandefuca Gate is the *harp*."

"How is the Wandefuca Gate the harp?"

"Yes, it took me a while to figure it out. It's because if you look at the shape of the gate, the long columns that we sail through are actually the strings at the top of a harp that is sitting upright in deep water. It may have even been standing at one point, like the Singer, but the rest of it was probably damaged or destroyed in the ICSM conflict and is now submerged. In other words, the Wandefuca Gate was at one point actually a giant statue, like the Singer, or Fan, but playing a harp."

There was a lot of head scratching. Lexie tried to imagine the Wandefuca Gate as a giant harp player, lying on its side in the sea. She had to admit, it was possible.

Dryden continued. "That means, if Warrick is right, if we split the defensive arc, we end up here, at the Fan. That's where the entrance to Pentapol should be."

Everyone was quiet. Feet shuffled and brows furrowed as they looked at the messy map. Finally, Lexie broke the silence. "Well, you certainly sound like a real egghead."

Cecile nodded, her eyebrows raised. "I admit, it's as good a hypothesis as any."

Ryder chimed in as well. "It's worth a shot."

"Who's going to go?" Lexie asked.

Cecile frowned at her.

Lexie said, "C'mon. I know we have our differences, and maybe we don't trust each other, but we should work together."

Cecile leaned over the table, studying Dryden's map. "If only it were that easy. I can offer you a ship, and Dryden should go, too, but I need to stay here with Rosalie to await our reinforcements. I will give you a communicator so we can keep in touch, but we will only be able to use it outside of retcher territory."

Lexie looked around at her group. "Count me in, Lex," Tarnation said.

After some hesitation, Keegan nodded. "It's not in Essentialist territory, and easily accessible by boat. I suppose it should be a straightforward mission."

Dryden cringed. "Yeah, well, we will have to take a ship, but it won't be easy."

"Why not?" Keegan asked.

"I think it's why Warrick said to *stay low*. You know the saying about the Fan. It's probably why Pentapol has never been found."

They all nodded. Some grimaced, including Lexie. Well, except for Cecile and Rosalie. They weren't from around here.

"What saying is that?" Cecile asked, her brow knitted in confusion.

"It's hard to ask questions of headless sailors."

—51—

Stay Low and Cut High

Dryden watched the sweeping arm of the Fan hurtle around in front of their ship. The huge blade of metal was angled down, but near the bottom it was bent out into a sharp edge pointed in the direction it was spinning. The ship was close enough that a blast of air from the arm's passage caught in the sail, first pushing them back, but then pulling them after the path of the blade. The sailors quickly went into action, trying to jibe back out to a safer distance from the perimeter before the next arm of the Fan would pass by.

This harrowing experience was enough impetus for the crew to get to work dismantling the sail and masts completely, because they would surely be cut off or cause the boat to capsize if caught in the blades. Despite their efforts, in the undulating sea it was hard to say if bringing down the masts would give them enough clearance.

Dryden felt pretty useless watching them go into action. He'd never learned much about sailing, or any other trade for that matter. He'd always had his nose in his books.

"Captain," Keegan yelled out. "We have company." The Gungivite moved past Dryden, walking hurriedly along the deck from the stern toward the bow. Dryden followed him. About a dozen people were standing at the bow, mesmerized by the sweeping arms of the Fan. These were mostly Gungivite militia that Keegan and Ryder had rounded up in Anacortes. Also joining them was the rather large fiefdom man with snakeskin tattoos named Tarnation, and the woman named Lexie.

This Lexie woman was some kind of merchant, or pirate, depending on whom you asked. She definitely knew her way around a ship. So they'd given her the mantle of Captain.

Lexie took Keegan's scope and returned with him to the stern. Dryden again trailed them, along with most of the passengers. "Yeah," Lexie said, staring into the scope. "Essentialist. Not coast guard, either. That's a war frigate headed this way."

Their passage through the Wandefuca Channel had been easy thus far. The ship had stayed glued to the southern coastline to avoid the eyes of the many patrol boats stationed near Victoria. Luckily, no ships had been coming north through the Seattle Strait that day, which would have been problematic. The only sign of activity had been two minuscule aerial drones in the distance, but they hadn't come close, on account of the drones being unable to cross into retcher territory.

But their ship had to head north to reach the Fan eventually, and that meant past the retcher line. In hindsight, Dryden realized the drones must have been keeping tabs on them from a distance—and called on this frigate to intercept them.

Lexie scratched at her cheek. She gazed toward the Fan, back at the frigate approaching, then toward their mizzenmast, which was being assaulted by men with axes on both sides. Soon it would be cut in half. "Well," she said, "we don't have many options, do we? I bet that frigate's got a motor on it, just like the Gungivites have. Let's drop the pontoon boats. We'll row them in to the Fan."

"I doubt they'll follow us," Ryder said, "but they may fire at us. Even if they don't, we could be revealing the location of Pentapol."

"Yeah, I know, but I've still got one trick up my sleeve."

The crew and passengers worked quickly, throwing bags into the two pontoon boats and then clustering inside. There were six passengers in each boat. Dryden was in one with Keegan and half his men. The other half went with Ryder and Lexie in the other.

Lines were cut, and they dropped into the water.

Dryden rowed with the rest of them. The pontoon boats were soon in the range of the sweeping Fan arm. The occasional ocean swell lifted them up to a disconcerting altitude. What would happen if they were on the top of the swell when the arm went by? He was pretty sure everyone else was wondering the same thing.

The arm swept toward them, humming from the friction with the air. "It's going to hit us!" one of the Gungivites said, and he jumped in the water. The rest didn't panic—or at least that much. They all ducked, keeping as low a profile as possible.

It washed over them like the giant wing of some pre-fall airplane, pulling the raft into a spin. Thankfully no one was hurt in either boat.

The man who'd jumped overboard was floating beside them. He called out, "Help!"

They pulled him out of the water and dropped him back in his seat. The other Gungivites didn't seem to think any worse of him for jumping.

"Row, dammit!" Keegan yelled. Dryden did, with verve. The Essentialist frigate was just outside of the Fan's sweeping range, and another ship appeared in the distance. It was coming closer.

Hopefully the frigate would give them a verbal warning, which would grant them time to close in on the center column of the Fan. Or maybe it would just wait on the perimeter, assuming this was just some suicidal escapade that would end once they wised up.

Unfortunately, for whatever reason, these Essentialists didn't have that kind of patience.

Broadside batteries lit up, followed a split-second later by a deafening booming sound and, just after, the clap of an underwater explosion and a torrent of water landing on top of the pontoon boat.

Keegan appeared undaunted. He was drenched, but his eyes burned with focus. "Row, dammit!"

They kept rowing.

Again, broadside batteries lit up, followed by a deafening sound.

This time, the world turned. Water, limbs and the hull of their boat were in orbit around Dryden.

And … agony. Searing agony wrenched at Dryden's left shoulder. He was underwater. There were men swimming, and men who had gone limp, and blood. Blood everywhere.

He tried to swim somewhere, anywhere. His left arm didn't feel right, but it moved. His head punctured the surface.

The boat—or the half that remained—had overturned. Men cried out. There were only two voices, though, and one of them was his own. His eye caught sight of the other pontoon boat. It was still afloat, and at the stern, Lexie was standing.

It was strange that she was standing with the Fan blades still circling above them. Dryden was so disoriented that he had trouble making her out. She held a blob of metal in her hand.

A swell of water hit him. He kept swimming while trying to focus on the boat, and on Lexie. It wasn't a blob of metal. She was holding a large weapon. A series of blue lights blinked on its side.

It fired. Pulses of energy seared steam up from the water. When Lexie achieved better control, the beam lifted up and hit the side of the Essentialist ship, pummeling into the hull.

The broadsides fired again, their ordnance landing just to the side of the remaining pontoon boat. Lexie remained standing, her teeth clenched, firing back at the ship.

The pulses did little damage. The hull seemed to absorb it. Black lines formed where the energy pulses passed, but otherwise it wasn't having much effect.

That is, until the energy pulse passed over a broadside battery opening.

Of the explosions he'd seen and heard that day, this one was the biggest, maybe because there was more than one happening simultaneously. He couldn't help but duck his head in the water as the ear-splitting detonations resounded across the seascape. When he pulled his head up again, the entire Essentialist ship was a floating inferno. The blasts must have set off a chain reaction after the first battery. Flaming men and woman were hurtling themselves off the upper deck into the water.

Dryden tried to keep his limbs moving, to stay pointed in the right direction. It was working, sort of. Or maybe the other pontoon boat was coming toward him. In any case, someone from the boat grabbed him. They threw him in the base of the boat, on his back, so that he was looking straight up into the sky.

His shoulder registered a violent surge of pain.

People around him tensed, and ducked low.

The arm of the Fan swept over again, passing directly over his field of vision.

"You're hurt," Lexie said. She loomed over him, obscuring his view. "You okay?"

He finally got up the nerve to glance at his shoulder. It was a mass of red, with a shard of metal sticking out, still steaming. His arm was still there. His fingers moved when he tried them, but otherwise he could barely lift his arm.

"I think so," he said.

"We'll patch you up soon." She stood up straight again to scope the horizon.

Dryden watched the sky. There were bright white clouds, billowing towers reaching high into the troposphere.

"Hold on," someone said.

The Fan arm swept over again. This time it was more surreal than frightening. Dryden even smiled as it went past, and chuckled deliriously, despite the pain radiating from his shoulder. He was alive. He wasn't drowning. They were low enough that the Fan wouldn't hit them.

The boat spun from the blast of wind, but it righted soon enough.

A tremor shook through the boat. They'd hit something.

Lexie was leaning over him again. "Okay, egghead. Last stop."

He forced himself to sit up, using his good arm as a prop. The others were stepping out of the boat onto a skinny metal platform, scaling steps that led up behind a metal wall.

The base of the Fan was wide, probably a hundred feet across. It was made of a red and orange metal casing. There was a lot more clearance from the Fan arms here. When Dryden looked up he could see why. The arms angled down closer to the sea only at the point when they extended beyond the circumference of the base.

Dryden followed them out of the boat and up the steps, trying to keep his left arm immobile. He knew that if it hit something, the pain would be excruciating. One of the Gungivite men stayed behind to tie the boat to a metal post.

At the top of the steps was a platform surrounded by a two-story-high external sea wall. Just inside this sea wall a number of human-sized statues had been placed—a dancer, a flautist, a singer, a guitar player, a pianist and more. They were red from oxidation, corroded and covered with fungi and barnacles. Some of the figures were playing instruments he didn't recognize. In the center of this platform was a column protecting the main mass of rotating metal. Ladder rungs had been built into the sides of this interior column.

They were already trying to cut into the floor, torches blazing. "I may need to blast it," Lexie said.

"No, wait," Dryden said. "This metal is probably too strong. Look how thick it is here." He showed them the sea wall metal near the opening, which was almost a foot thick. "I suspect these are to protect against the elements. They may even be armored. Warrick said to *stay low and cut high*." He pointed to the nearest ladder.

Lexie and Ryder didn't question him. They simply climbed up the ladder, one after the other. A couple of stories up was another platform that encircled the spinning column. Lexie banged on the floor of the platform. "Yeah, this is different—hollow-sounding. Go ahead, Ryder."

Ryder cut at it with his torch as she stepped away and put the scope to her eye to look out to sea. "Hurry up," she said.

Dryden walked over to the opening in the sea wall. In the distance he could see the second frigate nearing the periphery of the outer range of the Fan blades. It was turning so that its port side was facing them.

Dryden stepped back. "Let's all get back behind the seawall, on the other side of the column."

"We're through," Ryder said, just before the frigate launched its first rounds. They splashed before the column of the Fan, throwing up gushes of water onto the nearest statue arrangement. "Hurry," Ryder said.

They all rushed up the ladder, toward the makeshift hatch. Dryden was last up. He climbed slowly, one rung at a time, unable to lift his left arm in the process. It was tight at the top, barely enough standing room for seven people.

"Just jump in," Ryder said. He was already down through the hole he'd cut, in the gloomy interior of the chamber. "I'll catch you. The floor isn't far down." One of the Gungivite men jumped, and another.

Cannons blasted in the distance. Explosions sounded nearby, kicking up more seawater.

"I hope you're right about this place," Lexie said, frowning at Dryden. She went down the hatch. Tarnation jumped next. Another Gungivite man jumped in, and yet another.

Dryden was last.

Cannons blasted in the distance again.

He jumped.

—52—

Project Osprey

Hatsuo marched through the great hall of Diplopol, flanked by Communications Officer Fadina and Corporal Niko. The hall was like Haplopol's main courtyard but larger, recessed into the city beyond tower-lined roads and a number of automated manufacturing complexes.

Across from him, a huge pane of glass looked out to broad, hex-plotted gardens with trees, legumes, and fruits on the other side. The plants had all been experiencing rapid growth in their new home after being brought into the city. Shipping cylinders shot through tubes that crossed the expanse of the hall, like bullets through the chamber of a transparent gun. They would be delivered to other parts of Diplopol in seconds, moving machinery or supplies. Service robots and drones flitted about as well, but by now Hatsuo was so used to them that he paid them about as much attention as the floor tiles.

Several Prefectorate militia stood guard along the walls of the hall. They were some of his most loyal subordinates, and two of them were master shinogi wearing maroon armbands. Their orders were to leave the Prefectorate soldiers alone and interrogate only coastal Essentialists and foreigners. This would weed out any bad apples and ensure Prefectorate business took precedence. He'd insisted that they be outfitted with guns as well, even though shinogi often abhorred them, and many were not properly trained in their use.

Guns. Not more than a year ago the Essentialists would have raised a stink about the Essentialist edicts if a Prefectorate private was armed with a pistol or rifle. Now, with so many other technological marvels at their disposal, no one gave it a second thought.

He turned at the end of the hall, into the long corridor that led to the

Officiant's Office. A mass of people was coming out of one of the experiential rooms. Prefectorate guards parted the crowd for Hatsuo and his men so they could pass.

There were indeed hundreds of people inside Diplopol at any given time, mostly moving in and out of the experiential rooms. Fortunately, they were not accompanied by any of the virtual delegates, which he had always found annoying and intrusive.

The people of Diplopol were more tolerable than he would have expected. Tens of thousands had come to live and work in the area; still more came, and still the perimeter expanded. Having this many people in close confines, working at tough menial tasks, was usually a recipe for conflict, but almost everyone seemed content. Even outside the city wall, no one complained about the fifteen-hour days, the stench, the flies, the pestilence, or the bland food, which could at times be worse than sea rations. Perhaps the Essentialist people were finally learning the merits of obedience.

He entered the Officiant's Office and climbed the stairs to the command center. The room could easily fit thirty people, but Hatsuo wanted to minimize those in the know, so only Lieutenant Etzuka was there, swiping through display panels with his fingers. Behind him, the control junction boiled in its never-ending jet bath.

"Is everything ready for today?" Hatsuo asked in Japanese.

Etzuka turned to him. "The city says so, yes."

"Did you check for yourself?"

"I used to check, but the city is never wrong."

"So what are you doing?"

"I am observing. I may need to relay insights to you and others."

"I see—an important vocation." Hatsuo nodded with a smile. The man was useless. Hatsuo would have to begin using the communicator devices the city had advocated. Then he could reassign Etzuka to fighting duty and be rid of him.

"Oh, there was one thing," Etzuka said, as if he had just woken up. "A rogue Three Rivers clipper was approaching the Fan. Diplopol decided to issue the order for one of our frigates to fire on them. I'm not sure why."

The Diplopol speakers chimed in with a familiar feminine voice. "General, I have ascertained that these are dangerous spies that have advanced energy weapons. We should apprehend these spies if we can."

"Let me see."

The monitor showed the drone footage. It was hard to make out until Diplopol reconstituted the image and zoomed in. One pontoon boat made it to the middle of the Fan, but another was blown out of the water. In a remarkable display, a whole frigate was destroyed by a handheld energy weapon fired from the pontoon boat.

"Gungivite?" Hatsuo asked.

"Uncertain, but probable."

It definitely smelled of Gungivite influence. Diplopol had said before that they had advanced weapons. They were probably spies who had taken a wrong turn and were now stuck at the Fan.

"Have the remaining frigate keep watch, but not pursue," Hatsuo said. "Let's catch them if they try to get away."

"Should we send in more frigates to help?" Etzuka asked.

"No. We'll need every available unit today."

"Yes, sir."

"Speaking of which, let's get started," Hatsuo said. "City. Show us target locations for Project Osprey."

Three monitors in front of Hatsuo became an array of video feed panels showing various Gungivite locations—mostly ship placements across the Salish Sea but also warehouses in Duncan, patrolled ports of entry like the Sansum Narrows Bridge, and a number of strategic roadways.

"Good. Begin the first wave." New video feeds were superimposed on the others, showing hangar doors opening across Vicky territory. These were in Diplopol, but they also had some in Brentwood Bay and Sidney. Aerial drones of numerous shapes and sizes lifted off and swarmed out into the sky.

"Alert the men that Osprey has been initiated," he said to Etzuka. Etzuka began tapping out an electronic message.

"And you." Hatsuo pointed to Fadina. "Go on foot to be our live spokesperson. Remember, this is a pre-emptive attack in response to Gungivite aggression at the border." Fadina was one of the few coastal Essentialists besides Alayna he let near the Diplopol control junction. She had a horrendous crooked nose, but she was quite good at delivering news to the workers. Her family in Eugene was being "protected," so he wasn't concerned about her loyalty.

"Yes, sir." She saluted and left.

"And you." Hatsuo pointed to Corporal Niko. "As quietly as possible, I want you to arrest Supply Officer Alayna Menudos, Inspector Matias Caban, and Colonel Beetle Maplewood. Go in numbers and take them by force, but I want them alive. Bring them here under armed guard."

"On what charges, sir?" Niko was like a stiff board, standing tall, his chin up.

Hatsuo smiled. "Best to not worry people with confidential Prefectorate matters. I will formally lay the charges when they arrive."

"Yes, sir." And he left as well.

Finally, Hatsuo took a seat in front of the monitors, watching the attack unfold. He put his feet up on the desk and exhaled in satisfaction. This was promising to be one of his better days since he'd stepped foot on this barbaric continent.

—53—

PENTAPOL

Lexie landed in Ryder's arms when she jumped through the opening. It was a rug-burny wrap-around-the-waist thing where she slid through most of the way to the floor anyway. It would've been less awkward if he'd just let her sprain her ankle.

Only eight of them had made it: Lexie, Tarnation, Ryder, Dryden and four of the Gungivite militia that they'd inherited from Nillias. Tarnation lit up a lamp to properly see the space they were in. It wasn't anything special—just a circular metal-walled corridor with a number of closed panels on its walls. Just around the bend, there was an opening in the floor with a ladder heading down.

Before they tried the ladder, they hoisted Ryder back up to try to weld the top opening back together. He did a terrible job, but maybe it would buy them a few minutes if the Essentialists followed them into the Fan.

At the base of the ladder was a room with more closed panels, a few fancy contoured blue chairs and an imposing door. There was no handle on the door, just an indented circle with a skinny knob sticking out of it.

Ryder and a few others pushed and pulled at the knob but couldn't get the door to budge.

"Try the base of the control junction," Dryden said. "The knob looks similar in form to the placement nodes for the Haplopol and Diplopol control junctions." Dryden was wincing a lot, and his shoulder was drooping to the side, but thankfully his egghead brain was working fine.

Ryder took the control junction out from his pack and rotated it around in his hands. Noting his confusion, Dryden took it from him and placed it against the door so that the base was pointed toward the knob. The bottom of the orb opened up to accept the knob, and the door made a clicking sound.

The door pushed forward easily.

On the other side was a passageway out to a circular staircase that wound around the circumference of the spinning column. The group followed it down.

Lexie was toward the rear. She nearly ran into the Gungivite man in front of her when the column abruptly slowed. Up ahead, the walls around the staircase were opening up, and a shimmering light played on Ryder's back at the front of the line. They continued to move, and soon Lexie could see why they'd slowed. Above them, the ceiling turned to thick glass that appeared to be holding the ocean up above it. It must have been stronger than steel.

And below them …

They were at the very pinnacle of a massive underwater enclosure. In some ways it was similar to Tetrapol in form, but even larger, with walls made of high-strength glass holding out the sea, and with the column of the Fan rotating in the middle, in lieu of Tetrapol's stalagmite-stalactite spindle configuration.

The glass surface transmitted an oscillating glow from the ocean waters above—sunlight much dimmed by having traveled through great depths to reach them. It provided a somber tint to nearby objects, and little resolution of what lay down below.

As they continued descending the staircase, it gradually wound away from the cylinder in the center. Attached to the spinning cylinder were sculptures of glittering gold and silver, bobbing and weaving in a circular airborne dance driven by the Fan's rotation. They depicted musicians of all kinds—flautists, harpists, singers, and string instrument players. There were dancers in innumerable positions. There were mermaids and mermen. There were colorful fish, dolphins, whales, otters and seals. There must have been more than a thousand moving parts to the carefully choreographed airborne dance, sometimes connected by loose sectional staircases, or slides.

It was like a huge merry-go-round—but yeah, better than that. Lexie almost stumbled on the steps because it was so entrancing.

"Let's hurry," Ryder said from the front of the line.

He was right; they needed to move faster. They had been lollygagging, and they couldn't know if the Essentialists would send a team to follow them in. They might even try to destroy the Fan, although the metal structure looked to be incredibly well armored.

So far, Tetrapol was pretty bland compared to this.

But of course, nothing's perfect.

When they closed in on the city below them, after climbing down several hundred steps, Lexie began to see a variety of dead things. First was the forest. Lexie thought the trees might be more silver sculptures or perhaps parts of some kind of electrical plant. But no, it was a vast expanse of trees, stripped of bark, and no leaves littering the ground. The trees were well past the first stages of decomposition—like an army of standing driftwood.

Eventually Lexie could make out the details of houses and other buildings. They were all interconnected, more like adjoining levels of varying depth, rather than independent structures. There were a few shattered windows, and some of the housing lots were filled with ash.

When the group was close enough, she could see people, or what remained of them. Thousands of withered, skeletal bodies were littered about the streets and parks. Most were dressed in colorful suits and dresses; many still had their hair and nails. But all were dead and fully rotted out.

The stairs came to an end, depositing them at what seemed to be a main thoroughfare of the city. In the distance, at the end of this main artery, was perhaps the largest building in the cityscape, so they headed in that direction. The building looked something like a giant bird's nest made of glass, with shards sticking out, but it was so large that each shard was a building unto itself.

Dead people were scattered along this thoroughfare as well. Some had holes in their suits or uniforms, surrounded by dark stains; others looked to be half burnt.

"This must have been a last stand," Dryden ventured. "Maybe somebody stole the control junction from them and fought their way out."

"Fought their way out to where?" Lexie asked. "The stairs?"

"No. There's no sign of that. I don't know. I would try to follow the trail, but …"

He didn't need to say it. There was no trail, just lots of dead bodies everywhere. There seemed to be no pattern to those that had been shot or burned, either.

"What do you think, Tarn?" Lexie asked. He'd been remarkably quiet since they'd entered Pentapol. Usually he would at least be humming a tune.

"Place gives me the willies, *bae*."

Ryder said, "I don't see any defenses, or weapons of any kind. Wasn't this city supposed to act as a defense system for all the ICSM cities—for all of Kuvar Island?"

Dryden frowned. "It's true, I haven't seen anything like that. No weapons and also no industrial complex like we know exists at Diplopol. It could be deeper underground, I suppose, but if it had been destroyed in the last stand, or whatever happened here, we would probably see more burnt-out buildings, or destroyed machines. It's possible we were wrong. Our records are quite anecdotal."

"Oh, great," Lexie said, "so we almost got our heads chopped off for nothing?"

"We just arrived," Ryder said. "Let's look around before we jump to conclusions." But the wrinkles on his brow suggested he was just as concerned.

The arched doors of the glass nest building had been blown off, judging by the fact that one was lying flat on the ground and the other was shattered into pieces beside it. They had to walk carefully around the broken glass to avoid cutting their feet.

Inside was a large hall with more bodies. Most also had holes or burn marks in them. Charred metal machine parts were everywhere, presumably disembodied robots.

Dryden took the lead. He was staggering a bit, holding on to the elbow of his bad arm. "If I were …" he mumbled, and he moved deeper into the hall.

Here there was more of a pattern to the bodies, and a trail, which he seemed to be following. The pattern of heaviest destruction and concentration of dead bodies veered to the right and down another staircase. These Pentapol mucka-nuts certainly liked their staircases. At the bottom was a corridor layered in soot, so thick it was like the whole thing had been used as a stove.

Dryden moved through it cautiously, kicking up ash, and they followed.

Finally they arrived at the end, at a door with the words *Officiant Office* stenciled onto it. Inside the room was a single body: a woman clad in a sheer dress. Lexie made a mental note to not be laid to rest in anything sheer. It wasn't a good look when the dead skin pruned up real good.

"Okay," Dryden said, "we need water. Check that tap." He pointed to a sink in the corner of the room.

Tarnation tried it. Lexie was skeptical, but remarkably, after a few seconds' delay it worked. The first bit was orange and gave off a rusty smell, but then it seemed passable enough.

"Get that box over there," Dryden said, pointing to a plastic box on the shelf. "Fill it up with water, and dump it in the control junction compartment. We need to fill it up quickly."

Tarnation and one of the Gungivite men went to work. It was slow going until some of the others found some empty planter boxes to help fill it faster.

"Okay, that's enough," Dryden said when the basin was about half full.

Carefully, he placed the control junction in the bath they'd created, with the base over the node. It immediately lit up, and the water began to show tiny bubbles.

"Okay, fill it up all the way." Dryden sat down at a monitor that was caked in dust. He began tapping on the keyboard. "It might take some time to initialize," he said.

Tarnation kept filling up the bath around the control junction orb. The water began bubbling more vigorously, and the lights glowed correspondingly more bright.

Ryder said, "I wonder what's going on out there. Any word from Cecile?"

"Whoops," Lexie said, pulling out the communication device Cecile had given her. "I didn't think to check this." And why would she? She'd never carried one of these Old World doohickeys before.

She put in the code that Cecile had given her, and onscreen text appeared: *You have 1 unread message*. It was from a good thirty minutes ago.

Lexie pressed the triangle and the communicator played the message. Everyone gathered around to hear.

"This is Cecile," the device said. "I went offshore outside of retcher range to connect via satellite uplink. The news—it's not good, unfortunately. My feed shows that Diplopol has begun an attack on Ganges Island. They are fighting for aerial superiority, and Diplopol has at least five times as many aerial drones. I worry that this is just the first phase. They will send ground troops, or mechanized infantry. If Ganges Island falls, we may not have any hope here in the west. I don't know if you've found Pentapol, but if you have, I hope you can help.

"And you must know their attack will not stop with Ganges," she continued. "They may attack Anacortes again, or many other cities. I've seen this pattern too many times. They will always do more—take more than you expect—until there is nothing left to take.

"And … I'm so sorry, but that's not all. I wish it was, but it isn't. The reinforcements never came. They have been eliminated. And so, I can't stay here. I'm needed in the east. Our situation there is just as desperate as it is here, if not more.

"I know this is not what you wanted to hear. I only hope that you believe that I am with you—that we are on the same side—because we are. *Bonne chance, mes amis, et adieu*."

"What a load of rat piss," Lexie said. She felt like throwing the device against the wall. "I'm glad I never trusted her. Maybe Warrick was right. Maybe she is a witch."

She was just venting. The others responded in a much more stoic manner. Most were looking down, brooding. Ryder said, "The machines—they're always one step ahead of us, just like Nillias said they would be, but Lexie, it doesn't mean Cecile is evil."

"Evil or useless. Same thing to me," Lexie said. She clenched her teeth.

Screens were flickering to life, and Dryden tapped on the terminal screen in front of him. Lexie turned her attention to what he was doing.

"Okay, egghead, don't let us down," she said. She couldn't stop herself from rubbing the blond stubble growing on Dryden's head.

As video feeds started popping up, Dryden sucked in a long breath through his teeth. Something

told Lexie it wasn't just because of the pain in his shoulder.

—54—

Tears, Unimpeded

Hatsuo was sitting in the command chair, watching the display map light up as if it was teeming with fireflies. They had established air dominance over Ganges Island, and the majority of ground-to-air defense installations had been destroyed. Drones sank about half the Gungivite naval fleet, and the rest had no more air support so were cut off.

Every once in a while, a distant rumbling came from outside the city. Diplopol was on high alert, but none of the Gungivite drones had made it close thus far.

"Would you like to move forward with phase two?" Diplopol's comm system asked. "We have achieved the gating criteria for proceeding."

"Excellent. Yes. Move ahead."

Icons signaling ground units began blinking on the screen. Most of these were just outside of Duncan, but many were held in reserve, and only a few were heading into the city. Their strongest mobilized infantry were near the Sansum Bridge—the only land-based access point to Ganges Island.

"Show me Sansum Bridge up close."

The image popped up. There was heavy shelling on both sides, and so the area was obscured by dark smoke and fire. The Sansum Bridge was of sturdy construction—of ICSM origin in, fact—so Hatsuo hoped it would hold. They had a special package to deliver.

Essentialist ships began sailing northward as well. They would soon engage with the flagging Gungivite fleet, and some would be able to bombard the coast.

"General Hatsuo, sir."

Hatsuo's attention was pulled away by Corporal Niko entering the room. He was followed by Alayna, Caban and Beetle Maplewood, who were held by shinogi guards. Caban had a swollen eye. "How dare you," Caban said. "This is treachery against the Tucson Union. It will be the end of you, *and* the Prefectorate."

"Oh, there is treachery here, yes indeed, but you seemed to have misplaced it." Hatsuo sighed and gave him a pained look. "I try so hard. I try to be benevolent and fair, but I am forced into these ugly situations. The best I can do is to offer this: whoever steps forward to admit guilt, or offer important intelligence, will be treated with lenience."

Alayna's face was resolved, a cold mask. Caban remained defiant as well. But Beetle's head tilted to the side, and he stepped forward. "General, please forgive me. I do have intelligence that pertains to the conspiratorial activities of these two. I wanted to collect more information, to be more certain, but I should have come to you sooner."

"Go on," Hatsuo said.

"They have been meeting regularly, in secluded places. I have seen them talking, and I heard them mention the Groundwater movement, sir, and sabotage. Just the other day, I saw Alayna not use the typical mail depot. She was sending secret letters, outside of the normal military channels. I suspect they are recruiting Groundwater spies and saboteurs, sir."

Hatsuo smiled. "Beetle, thank you for stepping forward. You are very brave."

Beetle nodded, a look of grim satisfaction on his face.

Hatsuo continued. "Unfortunately, you are also conniving and craven. You see, Alayna has already named you both as traitors in a detailed letter to me." Hatsuo took Alayna's letter from his pocket, waving it in the air. "She has alleged that you are Groundwater conspirators, with the goal of gaining control of Diplopol, and that you have been pressuring her to participate in your treachery. We have confirmed her allegations with our drone recordings. It's really amazing what the drones can see, and hear, from so far away and even through dense concrete walls. It's all there: your coercion of Alayna, your plotting and bluster, your threats."

Caban and Beetle were looking at Alayna incredulously, but she did not meet their gaze. Her jaw was clenching as she stared starkly forward.

Hatsuo said, "So I suppose I should have asked who is *not* a traitor, but you see, I already knew the answer to that, and since you decided not to be forthcoming—"

Beetle snapped his head back, butting into the nose of his captor. He turned and grabbed at the man's holster, but it was closed tight and buttoned. Caban also struggled and pulled away from his own captor. His gaze swiveled between Hatsuo and the man he'd pushed away.

Hatsuo's heart jumped for a brief moment, but it was all quite hopeless for them. There were five of his armed shinogi in the room. Sure enough, blades whirled and one of them sliced Beetle's arm clean off. A second later, two other blades were nipping at Caban's throat.

Beetle screamed and crumpled to the floor, leaking blood and grasping at his fallen arm as if he might put himself back together.

"General?" one of the shinogi asked, his eyebrow up.

The question needed no clarification. "No, don't kill them. We may be able to use them, to ferret out more Groundwater spies, although I'm not sure Beetle will make it through the day." Beetle's face was white with shock, and he was still looking confused about his misplaced severed arm. "Let's have this cleaned up as soon as possible." He pointed to the pool of blood where Beetle was kneeling.

The shinogi nodded and escorted Beetle and Caban out of the room.

Alayna's eyes were wide. She was breathing deep, extended breaths, and she looked to be trembling as well. Her shinogi captors receded from her, leaving her to stand alone.

"Oh, you poor thing," Hatsuo said. "Please, have a seat. This is all such a sordid affair, but you did the right thing."

She didn't take the seat he offered. "I'm sorry, sir, I … have to go. Your men took me … I have another supplier meeting in a few minutes."

"Always so dedicated, and such a good Essentialist role model. Your efforts are truly appreciated, Alayna. And know that I am always here for your insights and advice. I deal with so many of the people around Diplopol, and you seem to be more present than the rest of them—more self-aware. I value your input."

She looked down, her eyes searching the floor. "I don't have any more specific intelligence, sir, but I do worry about some of the people that are closest to you."

The words surprised him. He hadn't expected her to take him up on his offer. He scanned the room. Only two of his shinogi were left, and Lieutenant Etzuka. Could they be traitors?

He couched his words carefully. "If you are concerned, write it down. It seems to have worked," he smiled.

"It's no one here," she said, looking nervously at the exit. "It's just that, the power you have needs to be protected, for the Prefectorate and all Essentialists. Groundwater wants to take control of Diplopol, and I doubt Beetle and Caban are the only perpetrators. They will infiltrate your ranks. I worry that someone might try to take control, or even try to assassinate you and leave a void."

It did make him think. It was true he needed to have a better control hierarchy, and a good proxy if he wasn't around. Until now it had been Binjai who had been mostly in control, and who had significant power over the city when Hatsuo wasn't there. And yet Binjai had been acting strangely, which was one reason Hatsuo had sent him to the front.

"Fine," said Hatsuo. "City, let's change the Officiant control hierarchy. We are an army, and this is war, right, so we will go by Prefectorate rank."

"Acknowledged," was the city's only response.

Hatsuo was glad of the change. It was less likely someone would try to kill him if there was a more rigid, predetermined control structure, one that couldn't be usurped by Groundwater spies.

"Well?" he said to Alayna.

She squirmed and said, "That is certainly better, but you should still be vigilant of conspirators."

He wondered if she expected him to put her in charge, maybe as second-in-command. Was it possible that, after all this, she wanted control for herself, that she thought if she proved herself he would find her worthy? You never really knew for sure with these Essentialists. No matter; he would never put a coastal Essentialist in such a position.

He walked over to her. She was flushed, perspiring. The tension was taking its toll on her. He put his hand up to cradle her cheek, and smiled. It was at that moment that he decided that when her usefulness was at an end, maybe when his army controlled all of the northwest, he would take her. This would be a big change for him; a courageous step. Prefectorate command asked him to blend in with the locals, and he would finally be doing it. Yes, she was still an Essentialist animal, but she was docile, and had other merits. She wasn't bereft of quality like the others. If there was one to try, it was this one.

Alayna took another ragged breath. "General, if I could go, please," she said. "If I miss this meeting, we may not be able to meet our supply shipment needs. We can't afford any idle time on production during war. We need—"

"Of course," he said, and pulled away his hand from her face. "Go, please."

He watched her backside as she left—definitely the better side of her—and took a seat at the strategic display console.

Things were progressing well at the front. His forces were inching across the Sansum Bridge, gaining ground on the one remaining Gungivite position on the other side. They would soon have access to Ganges Island.

The Gungivites had been ill-prepared. They couldn't compete against the rapidly expanding war machine around Diplopol. In truth, it would have been different if they hadn't taken the Gungivite Observer hostage. It was the city's suggestion, and it knew just what to do. It fried some kind of computer hookup that the Observer's brain had with an electromagnetic pulse, and tortured him for information.

As a result, many of the surprises the Gungivites had in store were neutralized, and the strategically important locations were taken. They didn't have much of a chance after that. And who knew that Tetrapol was actually situated below Ganges Island? The ICSM cities never ceased to amaze.

This was why the Sansum Bridge was so important. Their thermobaric bombs did damage above ground, but they were even more effective in enclosed spaces, like, for example, underground. According to the city, if they could find a good access point to place the bomb, the blast would tear through extended tunnels or caverns, using up all available oxygen to destroy everything in its path.

He could get used to this type of warfare. It was all so easy. He didn't have to tell troops what to do, or even move from this room. He could just sit here and be himself, enjoying the thrill of victory without any grand theater or handholding.

"Let's do Duncan now," he said.

"The unit is three minutes away from optimal position," the city responded.

"Good enough," he said, looking at the strategic map of Duncan. It was time to move forward. The people of Duncan were too devoted to their Gungivite beliefs. It was better to wipe them out before someone thought twice about it.

"Thermobaric detonation underway," the city said.

The screen showed a distant view of Duncan from the position of the entrenched Essentialist mobilized ground units. A huge fireball was expanding out from the center, leveling buildings in a broad radius. It was a sight to see.

If these bombs were supposed to be more effective below ground, he could only imagine what effect they would have on Tetrapol.

He had worked so hard for this, pandering to so many egos. He'd evaded so many ill-conceived political attacks. Finally, he was on the cusp of a major victory. He couldn't keep his eyes from welling up again. He didn't pick up a handkerchief, as he usually did. No, it was okay. He deserved this.

The tears streamed down his face, unimpeded.

—55—

An Uncomfortable Officiant

Pentapol came alive relatively quickly. The ground underneath Dryden hummed, some power source coming online. He heard distant music, like strings and horns and chanting.

The first question Pentapol asked was, "Are you my Officiant?"

Dryden cringed. He wasn't sure he wanted the responsibility.

"Makes sense to me," Lexie said.

Dryden said, "Yes, I guess so, until we can find someone better."

"Welcome. How can I help you?" the terminal asked.

Lexie said, "Let's make sure this city isn't going to steal our dessert before we order dinner, if you know what I mean. City, what is your objective?"

The terminal said, "To enhance the well-being of all human life without the use of synthetic stimuli, and to defend ICSM machine cities from internal or external threats."

Dryden spent a moment puzzling over the objective function. The synthetic stimuli reference was almost certainly to prevent the effects of the experiential rooms. Maybe it was some kind of attempt to get back to a more natural order of things.

Before he could fully digest the objective function, the terminal asked, "Would you like a tour of Pentapol?"

"Maybe later," Dryden said. "We've already had a brief—and rather harrowing—tour. We need to know what's happening on Kuvar Island, and Ganges Island. Do you have sensors, or drones or something?"

"I have visibility from latent sensors on the Singer and the Fan, but the Harp's sensors have malfunctioned. Regardless, all those locations are too far away to obtain the level of detail you may require. I am running diagnostics and may have more options soon."

Monitors began flashing on. These screens displayed views from the Fan and the Singer. From the Singer Dryden could see smoke and distant explosions in the direction of Ganges Island, but otherwise, Pentapol was right; it was too far away to learn anything useful.

"City, is anyone trying to enter Pentapol through the Fan?" Dryden asked.

"No. There is a great deal of debris within range of the Fan. One ship is leaving the vicinity. The access door you came through requires a node key, so it would be quite difficult without advanced weaponry."

"Okay, good."

The city said, "Officiant, do you approve of Ryder's request?"

Everyone looked at Ryder.

"Sorry," Ryder said. "I figured out how to interface with the city with my implant. I've requested that the city patch me through to Gungivite Command."

"Sure," Dryden said. "Approved." He was feeling a bit awkward having this level of authority. He was way out of his depth.

Ryder's eyelids started fluttering.

Meanwhile, a panel opened up in the back of the room and a small, cylindrical robot came out. "Officiant, you are hurt," Pentapol said. "Unfortunately it will take several hours to manufacture new pain medications, but I can begin repairing your shoulder mechanically. Should I proceed?"

"Um, sure," Dryden said.

A number of spindly arms popped out of the top of the casing and went to work on his shoulder. The pain wasn't that bad. It felt like several tiny needles were probing him, but no individual needle was excruciating. He tried not to watch as it poked at him.

Ryder's eyelids stopped fluttering. "Cecile was right," he said. "The Gungivites have been severely compromised and outmatched. In fact, they are asking for our help. Given that I am considered an outcast, it's saying something that they would ask *me* for help. They are planning another defensive push, but it's hopeless without air superiority. And I … and I …" His eyelids fluttered momentarily. "The city of Duncan has just been leveled by a thermobaric bomb. The Observers are worried they could do the same to Tetrapol if Essentialist ground forces move further onto Ganges Island."

"Did they say how we could help?" Dryden asked.

"The Observers said to use Pentapol, but they didn't say how. I'm not sure they know what to do."

"City, what weapons systems do you have here?" Dryden asked.

"There are no weapons here," the city answered.

"Why not?"

"There is an inherent danger in having weapons collocated within a place of habitation."

"So there are no weapons at all? It's in your objective function to defend the ICSM cities, and you have no defense system?"

"The defense system is outside the city."

"What do you mean? I thought the ICSM cities all had geographic constraints."

"In the case of Pentapol, the geographic constraints were expanded to include the defense arc, so that all ICSM cities could be protected."

The arc line Dryden had previously drawn appeared on a map depicted on the display panel.

"Is the tunnel system still usable?"

"Diagnostics are currently running. I have shown a schematic of the current status."

The main tunnel arc showed up as green with several yellow sections, where the words *Debris removal in process* were shown. There were several offshoots to the main arc tunnel that headed toward Haplopol, Diplopol, Triplopol and Tetrapol, but they were all marked red with the word *Impassable* next to them.

"The main defense arc should be ready within minutes," the city said.

Lexie asked, "What good are these tunnels if they can't access the other ICSM cities?"

Dryden had been about to ask the same question, and Ryder just shook his head, his brow furrowed. What were they missing? It was Tarnation who eventually spoke up. "We've got a superintelligent machine, bud. Why don't you ask it what it would do?"

"I guess it's worth a shot," Dryden said. "Okay, Pentapol, you've seen the feed from Ganges. Let's say we want to stop the people of Diplopol from destroying Tetrapol. How would you suggest we do that?"

"One moment, please."

These machines processed information at lightning speed, so when it asked for a moment, Dryden knew it was thinking very hard, perhaps running millions of simulations.

No more than a few seconds later, it said, "I have formulated a plan that should give you a non-negligible probability of success, but it requires the defense system be activated and an attack squad must head to the main tunnel junction below us immediately."

"But what can you possibly—"

"I have patched the plan through to Ryder's implant. A verbal explanation will take too much time, reducing your odds of success considerably. Rapid response is needed. Do you approve of the plan, Officiant?"

Approve what? Who knew what the city was going to do. Dryden looked to Ryder, trying to glean some idea what this plan was about. Ryder's eyelids fluttered momentarily, and his eyes opened wide. "Whoa," was all he said. Then, steadying himself in his chair, he said, "Yeah, it's the best chance we have."

"Do you approve?" the city asked again.

Seconds ticked away. How could Dryden know this wouldn't make things worse, that he wasn't about to cause more untold death and destruction? In the end, he had to trust Ryder. There wasn't much else he could do.

"Fine, I approve," he said.

Red lights started flashing everywhere. The text *Defense system activated* rolled across the monitors.

Ryder's eyelids fluttered again. He stood up and walked out, as if in a daze, only to pause briefly at the door, perhaps only now remembering they were there behind him. "Hurry," he said. "We need to go to the tunnels," and he jogged away.

Lexie looked at Dryden with a raised eyebrow.

"You all go," Dryden said. "I should stay here."

Lexie tilted her head, a cynical ridge forming on her brow. "You gonna make sure this thing cooperates?" she asked.

He only nodded grimly, and she jogged out of the room with the others.

—56—

Not a Good Day For a Trade Meeting

Alayna's breathing was erratic as she headed toward the operations tent. Tears threatened to pool in her eyes. Her legs weren't working properly. Occasionally a pitiful attack of self-doubt would hit her, and her pace would slow, as if she was wading through a swamp.

Caban's expression upon learning of her betrayal reverberated in her mind. And the blood, Beetle's arm ...

Had she made the right choice? She feared some grand retribution was in store for her. She imagined the flowers might wither around her, if there had been any left outside the city wall. Or maybe a rift would open up in the blue sky and a bolt of lightning would cut through it to strike her down where she stood. Maybe that's what she deserved.

"Eternal spring, I did this for you," she said under her breath. "It's the only way."

Commissioner Utep was waiting for her just outside the operations tent, with two of his aides. He was frowning. "You're late," he said.

"I'm sorry, I had an impromptu meeting with Hatsuo."

His face remained bitter, as if he had just eaten something distasteful. "There are things *exploding*." He arced his hand across the sky. "Not my kind of day to be out for a trade meeting."

Alayna didn't like Utep, but there was no one else she could trust. His allegiance was critically important. She decided to go with humility. "I'm terribly sorry, Commissioner. It won't happen again." And she bowed her head.

When her eyes met his again, she could see he was still unhappy, but he sighed resignedly. Perhaps her words had dulled the edge.

"Yes, well, I'm leaving," Utep said. "I want no part of this, and as far as

I'm concerned, I was never here." He turned about and walked up the hill toward the main rail station, his aides falling in line behind him to follow.

She took a deep breath and entered the tent.

—57—

THE DEFENSE ARC

Lexie wasn't comfortable deferring to the superintelligent city with uncertain motives that happened to be filled with thousands of rotting corpses—or trusting the judgment of Ryder the cyborg traitor hermit, for that matter. But it wasn't like they could just pick and choose options from a menu, here.

Ryder led them to a nearby lift that shot them down deeper underground at a disconcerting speed. She couldn't imagine this was how elevators worked in the Old World. It would be a lunch-losing experience for many.

The lift doors opened up to a bay where several vessels were lined up on monorail tracks. These vessels were similar to the one Dryden had described from Haplopol. Red lights flashed everywhere. Didn't the city know they were freaked out enough as it was? Maybe this was just standard protocol.

The door to the vessel opened for them, belching out stale air. "Hurry," Ryder said, "and put on your seatbelts."

"Yeah, yeah," Lexie said.

Lexie sat with Ryder in the front, while Tarnation and the four Gungivite militia sat in seats lined up along the sides of the rear compartment. She strapped on her belts, which automatically tightened around her body. These weren't like the seat belts Lexie had seen in Old World cars. They crossed over her chest from both sides as well as her waist. There were belts for her forehead and feet as well, but it seemed like overkill, so she ignored them.

"Masks, too," Ryder said. Face masks popped out from above them and dangled in front of their faces. She obliged. At this point the vessel was already moving along one of many rail lines that coursed through the broad tunnel.

The lines split, they went down a gradient, and the tunnel closed in around them so that the outer wall was just inches away.

"So what's the deal?" she asked Ryder.

"I … I can …"

She couldn't blame him for stuttering. Their speed picked up rapidly, as if they were being fired out of a cannon. The sides of the tunnel became a blur, and her face felt like it was being stretched back over her head.

"One minute until launch," a voice from the speakers said in a stark monotone.

Launch? Weren't they already "launching"?

She had more questions for Ryder, but yeah, she couldn't speak at the moment.

Her eyes caught a map display in the upper corner of the cockpit. It positioned the vessel in the Salish Sea area. They were travelling along the defense arc, and they had already passed Haplopol. Soon they would be at the Singer, and then what?

The vessel was approaching the Singer at a breakneck speed and still accelerating. Wouldn't they need to slow down soon?

They split off into a tunnel, angled down, and angled up, and up, higher and higher. Lexie was feeling lightheaded, but she tried to stay focused. This had to end soon, wherever they were going.

Suddenly the blur of the tunnel ended. Blue sky and clouds spun in front of her. She saw distant smoke on an archipelago of islands across an expanse of rippling water.

The vessel seemed to right itself, and finally there was relief from the oppressive forces of acceleration. A diagram on a display panel showed that their craft had actually transformed and sprouted wings. The display map showed them heading toward Ganges Island, with the Singer behind them.

She found the rear-view camera feed, where she saw the gaping mouth of the Singer spouting gray smoke while receding from view. Or rather, the Singer wasn't spouting smoke; their craft had literally been spat out of its mouth, and the smoke was its jet contrail.

But this wasn't the end of the assault on her senses. Explosions began rattling the vessel from below, so she looked through a small side window, down toward the water.

Okay. Now she understood why it was called the *defense arc*.

Rising out of the Salish Sea was a gargantuan wall, following the underground curve of the tunnel system. It was coming up in segments, rising sequentially in a southward direction. Each of these segments was as long as Diplopol. As they rose from the depths, the segments formed massive swells of water, some of which were capsizing nearby ships. Lexie could only guess this would result in tidal waves hitting the shorelines. These wall segments were also topped with lines of huge cannons and smaller guns. The cannons were already firing in the direction of Ganges Island. But these were not simple artillery shells. Their payload arced high in the sky and flowered into aerodynamic, self-propelled drones. The sky in front of their vessel was quickly becoming populated with them.

"Nifty," Tarnation said from the seat behind her.

Several different maps were showing up on the display monitors around them, with military units flashing in various colors.

"So what happens next?" Lexie asked Ryder, finally able to form words again. He'd been having regular bouts of eyelid fluttering since they'd launched out of the Singer's mouth.

"Pentapol has a limited supply of defense drones and munitions. Many of them have been destroyed in the previous ICSM war. It's throwing everything at the Essentialists so we can try to stop them from gaining access to Tetrapol here, at the Sansum Bridge." He pointed to a spot on one of the many tactical display maps.

It was pretty hard to make out. It looked like he was pointing at a zoomed-in picture of the center of a campfire, the image was so full of ash and smoke.

Ryder frowned. "Put on your other seatbelts," he said.

Apparently the wild ride wasn't over. Lexie again obliged, buckling the one around her feet and another over her forehead. The glass in the front of the craft became obscured by segmented metal that slid down from the top of the vessel, as did windows on the side and the back.

It wasn't a good sign.

She could see on the display panel map they were close to Ganges Island. Explosions sounded around the vessel. They chucked and jibed, the G-forces pulling her in several directions. She felt a major turn—maybe they were evading something—and the blasts around the craft became even more numerous. Some of them were earsplitting.

Lexie wasn't sure what happened next. The vessel was hit by something, and it must have started tumbling. As that moment, Lexie decided she preferred swashbuckling or cannon fire to these ICSM joyrides, pyrotechnics and gyrations. She couldn't figure out what was going on half the time. And they were moving too fast to make sense of the view screens.

The vessel was hit again. It tumbled even more violently and, straps or no straps, it was just too much for her to hold on.

She lost consciousness.

Lexie woke to Ryder shaking her. She was hanging upside down in her seat. The straps had been useful for something after all.

"You okay?" he asked.

"Yeah, I guess."

"We need you outside right away."

Ryder went to wake up another Gungivite militia man, who was seated next to her. At least she wasn't the only one who'd passed out.

She unmasked and unstrapped herself, being careful while undoing the last belt so as to not drop on her head. She righted herself and walked along the roof to the open vessel door. The vessel was remarkably intact inside. Outside it was a real mess, though.

They had crash-landed on Ganges Island, just uphill from a blown-out Gungivite artillery installation that looked over the Sansum Bridge. The bridge structure was intact, for the most part. Guardrails had split, and depressions had formed in the roadway from the bombing, but none had penetrated through to the other side. A few shells of tank-like vehicles burned along the length of it. There were splayed hands built into both sides of the bridge, reaching down into the strait below. Each of these was pocked with the markings of explosive ordnance, but they held their form remarkably well.

The bodies of Essentialist soldiers littered the area around Lexie, some of them bloodied, some severely maimed. Behind the vessel, a trench had been carved into the earth along the escarpment. The channel was deep enough to reach down to barren rock in places. Here, the stone had been scratched white from the passage of their vessel.

Above her, the sky was sullied by tornadoes of smoke, churning upward from all around her. The greatest of these was rising up in the northwest, in the direction of Duncan. Beyond these dense funnels the sky was a lattice of contrails, with no new ones forming. There was no buzzing, and the explosions, although still frequent, weren't anywhere nearby. Were the drones taking a lunch break or something?

Tarnation and three Gungivite men were positioned close to a stone cleft that overlooked the roadway. They were crouched down, so Lexie stayed low as she approached. Ryder and the last Gungivite man were quick on her heels.

When she came near, she noticed a metal box beside them, protected by the outcrop of stone.

"Don't touch that," Ryder said. "It's one of the bombs."

"How'd you get it?" she asked.

"We arrived in the area just as the Essentialists were crossing the Sansum Bridge. They were taking position on this side when our Pentapol drones attacked. We were hit by anti-aircraft guns and so had to crash-land. Pentapol steered us into the midst of the Essentialist ground forces, to maximize our impact. After we landed we overcame the remainder on this side and took the bomb."

"Any more of them left?"

"Yes, a small holdout over on the other side of the road. We believe they have another bomb with them."

"Why can't we just have our Pentapol drones blast them?"

"We've exhausted them all. They've been taken out by Essentialist drones and anti-aircraft gun batteries."

"And where are all the Gungivites?"

Ryder looked down at the ground. It was covered in a bed of ash and other detritus. He said, "Any Gungivite that was above ground didn't survive the Essentialist bombardment, or our crash landing."

She looked around again at the bodies and destruction. She wasn't surprised. "So what's the plan?"

"The remaining Essentialists are in a protected location—one of the Gungivite defensive positions built into the terrace of rock on the other side of the main road, similar to this one. Their only way out is toward us, or onto the road. About a half a kilometer down the road, there are turnoffs that could lead to any number of access points to Tetrapol."

"So we pin them down and wait for reinforcements?"

"Yes, but the problem is I'm not sure which side will have reinforcements first."

Lexie didn't have much time to ponder Ryder's words, because just then an explosion shook the ground beneath their rocky outcropping. She was worried the whole shelf might collapse, but it only shifted forward a few feet.

She wasn't hurt, but there was a cloud of dust in the air around her. When it cleared, she saw Ryder and the Gungivite men looking frantically through their scopes, probably to find the enemy position through the dust. By the time it cleared, she saw the Essentialists were well down the wall on the other side and were making a break eastward.

They didn't hesitate. Ryder moved to bound down the hill while brandishing his pistol. The others followed, as did Lexie. There were a few steep drops where she had to slow and slide down on her buttocks. Lexie still had Warrick's energy weapon in her pack, so she powered it up along the way.

The group all stopped in a line near the base of the wall and fired at the running Essentialist soldiers. A couple fell from the rifle shots, while Lexie cut an angular swath that blazed across two of their backs and went up into the sky. She was still getting the hang of the thing.

One of the Essentialists turned and hoisted some kind of rocket launcher onto his shoulder, with the sight placed neatly on his eye.

Lexie instinctively fanned out along the road, as did the Gungivite militia, to make for less concentrated targets. The rocket fired and hit behind them, again kicking up another cloud of ash and dust.

Lexie couldn't see the others, so she kept running toward the Essentialist position. Bullets fired, but she wasn't sure anyone could see who they were shooting at.

When she broke out of the dust cloud she was much closer to the enemy. Ryder shot the lead man in the front of the Essentialists—the man who'd been carrying the bomb box—and he fell to the ground. Fortunately, the bomb didn't seem to have a sensitive ignition switch, or they all would have been toast right then and there.

There were only four of the Essentialists left, as far as she could count. The rocket-launcher man was still reloading, but the others Essentialists were returning fire. Bullets whizzed past her. Ryder and one of the Gungivites crumpled where they stood. Fuckers. She lifted her energy weapon, aimed and pressed the trigger.

The weapon beeped at her. A red light was flashing on the side. It was out of juice.

What was amazing was that the Essentialists weren't shooting at Tarnation. How could they not see him? He was a real whirling dervish, with his bouncing bun and snakeskin tattoos. Maybe it was because he wasn't the one shooting at them, and possibly also because he was flanking them. The Essentialists didn't know him very well, obviously.

Tarnation slammed into one of the Essentialist gunmen from the side. He scooped the man up in his arms and cracked the gunman's back over his knee. The Essentialist with the rocket launcher turned to Tarnation, but by the time he did, his buddy's ragdoll body was being thrown at him. He fumbled with the launcher and had to duck down.

At this point Lexie was well on her way to the brawl. She tackled the third gunman, but he butted her in the head real good with his gun in the process.

The next thing she knew, the man was on top of her. He was a young Prefectorate officer, with a patchy moustache and a pear-shaped birthmark on his cheek. His knees dug into her side, pinning her arms while his hands reached for her throat. His face was pruned up with rage.

Now, this guy hadn't done do his homework either. He didn't know Lexie had a bit of a complex about Prefectorate men being on top of her, given what happened to her mom and all. Her scream must have sounded like a dog being run over by a horse cart, and it was just enough of a surprise for him to weaken his hold. That tiny bit of leeway allowed her to break one hand away so it could slip down to her boot.

That's right, after all that time being a pirate, and then with Nillias and the nutjobs, she finally got to use her boot knife. She stabbed him square in the temple, and she didn't stop there, either. She cut into his ribs a few times, and his stomach, even. She made a real mess of him, because she was in a frenzy and all, even after he'd stopped moving. As Warrick used to tell her, "If you can stab him once, you can stab him five times." *Thanks for that, bud.*

She pushed the dead soldier off and found Tarnation standing over her, smiling. His torso was covered in an apron of blood. He hoisted her up onto her feet and they turned back to survey the mess in front of them. There was only one Essentialist soldier left. He was running away down the road, toward the bomb box, until their last remaining Gungivite man shot hit him in the back. The soldier crumpled to the ground.

They'd lost three of the Gungivite militia, but Ryder was alive, a few steps away. He had been hit in the thigh, but it wasn't bad—probably just a flesh wound. He could limp along okay. "Well done, everyone," he said. "This should give the Gungivites a fighting chance." His eyelids fluttered.

"Let's get you fixed up," she said. After they'd grabbed the bomb box, Lexie and Tarnation took to each side of Ryder and helped him hobble back up the hill to their overturned vessel. "They got medical stuff in here or what?" Lexie asked.

"Yes, third panel on the left," Ryder said.

Tarnation sat Ryder down on the rock ledge while Lexie went to collect the box of medical supplies.

A minute later, as she uncapped a bottle of alcohol and unwound a roll of gauze, she saw that Tarnation was standing at the rock ledge, scanning the environs. She was glad he was doing it. Who knew if more Essentialists were skulking around, or even coming across the bridge. But he had an unusual expression. After a fight like this, she'd have expected Tarnation to be content, even jovial, but he looked concerned.

Lexie said, "Hey, Tarn, quit your worrying. We did good."

He cast a dark look her way. "The other big bomb—the one we had here by the ship. It's missing, *bae*."

—58—

Trivial Perceptions

Binjai was running along a well-tended path on Ganges Island, the bomb box in his hands. He was far enough away from Sansum Bridge that there were no more signs of the devastation they had wrought. The trees were full of verdure and covered with moss at their bases. It had been a while since he'd been in a natural setting, having been on Officiant duties at Diplopol for so long, but he hadn't missed all the flora and fauna. The only thing he missed now was the experiential room. There, he could enjoy settings that were far more stimulating than this one.

Ahead, at a road crossing, was a Gungivite soldier—thankfully not an Observer. The soldier was on his front, crawling away. His back had been torn up by shrapnel.

The Gungivite hadn't seen him, so Binjai put down the bomb box quietly and approached with stealth, his body level with the ground, just as he'd been taught in shinogi training. When he was close enough, he jumped ahead and slit the man's throat, cutting his windpipe in the process. The man bled out quickly and died without making a sound.

Binjai retrieved the bomb box and continued on, running across the road, and again along the same path that continued through the forest around a hillock.

Although he was using his shinogi training, he knew he was not being true to the shinogi way. Shinogi did not play dead when the enemy was attacking nearby, nor did they kill their comrades who urged them into battle. Some shinogi may have seen this as dishonorable, or a dereliction of duty, but it had been the best way to retrieve the bomb, and protecting Diplopol was more important than any of the trivial perceptions of honor or dignity he might have harbored in the past.

The path opened up into a field, with goats grazing nearby. Down a shallow slope was a farmhouse, and at the back, finally, a door labeled *Fruit Cellar*.

He knew he wouldn't enjoy the euphoric feeling of the experiential rooms again, but he was doing what was right—what he was destined to do. That in itself gave him a deep satisfaction. He could rest in oblivion, knowing he had contributed to the expanding influence of Diplopol and all who worked under its umbrella.

There was no one in the meadow, or at the farmhouse. He ran down the hill, heading for the fruit cellar door.

—59—

The Supply Meeting

Hatsuo slammed his hand down on the table. "Why did no one tell me about this confounded sea wall, coming out of nowhere? And more drones?"

Lieutenant Etzuka and Corporal Niko turned to him. Their faces were drained of color.

The city spoke through the intercom. "I did not know this was a possibility. There were no indicators to suggest these latent defenses were used in the last ICSM war."

It was probably the Gungivites who raised the wall. Maybe their captive Observer hadn't been told about these defenses. Hopefully this was the last trick up their sleeve.

The screen was showing him a battle between the downed aircraft and the remaining Essentialist troops at Sansum Bridge. It didn't look good for his men. "This image—it's from a drone, isn't it? Why don't you make it fight?"

"This is a reconnaissance drone, unable to attack. We only have five of these that are still active. We are building more attack drones in our factories, at a rate of one every five minutes."

It was extremely frustrating. They were so close, but now it looked like the chances for a quick, decisive victory were fading. Instead it would be a war of attrition.

He was still confident, though. The anti-aircraft installations around Diplopol were still unused. As long as the manufacturing infrastructure was working at full capacity, they would prevail.

"What about the thermobaric bombs we brought to Anacortes, and Port Renfrew. Can we still deploy those?"

"Yes," Diplopol replied. "They will be in position momentarily. For the Anacortes deployment, it is fortuitous that our galleon was east of the seawall before the wall was raised. In fact, it was behind an island, out of range of the defense wall guns, and also not affected by the tidal wave. I have had to reroute the vessel, but our schedule has only been impacted by twenty minutes."

"Good," Hatsuo said. "Let me know when they're ready." They might not eliminate the Gungivites today, but at least Three Rivers and the Kuvar Collective could be neutralized. That would leave only one last domino standing before the entire Salish Sea area was under his control.

And now that he was thinking about it, this new seawall defense system could be a good thing, in the long run. Once Ganges Island was taken, he could use it to keep out any external forces while Diplopol continued to grow its infrastructure and weapons systems. Eventually, the entire Salish Sea region would become a heavily fortified power base, a beachhead to allow the Prefectorate to move east and south as needed.

Etzuka said, "Sir, Alayna Menudos would like to gain entry to the Officiant's Office."

Hatsuo was surprised that she had returned so soon, since her supply meeting had just begun. It had to be a pressing issue, and he couldn't afford any inventory problems.

"Let her in," he said.

The door unlocked, and Alayna walked in. She was trailed by four shinogi, two of them hooded.

"Who are these shinogi?" Hatsuo said. "They are not needed here. And what's the problem? Make it brief."

Alayna said, "Sir, you asked for ways to ensure we could have the authority to continue our extensive supply lines from near and far, down the coast and beyond. I had to go to great lengths to secure the appropriate authority, and now they would like to speak with you."

He sighed. It was annoying that she couldn't handle it herself, but sometimes people needed to see the man in charge, even just as a formality. "Fine," he said. "Where are these people? Are they in the operations tent?"

"No, I have brought them here, for your convenience."

"No, they can't see all this," he gestured at the war room displays. "It wouldn't look good. We are about to crush Three Rivers and the Kuvar Collective. I assume they are just outside—in the Diplopol great hall? I will meet them there."

"Sir, I'm sorry, but they are already here, in this room."

The two shinogi in the back unhooded themselves. One was a woman. It was Commander Yasui.

Hatsuo's heart stopped.

"Hello, General," Yasui said, "and I apologize for the unannounced visit. I must say we are in good hands, though. Miss Menudos is an excellent supply officer. In fact, she has supplied me with a great deal of information about what is happening here at Diplopol, including a rather chilling rendition of your conduct." She withdrew a letter from her cloak. It was several pages long.

He'd been betrayed. Alayna could have revealed the false premises for the invasion of Vicky territory, or his initiating war with Anacortes and the Kuvar Collective without the Emperor's approval. He had communicated valid reasons to Yasui for these operations, but they were all manufactured, with dubious pretexts. Yasui had been too far away to learn their true origin, or perhaps to care, and his explanations only needed to delay her until he achieved enough of a power base that he could unseat her.

But here she was, and she knew too much.

She had to die.

He withdrew his katana and lunged at her neck, but she parried it, and held his blade at bay. In flashes of metal too fast for him to see, the other shinogi fought Hatsuo's men around them.

He only witnessed the aftermath.

One of his own shinogi guardsmen lay dead, stabbed in the heart, and the other was now prostrate on the floor, bowing to Yasui. Etzuka and Niko had both been decapitated.

Three blades nipped at Hatsuo's neck.

"City, eliminate Yasui and her guards," Hatsuo yelled out defiantly.

"They are traitors."

The city responded. "Commander Yasui is of higher rank than you, General. She has Officiant authority, by your command. Commander Yasui, do you wish that I eliminate you and your shinogi?"

Yasui laughed heartily. It was a throaty, multi-octave thing. She said, "No thank you, city." She was looking around at the walls as though the city was some absurd curiosity.

Hatsuo looked over at Alayna, who had receded to the back of the room. "You," he seethed. "You did this."

Yasui returned her attention to him. "You have not done your shinogi training recently, have you, General? I do it every day. It is an important part of my daily ritual. But you never were much for shinogi discipline, if I recall. When I met you, I remember thinking, somehow the Emperor allowed you to rise—and may regret it."

Yasui sighed. "Yes, Miss Menudos' letter has been enlightening indeed, but to be frank, I found it hard to believe—until now. She convinced us to confront you, and she was right."

Yasui looked at the letter again. "Let's see: insubordination, treachery, fraud. There is a long list of crimes against the Prefectorate, but some of these could have been dismissed or forgotten if you were pursuing our agenda—if you demonstrated an adequate level of success. We have been known to be flexible, in extenuating circumstances, but you miss the bigger picture. This," she gestured at the room, "this is not what we came to this continent for. It sickens me. We do not want to occupy a continent filled with machine-filth. What point is there to conquest if what you conquer is without soul? We do not want drones and factories. We want dojos and gardens. Could you imagine the Emperor coming to this place?"

"I see now that I have erred," Hatsuo said, finally dropping his katana to the floor and bowing his head. "I am ashamed, but there is much that can be salvaged here. A leader of your great vision can surely—"

In another lighting-fast motion, Yasui's katana sliced at him.

Hatsuo's hand fell to the ground, and blood cascaded from his wrist. Searing pain gripped him and he fell to his knees.

Yasui said, "Enough of your toxic niceties. This seems a fitting punishment, to begin with, since you have bestowed it on so many others, but we cannot afford to extinguish you just yet. We may need you, and for a deception as great as this, you must stand proper trial, so our allies can see that justice is being done. They need to see that you were a lone wolf acting in dereliction of duty."

Hatsuo was in agony, barely registering the words. He fell to the ground, holding his wrist below where his hand used to be, watching the blood course out.

"Take him away," Yasui said, "and keep him alive." The shinogi in the room were all shifting around him like shadowy apparitions. He could only see them in his peripheral vision as he stared at his truncated arm.

A stone-faced shinogi tightened cloth around his upper arm, wrapped his stump in bandages, hooked him under the armpits, and pulled him up on his feet.

Before he was dragged from the room, he heard Yasui say, "Now, Miss Menudos, how can we rein in this abhorrent machine?"

—60—

Binjai

Binjai stopped at the fruit cellar door and began unlatching the protective casing around the thermobaric bomb. He wanted to be ready to detonate it in the event he encountered resistance underground.

The burn on his hand from the control junction had healed, but not perfectly. As a result, his hand hurt when he performed tasks requiring manual dexterity. The skin was stringy and taut, and prone to rupturing. It was ugly, but he wore the scar with pride.

When he had removed the casing, he noticed that instead of flashing an orange *Armed* light, the screen readout said *Remotely disabled.*

How was that possible? He wondered if it was some Gungivite trick. Maybe there was some way to hotwire it. He looked for a way to access the bomb casing, knowing in his heart the chances were slim that he could still proceed.

He heard buzzing high above. It must be a Diplopol reconnaissance drone. Maybe that was what sent the *Disable* signal. He took out his communicator device and turned it on, knowing that it might reveal his position. Maybe he could talk to Diplopol and get the drone to reactivate the bomb.

Aside from the occasional glance, he hadn't been paying attention to the farmland around him. His ears were trained to notice footsteps, and these Gungivites were lumbering oafs compared to shinogi. He wasn't worried.

But this was something that made much less sound—something even quieter than shinogi.

The next time he looked up, standing no more than a few feet away was a gigantic mountain lion, its eyes focused, its maw open, saliva dripping from long incisors.

The Observer they captured had made reference to these cats. It was intimidating, but still some kind of pet. He would befriend it and it would leave him alone.

He slowly took some jerky ration out of his pack and threw it at the cat.

The cat's maw closed. It sniffed at the jerky.

"Now go," Binjai said, and motioned for the cat to leave.

The cat ignored the jerky. Its jaws opened again, and it advanced on him.

He scrambled for his weapon, but it was too late. His world became an agonizing frenzy of teeth and claws. His throat was breached, and his life slipped away soon after.

—61—

QUALIFICATIONS

Ryder's eyelids were fluttering again. "It's true," he said. "Diplopol is seeking a ceasefire. In fact they sent us images of the rogue Essentialist who stole the bomb. We don't need to worry about him—the cats found him. And I'm in contact with Dryden. There are more Pentapol drones coming all the way north from the Fan. There should be enough to ensure we have air dominance, if we need it."

Lexie was siting with Ryder, Tarnation and Ulrig—the last Gungivite militia man–near the blown-apart Gungivite gun placements, looking over the Sansum Bridge. The smoke and fires were dying down. Or at least, the winds were calming, and so the plumes billowed straight upward instead of in erratic spirals. In the west, over the undulating lands of Kuvar Island, the sky was turning amber, and the contrails took on a purplish color.

"So what now?" Lexie asked.

"The Observers are coming to meet with us," Ryder answered.

A few minutes later, an armored vehicle drove down the road, in some cases bulldozing charred mechanized units to the side to get by.

Three men exited the vehicle and made their way up the incline. At first Lexie wasn't sure they were Observers. Gas masks hung from their necks, and they were wearing helmets and flak jackets. She wasn't used to seeing them like this, without their baggy linens and sleek wigs, but she did recognize Olint right away. His icy gray eyes were easy to spot.

"Well, hey, let's see a smile, nutjobs," Lexie said.

There were no smiles, of course.

"Our victory is marginal," Olint said. "We don't know the stability of the new leadership in Diplopol, and we can't be sure the situation won't deteriorate."

Lexie said, "Well, maybe you're going to have to live with a little uncertainty."

Olint ignored her. "We came to discuss the transition of Pentapol Officiant authority to us." He pulled a metal device from his pocket and placed it on the rock ledge beside them. "Dryden is on the line."

Ryder was frowning.

"Isn't that a little bit presumptuous?" Lexie said.

"None of you are qualified to be an Officiant. We need people who can be responsible for preventing the misuse of machine intelligence. This is our mission as Observers—what we are trained for. It makes sense that Pentapol is under our control for the greater good."

"They have a point," Dryden said through the communicator device.

Ryder scratched his temple. "What if we say no?"

"There would be grave consequences," Olint said. "We would not have confidence that Diplopol and Haplopol could be adequately contained, so measures would be taken."

"What measures?" Lexie asked.

"We have additional defenses of which you are unaware. These would have been deployed in the event of Tetrapol's destruction. In the splayed hands you see here," he pointed down to the bridge, "and across the islands, there are canisters containing toxic gases. When released, these gases will euthanize anybody within a radius of several miles. There are also underground depots of this gas that, upon our command, will be released through the earth at strategic locations. With these, we have the means to neutralize human agents at Diplopol and Haplopol, as well as the surrounding populations."

A bird cawed overhead, but it did not sway anyone's attention.

Dryden said. "I don't understand. Why is it necessary to … kill all these people?"

"The other ICSM cities will have to be decommissioned eventually, but we do not have the means to do so at the present time, given their defense systems. The major threat to us in the near term are the human actors developing munitions, drones and mechanized infantry outside of the city walls, and recruiting more people to be put under the sway of the experiential rooms. Without these human actors, the cities can be made benign due to their geographic constraints. With the control of Pentapol and its substantial defense capabilities, we would feel more confident that this harsher step would not be necessary in the near term."

"In the near term ..." Lexie said. The discussion was making her skin crawl. The Gungivites had such a bland manner that it was hard to tell if they were hiding something, or being malicious. She had always known them to be cold and calculating, but something was different this time.

Dryden said, "You've done this before, haven't you? The gassing, I mean."

"We have no direct evidence or records, because Tetrapol's memory was wiped clean after the last ICSM war, but it is likely the splayed hands have been used before, based on our census of the remaining gas inventories."

There was a tense pause in the conversation. The Observers were awaiting their decision.

Dryden said, "I'm an anthropologist, not a judge, or an ethicist. I'm certainly not trained in the governance of a machine city. Bottom line, I don't want those deaths on my conscience."

Ryder's head had been tilting side to side as he wrestled with the question. Finally, he looked to Lexie and said, "Who are we to say what is right?"

Lexie couldn't answer him. She gritted her teeth and took a few steps away, towards the amber sunset. She looked down to the road below. Tarnation was there. He hadn't wanted to be part of the conversation. Instead, he was working with Ulrig to haul bodies into a pile. They were doing it carefully, respectfully, drawing his fingers to close eyes where necessary.

Ryder's words gnawed at her. *Who are we to decide what is right?* The Gungivites were indeed trained to control these machine cities, and yet they were whimsically threatening the lives of hundreds of thousands as if it was nothing—all part of a day's work. Her lessons with Nillias were also coming back in full force, but not just the academic parts. She remembered him lecturing her while she counted his moles. She saw his pathetic smile, those few times it ever materialized, and his gaze up into the sky before the retcher came to destroy him.

"Just no." She said it quietly at first. And then she turned back toward the group and yelled it out. "Just fucking no!"

All eyes were on her. She collected her thoughts, took a deep breath, and spoke. "I get the difficulty in defining goals for these machines. I know value-loading, in particular, is a real challenge. The built-in constraints are flawed, and the machines often find ways to get around them in unintended ways, like the use of human agents outside of Diplopol, for example. So yeah, I understand why you Observers do what you do. It's important, and somebody's got to police the cities. I also understand that sometimes you've got to be a hard-ass about it, and that's you.

"But Nillias also taught me about bias. The values we give these machines are a reflection of who we are, even if we don't intend them to be. Nillias was worried about confirmation bias, in particular—that you were justifying your own existence as Observers with untested assumptions."

"We had discussed this at length with Nillias," Olint said. "We are not seeking additional power for power's sake; we are seeking it to fulfill our mission. Since Nillias left, we have given the matter due consideration. We set up an independent simulator to analyze our ethical guidelines. Confirmation bias is not an issue."

"Listen to yourself. *You* set it up, but what if *you're* part of the problem?"

She was met with a lot of confused looks.

"What I mean is … I don't think you're really human anymore."

This raised a lot of eyebrows. It only seemed to amplify their confusion.

"How do I know this? You take children away from their parents, traumatize them and gut their emotions, turning them into cyborg-zombies whose only purpose is to pray to your altar of machine hate. You force them to live in fear of untamed, ferocious animals. You people can't even have a proper marriage—just loveless baby-making. Is that how humans act? Is that your vision of compassion?

"I also know this because Nillias was *ashamed* of who he was. He couldn't even talk to his own daughter, because he was afraid she would find him too hollow, too inhuman. And because Ryder here has had to live his whole life in exile, just to live any kind of life at all. He never knew his family, or his parents, just a cousin who barely spoke to him.

"Ask yourself, how much time do you spend living, laughing, loving, experiencing life instead of grinding data with that implant brain? The only time Nillias seemed halfway human was when he was able to be disconnected."

She let out an exasperated sigh. "And I know this most of all because here you are, willing to kill all these people in a snap. Humans don't do that. They look for alternatives. Humans don't give up when that many people are on the line. These brainwashed people might be changed back somehow, or maybe they can be stopped *without* killing them, but you won't wait to get all the answers before you strike down the very people you claim to want to save.

"So yeah, we need machine police all right, but *you're* the ones that aren't qualified, as far as I'm concerned. How can someone who no longer knows what humanity *is* anymore, who is so callous towards their own people, say what's right for all humans? After all the nutjob games and tutorials, this was the final lesson Nillias gave me. I don't think he meant to do it, but it might be the most important lesson of all."

She had worked up a real head of steam at that point, while the Observers were all still staring at her blankly. Even Ryder's face was expressionless. Maybe he was in a state of shock. Had they heard her? Did they even understand her?

She said, "You go ahead and try to gas these people, but why don't you take a good look in the mirror before you do? And you can bet at least this one human will try to stop you."

She stomped away, down the decline. She'd said her piece. Let them figure it out.

They didn't stop her, and they didn't say a word for quite a while, in fact. She soon realized, however, that their conversation had probably gone quiet because they could connect to Dryden through their implants.

When she reached the roadway she helped Tarnation and Ulrig with the bodies, piling them neatly, both Gungivite and Essentialist. Somebody would have to tell their parents, and their children. For some reason she thought of Keegan, even though he'd died at the Fan and not here. He had four girls. Would the Observers take care of them? It was hard to say.

Maybe it was all the dead bodies, or maybe it was the heated discussion, but tears threatened to pool in her eyes again. She tried to distract herself by moving faster, and she forced the emotion to retreat.

"Hey Tarn," she said. "Just curious, why aren't you scalping these people?"

He frowned at her, and shrugged. "Wouldn't do much, *bae*. You can't scare a machine, so *death of ambition* doesn't work."

She could see the sense of it, at least from Tarnation's unique perspective. Scalping wouldn't scare anyone in this conflict into pacifism because it was all orchestrated by the ICSM cities. The thought only heightened her concern. Without fear, was there any line these machine minds wouldn't cross?

Every once in a while she would look up at Ryder and the Observers, who were standing silently above them. Ryder was the only one with any expression, and it was difficult to decipher—a few small frowns and some raised eyebrows. On occasion the Observers would look down dispassionately at her, but only for a moment.

The group eventually broke apart and made their way down the hill. The Observers split off toward their vehicle, not saying a word, and Ryder turned toward her. She imagined any number of outcomes. They might still kill all those people. Maybe they would kill her and Ryder, too. She had no idea.

When Ryder reached her, he looked tired. He said, "We have agreed to act independently, for now. I will be Officiant. We will work closely together, and they have agreed to hold off on any gassing."

"Huh. What do you know," Lexie said.

"I'm not sure you swayed them, Lexie. The Observer culture is an entrenched doctrine—a way of life. Hopefully, in time, they will take that look in the mirror, as you suggested. But, Lexie, you *did* sway me, *and* Dryden, and that matters more. The Observers have lost their way. Someone has to watch the watchers. That's going to be us, for a while."

The Observer vehicle pulled away as she was processing Ryder's words. She noticed Ryder's eyes were intently focused on her, and so were Tarnation's. They were waiting for her to answer, for some kind of approval of the outcome. Didn't they know she was a pirate? Who cared what she thought?

She said, "I can't believe they just left like that."

"Why is that?" Ryder asked. "They will be sending a separate car for us later."

"No, it's because after all that, they didn't even give me my nutjob diploma."

—62—

THE MONTEVERDI

Dryden was sitting with Ryder's team in the Monteverdi bar—a low-key establishment with soft ambient lighting and a constant backdrop of upbeat classical symphony music. Dryden had thought it a good place to welcome them all to Pentapol.

"What's that one?" Abernathy asked the bar droid, his eyes wide. He was pointing at a blue drink with red flecks in it that was perched among the hundred or so other options along the bar wall.

"That is called the blue lion," the bar droid said, its transponder mouth flashing with every syllable. "It is a synthetic version of a Tucson Union spicy margarita."

"Yes. That one, please." Abernathy smiled. Abernathy was tall, with a square jaw and short haircut. He was one of the team members Ryder had brought with him to Pentapol.

They were certainly enjoying the variety of cocktail options.

"And so what's in there?" Ryder said, pointing to Dryden's binders, which were perched on the countertop.

"These are for you," he said. He handed the top one to Ryder. "Your team should read them before you all settle in."

"Why not just let the city brief us?" Ryder asked, opening the binder. "Doesn't it have detailed plans of its own? I'm sure it could have made us introductory packets like these."

"I wanted to give it some personal touches," Dryden said. "There are places you should never go, and places I'd like you to stay away from until we have time to properly study them."

"Like what?"

"I've explored most of Pentapol at this point. It goes deep underground.

There are three other large cavities that also have oceanic ceilings. In these sections there are huge, colorful tapestries, dance halls, and cinemas, but I haven't used any of city functions in those rooms, and I recommend you stay away. Even though none of these venues looked like the experiential rooms of Diplopol and Haplopol, I'm paranoid that any one of them could warp our minds."

Abernathy had a skeptical frown on his face, but Ryder nodded gravely.

"And there's more," Dryden said. "I think Pentapol and its citizens appreciated more physical manifestations of the arts. You've seen the statues and monuments, but there also rooms filled with musical instruments, eccentric clothing, sculpting materials and other craft supplies. I've roped off a few sections that contain many of these items, to preserve them for further study."

Ryder nodded and took a sip of his drink. Abernathy was losing interest. He walked over to a group that was laughing at a nearby table.

Dryden had taken Leo's words about his Haplopol paper to heart. He'd been sloppy, and now he was going to do it right. He would hire a well-trained team of scientists, anthropologists and archeologists, and they would meticulously examine the city, and until that team was ready, none of the points of cultural interest would be disturbed.

There was one area, in particular, that he'd insisted the city wall off completely—one area that he didn't even want Ryder's team to know about.

Unlike the other ICSM cities, Pentapol contained a library. It was filled with paper books and electronic tablet readers. It wasn't big—more like a large study than a fully inventoried library. It probably only had a few thousand books. But on one shelf Dryden had found a book that made him almost fall to the ground.

The book was titled *A Brief History of the ICSM*. He had the city make him a copy just before he had the library walled in. It was rich with information and answered many questions. Most notably, it chronicled the timeline of the founding of the ICSM cities. According to the book, Tetrapol and Pentapol were founded after initial conflicts developed between Triplopol and Diplopol. These conflicts were mostly squabbles related to controlling a port at Brentwood Bay—a community that no longer existed—and scuffles between the citizens outside the cities as they pursued scarce resources. At the time of publication, dubbed the golden age of ICSM, these conflicts had ostensibly been resolved, and all was in balance.

Obviously not balanced enough. The conflicts must have materialized again, or maybe new ones had arisen, culminating in the intercity war that left Triplopol vaporized and, eventually, the majority of the inhabitants of the other cities dead. Dryden wasn't surprised none of this final conflict was described in the book. History is written by the winners, and from what he could see, there were no winners.

Ryder leaned in and asked, "Besides that, is there anything we should be worried about?"

Dryden could tell that Ryder was genuinely concerned. It was reassuring to know that he was leaving the city in the hands of someone who understood its true power.

"Not that I can think of," he responded. "The control system of Pentapol is more like Tetrapol compared to, say, Diplopol. It will ask clarifying questions about what the Officiant wants, and it has more safeguards. Maybe they finally got it right with this one, but the past came back to haunt them."

"That's good to hear."

"But just because I can't think of it, doesn't mean there isn't some misalignment somewhere. There's a lot I don't understand. Keep the city in oracle mode. You should always be watching out for unusual behavior."

Despite all he had discovered, Dryden still had countless questions about the ICSM cities, and even what had happened in the last year. He pondered these questions often, listing them in his binder and annotating them with hypotheses and ideas.

Perhaps one of the biggest unknowns was where the drone that had awakened Haplopol originated. He had recently made a disconcerting find related to this. Lexie had left him one of the energy weapons, in case he needed to defend himself. One night, when he wasn't preoccupied with his Pentapol notes, he examined it. On the base he found an imprint of a shooting star formation. It looked like an Old World logo, exactly like the logo he'd seen on the drone attached to the Haplopol control junction.

It raised troublesome concerns, especially with respect to Lexie's friend Warrick, the keeper of these weapons.

Regardless, whoever did it, or *whatever* did it, still might have designs on the ICSM cities. It was possible that this machine power in the east might still have some influence over them. The city Officiants would need to remain vigilant.

"Should we try the food in this place?" Abernathy asked, returning to the bar. "I could go for some of the mutton we brought."

Dryden cringed. Whenever mutton was mentioned he remembered his meal with Maxwell. He had been through so much and could only hope it was an aberration—that he wouldn't have to resort to violence like that ever again.

"No thanks," Dryden said, "but you go ahead. The food *should* be good, now that you've brought supplies that aren't synthetic. The only stuff I've been eating has been decades-old stores that are basically mush."

The bar droid shifted on its tracks to stop in front of him. "Would you like another glass, Dryden?"

He'd barely touched the beer in front of him. "No thanks," Dryden said, standing up. "Ryder, you should have all that you need. I've transferred Officiant authority to you. I need to pack my things. I have a commitment to keep."

—63—

A Day Off

A lot had happened in the last week.

Lexie had returned to Anacortes and been named Pentapol Ambassador. It sounded like a job for a real softie, but it did keep her busy. There were a lot of folks concerned about the huge seawall and guns pointed their way.

In fact, Pentapol had opened a hole in the base of the defense wall near Anacortes, to let shipments through. That meant sea traffic through Anacortes was going to become even more important. Sure enough, the half-drunk skunks started ripping people off with higher tariffs the next day.

That is, until Lexie had gone over to the municipal buildings with Tarnation. They changed their minds about the tariffs in a hurry. It could have been because of Tarnation's dirty looks, but it was probably because Lexie threatened to close the door in the defense wall. Maybe the guns helped, too. But yeah, that was the kind of thing she had to deal with.

Ryder, the Essentialists and the Gungivites were hammering out some sort of treaty. Lexie wasn't involved much, and she doubted it would last, but for now people were playing nice. Three Rivers was a bit put out by not being a part of the negotiations, so she had to unruffle a lot of feathers. That, or mention the guns.

Today she had taken a day off, so she was out with Margaret for a walk. They headed east until they were well out of the city. There was too much hammering and yelling with all the rebuilding, so it was good to get away.

Wow, did Margaret ask a lot of questions. Were all kids this way? She also laughed a lot, too. Sometimes it was real hard to see how she was related to Nillias.

They had passed a number of open fields, filled with corn or wheat. The farmhouses had all their shingles and the horses weren't all spooked out, like in the city. It was nice to see a part of the world that hadn't been beaten up. It was unlike anywhere else she'd been recently.

The road passed through a lick of forest, and the ground sloped up to an old blue farmhouse on a hill. Here, there was a field on a gradient, full of trees filled with shining red apples. A table stood just off the road, with a few wicker baskets on top. A sign on the table read, *Pick then pay.*

"Your dad liked cherries and plums more than apples," Lexie said, "but they're not in season very long. Apples will do us just fine."

Margaret daintily picked up a basket and placed it under her forearm. They walked over to the nearest tree and Lexie watched while Margaret climbed up the ladder. Margaret said, "Why do you always talk about my dad? My nanny used to say he wasn't important—that not everyone needs a dad."

"Oh, I don't know about that. Everyone needs someone to look out for them, and even though you never knew him, that's what your dad did. He wasn't exactly a teddy bear, but he was important all right—a real straight shooter."

Margaret had already picked a good ten apples. She moved up higher in the tree. "Who is your dad, Lexie?" she asked.

"There was someone who was with my mother, but it wasn't her choice. He may have made a baby, but he's not my real dad."

"So, who's your real dad, then?"

"I don't have one."

"You just said everyone has someone who looks out for them."

"Not me, I don't … well, actually, now that I think about it, maybe I kind of did. He's a bit of a mess, though. He doesn't remember much, and I don't know where he is. He's out there somewhere."

Margaret handed her full basket to Lexie and stepped down off the ladder. "Maybe your dad needs your help," she said.

Lexie looked up from the basket and into Margaret's eyes. They were wide, unassuming. Her brow had ridged into the tightest of frowns. What was with this kid and all her questions?

There was no easy way to respond. Lexie could only think of one thing to do—give her the right answer.

"You know what, kid, maybe he does."

—64—

Portland

More than a week passed before Dryden heard anything about Alayna. It was unnerving. The Essentialists hadn't permitted her to speak with him when he was Officiant of Pentapol, so he didn't know if she was even alive. All he knew was that Hatsuo was under arrest and that Commander Yasui was taking over Diplopol operations.

Finally Dryden received a military communiqué at his doorstep in Hood River. It was curt:

Alayna Menudos is under Prefectorate protection. She will testify in the trial of General Hatsuo.

And that was all.

Prefectorate protection often meant some form of detention center.

Another piece of mail arrived the next day. It was hand-delivered by a courier from a merchant that frequented the Columbia River. Inside the decaying envelope was a torn piece of paper, ragged at the edges. It was pulpy, the kind of paper you would find in Alayna's notebook. Dryden immediately brought it to Nate and they read it together. There were no names, and no addresses, but it was definitely from Alayna. It was one of her odes to Essentialism, so not much could be gleaned from it, but it was clear from the words she used that she would be traveling across the Pacific to the Prefectorate motherland.

That was arguably worse than any detention center.

Nate was miserable.

Nate felt the seams of the fuselage. He looked under the wing, and poked at the rivets with his fingers. "It's so smooth, so precise," he said.

Nate wasn't supposed to touch the exhibit, but Dryden couldn't bring himself to say anything. Instead, Dryden looked up and down the museum hall, watching for museum staff.

"And you said you saw one of these in action, up north?" Nate asked.

"No, it wasn't a commercial aircraft like this. It was more of a subway car that could convert into a compact plane. Some friends of mine were in it."

Nate nodded. His expression was halfway between confusion and awe.

"Okay, we should go," Dryden said. "It's been four hours. One more exhibit, and then I want to show you one of the skyscrapers downtown. You can see all of Portland from there."

"All right, Dad."

The final exhibit showed all the components of a computer motherboard spread out on a large contoured table, with each piece labeled. The Essentialist authorities would never have allowed anything like it in Hood River. "No touching," Dryden said, as Nate was reaching in. He was quite sure these artifacts would be more fragile than the airplane, and besides, one of the museum attendants was watching.

They left the museum shortly afterward.

There was spitting rain outside, so they walked quickly through the streets to Vista Tower, as it was now called.

They paid at the entrance and were guided to a narrow flight of stairs, which had obviously been a fire escape at one point. They huffed and puffed up thirty levels to reach the top.

The viewing area patio was full of people. It took them a while to have their turn at the front.

Fortunately, it had stopped raining by that time.

It turned out Nate wasn't that interested in the view across the city. He only looked out for a few minutes and sat back at one of the tables, leaving Dryden at the outer railing.

"Curried goat sausage?" an old man with a gray beard offered, showing a bag full of wrapped sausages. Some of them looked burnt, and so did his mouth. His smile revealed a motley array of blackened teeth.

The place was a more of a tourist trap than Dryden had remembered. "No thank you," he said.

The man moved on.

Dryden receded to sit with Nate, relinquishing his spot at the railing to a young couple.

Dryden said, "Your mother and I came here once, you know."

"Yeah, you told me."

Nate seemed in a mood again. It wasn't bitter, exactly, but he was quiet, as if it wasn't worth his time to express himself.

Dryden let him be. He watched the people at the railing more than taking in the view itself. He enjoyed their enjoyment.

Eventually Nate said, "When do you think Mom is coming home?"

"It'll be a while. The trip alone could take a few weeks, and I don't know how long a Prefectorate trial like that might last. It could be months, unfortunately."

Nate frowned.

"There are a lot of things that are out of our control," Dryden said. "You saw her note. She's doing what she can; she wants to get back here as soon as possible."

Nate took Alayna's note out of his pocket. He read it, and his expression turned sour. "But you're here," he said. "Must be nice for you."

Now he understood. Nate thought it was Dryden's fault that Alayna had to go away. Dryden must have screwed up, and Alayna was fixing some problem he'd created. Dryden couldn't blame him. It was a conditioned response, one that had been right all too often.

"Let's go," Nate said. He stood up and threw the note aside in an act of defiance.

Before it hit the ground, the paper was taken up by a gust of wind, swirling and darting around the patio. Dryden jumped up and grabbed it just before it went over the railing and was gone forever.

Nate was frowning.

Dryden didn't rebuke him. He just stuffed the note into his coat pocket and followed Nate off the balcony toward the stairwell.

It would take a long time to regain Nate's trust.

That was okay. He would take the time.

Nate didn't want to eat together, so Dryden went out for a run just before dark.

It was still wet out, so his shoes were kicking up spatters of dirt onto his legs. He wore a tattered fleece, full of holes, with threads hanging off.

The people of Portland paid him little attention. They were busy making horseshoes or selling fruit or repairing Old World buildings, and unlike the Salish Sea people, they weren't paranoid—they weren't strained. He'd seen so many strained people around the Salish Sea. People who'd lost loved ones, people who were fighting for their lives, and people who were serfs to an insatiable machine.

It was a relief to see these unsuspecting people, but also unnerving. The people of Portland didn't know what could have been—or what could be—with all that was going on up north.

He ran down many streets he knew, and some he didn't. Eventually he ended up by the river. A path meandered alongside it. It was a solitary jog. No one else wanted to brave the wet path just before dark.

He found the spot he was looking for. There was a small inlet here, close to the water, and a bench. He'd been here with Alayna many years ago. It had been bone-chillingly cold, but they had both put their feet in the water, probably longer than they should have.

He sat down on the bench, took out Alayna's note from the pocket of his fleece, and read it once again:

I have climbed along the trunk of a narrow tree; slick with grease, dark exhaust choking through knotholes, and bleeding sap from the infliction of terrible wounds. The tree spanned the broadest of rancid rivers, and never once did I dip my foot in that unhealthy brew. I hoped to see you on the other side, but instead it brought me here, to this great water unraveling before me. The ocean is daunting and vast, but it is eternal, and it is who we are; it is essential. As I ponder its dark depths, I can only hope it is also grateful for what I have done, and that it graces me with a safe journey.

There is much I have seen and learned. I could tell you, but it would only burden you as it burdens me. There is one thing that you must know, however. Know that the old saying is true.

There was a picture of a butterfly in flight, chasing another butterfly across a meadow. And below it were the words *the strongest rivers are made of streams from distant lands.*

He folded the paper neatly up, and stuffed it back in his pocket. Then he knelt down and dipped his hand into the river. The cold waters rippled energetically as he wiggled his fingers.

"Thank you, Alayna," he said, and he continued on his run.

Acknowledgements

A sincere thank you to my editors Tim Major, Doreen Martens and Julia Gibbs, and much gratitude to Art and Sarah for their first look and words of encouragement. I would also like to recognize all those who provided thoughtful feedback on Detonation—Proliferation might not have come to fruition without it.

If you enjoyed Proliferation, I would greatly appreciate a review on Amazon or Goodreads. As a self-published author there are limited options for reaching online reviewers, and they are so critical to achieving even moderate levels of readership.

Thank you for your interest in my work,

Erik A. Otto

About the Author

Erik A. Otto is a former healthcare industry executive and technologist, now turned science fiction author. His works of fiction include A Toxic Ambition, Detonation, Transition, and the Tale of Infidels series. Detonation has been named to Kirkus Reviews Best Books of 2018, and was a finalist for the Foreword INDIES Book of the Year Award for 2018.

In addition to writing, Erik is currently serving as the Managing Director of Ethagi Inc., an organization dedicated to promoting the safe and ethical use of artificial general intelligence technologies. He lives in Charlottesville, Virginia, with his wife and two children.

Visit *erik-a-otto.com* for more information or to sign up for updates on new releases.

CPSIA information can be obtained
at www.ICGtesting.com
Printed in the USA
LVHW021204100921
697438LV00013B/868